Black Noise

Pekka Hiltunen

*Translated from the Finnish
by Owen F. Witesman*

nova

I
The Falling Tree

I.

Personal messages from the Devil.

The words had rung in Lia's head all day.

When the dark videos appeared, they were like personal messages from the Devil.

Lia had noticed the short item about the videos in her newsfeed that morning when she arrived at work. Apparently someone had hacked the YouTube accounts of two English teenagers to upload some videos. The teenagers didn't know one another, they lived in different parts of the country and they didn't have the slightest idea why they were targeted or who had done it.

The strangest thing was that the clips were essentially blank – no picture, no audio. Just a black screen.

A reporter had interviewed one of the teens. He said the videos scared him. Staring at the soundless darkness had felt strange and funny at first, but when the nothingness just went on and on, it turned frightening. It was like getting coded messages or personal threats from the Devil, the boy had said. That was why he had contacted not only the YouTube admins but also the police and a newspaper. In the picture, the boy looked rather more pleased with the attention he was getting than racked with terror.

As a joke, the video stunt was dismal; as vandalism, ineffective; but still some significance seemed to lurk behind it.

The hacker had uploaded ten black videos under each teenager's name, their lengths varying from a couple of minutes to nearly six. The videos had been taken down, and YouTube was currently investigating how the hack had occurred.

A marketing stunt perhaps? Lia thought.

But what kind of company would want that sort of publicity? And YouTube would be sure to take to court anyone who used hacking for advertising.

By the end of the day, Lia still couldn't work out what the videos were about. She left the office early because she had another, less orthodox job to do before the evening.

Only once she was safely out of her magazine's building on Fetter Lane did she pull on her gloves. They felt soft and protective, and signalled that something new was happening.

Lia wore gloves when she ran only on the chilliest winter days. She had a runner's circulation and a Finn's tolerance for cold. It was March, and London was already past the worst of its bleak spring, but today she still had to have gloves. With them on, she wouldn't leave any fingerprints.

She looked at the thin, white fabric. The touch of cotton on her skin made the change concrete. She had entered into a new phase of an undertaking which had required long, painstaking planning. Now it was really happening, and there was no turning back.

Lia had chosen the gloves with care. She had looked at the range of a few department stores and chosen a brand sold at several. Even if they left fibres behind, tracing them would be impossible.

She checked the envelopes one more time. There were five small ones, their addresses printed on labels, their postage stamps affixed with glue. There were three larger, thicker envelopes, prepared in similar fashion. Each envelope, label and stamp was different.

Resealing the plastic bags she was using to protect them, she placed the envelopes in her rucksack.

Lia had decided to run her round. She had checked the locations of the postboxes and post offices online and carefully planned her route so the envelopes would go through different sorting facilities and arrive on three different days. If someone ever investigated the letters, connecting them to each other would be difficult.

Starting from the City, running the route would take her a good three hours, but it felt like a good use of her time. Every last detail had to be perfect. A person's whole life was at stake, and the Studio would also be affected.

My lovely, peculiar second home.

The Studio had given her day-to-day life a new dimension – caring for other people. You could commit to a job like that more than to other things. Lia wanted to do her day job at *Level* magazine well too, but for more selfish reasons, to be thought professional perhaps. At the Studio she was doing things for other people, so the tasks became emotionally important. Doing these jobs made her stronger as a person.

Running through Clerkenwell and Finsbury, she headed towards Islington, taking in one of her favourite streets on the way. On Essex

Road her eyes took in every little launderette, shoe shop and under-taker's, everything she had time to notice as she ran seemed to touch her lightly and spur her on as she passed.

The rucksack on her back grew lighter as she dropped each enve-lope in its appointed postbox. An almost melancholy feeling came over her. Off went all their meticulous hard work.

Whenever she stopped at a traffic light, she continued jogging slowly on the spot. People smiled, and Lia knew what they saw: just a young, blonde woman out for an evening run. Energy in motion, silent determination.

She thought of the envelopes she had posted and the routes they would travel. Each of them had a different destination but one and the same purpose.

In her mind she saw the letters' journey. Postal workers fetching them, piling them onto moving conveyor belts, machines sorting them and sending them off in different directions. Then they would be delivered around London. The envelopes would travel in mail carts in buildings, making their way to secretaries' desks and then to their intended recipients.

How long would they wait to be opened? And when they were opened, would they serve their purpose?

She dropped the last envelope near Primrose Hill. The round, red postbox swallowed it without a sound.

Home was a few kilometres away still. Accelerating, she felt her breathing speed up. Her step was light, so light she was almost floating in the air. As if she were breathing herself forward in the darkening evening.

When Lia arrived in Hampstead, she could recognise every hedgerow and garden gate. She knew exactly where and how to run so she wouldn't need to slow down and could keep her heart rate steady at just the right level. On her street, Kidderpore Avenue, she finally slowed to a walk.

Right now she was powerful. An unusually long and winding run, just the right amount of exertion and the euphoria that accompanied it. The knowledge that the envelopes were on their way and that important things had been set in motion.

Her warm body. The chill evening. The contrast produced a physical pleasure that tickled a special place somewhere in the depths of her brain.

Stopping at the small park next to her building, Lia started moving through her familiar post-run stretching routine. Next to the large, dignified statues in the park, her slender body was a fragile blade of grass. But Lia felt vigorous and confident, utterly alive.

That evening she didn't notice the news that someone else had discovered their YouTube account had been hacked. The Devil had sent more of his messages. Another ten videos had been uploaded to a Scottish woman's account, again showing nothing but black silence.

2.

As soon as Lia opened the door to the Studio, she heard quick, alert steps start towards her.

Tap, tap, tap. The well-groomed claws barely touched the floor. Kneeling, Lia accepted all the warmth a dog's greeting could give.

Gro always knew when she arrived before all the others did, perhaps even a split second before the Studio's surveillance systems. And Lia always wanted to greet Gro as thoroughly as the dog wanted to greet her.

'You're going to spoil her rotten,' Mari used to say. 'What kind of a guard dog is she going to be now?' But Lia defended herself saying that she was only petting and wrestling with her, not feeding her too much or teaching her bad habits. In reality Mari was almost as taken with Gro as the rest of them.

Gro was Berg's dog. Berg was the Studio's carpenter and set designer, who could create almost anything for their operations: documents, identity cards, tools, objects. If necessary Berg could create a whole flat that looked like it really belonged to someone.

Sixty-something, Berg was half Swedish and had named his dog after the former Prime Minister of Norway, Gro Harlem Brundtland. Berg wanted a woman's name for his girl dog that exemplified Scandinavian values.

'Gro doesn't sound very dignified,' Lia had said, teasing him. 'It sounds more like a dog's growl.'

'But I know where the name comes from,' Berg had said. 'Since she has a name I respect, I never say it without that respect.'

Why not name her after a Swedish woman? Lia had asked. Greta Garbo? Ingrid Bergman?

'No,' Berg had said. 'She looks like a Gro.'

In addition to serving as Prime Minister, Gro Harlem Brundtland had been a doctor, a party leader, director-general of the World Health Organisation and much more. Her black and white namesake also had a diverse background, but the breed she most closely resembled was a pointer. She was a stray Berg had adopted from an RSPCA shelter. After teaching her basic obedience and building her trust at home, he had gradually introduced her to the Studio's team.

At the Studio Gro lived in the Den, which, despite its name, was an enormous space. That was where Berg worked, and it took time for Gro to learn not to chew on things she found on the shelves and desks and not to sniff at the cupboards in the kitchen area in the corner of the room.

But the dog worshipped Berg, and before long she learned her boundaries in the Den and the Studio at large. Eventually Berg even trained her to stay out of the kitchen.

Following a brief discussion, Mari had agreed to let Berg replace some of the Studio's interior doors with lightweight swinging ones so Gro could move from one room to another by pushing doors open with her muzzle.

'It'll be easier for her to guard the place this way,' Berg argued, although they all knew the Studio didn't actually need any more guarding. The CCTV cameras, motion sensors in the floors and computer surveillance were quite sufficient.

Two places were off limits to Gro. One was Rico's large office, dominated by dozens of computer racks and other delicate devices.

'Gro Harlem is welcome in my home any time but not near these cables and instruments,' the Brazilian IT genius said. Calling the dog by her full name amused him, what with its entirely non-Scandinavian reference.

Gro was also never allowed in Mari's office. Lia wasn't entirely sure why, whether it was meant as a sign of deference to Mari's position at the head of the Studio's little team or whether she just wanted to be left in peace, but Gro accepted this rule quickly too. Even though Mari's door was often open, she never tried to go in.

'She recognises natural leadership, who the pack leader is,' Mari once observed to Lia, who was slightly irked to have to admit to herself that Mari was right.

Even though Gro had been a stray with some trust issues, she settled into life at the Studio significantly faster than Lia had herself. For the dog it took a couple of months, for Lia it had taken more than a year.

The Studio was a place the like of which Lia had never imagined existed, and she couldn't talk about it to anyone. It was a large, eight-room space occupying nearly an entire floor of an office building in

London's Bankside, and the jobs they did were always interesting and unusual. Mari always chose projects that would move the world in the direction she wanted. Sometimes it was behind-the-scenes charity work, but occasionally the jobs were stranger and more frightening.

For Lia the Studio was like a second home or office where the lines between friendship and work overlapped and intertwined. By day she worked as a graphic designer for a biweekly magazine named *Level*. In the evenings and at the weekends, she spent most of her time on Studio business.

Mari was her best friend, an exceptional woman who had suddenly appeared in her life after nearly six years living in London. Their shared Finnish background united them, along with an ability to drink with abandon when the opportunity presented itself and a feeling that they could get along in the world on their own but had to be thankful for true allies. Berg and Rico worked for Mari, but like Lia and everyone else at the Studio, they were also Mari's confidants. The team's two other members were Brits: Maggie Thornton, an actor in her fifties, who did background research and played characters in their operations as necessary, and Paddy Moore, a security specialist and private investigator.

Lia didn't know how many of the Studio's jobs required specific detective skills or led to illegal acts. Although she and Mari had become quite close, Mari remained tight-lipped about much of what her group had done over the years.

Lia stepped into Mari's office and Gro returned to the Den, back to her master.

'How did it go?' Mari asked.

'Well,' Lia said, taking her usual place on one of the large sofas in Mari's office.

She knew such a brief report wouldn't be sufficient for Mari, who always wanted to know everything down to the tiniest detail. Lia had learned that it usually paid to tell Mari everything, because even the smallest-seeming bits of information could turn out to be worth their weight in gold once they had percolated for a while in Mari's brain.

So Lia recounted the letters' progress over the previous day. Of the five thin envelopes, three had been delivered today to the editorial offices of large newspapers. The rest would arrive tomorrow. The three larger, thicker envelopes were still en route, one of them on its way to the editor-in-chief of a magazine and two to the offices of TV channels.

They had considered the number and manner of delivery of the letters for a long time, weighing the likelihood that each editor would make the contents public and which media outlets it was most important to reach. They debated whether to approach the newspapers by email or using more old-fashioned means. They decided on letters because these days those always made more of an impression on their recipients than emails, and concealing the true identity of the person sending a letter was easier.

Each of the five thin envelopes contained a letter to the editor. They all dealt with the same topic, although they were each written differently and sent using a different name.

Mari had written them with Lia's help. From her day job at *Level*, Lia knew a little about what kinds of opinion pieces newspapers and magazines wanted to publish, but Mari had only needed a little help polishing them. Making sure each had a unique authorial voice was critical so the letters could never be connected to each other.

Together with the Studio's other employees, they had also created contact information and an online history for the writers. If the newspapers checked up on them before the letters were published, the enquiries would come to the Studio. There Maggie and Rico were prepared to play the appropriate parts over the phone or via email.

Newspapers rarely checked opinion letter writers' information, Lia knew. Mostly only when politically significant issues were in play. The editorial offices of the larger, more prestigious papers did look online and in the telephone directories to verify whether the senders existed and seemed like normal, respectable people. But that seldom led to even a phone call.

In the thicker envelopes were larger packets of information, and creating them had required more of the Studio. They had needed to set up an entire fan site. It was very small, built so one person could operate it, but in addition to a website it also required content with a range of dates and references to it elsewhere online. Berg and Rico had handled that.

All of the preparations had taken a little more than a week, in which time quite a bit of other planning also went on. That still amazed Lia. She had been working with the Studio for more than a year but still struggled to keep up with the rest of the group.

'What now?' she asked Mari. 'Just wait for a couple of days?'

Mari nodded. Now they waited until the letters served their purpose. Then the next stage would begin.

Lia had learned at the Studio that Mari's plans worked. And although waiting felt hard, she knew it was easy for Mari. She would use this time to plan too, always something new. For her, the world was a place that could be changed – you just had to choose what you wanted to change.

Fortunately Lia knew what to do while they waited.

'I'm going for a jog,' she announced and then left to make two creatures happy for the next two hours: the dog and herself.

3.

They waited for Craig Cole a few blocks from his flat so he wouldn't think them pushy.

Cole walked briskly. He had hidden his red, puffy face behind dark glasses. The swelling of his face was not a result of drink, Lia and Mari knew. This was a man who now cried every day. Sometimes several times a day, without the dignity or self-control that had previously been a foregone conclusion in his life up to this point. Until the catastrophe struck.

Craig Cole had become a man who cried every day when a fourteen-year-old girl named Bryony Wade called his live radio show and announced before an audience of millions that Cole had made advances on her.

Of course the staff at Radio 2 screened that call, just like all the other calls that had been made to the show that day three weeks ago. An assistant producer talked with Bryony Wade before connecting her to the broadcast. She was supposed to request a Justin Bieber song and chat with Cole about her friends' favourite websites. Instead she dropped a bombshell. She said that her parents had encouraged her to ring and tell him that the whole family intended to go to the police.

'You dirty old man,' Bryony Wade said live on the air. 'You should be in prison.'

Cole's twenty-six years in radio did not save him. He lost crucial time by thinking that the call had to be some sort of sick joke. This sort of thing simply didn't happen.

'Come now, Bryony,' he said. 'We've never even met. I think it's best we end the fun right here.'

'Last night you shoved your hand under my jumper and touched my tits,' Bryony said. 'You promised me money if you could grope me. You dirty old man. I'm only fourteen.'

The producers cut off the call, but 1.6 million listeners had already heard one of the most popular radio personalities in Britain knocked speechless. All that came over the airwaves was the muted music that was supposed to play in the background of each call. It continued to play for nearly thirty seconds before Cole had finished screaming at the production team behind the glass and returned to the microphone. All that was missing was the audience hearing his screams.

Within ten minutes the incident started spreading online, replaying over and over the clip of a fourteen-year-old nobody accusing a fifty-two-year-old radio star of groping her breasts and saying he should be locked up in jail.

The tabloids took about an hour to find Bryony Wade and get her on the phone. She told them she and her parents were heading to the police station to file a complaint. And thus, the catastrophe was complete.

They never filed a criminal report. Bryony and her parents never went to the police station. They started giving interviews through the window of the family car and then at home.

Perhaps the Wade family had never intended to go to the police at all, Craig Cole had thought. Their target might have been something else entirely – such as the national media attention.

Cole quickly realised what an easy target he was. It turned out that he had been at the same event with Bryony Wade the previous day, and he had even been seen alone with her for a moment in the same place. They had both been participating in a fundraiser for the Elizabeth Simms School in Newham – Craig Cole as a celebrity guest whose presence would draw in potential donors, Bryony Wade as one of the school's numerous volunteers.

As Cole waited in the dressing room for his turn on stage, Bryony was also seen backstage, on her way to the dressing room and then coming out a little later. Cole didn't know what the girl had been doing in the room, but he did know he had never seen Bryony, let alone touched her.

'Why didn't you report the groping to the teachers?' the reporters asked Bryony.

'I was in shock. I'm only fourteen,' she replied.

I'm only fourteen. The girl repeated that over and over, and it had its effect, as if her age confirmed her accusation, practically proving it was true. Every headline, every interview in which Bryony called attention to her fourteen-year-old innocence cut a little piece from Cole's reputation.

'I've never met this girl. I would never do something like that,' Cole repeatedly told the reporters. 'I have a long, happy marriage, and I've been working in radio for twenty-six years. I can't understand why any young girl would even want to allege something so grotesque.'

His confusion and the girl's age was enough to ensure a spot on the front page of every tabloid in the nation. Inside, their interviews were often printed side-by-side, which dismayed Cole even further: as if the girl's absurd story could be taken seriously. In the *Sun*, a four-page special report related Cole's distinguished career, while the Wade family received six pages.

Gropegate the papers called it. The word left no room for doubt, talking about it as if it had actually happened. When Cole saw the phrase for the first time, he knew he was sunk.

Cole cried for the first time three days after the catastrophic phone call. He cried over how exhausted he was, that he no longer had the energy to declare his innocence to even one more person and that a twenty-six-year career didn't seem to protect him from anything.

The more serious news outlets gave the case a few columns, in which they also stated that Bryony had not yet gone to the police.

But the gossip rags couldn't pass up the opportunity. Day after day Gropegate continued as they assembled expert commentary on how common sexual harassment was and dug up old friends of the Wade family who swore that Bryony was a normal, quiet girl without any reason to make claims of this sort unless they were well founded.

Cole asked himself every day what the 'foundations' could have been. Why had this teenage girl and her family pulled such a dirty stunt?

There were many possible answers. Perhaps she had been infatuated with him. That happened sometimes, Cole knew from his fan mail. Perhaps his presence and sense of humour on air had made him a target, inexplicably important somehow. Perhaps the fact that the listener never sees the speaker only intensifies the attachment, allowing them to fall in love with their own idea of the person behind the voice, with their own emotions when listening to him. A pleasant voice could be a powerful draw.

Or maybe the family just wanted to become famous. Maybe they thought they would get money from it. Maybe they wanted all of this fallout and something more. A feeling that they were somehow important.

When Mari and Lia went to meet Craig Cole, they knew they would find him near his home. Cole didn't have anywhere to be during the day any more.

The network had shelved his show after five days of sensation. The listening figures had actually gone up because of the scandal, but so many prank calls were coming in accusing Cole of being a paedophile and child rapist that screening for normal callers was nearly impossible. And even the normal callers usually just had one thing on their minds, how terrible what had happened to Cole was. You couldn't make an entertainment programme out of pity calls. The producers had encouraged Cole to file a criminal complaint against the girl, but he wouldn't agree to that or to the BBC doing it on his behalf. So Cole had been forced to leave the station.

They stood face to face, two women with expectant looks and Craig Cole steeling himself for the wave of outrage that had to be coming. Cole lived on Radnor Walk in Chelsea, which was dominated by the restrained atmosphere that often accompanied wealth, but perhaps the aggression against him had reached closer to his doorstep than he knew.

'We don't know each other, but I have a matter to discuss with you,' the woman with darker hair said.

'Yes, you're right, I don't believe we do know each other,' Cole said, trying to keep his voice friendly.

So many people had approached him this way. People who wanted to stand in judgement on the street, in the shop, in the pub, in the lobby of the radio station. The worst had been a man who attacked him in Currys, shouting that people like him didn't have any right to be walking around free. When the salespeople intervened to save Cole, he fled immediately, without buying anything, avoiding the stares and wondering how long it would take for someone to pull out their camera phone and put him back in the headlines: *Cole Beaten Up in Currys*.

These women seemed civilised enough, but their purposeful bearing didn't bode well. He had to assume that any complete stranger walking up to him on the street might be trouble. Perhaps they were mothers and some pervert had messed with their children and now he was going to get a taste of their rage.

'My name is Mari Rautee,' the dark-haired woman calmly said.

'Yes?' Craig said, raising his eyebrows at the foreign name as he looked around for an escape route.

'We can get you back your reputation.'

After an hour of conversation, the impossible was starting to feel possible again.

Not probable, Craig thought, not something you'd dare put much money on, but it was starting to seem at least faintly conceivable.

'The most important thing is that you stay absolutely calm and stick to the logic of your story,' the Finnish woman said.

'My story?' Craig repeated.

'Yes.'

The woman's gaze was sharp, almost piercing, like her entire attitude. The other woman, the blonde one, mostly kept quiet, but the dark-haired one named Mari was more than enough of a challenge. If they hadn't spent the past hour talking as they had, Craig Cole would have avoided that gaze. He couldn't have borne it in his present condition.

'Does it feel strange for you that I call it a story?' Mari asked.

'Yes, it does. This whole thing is strange.'

But Cole had to think about it that way, Mari argued. He had his own life, a good life that had been interrupted because he had been thrown into a strange story. Someone had invented this lie, and now that meant the actual reality of Cole's life wasn't enough. They had to create another narrative. They had to attract attention to another story that was just as powerful and interesting as the one to which Cole had fallen victim.

'The truth isn't enough right now. The truth needs some help.'

The woman with the strange name spoke well, Cole thought.

When she had introduced herself on the street and offered to help him with damage control, Cole's first reaction was to try to get away. PR consultants weren't going to do him any good, and any PR firm sniffing at his carcass wasn't going to want anything but his money.

But the woman had said they were prepared to work for him pro bono. Cole stopped and listened. After listening he asked the women into his home.

The house was large and silent. Cole's wife, Gill, had been on personal leave for a week due to Gropegate, but now she was back at work. Cole put the kettle on as they sat in the kitchen.

'Did you see the morning paper? The letters page?' Mari indicated *The Times* lying on the table.

'No,' Cole said.

He hadn't been able to read the letters pages for days. His name came up too often.

'It might be worth a look,' Mari said, opening the paper to the right page and handing it to Cole.

Reputation is the most important means of communication people have these days, the long letter began. *Not a social media platform, not a mobile device, but rather the overall picture that forms of each of us through all different channels. Because reputation comes from so many sources, you might think that ruining it quickly and almost by accident would be difficult. But it is not. It is actually very easy. Too easy. And this appears to be what happened to Craig Cole.*

The letter described how single, chance occurrences could destroy the reputation of a public figure, possibly for entirely the wrong reasons. Cole looked at the letter-writer's name: Jane Woolstone, a communications consultant from London.

In the surge of emotion, Cole could barely speak. Mari and Lia waited quietly while he reread the letter.

As she looked on, Lia's eyes fell on another page of the newspaper lying open on the table. There was a short, one-column story: strange black videos had appeared online again under a hacked identity, this time on MySpace. Again ten videos like last time. Apparently whoever was behind the stunt knew how to cover their tracks in such a way that even the largest web services in the world couldn't track them down.

The letter to the editor in *The Times* almost brought Cole to tears again.

'I never would have believed anyone would write something like this about me any more,' Cole said.

'There are other people who think this way too,' Mari said. 'We have to give them a voice.'

Cole listened in confusion as the dark-haired woman with the strange name pitched her PR campaign. It was the strangest thing Cole had ever heard.

When the woman reached the conclusion of her presentation, Cole thought for a moment. Then he asked, 'Why would you do all that?'

Mari smiled. 'I like the truth. And sometimes a chance comes along for me to help it.'

4.

All five of the Studio's letters were published at almost exactly the time Lia and Mari expected. Only the *Daily Mail* took a day longer than planned.

The five letters to the editor were the first positive things written about Craig Cole in weeks. Each of them presented its own arguments for why the Gropegate accusations should be considered suspect. And all of them suggested that Cole had been defamed.

Each letter sounded reasonable and measured. Mari and Lia had polished the language knowing that there was no sense trying to suppress the frenzy against Cole with passion. Instead, it had to be turned by quiet conversation, by creating conditions favourable for his defence.

Of course the writer who had defended Cole in *The Times*, Jane Woolstone, didn't exist. The Studio had created her, just like the other four writers.

Rico had doubted the plan. 'Do people read the letter pages much any more since so much happens online? Do letters like this have any real impact?'

They weren't looking for any dramatic change from five letters though, Mari explained. They were just an opening, a way to lower the temperature of the conversation. And they would give Cole himself a little hope for the future.

Given her line of work, Lia was able to assure the others that people still read the letter pages. Everyone in newspapers and magazines knew it, and reader surveys had confirmed it. At *Level*, they didn't publish very many messages or letters from readers, but those they did were still among the most popular content.

And the main audience for the letters wasn't just the general public, Mari said. By writing in Cole's defence to the five big papers, they would also create the impression in the rest of the media that the wave of anger against the DJ might be subsiding.

At the same time as the letters were coming out, the larger envelopes reached their destinations at three selected editorial offices. In each was a scrapbook, every one different, containing copies of magazine articles and newspaper headlines spanning Craig Cole's career.

Cole Opens New Prize Gala.
Radio Star Relaxes at Pub Quiz Contest.

The fact that the Studio could only find warm or neutral news stories about him over the years was a testament to Cole's irreproachability. He had participated in hundreds of events in his work and free time – he had had a lifetime of opportunities for dalliances or ruffling feathers.

The public record created an unstintingly positive picture of him, and the books of clippings showed that. They had his quips to the paparazzi at film openings, his speeches at charity events, even a story about the only crime he was known to have ever committed: he had been caught trying to smuggle a piece of jewellery made from a rare turtle shell from Morocco back to England. Even that entanglement turned out positive once it came out that he had done it at his daughter's request since she was so smitten with the piece.

Lia was relieved when Cole's past turned out spotless. When Mari initially announced at the Studio that she was going to try to help Cole, Lia had been floored.

'We need to intervene. Cole didn't do it,' Mari said the day Gropegate hit the news.

'What do you mean he didn't do it? How can you be so sure?' Lia asked curiously.

'He just didn't.'

Lia often had a hard time accepting the absoluteness of Mari's opinions, but she had seen her friend's special ability in action before: all Mari had to do was look at a person to read their innermost thoughts. Sometimes Mari's gift felt almost supernatural, although she claimed it didn't have anything to do with clairvoyance or anything else otherworldly. Mari was a psychologist by training and a researcher by disposition, and she didn't believe in the supernatural. She took a very practical attitude towards the jobs she took on at the Studio, devoting herself to them nearly round the clock. Part of that was because she seemed to perceive so much more about people than the rest of them.

They had a lot in common. They were roughly the same age – Lia twenty-nine, Mari thirty-three – and both had left their home country to look for work and something new.

Lia had told Mari nearly everything about her background except why in her early twenties she had suddenly wanted to get as far away from Helsinki as she could. She had been in a relationship that had turned nightmarish. Lia didn't know whether Mari could see that unpleasant experience in her. Sometimes she was convinced Mari didn't know but other times it seemed obvious that she did. She could never be sure with Mari.

The operation began in earnest when the network shelved Craig Cole's show. As the first order of business, Mari asked Lia, Rico and Maggie to help her investigate both him and Bryony Wade. Lia focused on newspaper articles in the digital archives, Rico on web sources and Maggie looked into official records and conducted interviews. Every couple of days they reported back to Mari and each other.

Cole's past was squeaky clean, but so was Bryony's. Nothing suspicious about her or her family turned up, and the accusations against Cole were the first time the family had appeared in the public eye.

'The girl is lying,' Mari said after watching Bryony appear in a TV interview and listening several times to her call to Cole's radio programme. Something had made the girl direct her anger against Cole, but the reason was a mystery.

Craig Cole's feeble attempts at self-defence were strange too, Mari said to Lia one night. He hadn't even filed a police complaint about her accusations, instead just waiting apathetically for the truth to come out.

'This whole thing has gone too far,' Mari said. 'No innocent person should have to endure something like this.'

She also wanted to get involved because she detested the exaggerated fuss some newspapers made about sexual harassment. For decades the issue had been virtually taboo in the UK, as elsewhere, but in recent years more and more cases had come to light where someone accused a famous person of sexual abuse. Entertainers, artists, long-established politicians. The revelations had shocked the nation time and time again. When the incidents kept coming, people had started learning to approach the issue in a new way, breaking the systematic silence. Brushing it aside was a thing of the past.

But these accusations were a dangerous temptation for the media. Witch hunt was often an understatement, and sometimes innocents were harmed. Serious, aggravated sexual harassment occurred every day, and sensational stories only made it harder to do anything about the real problem.

Lia agreed completely, but she still had a theory about why the Craig Cole case touched Mari so deeply. Perhaps Mari was partially trying to make up for the Arthur Fried incident. A year earlier the Studio had taken on two jobs, the ones that had drawn Lia into the team. While investigating the activities of far-right politician Arthur Fried, they had also begun looking into the death of a woman brutally slain in London.

Participating in those jobs changed Lia's life. She had never believed she could do anything like that or even thought about grim crimes in detail. But after meeting Mari, her ideas of what was possible for a normal person had broadened considerably.

However, they had come to loggerheads about what Mari had done to Fried. It had taken time for Lia to get over their disagreement.

But now here she was, at the Studio. Their little band had become very dear to her, as had their office building's expansive views of the Thames and the old industrial blocks of Bankside.

Mari and she rarely talked about the events of a year ago and especially avoided talking about the Arthur Fried incident. Lia knew it was better to let things lie.

Maybe Cole is Mari's way of balancing something out. Help one man regain his reputation because she made the wrong decision about another.

But what do I know? Mari probably doesn't regret her decisions one little bit. Maybe that's only my wishful thinking.

5.

The first phone call the Studio arranged in Cole's defence went through to a live broadcast on Radio 2 at 8.52 a.m.

'And who do we have on the line now?' asked the woman hosting the morning talk show, her voice so soft and friendly you could have packaged and sold it to spread on toast.

'Dave here,' the caller replied.

'Dave, you're calling from Ipswich?'

'You got it!'

'Goodness gracious, we certainly are perky out in Ipswich this morning, aren't we? So what's your take on the question of the day? Should the licence be changed to reflect how many TV broadcasts a person really watches?'

'No, I don't think so. I'm perfectly satisfied with the current system. But what I'm not satisfied with is that last night when we met, you started groping me.'

The presenter's silence only lasted about ten seconds.

'OK, Dave…'

'It's not OK,' Dave interrupted. 'People need to hear this. It's the easiest thing in the world to ring a radio show and throw out any old bollocks.'

'OK, you've had your fun.'

'Don't OK me. I'm twenty-eight years old. You're forty-seven, and I'm twenty-eight.'

From the presenter's voice, it was obvious she was losing her temper.

'Repeating ages like that isn't funny. You're just trying to allude to Bryony Wade,' the woman said.

'The purpose isn't to be funny. The purpose is to prove something.'

'Great, you've proved something.'

'Thank you!'

'Ladies and gentlemen, that was Dave from Ipswich who wanted to talk about something other than the question of the day and who –'

'And who is twenty-eight years old,' Dave interrupted.

'Very funny,' the presenter said, disconnecting the call and continuing her programme.

The Studio staff made four similar calls during the day, each to a different radio programme. In addition to Dave, age twenty-eight, there were Lisa, thirty-two, Terry, sixty-seven, and Shane, forty-four. Adult callers who repeated their own age several times, claimed the host of the programme had harassed them and talked about how easy it was to get on a phone-in show and say absolutely anything.

In each case the presenter stumbled for a moment at first before recognising the connection to the Bryony Wade case and ending the conversation as quickly as possible. The calls attracted a lot of attention anyway. Subsequent callers wanted to comment too, and soon Craig Cole had become the main topic of discussions on other programmes as well.

That afternoon a news editor for the BBC rang Cole and asked whether he knew about these surprising phone calls. 'Yes, I've heard,' Cole replied. 'I don't know the people calling, but it is awfully nice that people want to get involved. It gives you the feeling that people really care.'

That was the answer Cole and Mari had agreed upon.

The Studio's letters to the editor about Craig Cole did their job, quickly spawning online chatter, and Lia noticed it was getting the reporters at *Level* talking too. The topic of Cole even came up in their editorial meeting, although they decided not to do a story because they already had other crime pieces in the pipeline. That was a small disappointment for Lia, but, on the other hand, she was pleased that *Level* didn't grasp at scandals just because the headlines would sell magazines.

The fake Cole scrapbooks had an even more profound effect. The intent was to create a specific impression: a collection of clippings collected lovingly over the course of years, a book an admirer might piece together about a revered, trusted person. All three of the media outlets which received them took notice. So unusual were they that they were treated to a thorough review. Yes, people smiled at them, but they also started thinking.

The first media outlet that took action was Sky News. Calling the number that accompanied the package, one of their background reporters said that the host of their Sunrise programme, Eamonn Holmes, wanted to do an hour-long special broadcast about the life and career of Craig Cole. Maggie answered at the Studio playing the part of the book's sender, someone who maintained a Cole fan site.

Mari was over the moon.

'I knew the scrapbook would work!'

Lia watched her enthusiasm with amusement.

She thinks she's always right. Which she is, nearly always.

What she didn't understand was why Mari had wanted to meet Craig Cole herself, face to face. As a general rule, Mari avoided direct contact with the targets of the Studio's work, and Cole was a national radio personality, so being seen with him could arouse unwanted curiosity.

'He needs me,' Mari explained.

Cole had fallen from so high that his emotional reserves were almost exhausted. All of his energy was going into getting through each day, keeping himself together. In order to accept someone's help, Cole would have to trust them completely.

An acquaintance with a person like Cole also had its good points, Lia thought. The network of important people he knew had to be large even if it hadn't held up when he had needed it.

Mari chose her friends and associates at the Studio carefully. Thanks to all the relationships she had developed over the years, Mari had so much money she never had to skimp on expenses in their work. And Lia could never stop admiring the talents of the people Mari assembled around her.

Berg made a particular impression on Lia while they were searching for articles about Cole for the scrapbooks. When their haul from the specialist shops that sell old newspapers had proved too small, Berg had the idea of looking for real Cole admirers and convincing them to sell parts of their collections. Lia went along when Berg went to meet one woman.

A twenty-six-year-old paraplegic, she spent her days lying in a nursing home. Thinking the woman might feel uncomfortable with a strange man visiting, Berg asked Lia to accompany him. But Lia didn't have to do anything during the visit, just watch as Berg deftly handled everything. He didn't offer the woman pity for her condition or talk to her with exaggerated warmth. He was just disarmingly sincere.

Sitting at her bedside, they talked about Craig Cole for quite some time. The woman had taken a shine to Cole years earlier, initially because of the sound of his voice. Now after the Gropegate scandal, she didn't know what to think of Cole but hesitated to throw away the magazine stories she had collected.

'I don't want all of them, just a part,' Berg said.

The woman went silent and stared at Berg in confusion.

'I've always liked all sorts of TV and radio people,' Berg said. 'Like some of the news anchors or Stephen Fry – it doesn't matter what he's talking about or what show he's on. When a person does something like that well, it just brings people joy, you know? And it's totally different from liking a singer. They can give you opinions, life experience. It's a little like having a friend who knows loads about all sorts of things and is always trying something new. They just make the world a little more fun and open.'

Lia saw on the woman's face that those words had earned Berg a stack of clippings about Craig Cole.

On the way back from the nursing home, Berg drove Lia back to Hampstead. Once he had turned the Studio's grey van around and driven off with Gro staring out the window wagging her tail, Lia couldn't help thinking that Berg had just as much warmth and natural wisdom as any of the famous people they had just been talking about.

Berg is one of those people who always makes everyone feel better.

But unlike some famous performer, Berg's wisdom wasn't to be shared with everyone. It belonged to the Studio, and to Gro.

That thought led to another, more melancholy idea. Had Berg adopted the dog because he felt lonely? Lia knew a little bit about everyone at the studio. Maggie had one marriage behind her and was currently seeing someone. Rico kept personal things private but was active on the London night scene. Between Mari and Paddy there was a clear, mutual interest, but so far neither of them had made a move – and both of them engaged in other occasional relationships. During her years in London, Lia had felt a gnawing loneliness that led her to seek variety by picking up men in bars, but now she was living a sort of intermediate phase in which the most important things to her were work and the people at the Studio.

But, as far as she knew, Berg had never been married or had children and didn't seem to be looking for that. Besides Mari, Berg was the only person at the Studio who had ever talked to her much about relationships – actually he had asked her about the subject very directly once.

'What's a young woman like you waiting around for?' Berg asked her one night in the Den kitchen when no one else was around.

'What do you mean?' Lia asked evasively, guessing what he was getting at.

'Why don't you have a man?' Berg continued.

Coming out of anyone else's mouth it would have sounded rude. But Berg lived alone himself, and his attitude was so open and accepting that Lia knew he was only interested in a straightforward answer to the question.

'I guess I'm just going through a phase. Like I'm between two places in my life,' Lia said. 'I'll find someone who's right for me. Someday.'

'Good,' Berg said.

He hadn't laboured the topic by making jokes or offering advice. That made Lia like him even more. They could talk about complicated, even painful things. Berg might be lonely sometimes, but even in his solitude there was an unusual peace.

We are all a little like Gro, lucky that a person like that happened to cross our paths. We were all lucky to end up at the Studio.

You need one or two really good strokes of luck to protect you from the bad things that always come.

6.

Lia's day at *Level* was busy. After putting off her work to go to a series of meetings, she had to get her layouts done quickly. The hour hand was already creeping up on three o'clock, and in situations like this Lia usually shut everything else out of her mind, but something in one of her colleague's voices made her turn and look.

'Dear God,' said Sam, the reporter who sat at the desk next to her.

Staring at his computer screen, Sam was as white as a sheet, with his fists pressed to his mouth.

Lia rolled her chair over next to him. On the display was a video. There was no sound because Sam had headphones plugged in.

The images in the video changed at a breathtaking pace. Something was happening, so confused and violent that it was hard to comprehend.

A person lying on the ground was being kicked. Lia wasn't sure whether the victim was a man or a woman, the images shifted too quickly. The feet doing the kicking looked like a man's, but being sure of the number of kickers was impossible.

Kicking legs surrounded the person on the ground.

Dear God indeed.

Occasionally the kicker would take a step back to get more force. Flying into the victim, the kicks sent the poor person sprawling into unnatural positions.

The video was shot and edited in such a way that the kicks became the main focus, sometimes also moving into slow motion. It was the world's most disgusting work of videography, starring a pair of feet mutilating a helpless person.

'That's the sickest thing I've ever seen,' Lia managed to say.

Sam shoved his chair back, pulling his headphones out. When their cord came out of the computer too, Lia realised that the video didn't have any sound.

Sam was speechless. He was so shocked that he had to stand up and walk around a bit.

'How did they make it?' Lia asked. 'Why would anyone do something like that?'

She looked at the video and hated it. As the kicks flew home again and again, watching became too repulsive.

Reaching over to the keyboard, Sam stopped the video. On screen froze an image of the feet mid-motion and the victim, a dark, lifeless mass against a grey background.

Lia stared at the frozen frame on the computer and then turned to look at Sam. Seeing his expression, she realised what he was thinking.

What if those images aren't staged?

Listening to Sam and the others in the office following the story as it progressed made it difficult for Lia to concentrate on her design work.

The editorial staff at *Level* was a male-dominated group that was hard to faze, but the video made them all shake their heads. Most of them couldn't watch it all the way through, even when it was still online. According to the news broadcasts, the aggressive kicking video had been uploaded by an unknown hacker to a woman's YouTube account. By the time YouTube removed the video, it had been copied to countless other servers and continued spreading.

'Rather gruesome for a viral stunt,' said the editor-in-chief of *Level*, Timothy Phelps.

What was the purpose of the kicking video? That was the question that began to crop up on the Internet discussion boards. And did it have anything to do with the earlier, black videos?

It would take a really sick person to want to spread these images around, Lia thought. There was nothing artistic about the video. It was all too ugly, too frighteningly real.

If it was meant as a protest against violence in films or video games, it completely overshot its mark. All it did was make viewers sick.

By the time Lia arrived at the Studio, it was almost seven. This time both Gro and Rico greeted her in the hall.

'You've seen the video, right?' Rico asked. 'Did you hear the news though?'

'What news?'

'The police think it really happened,' Rico said.

Not waiting around for Lia's response, he walked back to his office carrying his custom-built tablet. Lia quickly patted Gro and then followed Rico with the dog obediently backing off at the door to Rico's kingdom.

Rico's office in the Studio was a large space mainly dominated by the dim flashing lights of workstations and server racks. Rico always wanted the light set optimally for his machines and the work he was doing. There were dozens of custom-modified computers in the room and shelves of supplies he used to assemble other devices.

Rico showed Lia the ITV news broadcast. It had just been released, and while Lia watched it, Rico set his tablet in its cradle. He called it the 'Topo', a Portuguese word that meant 'top' but also 'done!' when used as an interjection. The little machine was Rico's pride and joy, the subject of constant upgrading and tweaks. Somehow he had managed to pack more processing power into it than a normal desktop computer. He never went anywhere without it.

Video Violence, read the headline over the picture. The image was familiar to Lia – this was the thing she and countless other people around Britain had been staring at in shock for the past few hours.

Cruel kicks at a person lying helpless on the ground.

Lia watched the news report in silence. The newsreader spoke about the outrage the video had sparked, its removal from YouTube and the statement from the police. The authorities suspected that the video might depict an actual assault. The images had been cut so little was visible of the people doing the kicking or the location where it occurred, but, according to experts, the footage seemed real.

The video had been uploaded by the username Dina81. That account belonged to a woman in her thirties of Algerian descent living in Bristol. Her only other videos were four clips from rock festivals recorded on her phone. The woman was devastated that the video had showed up online under her name and, according to the police, she didn't know how it had happened.

Once Lia finished watching the broadcast, Rico moved over next to her. He hadn't wanted to see it again.

'Couldn't it still be staged? Could it be fake and still look so real?' Lia asked.

Rico knew a lot about making videos and manipulating images and sound.

'If that was staged, the people who did it are some of the best in the world,' he said.

Lia sensed the anxiety in Rico's voice.

This video has us all shaken up. The people at Level, *here at the Studio, everywhere.*

Soon the whole world is going to know about it. What a revolting, sick thing. A visual virus.

They held the meeting in Mari's office. Everyone from the Studio except Paddy Moore was present.

Their work on Craig Cole's behalf had borne fruit. The TV stations had aired their shows about the Cole incident, attracting widespread attention. The newspapers wrote about the programmes before they aired, and the broadcasts themselves had high ratings. *The Times* even dedicated one of its lead stories to a discussion as to whether it was too easy to stigmatise a person in public without any basis in reality.

'Then comes the best news,' Maggie said.

Cole had received a job offer from Smooth Radio, one of the biggest independents in the country. The station was launching a new programme, and Cole would be one of the celebrity guest hosts who would work with the regular presenter and run the show himself once a week for the next month.

Berg whistled while Lia and Rico clapped. Mari nodded, looking satisfied, but she still had more information to add.

'Unfortunately Craig doesn't plan to take the job,' she said.

Mari had just talked with Cole about it on the phone, and couldn't convince him to change his mind.

'Why on earth not?' Lia asked.

This news was a disappointment since they had expended so much effort to get Cole back his reputation. That job would be that much easier if he returned to the work he was known for.

'I think I understand where he's coming from,' Mari said.

Cole had several reasons for his decision. His reputation still wasn't clean, and in such a visible position he would still be forced over and over again to defend himself. He had also already been working for twenty-six years – he would have to stop doing daily shows before long anyway, and he had started to get used to that idea.

'That's absurd,' Maggie said. 'We worked for weeks to patch up his reputation, and then right when it starts getting back a little shine, he doesn't want it after all? Or at least not the same status he had before?'

'This happens sometimes,' Mari said. 'But we'll keep in touch with Craig. This isn't over yet.'

Did Mari have some kind of plan for him? Lia asked.

'Well, let's just say I have some ideas brewing,' Mari said. 'But now we need to give him some space for a while. Falling from stardom was a big change. All of this takes time.'

'I think we can be pretty satisfied,' Lia said once the meeting ended.

Mari smiled. Berg gave a thumbs-up and hurried down the corridor to call Gro for her evening walk.

Rico didn't say anything, and Lia could see that he wasn't listening any more. Instead he was looking at news and commentary about the kicking videos on the Topo. More just kept coming.

7.

Mari glances at her computer screen and sees the front door of the Studio closing. The others have left, Rico last of all. Information from the Studio's access control system is visible on Mari's computer in real time – she doesn't always watch the others' movements, but it's good to know that they go home to sleep sometimes.

The evening has been discouraging. Some were disappointed in Craig Cole's decision not to return to the radio. And the gruesome video haunted everyone.

Mari isn't disappointed in Cole. Quite the opposite. She knows he has reasons he couldn't express out loud.

They have just saved Craig Cole's life. Mari didn't say that to the rest at the Studio, but they all sensed it in some way, at least Berg and Maggie did, mature adults who know how much sorrow in life gets hidden from others and borne alone. Perhaps Lia and Rico didn't recognise it because their thoughts were too occupied with the video.

When Mari and Lia visited Cole together, Mari realised he was contemplating suicide. His thoughts about it had already reached the point of considering what method to use. Afterwards Mari asked him directly and in the resigned condition of a man bereft of hope he told her that he was considering using his car, either by means of the exhaust fumes or by driving himself into some ravine, not retaliating against anyone for his misfortunes.

But now Cole had a future, he just didn't know what kind. They couldn't rush him, no matter how good even more progress would have felt.

That is sometimes the hard thing about Mari's work: the endings. You had to be able to take a breather and watch to see how far you've got, especially when you're dealing with someone else's life.

But then there is this video.

Mari has watched it three times during the course of the day. It has an almost hypnotic effect, exciting the viewer so that, despite the revulsion, you want to watch it again and try to work out if it is real. It shocks the viewer over and over with its incomprehensible composition; the raw power of the legs appearing almost as a dance.

Mari has stopped watching the video after realising that this is exactly what the people who made it want. They want people to watch, to make them all voyeurs of violence. They want to give the audience a new kind of viewing experience, to change the way people browse online for cat clips and music videos, and suck them into this work that will leave them all shell-shocked.

That was what the people who made it took pleasure in – perversion, twisting things into grotesque caricature. And their own skill and aggression – those were important to these people too, wanting to elevate them to something superhuman and impress others with them.

The kicks had only been a tool the men who made the video used.

And they are men. The men who did the kicking and shot the video wanted everyone to witness their masculine power. That is integral, Mari can tell that just from seeing the images.

And just as integral are the previous videos, the black, mute ones. A collection of dark films whose purpose is to arouse confusion and fear. Although you couldn't see anything in them, they nudged open the door to some frightening place.

And although the videos were completely soundless, there was noise that went with them. It welled up from the confusion of the viewers, from all the astonishment and conversation the videos spurred. The sounds of disbelieving revulsion and shock uttered when you watched a video of someone being kicked.

Mari didn't want to watch the kicking any more because she understood more about the people who made it than she wanted to. And if she knew one thing, it was that this would not end here.

This wasn't staged. They have all witnessed the beginning of something that will grow larger. Into something very evil.

8.

'Not a bad number. But too average, just good writing that doesn't really stick with you after you're done flipping through the mag. We can do better,' Lia said.

The staff of *Level* listened quietly, and as Lia wrapped up her remarks, the editors and reporters gathered in the conference room gave appropriately brief applause.

Every two weeks the magazine evaluated the previous edition, and this time Lia had done the assessment. Previously the assignment had made her a little nervous but not any more. Although the Studio was taking up an ever increasing portion of her life, she had noticed that her day job at *Level* wasn't necessarily suffering. If anything, she had become more purposeful.

And that was a big help with the goal she had recently realised was within reach: becoming the magazine's next AD, art director, when her boss, Martyn Taylor, retired in a few years' time. *Level* was a smart combination of culture and politics, and, despite its limited circulation, it held considerable prestige in the industry. The AD job at *Level* was a sought-after position. How close Lia was to that goal was difficult to determine. But she knew she was taking a more active role in editorial discussions and voicing opinions about the overall performance of the magazine.

Level and the Studio. Lia's life was full of work, although the Studio's business was so interesting that you couldn't really compare it to wage labour. It all took time though: all that was left of Lia's leisure-time activities was running. She didn't do the rounds of the bars as she used to. Or meet men. That had been one of her longest-lasting pastimes after moving to London seven years before. Now she had a hard time remembering the last time she was in one of those bars.

In her parents' eyes, a twenty-nine-year-old woman living alone was in serious danger of becoming an old maid, which was precisely one of the reasons her contact with them was so infrequent. But that image of the future had started popping into Lia's mind recently too.

It was just impossible to start worrying about something like that when she didn't feel alone at all. With her colleagues at the Studio,

Lia had found a feeling that went beyond friendship. She had never felt such camaraderie before. Beyond ideas related to work, Lia only shared superficial things with the people at *Level*. But she could tell her Studio colleagues anything.

Lia was setting an article about the rise of three new prescription medications as the latest recreational drugs of choice in Britain when editor-in-chief Timothy Phelps' voice rang through the office.

'Channel Four! Turn it on, now!'

Quickly a group gathered around the large television screen on the wall to gape at the startling news. Another kicking video was spreading online.

'We won't show the video in its entirety because the goal of the people who made it is obviously to garner as much public attention as possible. But the copy of the video obtained by our office demonstrates that it bears a striking similarity to the previous example,' said the Channel Four newsreader.

A disbelieving stir went through the office when a clip from the video started running on the television screen.

The kicking looked the same as in the previous video, Lia thought before the excerpt ended. But this time the victim looked like a woman. It was hard to tell but it seemed that the victim's hair and clothes were those of a woman, and the lips appeared painted judging by the way they stood out so vividly from the rest of the face. This was probably a woman being kicked.

Horrendous. Poor thing.

The newsreader said that the video had been on YouTube for less than an hour before the admins took it down. There was no word on the authenticity of it yet, nor had the final word come in on the previous one. The police had no record of any victims of violence who had been abused like that.

This time, the video had been uploaded using the account of a man living in London. The police were currently interviewing him, the newsreader said.

A Channel Four reporter interviewed a police detective live over the phone.

'How does the new video change the situation?' the reporter asked.

'At this early stage, it's impossible to say how this changes things,' the detective replied. 'But it does.'

'Is the victim in the new video a woman, as it appears from the images?'

'We can't comment on that.'

As she watched the shock the second video caused in her office, Lia realised that the same emotion must be spreading across all of the UK and the world.

Several people in the office tried to find the video online to watch the whole thing. Lia didn't.

Soon avoiding images from the video became impossible. Various websites spread them online, and the video became the main topic of conversation in the media.

A little before the end of the day, Mari rang. 'Can you come over?' she asked.

'I'd be half an hour, maybe a little more,' Lia said.

'Come as soon as you can.'

'What's the rush?'

'I don't want to talk about it over the phone.'

She could hear the agitation in Mari's voice. Lia waited for her to continue nonetheless.

'You've seen the news about the second video?' Mari asked.

'Of course.'

'There are really three of them. They just haven't made the third public.'

Lia made it to the Studio in just over fifteen minutes. The fastest way was by foot, taking the footbridge over the Thames. Public transport at this time of day would have taken at least half an hour.

A serious meeting was in progress in Rico's office. This time, Paddy was there.

On the Topo's remote screen, a video was running which Lia hadn't seen before. The sight was familiar though: a figure lying on a floor was being kicked.

Paddy was the only one who kept his eyes on the video. All the others had to turn away occasionally. The victim looked like a man, Lia thought.

Two men and one woman. Does that mean anything?

'As bad as this feels, this is just part of something larger for whoever is doing it,' Mari said. 'They want to get people used to watching videos of actual murders as if they were music videos.'

'How do we know the victims died?' Maggie asked quietly. 'Or how recent the images are?'

'All three videos were filmed the same way, and I think the footage had to be made specifically for this,' Mari said. 'And if the victims were alive, they probably would have been found and taken to hospital somewhere. I think it's highly unlikely they would still be alive.'

The end of the video was particularly gruesome. Even though the body was covered in blood, the abuse continued.

When Paddy started showing the video to Lia again, Rico bounced out of his chair and tried to say something. He couldn't get his voice to work though and had to leave the room.

Paddy leaned over to stop the video and close the whole window.

'People put snuff films online sometimes,' he said.

As Paddy continued his explanation, Lia wished she could follow Rico and escape.

'That's what they call videos like this of actual killings,' Paddy said.

Most videos going by that title were actually counterfeits. But civil authorities around the world knew that occasionally they were real. Paddy had served as a police officer years before, and although he hadn't specialised in murder, he knew plenty about the subject. The police always carefully investigated snuff films whether they were bogus or real because in either case the imagination behind them was sick. The participation of the makers of the films in actual violent acts was always a high probability.

'I've never heard of anything like this before though,' Paddy said. 'Making a snuff film this artistically. Usually just shooting the attack is shocking enough.'

'These people want to give their viewers an experience of extreme weakness and subordination,' Mari said. 'No matter how insane they are, they planned all of this. There are things here they're aiming at we don't have a clue about yet.'

'How did you find the video?' Lia asked.

Mari related the chain of events: Rico had found the video. When the other video appeared on YouTube earlier in the day, the one with the female victim, they knew they weren't dealing with an individual random event. And Rico had a place to start.

Hacking into YouTube, he searched the database of all videos removed by the server administrators over the previous weeks. Their number was considerable, but he had good search criteria: he set his image recognition program to pick out all the ones with lots of pictures of moving feet.

There were only a few dozen of those. This had been one of them.

It had been removed from YouTube quickly, less than an hour after upload. The video was originally uploaded using the account of a teenage girl from London, a couple of days before the other kicking videos. The girl's friends had discovered and reported it.

'Do the police know about this?' Lia asked.

'They must,' Paddy said. 'YouTube must have informed them.'

'I wouldn't be so sure,' Rico said.

He stood at the door, pale and still out of sorts.

YouTube and the other similar Internet services weren't nearly as public-service minded as one might imagine, Rico said. Because they couldn't censor in advance what was uploaded onto their servers, they mostly trusted in notifications from their users to weed out anything illegal. Any user could make a complaint about question-able content, which the administrators then investigated.

In theory the services had many ways they could screen content themselves too, Rico pointed out. The administrators could track which videos gained views abnormally quickly and which ones elic-ited the most comments. Software programs existed that could sift through the words used in comments or the videos themselves and sound the alarm if things got too vicious or references to weapons or hate groups started showing up.

'But they don't use them. YouTube and the others are focused on making money and attracting users. They aren't interested in the content,' Rico said.

The editing and camera angles in all three videos pointed to a professional job.

'The people who did this have made videos before,' Rico said thoughtfully.

He listed the things that revealed the creators' previous experience. The focus of attention was always selected carefully. The pauses always came in just the right spot, making the viewer wait for the next image, subconsciously watching more than they would otherwise. You didn't notice the cuts, meaning they had been made just the way they were supposed to be. Still it appeared the videos were all filmed with one camera, which didn't seem particularly high quality.

'The police have to know about this one,' Paddy said. 'It's so similar to the others. The police must have learned about it from YouTube or the person whose account was used to upload it.'

'Why didn't they say anything about it on the news then?' Lia asked.

The police probably wanted to protect their investigation, Paddy guessed. Three videos, three murders. That would have to set off one of the largest police operations the UK had ever seen.

'And they don't want to scare people any more than they already are,' Berg said. 'This is gruesome enough as it is.'

Lia sat in the statue garden on Kidderpore Avenue and looked at the building she lived in. It was late evening, and the students who lived in the King's College residence hall were all home. A light burned in nearly every window.

Lia saw movement in the window above her own flat. She lived in a small room on the basement level, below the building's caretaker, Mr Vong. The name was Lia's own abbreviation of the original Laotian name, Chanthavong. Mr Vong had accepted it with friendly, restrained grace, as he did all of Lia's actions.

Their friendship was quiet, based on coexistence and mutual respect and the occasional long card-playing session. Mr Vong had taken her in, giving her the small room very inexpensively, and once Mr Vong had even saved her from a very scary situation.

44

That had been connected to the discovery of a dead woman in the City, and as she remembered it, Lia realised she was going through the same feelings now as then.

These snuff films. All of the UK had seen two of them. Not many knew about the one that had appeared first though.

Lia needed to talk about them to someone. Mr Vong or the statues around her. Sometimes she told them the thoughts she couldn't really share with anyone else.

But she couldn't unload something like this on Mr Vong, and saying anything to her beloved statues didn't feel quite right either.

If I talk about this out loud, that only makes it more real. Then the people who did all this have won.

She had to interrupt these thoughts. And she knew how to do just that.

'You Finnish girls,' Berg said, tut-tutting on the telephone. 'Always making me traipse around in the middle of the night answering your calls.'

Berg's voice was immediately comforting. Mari was the Studio's leader, but Lia knew that with their greater life experience, Berg and Maggie were the group's emotional stalwarts. With their help the others could always work through anything, and everyone felt a special companionship particularly with Berg.

'Would Ms Brundtland like to come out for a walk?' Lia asked.

'She does like going out on the town at night,' Berg said. 'But where are you? An old man like me isn't going out at this hour, and I wouldn't be able to keep up with you anyway.'

Lia went to change into her running clothes and then took the Tube to Berg's place in Barnet. She ran under the streetlights of Woodside Park, Gro at her side, keeping the leash just loose enough that the dog could jog properly but while it still tied them together.

Running at night calmed her. On the way home she was able to shut the evil images out of her mind and smile at passers-by. Even on weeknights an endless flow of people streamed through London in high spirits, on their way to clubs and bars, searching the night for a connection to someone else.

9.

The voices of Lady Gaga and Marc Almond alternated in the song like an old married couple having a heated conversation, and when either voice rose in the chorus the hands of the crowd swaying on the dance floor went up in the air.

Brian Fowler stood at the edge of the floor, in the line of men who weren't dancing, each with his eyes fixed on someone in the moving mass. For now, watching was enough.

Gradually he noticed that he was also being watched. A man in a leather jacket off to the side was casting brief glances his way. The man never smiled, Brian noticed.

That wasn't abnormal. There were ones who didn't smile. For some of the customers at the Black Cap bar, keeping in character was important. These men never laughed and were never their true selves at the bars. That was part of the attraction, part of their promise of masculinity.

Brian never quite trusted serious, unsmiling men who sought company by pretending to be rougher than they were. Generally he considered them insecure, small people in whom there was no point taking any interest.

But this man in the leather jacket looked powerful.

Brian Fowler wasn't sure what kind of men he trusted. Thirty-four years of life hadn't made it any clearer. He did know what kind of men he liked though, and the man in the leather jacket fitted in that group.

Brian had come out as a sixteen-year-old, revealing his homo-sexuality to his parents on Mother's Day, gifting them with the knowledge of something they had always known on some level but which had been too hard to think about. A week later he crossed another line and started visiting the clubs in Manchester. Later he moved to London, meeting more men than he could remember as he greedily drank in the feeling he got from them, a feeling he could not name. Perhaps it was some sort of precursor to love, the expect-ation of deep companionship. In due time he swallowed the pain of two long-term relationships that didn't last. Now, he was more than ready for commitment. Of course he didn't come to the Black

Cap for commitment, but a gay man living in London who spent his days dedicated to his work always had a difficult choice of evening entertainment: going out to clubs or home to curl up feeling like you were wasting your life.

And Evelyn wanted to go out. Her endurance for partying was in a class of its own. Evelyn always wanted to go out in a twosome, preferably three nights a week, which outpaced her many gay friends' motivation for clubbing, so Evelyn had to take them in turns. Brian had promised her this night. Sometimes you just had to go even if you didn't want to, because that's what he and Evelyn did for each other, create opportunities. A big part of their friendship was pushing each other out of the door to experience the feelings they came here for: the longing for people, the knowledge that anything could happen.

Brian had put on tight black jeans and, after a brief hesitation, his Vivienne Westwood shirt, the right side of which was completely black and the left side of which was bright red, the collar black and red stripes. He had paid a lot for it, and it was a little too small, but sometimes he just had to wear it. To stand out from the crowd if nothing else.

The man in the leather jacket didn't smile. But occasionally, very briefly, he looked Brian in the eyes. There was strength in that look.

Half an hour later Brian had drunk two drinks, lost sight of the man in the leather jacket and realised that Evelyn was also going to disappear somewhere too if he wasn't careful.

Bars made Evelyn too boisterous. Brian caught sight of her laughing face every now and again as she appeared in his field of vision always in the middle of some new group of friends, and then disappeared again.

Feeling a light touch on his shoulder, Brian turned.

The man in the leather jacket was there next to him. The man was older than Brian had thought. But he was also in fantastic shape, Brian could see through his shirt. Muscles.

The man did not speak.

'Hi,' Brian said.

The man still didn't say anything. He just looked. Brian had never seen eyes like that before. The man's gaze devoured him.

Brian smiled quickly. What was the man waiting for? Was he one of the ones who didn't want to talk at all? Something was wrong. Instead of telegraphing desire, the man's eyes seemed to be appraising him.

'What do you like?' the man asked.

A deep voice. Sexy, Brian thought with relief. A manly voice.

'Lots of things,' Brian said.

Did the man just want sex? That would be a small disappointment – but maybe OK too.

'And you?' Brian asked.

The man did not reply. Slowly he extended one of his hands towards Brian. The motion was controlled and calm – he didn't want to startle Brian when he touched him.

The man lightly rested his hand on Brian's shoulder. Brian felt as the man probed his shoulder and shirt. Maybe he was feeling to see if he worked out. What a strange situation – did this guy choose his companions like squeezing fruit at the greengrocer's?

'I like the dark,' the man said.

Brian stared in confusion. He didn't know this code word. It sounded intriguing but strange.

Then the man left. Just like that, disappearing as quickly as he came.

Brian stared into the mass of humanity in the middle of the dance floor, hurt, rejected, useless.

Two hours later he had had enough.

The night had not been good. Not bad, since Evelyn and other people he knew had been around, but nothing had led anywhere. He hadn't seen or wanted to see the man in the leather jacket any more, and the two others who caught his attention hadn't shown any signs of interest. Evelyn had confided in him about worries at work – she was having a hard time getting past the open disdain one of her colleagues showed for her – but there was nothing new in any of this. Evelyn was always having some problem at work, and there were always men in the bars who were destined to be nothing more than eye candy.

Walking to the door, he wiped the sweat from his brow. Adele was singing one of her songs that you felt through your whole body. Brian waited to hear the end.

Once Adele's confession was complete, Brian found Evelyn smoking outside. Two boys were bumming fags from her. Too young for Brian.

'Ready, Evie?' he asked.

In reply he received kisses, one on one cheek and then another on the other. Evelyn was drunk, almost too intoxicated to walk.

'*Completely* ready,' Evelyn sighed.

'*Complete* idiot,' Brian said affectionately.

If nothing else came of these evenings, at least they brought the two of them closer together.

Evelyn was in no shape for the Tube, so they would have to get a taxi. Brian glanced up and down Camden High Street, but no taxis were anywhere near. What he could see were men standing around.

There were always a few standing around outside gay bars like the Black Cap looking for company. The ones who didn't dare go inside or who didn't want to for one reason or another. Some of the guys loitering outside were always hopeless cases, and sometimes they were prostitutes looking for clients who hadn't found anyone to go home with in the bar.

Walking past these men was a sort of little test. You had to be looked at, to have glances follow you. Sometimes someone approached him, but Brian wasn't looking for that – the man of his dreams wasn't going to be hanging around outside a bar like this.

But if no one even looked, that would also be a sign. Brian was well over thirty, but still a good prospect for a while yet. How long exactly would be measured here, among other places.

Slowly he walked along the street, looking for a taxi and keeping a lazy eye on the loiterers. One looked. Then another. Thoroughly. That one would have come over to chat if he had looked back.

Brian's shirt might be a little too small, he might never have been able to make a relationship work and now he'd been on one more night out he would never remember, but he still had a future at least.

Then, far ahead, he saw the man in the leather jacket, waiting on a street corner. The man was looking at him, waiting for him. His eyes burned even at this distance.

Bing. Round One. It was as if Brian heard a real sound in his head, the bell at the beginning of a boxing match announcing one and only one thing: sex. In two steps he turned from a tired barfly into a prize-fighter tensing before a bout, stepping into the ring where there would only be the two of them, he and the athletic, taciturn opponent with the hard eyes.

Let him be a little strange. At least he would get some sex.

But he had Evelyn with him. Evelyn was waiting at the door of the Black Cap, propping up the wall. Brian looked back. If he got Evelyn a taxi and went it alone, what might the night have yet to offer?

Turning, he walked straight towards the man in the leather jacket, towards the match.

The man did not smile, but looked him in the eyes. *Bing bing.*

The man disappeared around the corner. Brian's breath caught, and he turned one more time back to the Black Cap. Evelyn was waiting there, and Brian saw Evelyn see him – Brian waved, hoping that Evelyn would understand that she should wait while Brian arranged his entertainment for the night.

Striding around the corner, Brian found the man waiting for him, in the alley, still not smiling, just with that look. Brian looked the man over again, finding his previous evaluation accurate. A worthy opponent.

Brian heard the bell ringing inside him *bing bing bing bing* and thought: Evelyn isn't going to come barging in here. She'll know to wait. And then the man in the leather jacket extended his left hand. Brian looked at the hand, which was empty, and wondered why he was doing that again. Then an unimaginable pain struck Brian's shoulder.

He felt the man's other hand at his throat, a crushing grip. Brian groped for his shoulder – he had never experienced anything like this. Did pain like this really exist? He tried to scream, but no sound came. The man's stranglehold prevented him from crying out.

The man held him in his grasp. Brian saw his eyes and felt a rending pain.

He tried to hit, to flail, but the man's squeezing sapped his strength.

Air. He gasped for air, but the man's grip held. Second by second Brian felt himself suffocating.

Movement at the corner. Someone was coming. Brian recognised Evelyn – drunk Evelyn was coming to look for him. The man in the leather jacket released his grip on Brian's throat, but the squeezing in his shoulder was spreading inside, something horrible was spreading through him. He had to warn Evelyn, he had to scream, but the sound wouldn't come out.

As he fell to the ground, Brian saw the man in the leather jacket turn towards Evelyn.

The discovery of three bodies at one time shocked the entire country. Left on the street in different parts of London during the night, they triggered special reports on every television channel. The police cordoned off the surrounding streets for their investigation and called in dozens of detectives from various police divisions in the Greater London area. Dubbed Operation Rhea, the authorities said the police inquiry would be one of the largest London had ever seen.

Most people had no points of comparison for the murders. They had a place in their minds for alcoholic fathers who went crazy and shot their families and then themselves. Cases like that fell into a certain category, just like cars skidding off the road, individual gangland assassinations and people freezing to death sleeping rough in the winter.

But three bodies at once, thrown out on the street like rubbish? Things like that didn't happen. The idea was difficult to accept. This was London, a city of order and culture, a collection of tiny old villages that grew together and spread into a metropolis, attracting a population of millions while still preserving its feeling of peaceful coexistence. This was England. They weren't living in the middle of a South American drug war or riots in India.

Three murdered bodies was news for which everyone wanted an explanation.

Not particularly well concealed, the bodies were nevertheless left in places where no one would notice them other than at close range. The male victim left in Vauxhall was sprawled on the pavement in the doorway of a deserted warehouse near the Tube. In the West End, near Charing Cross, there was a man in a small alleyway, and in Camden a woman had been shoved between two rubbish bins in a side street.

Because there were three bodies, the police soon announced that there had also been three videos.

There was no doubt they were the same people from the videos, the police announced. The marks from dozens of kicks were clear. Covered with abrasions and bruises, they were unmistakable, although two of the victims had been killed several days before and post-mortem changes in skin colour and bloating were already significant.

At home in Hampstead, Lia watched the live morning broadcast in which the Operation Rhea detectives attempted to negotiate the siege of reporters. Whenever anyone interviewed a police officer in the media, she remembered her meetings the year before with Detective Chief Inspector Peter Gerrish of the City of London Police. Gerrish had told her some details about the investigation into the woman's murder, and in turn Lia had helped him with information the Studio was able to gather about the case.

Gerrish was not investigating the videos, but what little she knew about the work of the police gave her the feeling she knew something about what was happening behind closed doors. If nothing else then the enormous amount of work that was going into solving these murders.

That workload was visible in the focus of the police on the TV news, in the seriousness of their demeanour and the curt comments they gave to the media: the investigation was ongoing; they were only just getting started. They didn't have any answers, and they were just trying to get through the questioning without saying anything.

Lia went to *Level* for a few hours and then took the rest of the day off. Her boss agreed to requests like that these days without complaint because he knew Lia would make sure her work got done. And Lia knew she wanted to be at the Studio.

'The most frightening thing about this is that it was all so well executed,' Mari said.

The whole Studio had gathered in Mari's office. On the large TV screen on the wall was a frozen frame from the first video. They had all seen the video enough times, and no one wanted to see it again.

'This was planned,' Mari said. 'Nothing like this happens on the spur of the moment.'

Leaving the victims in different parts of the city on the same night told of startlingly cold calculation. The perpetrators had saved up two of the bodies for several days.

'Have there ever been cases like this before?' Lia asked.

Maggie had just looked into that.

'Several murders occur in London every week. Sometimes we even have brutal beatings with a whole group involved in the killing. But usually those are gang fights or drunken brawls. This is different. This has the hallmarks of a serial killer,' Maggie said.

'These killings were planned to be caught on video,' Mari said.

'How can you tell? Lia asked.

'From the amount and quality of work that went into it,' Mari said.

Shooting the videos probably hadn't taken long, but editing each of them to create the taut rhythm of the final product would have taken even an experienced professional hours to complete.

'They also finished the job somehow,' Paddy said. 'Kicking a person to death is more difficult than you would think.'

In theory it was possible to kill someone with one or two kicks if they landed right, Paddy explained, listing the dangerous places. The temples were a dicey spot, as was the rest of the head, and a rupture of the spleen or liver could lead to death even after a short beating. But usually it was hard to kill someone that way. Even striking someone with an edged weapon could leave them with hours to live.

The killers wanted all of the bodies to be found at the same time, Mari pointed out. People who acted that systematically could have disposed of the bodies without anyone noticing, but instead, they dumped them near busy streets, intending that they be found. The awful violence and then leaving bodies in the street – the killers must have either truly hated these victims or been looking for shock value.

Lia didn't say out loud what she was thinking.

Paddy knows about these things from his old police experience, but Mari can only draw conclusions from what she sees. Mari would have made an unbelievable detective.

'I don't want to think about this any more,' Mari said.

Lia blanched. Had Mari guessed what she was thinking? But Mari didn't even glance at her.

'I don't want to investigate this or get involved in any way,' Mari continued. 'The police have their work to do. Three bodies and three videos. And all the black videos uploaded before this. We still have Craig Cole – that isn't over yet. And I have some other plans as well.'

Lia sat for a long time in the Den rolling a ball for Gro. That was their game – she rolled the ball and Gro took off after it when she gave the signal, a small nod of her head.

The dog loved balls, but Lia was really playing with her because she wanted something to do. Anything. Berg was pottering around on the other side of the Den – after a day like that, neither of them really knew how to react, but they had to have something to keep them busy.

Hearing the sounds of the Den was calming, and Lia realised something she had never thought before: Berg was the only one whose work started with such clear, concrete sounds. Hammers, drills, sewing machines. With Rico an entire virtual world surrounded you, invisible and inscrutable, but spending time with Berg gave you the feeling that anything could be built or mended. With Mari... Around Mari it felt like force of will was enough to change the world.

'Shall I brew up some Bettys?'

Berg's suggestion snapped Lia out of her reverie. 'Yes, thanks,' Lia said.

Bettys and Taylors was Berg's favourite tea, and offering it was his way of telling you to calm down and take it easy. Plenty of coffee and tea were brewed at the Studio – coffee for Lia and Mari because of their Finnish roots and for Rico since he was from Brazil, and tea for the others. Berg knew the moment when offering Lia a teacup was more appropriate than a coffee mug.

When Berg left for home with Gro, Lia thought about going for a run. A beep from her mobile phone interrupted the thought though.

It was an instant message from the Studio's internal communication system. Rico had sent just two words: 'BBC News' and a link to a news item. Lia found the nearest computer and opened the BBC News homepage.

The Operation Rhea investigators had discovered the identities of the victims and published their names. Evelyn Morris, Michael Cottle and David Wynn. All three previously reported missing in London. According to initial information, the victims did not know one another, but one thing did connect them: they had all disappeared within the past week after nights out in clubs or bars in London. Their bodies had also been left on streets close to the sites of their disappearances. In the cases of Wynn and Cottle, the bodies were within sight of the bars, and Morris was found a few hundred metres from the pub where she was last seen.

After reading the article, Lia walked straight to Rico's office and found him at his desk. The expression on Rico's face was difficult to interpret.

He pointed to the names of the clubs in the BBC story on his tablet display. RVT, Heaven, Black Cap. Lia only recognised one of them.

'Heaven is an old gay club,' she said. 'I went there once for a work friend's farewell party.'

'I go there,' Rico said quietly. 'Not often, but sometimes. I've been to all these places. At one time or another. They're all gay places.'

Lia stared at Rico. Their brilliant, nerdy hero. With his boyish Brazilian features, Lia had always found Rico attractive and sweet, and now that he was implying he was gay, Lia found him attractive, sweet and suddenly a little vulnerable.

'I've been with men and women. Usually men these days,' Rico clarified.

'OK,' Lia said, slightly flushed.

Rico didn't need to explain his sexuality to her. Still, Rico wanted to say it out loud.

'They'll find who did it,' Lia said. 'They have the videos and everything. No one can pull something like that off without leaving any evidence behind. Maybe someone saw them throwing the bodies on the street, or maybe the kidnappings got caught on CCTV.'

Rico nodded.

'Of course they'll get caught,' he said. 'It isn't that.'

After seeing the victims' names, Rico had looked to see what he could find out about them online – as countless other people around the country were no doubt doing right then too. He had seen pictures of all three.

'I think I know one of the men. Michael Cottle. I think he's a Mike I talked with sometimes.'

Rico hadn't known Cottle well, they weren't friends, but the man's murder still hit close to home.

'There isn't any big, like... feeling of community at those bars, nothing that deep anyway,' Rico said. 'But still it feels like even though this didn't hit *me*, it hit *us*. It could have been me. They killed my people.'

Mari changed her mind about standing aside once the police spokespeople announced that the kickings weren't necessarily hate crimes.

The determination and speed with which she took up the case showed how angry she was.

Immediately after the updated police press conference, Mari called them all to the Studio, and as she walked to Bankside, Lia already knew what was up.

'Idiots,' Mari said, meaning the police.

All six of them were sitting in her office. Rico had the victims' names up on the television, broadcasting from the Topo. Evelyn Morris, Michael Cottle, David Wynn.

All disappeared after spending an evening at a gay bar, including Evelyn Morris. The men were known to be homosexual, but because police information indicated that Evelyn Morris had only had boyfriends over the years, they didn't want to classify the cases as anti-gay crimes.

'It is possible these are hate crimes, but the victims may also have been chosen at random,' the police spokesperson said.

'They were all grabbed coming out of gay bars,' Mari said. 'And their bodies were brought back to the bars. How stupid do you have to be to think that this woman's sexual orientation is the deciding factor here?'

Maybe the police wanted to avoid fanning fear among the gay club clientele and spreading hysteria in the media, Rico suggested.

Mari already had tasks outlined for them.

'We don't have time to spend weeks planning this. We have to act quickly,' she said.

Rico would inspect the videos again, sifting through them frame by frame with his software so nothing would go unnoticed. Were there technical details in the videos that could be used to track down whoever produced them? Did the images contain anything recognisable?

'We need enlargements of anything even remotely identifiable,' Mari said. 'It might be something on the floor or ground or in the background on the wall or on the kicker's clothing or shoes. Or on the victim.'

'The police have already done that work, or are doing it,' Rico said. 'And sifting through the CCTV footage from around those bars. If I could get into the police database, that would be helpful.'

'Can you get in?' Mari asked.

Rico rolled his eyes.

'Maybe,' he said.

One of his hacker contacts might know how to break the police systems' protection.

'That will take time, and we can't know whether it will lead anywhere,' Mari said. 'But at least we can examine the videos now.'

Maggie would get to interview the staff in the bars where the victims were last seen, and Paddy would reach out to his contacts in the police to see if any theories were circulating about the murders. Berg would help Rico with the videos.

'Lia, I have a meeting set up for you in two hours, so you'll have time to prepare a little.'

Lia looked at Mari inquisitively.

'It's with a woman who knows everything there is to know about anti-gay crime in Britain.'

'Why are we in such a rush? We can't know for certain that more of these murders are going to take place,' Lia said.

'I'm afraid we can,' Mari said, nodding to Rico, who pulled up some sort of number list on the display.

'Here are the durations of all of the black videos,' Rico said.

The shortest of them was a little over two minutes, the longest almost six. The three snuff films perfectly matched the lengths of three of the black videos.

'They're going to make ten of them,' Mari said.

The offices of Gallant stood on King's Cross Road, an area Lia didn't know particularly well due to its old reputation as a home to drug dealers, prostitutes and heavy traffic.

She didn't exactly have to look for the organisation's building since the entrance was pasted with rainbow flags and posters of people with serious, accusing faces. The woman Lia had come to meet looked hard too. Annie Bayhurst-Davies' face was full of piercings, and her ample body was more covered by tattoos than her thin tank top. It was as though she wanted to say as much as possible about herself at once using her appearance.

Lia had assumed that she would have to explain her visit to the executive director of Gallant, but Bayhurst-Davies didn't ask. Instead, she was more interested in the way Lia had arranged the meeting.

'This morning I received a call from the one person in the world who never has to ask anything of me. All she has to do is tell me what she wants,' Bayhurst-Davies said once they had shaken hands and taken their seats in her office. 'My teacher at Lancaster University in the gender studies department. My dear, dread guru.'

Lia concealed a smile. Mari had gained them access to the head of Gallant in a way she couldn't refuse.

'I really appreciate you taking the time to meet me,' Lia said.

'My old teacher is the worst shrew in all of Lancashire, a real shrew. She doesn't do favours,' Bayhurst-Davies continued. 'How did you know to contact her, and why was she willing to vouch for you?'

'I know a person who knows people,' Lia said.

Gallant was a London organisation that opposed violence against gay and lesbian people. Like many other gay organisations, it also reacted against any attacks on other sexual and gender minorities. That was why the clumsy acronym LGBTI often appeared in the organisation's press releases: lesbians, gays, bisexuals, transsexuals and intersexuals, i.e. people who had physical characteristics of both sexes. Towards the acronym and Annie Bayhurst-Davies, Lia felt both great empathy and some degree of hesitation.

Rights for everyone regardless of sexual orientation or gender identity, yes. But there were times, Lia had to admit to herself, that the ways people exposed their bodies, aggressively asserting their queer identity, made her ever so slightly uncomfortable. She wanted to understand though.

'This morning I've had three TV interviews and one big press conference. Tonight I have another event and a slew of interviews, and I'm supposed to be issuing statements for the foreign press,' Bayhurst-Davies rattled off.

The message was clear: *Don't waste my time.*

'I may be able to help you,' Lia said.

The woman looked Lia over.

'Good,' she finally said. 'What do you want to know?'

Lia began with the most important thing: why would anyone want so desperately to attack gay people that they would kick them to death and then stream videos of the murders? Who would do something like that?

'I don't know,' Bayhurst-Davies replied quickly. 'These killings are in a category of their own. We've never seen anything this methodical.'

Not necessarily in their brutality though, she went on to point out. Most of the crimes against sexual minorities in London and the UK in general were small and undramatic. But savage murders happened every year too.

'How many?' Lia asked, making some quick notes.

The number was difficult to pin down precisely, Bayhurst-Davies said. Greater London police recorded some 1,200–1,500 crimes as homophobic each year, but researchers estimated that a much larger number never came to light or the connection to homophobia was unclear. Every year two or three murders occurred in the area with apparent anti-gay or anti-gender minority sentiment.

'But usually it's impossible to know how much the victim's sexuality had to do with the case,' Bayhurst-Davies said. 'Like what they did to Stuart Walker in Scotland.'

Lia remembered the news reports well. The brutal murder of a thirty-year-old gay man in a small village had shocked the whole country. A barman by trade, Walker's family became worried when he failed to show up at his grandmother's birthday party. His body was found in an industrial estate on the outskirts of town. During the night he had been tortured, killed and his body set alight. Walker had been well-liked, and his homosexuality was public knowledge, but the police avoided talking about the case as a possible hate crime for as long as they could.

Suddenly Bayhurst-Davies stood up behind her desk.

'Excuse me,' she said, and then began riffling through a filing cabinet in the corner until she found the paper she was looking for and handed it to Lia.

'This is how it looked at first,' she said.

Lia stared at the enormous headlines. GAY MAN KILLED IN SCOTLAND – TIED TO LAMPPOST AND TORTURED.

'Fortunately that wasn't true – that they found Stuart tied to a lamppost,' Bayhurst-Davies said. 'That detail was wrong. But the rest was right. He had been tortured. He had been violated. Just think – a grandmother was waiting for her grandson to come to her eightieth birthday party, the boy who had always been the family comedian. Walker was like that, always talking. Making people laugh, bringing joy.'

Walker's murder had sent the whole village into mourning, and nearly a thousand people attended the funeral.

'That's how it always is,' Bayhurst-Davies said. 'There's always something not quite right in the initial information, but the general picture almost always is. And there is always a village worth of people left suffering. The funerals aren't usually that big, but every one of these cases affects dozens if not hundreds of people.'

Big murder cases where the motive was homophobia were rare. But Gallant had always known they happened regularly. And nothing indicated they were on the decline. If anything, the opposite was true. Violent attacks on gay people were a serious problem all around the world. Although the most brutal acts usually occurred in developing countries where homosexuality was completely banned, the West didn't have any room to flatter itself that it didn't have a problem too. Violence against women and ethnic minorities had diminished in many countries, but in some areas gays and lesbians were in greater danger than ever before.

Statistics on hate crimes in general in Britain seemed to show a decline. But it was hard to trust statistics because a large percentage of cases were never recorded.

'Who is behind the attacks?' Lia asked.

Usually relatively young adult men, Bayhurst-Davies said. For a long time skinheads were the major culprits, but nowadays the skins were telling the police that Muslim extremist youths were doing it more.

'We don't have any evidence of a change like that, but there have been cases. It's hard to classify these current attackers since they're all so different.'

Before Stuart Walker and the videotaped killings, the gay murder that had received the most publicity was Ian Baynham in 2009. It happened in the centre of London, near the place where David Wynn's body had been found now. Baynham's killing attracted the most attention because the main perpetrator was such a surprise: a nineteen-year-old girl, Ruby Thomas. Thomas, a drinker with violent tendencies, had been flirting with men on the street. Encountering Baynham, a sixty-year old out with his male friend, the girl started a row. Baynham became indignant when Thomas began using homophobic slurs. Shouting and arm waving ensued, and the girl attacked Baynham. Thomas's former boyfriend, who was also on the scene, struck Baynham to the ground, at which point the girl and her friends began assaulting him. Sneering all the while, she continued beating him even though he was already lying on the ground unconscious, with blood dripping from his head. Later the group joked about the incident on Facebook.

Thomas, who grew up in a violent family, received a sentence of seven years, which included an extra year for committing a hate crime. The boyfriend who knocked Baynham to the ground received six years. Many criticised the light sentences, especially since everyone knew they would only serve part of them.

Lia remembered reading about the case in the news. Then, it had felt like an isolated act. Listening to Bayhurst-Davies talk was starting to give her a more coherent picture.

'People always want to explain away hate crimes,' she said. 'It's easy to say that Ruby Thomas was drunk and came from a horrible family so that's what really matters. Or that everyone in Stuart Walker's home town liked him and that no one wished any harm on him. But in all of these cases the sexual orientation of the victim was a key factor. The circumstances surrounding a crime blur people's vision, but they don't reduce the destructive effects of homophobia. If we always find some other explanation, it's never going to go away.'

Bayhurst-Davies praised the London police for their actions in recent years. Each police division had at least one officer assigned specifically to LGBTI issues. But they were also seeing a backlash: as these groups' rights received more attention, the opposition to them only hardened.

'And the fanatics are getting better and better at it,' Bayhurst-Davies said. 'They usually know not to reveal their attitudes publicly. A local councillor can advance his ideology by soliciting funding for far-right Christian groups. The police can fail to list crimes as homophobic.'

Investigating homophobia was usually quite complicated. Sometimes the police justified not handling cases as hate crimes as an attempt to protect the victims. There were times when covering things up did protect them, Bayhurst-Davies said, but at the same time it prevented the overall problem from being addressed.

They had been talking for nearly an hour now, and Lia could see that the woman wanted to move on to other work.

'That's how it is,' Bayhurst-Davies said. 'Whenever someone attacks gay people, we get flooded with work.'

Usually the victims didn't have lawyers, and Gallant would try to find them one. They helped arrange medical care and found the victims and their families safe places to stay. Often the victims needed shelter just so they could testify against their attackers. Sometimes the organisation had to put pressure on the police, and representatives were constantly waging a public opinion battle in the media.

'People only want to see happy gay and lesbian people. After all, think how much they've already given us by legalising homosexuality and making gay marriage possible in some countries. And TV shows are full of cute, cuddly gays, so what do we have to complain about any more? But we aren't just a harmless little minority. Every day I meet people whose lives are being made intolerable by homophobia.'

Did Bayhurst-Davies believe homophobia was behind the video murders, Lia asked.

'Do I believe that personally? You bet your sweet tiny arse I do,' she snapped. 'Three people snatched outside of gay bars end up dead. How could the connection be any clearer? Publicly what I would say is that I expect the police to investigate the incidents with utmost speed and care.'

Did Gallant have any idea who could be behind something like this?

'No. Only guesses.'

Watching the kicking videos for the first time, Bayhurst-Davies had automatically thought it must be skinheads.

'Skins are still a real threat to a lot of us,' she said. 'In London gay and lesbian people don't have to be constantly afraid for their safety, but there are still groups of people it's best to keep your distance from. Like skinheads.'

But over time Bayhurst-Davies had started to get the feeling that the videos were too much to be the work of the skinheads.

'Violent skins like simple things. Slogans. Petrol bombs. They wouldn't have the patience to make videos like these. The people behind this are... stranger,' she said.

There had been a few serial killers who had targeted gay people in Britain in recent decades. Allegedly, the worst of them had managed to kill fifteen men before his arrest.

If this was a serial killer or some new homophobic group, that would be a serious setback for organisations like Gallant and the whole country's sexual minorities, Bayhurst-Davies observed solemnly.

'When things this big happen, people start to get afraid. And living in fear limits your life. Whatever position we've managed to achieve in the past, now we slowly have to rebuild it all over again.'

12

'I don't know if there's any point in doing this,' Paddy said, staring at a series of enlarged frames from the kicking videos hung on the Studio conference room wall. Lia knew what Paddy meant.

This is like a police incident room. Their investigators must have exactly these same pictures posted on their walls.

'What do you recommend?' Mari calmly asked Paddy.

Paddy shook his head.

'I don't have any recommendation. I just don't know if this is a good idea.'

Mari looked at them each in turn, Paddy, Lia, Rico, Maggie and Berg.

'We've never really done anything like this,' Mari said. 'We usually keep our distance from violent crimes. And last year we got our fill of that side of things when Lia came to us.'

Lia recognised Mari's familiar, cool analytic gaze, the one that always came out in moments of crisis – and, unfortunately, occasionally also at times Lia would prefer not to see it.

'I haven't been thinking in terms of doing the police's work for them,' Mari said. 'But if they aren't getting anywhere with this, I want to know. If one of you thinks this is too dark for us to look into, it would be best to say so now.'

None of them had anything to say to that.

Only one day had passed since they had received their assignments. Lia reported on her meeting with Annie Bayhurst-Davies at Gallant. Rico went through what he had found in the videos.

The videos had all been shot in dimly lit interior rooms. In the images they could make out a dark, stained floor and a lighter wall, but no clear details were visible. It could be the same place in all three videos.

'Whenever something new or identifiable may be coming into the background, there's a cut,' Rico said. 'The editor really knew what he was doing.'

Determining the number of kickers was difficult, but their movements most likely suggested a slender adult man or men.

'And strong,' Rico added. 'They kick their victims like they know how and where to kick. Like they've practised and know how to channel their anger with precision.'

Lia stared at Rico in surprise, and he clarified.

'Street brawlers. This isn't their first time doing something like this.'

Paddy had heard from his contacts in the police that their thinking was in line with what Lia had heard from Annie Bayhurst-Davies.

'They could be skinheads.'

It was impossible to make out anything specific about the kickers' clothing other than narrow-cut trousers and heavy shoes. Skinheads often dressed like that.

'If it is skinheads, they wouldn't be stupid enough to let their gang insignia show,' Paddy said.

Rico listened to Paddy, looking serious.

'Skinheads do seem like the most likely culprits right now,' he admitted. 'I wonder about the production values though. The editing seems a bit too slick for them.'

And it wasn't just the video. All kinds of people belonged to those gangs. There had been gay skinheads, Rico said, and in some gangs they were even out and open about it. The skins vs. gays setup wasn't as black and white as it used to be.

Paddy hadn't heard much else from his police contacts, only that the authorities believed the deaths had occurred in London. The victims were taken from London clubs, and they were brought back to the same locations – nothing indicated that the murders had happened very far away.

During the day, Maggie had visited the owners of the three gay bars where the victims were last seen. She had presented herself as the director of a PR firm scouting locations for new product launch events. The bar staff had just been through their police interviews, so Maggie had an easy time getting them to pour out their troubles to her. One hate crime victim close to home was bad enough, but suspicions about three had them completely unhinged worrying that their customers would be too afraid to come out at night.

'And there's more,' Maggie said, glancing at Rico.

The shift managers at the bars were genuinely devastated about the violent deaths. Maggie had got the feeling that they mourned the victims almost like family.

'One of them said that when the police came the feeling in their place changed,' Maggie said. 'Like they had released sniffer dogs there. All the anger they knew existed somewhere against them had been let in when the police came and started asking their questions.'

The bartenders hadn't known the victims well and mostly just had second-hand information. According to them, the victims had been normal customers: regular partygoers out meeting friends.

All of these people had come back with them to the Studio, Lia thought. Annie Bayhurst-Davies from Gallant, Paddy's world of policemen and skinheads, and Maggie's bartenders living the nightmare that had suddenly taken over their lives.

And then there are the others in Mari's head. The ones who did the killing and made the videos.

Maggie thought they should go back to the gay bars at night and ask about the victims. That would make it more likely they would find people who knew them better.

'That's too much work for one person to handle,' Mari said.

Rico and Lia volunteered to help, and Paddy said he was ready to go too. Berg looked unsure.

'I don't know how well an old guy like me would fit in there,' he admitted.

A quick smile flitted across Rico's face.

'You'd make a great gay bear,' he suggested. 'One of the ones with a beard and black leather and some belly to go with it.'

The thought bewildered and amused Berg. But Mari thought four people would be enough and that they could go as themselves without any cover identities.

'I think it's safe,' she said. 'Three victims, three different bars in different parts of London. The perpetrators changed locations so they can't be traced.'

'When are we going?' Lia asked.

Mari's glance at Rico contained a question.

'Now,' Rico said. 'Early in the evening people are in better shape to talk.'

13.

The thumping of the music was audible on the street as Lia, Maggie, Rico and Paddy approached the Heaven nightclub.

Lia recognised the music. It immediately brought two things to mind.

Ages had passed since she had been out dancing or looking for companionship. The pounding rhythm caused a physical reaction, an almost painful longing to get out on the dance floor. Music was the best thing for tying together memories of nights out partying, she thought. Years later you could hear a song and know the time a specific memory belonged to. The nights and the people and the events at the clubs all ran together, but the songs served as temporal landmarks.

The song playing now was a new club mix of Adele's hit 'Rolling in the Deep'. As they entered Heaven, it washed over them, seeming to go on forever. Ten seconds into the middle of the thundering and Lia was wondering where she had lost the intense high bars and dancing used to bring her.

That nostalgia disappeared with a single thought.

David Wynn had been here just a few days before. 'Rolling in the Deep' had probably been playing that night too.

Before scattering into the clamorous, swaying mass of hundreds of people, they divided up jobs. Gay men for Rico, women for Lia. Maggie and Paddy would take the bartenders and bouncers, after which they would help Lia and Rico.

Getting people talking about David Wynn was no problem, but only a small number of the club's patrons and staff seemed to know him.

'He was still just a boy,' a large bouncer told Paddy. The rugged-looking man fought back tears for a moment talking about Wynn. 'I just can't imagine how he could have given anyone a reason to do anything like that.'

The club staff were worried about the murders, but the customers didn't believe they were in any danger. Only some of the revellers were regulars at Heaven, and there were a lot of foreign tourists and occasional drop-ins. At such a famous club, a good part of the crowd was straight too, and the central location meant the surrounding streets were crowded every night. One macabre murder touching a mass of humanity this size seemed strangely distant, almost random. Some people might even find the video killings exciting.

Lia watched Maggie's progress through a group of carousing young men out of the corner of her eye. Vociferously admiring Maggie's self-confident style, they surrounded her to get better acquainted, but Lia heard her giving two of the young men a thorough dressing down for treating David Wynn and the other two murders too lightly.

'None of us is invincible, boyo,' Maggie said to the mouthiest of the men. 'You may be able to squeeze into those Dolce & Gabbana jeans and even dance a little in them, but that isn't going to protect you from bad people.'

'Will you protect me, Mummy,' the man threw back.

'No. Your only protection is very small, and it isn't located in your trousers, although I'm sure that's small too. The thing that might keep you safe is seventy centimetres higher up, and you seem to be doing your best to put it out of commission with illegal stimulants.'

The man's drivel drowned in the cheering of the rest of the crowd.

In Camden a completely different place awaited them, a world away from the cosmopolitan Heaven. The Black Cap pub was more relaxed and the concentration of gay people was higher. Here they quickly learned all sorts of details about Evelyn Morris, who had been a regular visitor. In addition to her own boyfriends, she was known to have had a large circle of gay acquaintances.

'Fag hag,' Rico said to Lia.

To those who knew her, Evelyn Morris had been the perfect queen bee: her best friends had been gay men and she loved partying with them. Morris was even known to have cut short a couple of her own dating relationships when her boyfriends couldn't get along with her gay coterie.

Lia listened to these accounts of a woman she had never known. Evelyn Morris had been younger, more animated and more rakish than her.

Evelyn had enjoyed a much larger circle of friends than her. But Lia could also imagine herself in Evelyn's place at the club.

The Black Cap played the same songs as Heaven. What did Evelyn do that night?

'Rolling in the Deep' is playing in the background. Evelyn goes out to get some air and cool off.

Lia slowly made her way to the door and slipped out. The night was chilly. Outside on Camden High Street a group of a few men were smoking, and further off stood other solitary figures.

Inside, Adele's raspy, passionate voice ached for a relationship gone bad.

Lia thought of her lonely life.

Was Evelyn thinking about the same sorts of things? Did she leave here alone that night or with friends?

Lia felt someone walk up next to her.

'We must have been thinking the same thing,' Rico said. 'Shall we walk?'

Strolling along the street, they looked all around. Mostly small shops, hairdressers, offices.

Maggie had attracted a group of admirers in the Black Cap, Rico reported. Paddy was getting his share of flattering looks too, but no one had approached him directly yet: the regulars could recognise a hetero man who wasn't just there to have a good time, and asking about Evelyn Morris didn't increase the other customers' enthusiasm to make his acquaintance.

When they reached Ferdinand Street, where Morris's corpse was found, a dreary sight awaited them. No doubt it was a bleak stretch of road at any time, but with the crime scene cordoned off by the police, it was startlingly harsh.

Entrance to the cul-de-sac of Ferdinand Place was cut off by plastic tape stretched between traffic cones, and a uniformed officer stood guard to prevent passers-by from getting too close. Lia and Rico couldn't see exactly where the body had been found, but its location was easy to tell: even at this time of night several police investigators were still hard at work under large floodlights.

Their brilliance created an unreal, separate space in the dark night.

Lia glanced at the shabby buildings bordering the street. Miscalculating distances was easy in the dark, but her internal sense of direction told her they were about six hundred metres as the crow flies from the pub.

They watched the police work for a few seconds, the policeman on guard eyeing them warily. It was possible another officer was lurking somewhere nearby taking pictures of anyone who seemed interested in the crime scene.

Lia nodded to Rico, and they continued their walk. Turning at the next corner, they started making their way back to the pub by another route.

'That place was a good choice,' Rico said. 'I doubt that cul-de-sac gets much traffic at night. There is probably CCTV somewhere nearby, but otherwise you could do almost anything you wanted there.'

When they arrived back at the pub, Rico stopped. For a moment he watched the stream of cars and pedestrians flowing along Camden High Street and then noticed a small alley between two buildings.

The alley was so small it didn't even have a name.

'Look,' he said, motioning towards the pub.

From the corner of the alley one could see the door of the Black Cap and observe anyone coming or going. But from the pub you wouldn't be able to see someone watching you from around the corner.

The only doors visible in the alley looked like emergency exits, and it seemed unlikely anyone ever used them under normal circumstances. Rico looked for security cameras on the walls. There were none.

'If they chose their victim specifically, they could have waited for her here,' Rico said.

Lia watched the pub, lit up in the darkness with the din of music pouring out whenever the door opened. The thought that they might be standing in the same place as murderers lying in wait for a victim sent a chill down her spine.

A mobile beeped. Maggie had found something.

Paddy made it out of the pub onto the street quickly, but the three of them had to wait for Maggie for a few seconds. When she arrived, she brought news.

'Evelyn Morris might not have disappeared alone,' she said.

Two men Maggie had just talked to claimed that on the night of her disappearance, Morris had been in the company of her friend Brian Fowler. Fowler had been going to the Black Cap and the other London gay hotspots for years, so all the regulars knew him. But no one had seen him since that night, and one of the men Maggie talked to had heard that Fowler hadn't shown up at work at his marketing firm and no one could get hold of him. His phone was switched off.

'The police must know he's missing,' Maggie said. 'They just haven't made it public.'

Paddy said out loud what they were all thinking.

'Four victims. Or perhaps Fowler is one of the killers.'

14.

Mari made her plan instantly after hearing their report.

They had to go and check the areas surrounding the other two bars immediately to see if any similarities existed with the Black Cap. Dividing into pairs, Lia and Rico headed back to Heaven in the centre of the city and Maggie and Paddy went to the Royal Vauxhall Tavern.

'We're going to be exhausted soon. It's dark. We'd be better off doing this in the morning. If this Brian Fowler isn't the killer himself, isn't he probably already dead?' Lia asked Paddy in hushed tones before they split up.

That seemed likely, Paddy said. 'But we can't think that way. We can't start from that place,' he continued. 'You always have to hold on to the possibility that the person you're looking for is alive. That's how you find people alive who no one believes could have survived that long.'

Lia and Rico took the Tube, and Paddy and Maggie went in his car.

Those travelling by car arrived first. Around midnight, the RVT was still hopping, but people were starting to trickle out, some alone and others in pairs.

Instead of going in, Maggie and Paddy began inspecting the surrounding area. It was only twenty or thirty metres to the site where Michael Cottle's body was found on Goding Street, a dreary service road where, again, police stood on guard as crime scene investigators did their work. The area was not restricted as widely as the street where Evelyn Morris was found though. Maggie started to move closer to get a look at the police investigation, but Paddy jerked her back.

'The car, there, in front of us,' Paddy said quietly.

Within a nearby parked car sat two police officers, one with a camera taking pictures of everyone who paused at the scene.

Maggie and Paddy walked by the cordoned-off area calmly like a couple returning from a night out. As they passed the spot marked by the police line, Maggie pressed a button on her phone to mark the precise GPS coordinates, which instantly went back to Mari at the Studio.

Finding their target took Lia and Rico a while. The site where David Wynn was found was not blocked off as visibly as those of the other two victims – on the buzzing streets of the West End, police investigations always attracted heavy crowds. Tiny York Place was a minor lane a couple of hundred metres from the entrance to Heaven. Guarding the mouth of the lane were two men whom Lia and Rico recognised as plain-clothes police officers just by the way they stood.

The entrance to the nightclub was located below street level in the railway arches beneath Charing Cross station. The arches also led to several restaurants and other businesses, so no one could hang around long watching club-goers without being noticed himself, Rico guessed.

'Maybe they went inside the club to choose their victim,' he said. 'And then waited on the street for him to come out and followed him somewhere.'

Lia felt her skin tingle with a rush of anxiety at the knowledge that someone had been snatched from these streets to be beaten and murdered only a few days before. And with the feeling of how quickly the situation was changing, that they were in the middle of events.

We aren't far behind the police. In some areas we might be working in real time with their investigation.

Strangely enough, along with everything else, that also gave her a feeling of satisfaction.

Mari asked them to record as inconspicuously as possible everything about the streets and buildings surrounding the bars.

'Take down absolutely everything. Where are there doors? Where are there stairways? The names of the businesses and offices. Is there rubbish? Have the streets been cleaned? Everything.'

Paddy and Maggie walked around the RVT searching for a place the killers could have kept watch on the bar unnoticed. Right behind the club was the last patch of an old amusement park, Vauxhall Pleasure Gardens. The name felt like black humour – in recent decades the 'pleasure garden' area had been known for drug dealing, free sex and vagrants.

'Too restless a place if you wanted to watch the RVT in secret,' Paddy said.

Even in the dark a surprising number of people were about in the park, and police patrols made regular rounds.

'And all those cameras,' Paddy said, pointing out the CCTV installations on the walls of the buildings and the brick walls of the elevated railway that cut through the area. The entire locality around Vauxhall station was full of cameras.

'Cameras don't help though if the people watching the bar are indoors,' Maggie said, pointing at a bare window in the brick wall rising from South Lambeth Road.

'What is it?' Paddy asked.

'Not a clue.'

Paddy took less than a minute to pick the lock that led into the empty space under the railway. Apparently some kind of business had operated in the space at one time, but the place seemed too uninviting for anything to succeed there.

They found the small room containing the window Maggie had seen in the brick wall. On the floor by the window was a stool, which gave the impression of having been put there precisely so someone could look out.

When they took turns standing on the stool, they could see directly over Kennington Lane to the entrance of the RVT. No one in the bar could have seen them, and no one on the street running below the window could see them either if they stood still.

They watched the police investigating the crime scene on Goding Street and the crowd milling outside the RVT.

'If the killers wanted to choose their victims unnoticed, they did it from here,' Maggie said.

Both teams were keeping Mari apprised of their progress by phone.

'Come on out,' she finally said. 'Gather back here when you're ready.'

It was almost three in the morning by the time they arrived back at the Studio.

Rico uploaded the pictures they had taken to the Topo, and they all typed up their notes. By three thirty everything was ready, and it was time to draw conclusions.

'I think we have four victims,' Mari said. 'We can't know whether Brian Fowler is already dead, but he isn't a killer.'

While the others were walking around the crime scenes, Mari had looked for what she could find out about Fowler online. Not much. Brian Fowler worked at a marketing agency as an account manager. Mari found references to his schooldays and participation in gay sporting events, including a couple of prizes in Gay Aerobics competitions. For several years he had been involved with organising a fundraising drive for a foundation benefiting children with cleft palates.

Fowler hadn't had a cleft palate himself as a child, but his sister had, Mari reported. 'I even found a picture of him with Evelyn Morris at a fundraising gala.'

Mari showed the picture she had found online. They looked at Brian Fowler and Evelyn Morris hand in hand, radiant in their formal attire. Their eyes gave away that they were a little tiddly.

'That man isn't behind all this,' Mari said.

The crime scenes where the bodies were found didn't seem to have told them anything about the perpetrators. Maybe the police would learn more, which they would hear in due course.

'We made a lot of progress today,' Mari said. 'Now we have two options. Either we go to sleep or we soldier on.'

'What can we do in the middle of the night?' Maggie asked.

Mari pointed at the pictures and their notes.

'We can catch them using those,' she said.

Rico stood up and made a tired sound. The others watched as he paced restlessly, placing his hands on his head.

Rico stared at Mari.

'It's an impossible job,' he said.

Mari just stared back at him.

Rico squeezed his head with his hands, as if trying to prevent himself from thinking something.

'Do you understand how many variables we'd have to program?' he asked Mari.

'I understand.'

'And even if I could program it, it still might not be any use,' Rico objected.

'That is a possibility,' Mari admitted.

'You mean a computer program that would calculate possible future crime scenes?' Paddy asked.

Mari nodded.

Rico squeezed his eyes shut before the hopelessness of the task.

'All three of these are gay bars,' Mari said. 'That's one variable. Each one has an Underground station nearby. The killers could have visited the area several times and used the Tube. That could be another variable. And then there's the fact that the bars are in different parts of London and all have small alleys nearby without any flats or shops at street level. And there must be other variables.'

'That's pure speculation,' Paddy said. 'There must be hundreds of places like that in London. Maybe more.'

Rico sighed.

'We should still do it,' he said. 'If we can do it, it will give us probabilities.'

'We can do it,' Mari assured them.

'How can you know that?' Lia asked.

'It's already been done,' Mari said. 'The killers have already drawn the same extrapolations. We just don't know all of the variables they're considering.'

15

Rico stayed up all night working on the program, while the others got some rest. Running on just a few hours of sleep, Lia did a full day's work at *Level*, but all she could think about were the events of the night before, canvassing the clubs and Rico slaving away at his Sisyphean task.

The news channels had already christened the murderers the Video Killers, and the media was full of reports about snuff films.

For makers of snuff films, the cinematography was part and parcel of the killing, a BBC news broadcast reported. Visual recordings of serial killings were extremely rare, but serial killers were known often to be interested in snuff films.

'Some of them may even practise their crimes in a macabre way by looking at pictures of people dying,' the newsman explained.

The videos gave the violence a strange new dimension, Lia noticed as she watched the news. Because it was filmed, the killing became less real.

It's almost as if it's harder to accept that this actually happened because we can see it on a video like that. As if the whole purpose of the act wasn't the killing but the video.

'We're still talking about a serial killer, though,' Mari observed at the Studio when Lia arrived at six in the evening. 'To them, all the details are important: the kicking, who they kick, the videos and the horror they evoke. And that people are watching them.'

Rico was so tired that his head kept nodding the whole time they were trying to hold a progress briefing on the sofas in Mari's office. Everyone was there except Paddy, who was joining them later.

The program was still in process. The number of variables was huge, and data gathering and analysis was slow. Most difficult was collecting information about CCTV camera placements. The authorities had cameras, but private parties maintained them too, especially security firms, and some of the cameras installed in public places were dummies not connected to anything. Rico had access to some surveillance systems through his hacker contacts, but no one had a complete map of London's countless CCTV cameras.

Maggie, Berg and Mari had helped collect information, but they still didn't even have a complete list of the gay bars and clubs in London. They had found data on more than a hundred gay gathering places, but there were more.

'Maybe we don't have to list all of them,' Mari said. 'Maybe it's enough that we include the well-known ones. Those are the kinds of places they've targeted so far.'

On Saturday morning two messages were waiting on Lia's phone.

One was from Mari, who asked her to come in to the Studio before lunch. Lia looked at the message sent time. Two o'clock in the morning.

The other message was from Berg and had come at a more sensible hour, half eight.

We have Swedish pancakes. And a new jogging lead.

'You know Swedish pancakes have nothing on Finnish, right?' Lia said when she rang Berg on the way to meet him at his flat in Barnet. 'They're so sweet.'

'*Javisst,*' Berg said. 'They're still pancakes though.'

Berg had inherited his name from his Swedish father – Bertil Berg – along with his rare talent for set making. He had adapted to British life completely, having lived here since he was a small child, but his Scandinavian roots were important at the Studio, linking him emotionally to Mari and Lia.

At breakfast, they ate most of the pancakes, and Lia knew that when she left Berg wouldn't be able to resist giving Gro a piece.

The three of them left together. While Lia did little sprints with Gro, Berg satisfied himself with a brisk walk.

The day at the Studio was going to be hard, Berg said.

'Sometimes I worry about all the things Mari decides to take on,' he said. 'Not because of anyone else, but for her. She doesn't know how to let go of work.'

Lia smiled. Berg had such a way of supporting the people he cared about.

'The miracle girl,' Berg said, and Lia knew he meant Mari.

'That's what I called her years ago when I joined the Studio,' Berg related. 'Miracle girl.'

Lia saw her opportunity.

'I've never heard how you ended up at the Studio,' she said.

Lia tried to make it sound light, as if she were simply mentioning a fact in passing, but the significance of the question was not lost on Berg.

'Mari hasn't told you about it?' Berg asked.

And he told her the whole story. Perhaps Berg felt the moment was right because the Studio was constantly on both of their minds. Berg and the others were gradually taking Lia in, making her part of the Studio, and these days the bond between them was strong. Feeling like she was one of the group helped.

Years before, Berg had landed a job working on a big period drama, which was celebrating the anniversary of the founding of a large theatre in Liverpool. The production had dozens of workers back stage. Unfortunately everything went wrong. Berg was too gullible, trusting others too much. Construction fell behind schedule. Someone broke into the set storeroom, stealing props and damaging half completed backdrops.

The whole project was on the verge of collapse, and all of the blame was landing on Berg, whose work was most prominent.

'They liked the sets and props, the ones we were able to get into rehearsals,' he said. 'The director said he could almost faint with joy when he looked at them. But that didn't matter when the whole production was about to crumble in on itself.'

Berg had agonised over his options. He could resign and give up his budding career as a set designer. Then Mari appeared. She had heard about Berg from Maggie and came to Liverpool to see his work.

No one told Mari, an outsider, what trouble the play was in.

'But somehow she pieced it together,' Berg said and looked at Lia.

Mari never revealed to Berg everything she did to help the play. It was a lot – that much Berg knew. A new investor appeared on the scene, a Londoner Mari knew. With his own money he hired two carpenters to work around the clock and ordered new materials, some of which had to be flown in from overseas. For two weeks Mari and her acquaintance poured in money and support, until the play was back on its feet.

The show opened. Berg was able to walk away with his head held high. Only a few days later, he received a call from Mari asking him if he would come to work for her.

'The miracle girl,' Berg repeated. 'I said that to her as soon as I realised what the Studio was about. Rico was already involved then too, and he was already quite the miracle worker himself.'

Berg fell silent for a moment, lost in his memories. Lia considered what she had just heard. Mari had helped Berg just like she had helped Lia. Had Mari done some great service for everyone at the Studio? If she had, was it altruistic or did she want to bind them to herself – or both?

'*Herregud,*' Berg burst out and then started walking faster again.

The Swedish was a signal to Lia and made her grin. It was one of their inside jokes when they were out walking. They would always speak English with Scandinavian accents and complain about goings on in Woodside Park like they were fresh off the boat and couldn't let go of their homelands. Lia didn't remember where the characters came from, but she loved these conversations.

'These Brits,' Berg said. What Britain needed, he cried, was cottages, summer cottages, hundreds and thousands of proper summer cottages, one for everyone like in Scandinavia.

'This nation spends far too little time wearing thick woollen socks huddled around a wood stove,' Berg said.

Yes, they needed proper cottages, Lia agreed, with proper cottage life where women were in charge.

'Cottages, where the women get to be in charge, and the men get to build things,' Berg continued.

'Cottages, where the women get to spend a holiday watching men building things,' Lia added.

At the Studio, Rico had made significant progress. After getting a good night's sleep, he had come in early and, at Mari's suggestion, narrowed the scope of his task.

'Run the program with the information we have,' Mari said. 'We'll see how the results look.'

Any list of probable future crime scenes was better than just waiting for what would happen. They gathered in Mari's office to go over the results.

'It's really a simple program. It just calculates probabilities. The difficult thing here is knowing what the right criteria are to put in and how to weight them,' Rico said.

Rico's program had produced a list of 264 sites on different streets of London.

'Of these, twenty-three are places that fit all the same criteria as the previous ones,' Rico said. On his list, he had labelled these as 'hot spots'.

They looked at the list and inspected the hot spots on a map of London. Even twenty-three places felt like impossibly many.

'Should we give these calculations to the police?' Lia asked.

'No,' Mari said sternly.

Lia understood. Mari always wanted to avoid the attention of the police to protect the Studio. Now Mari had another reason too though.

'Their attitude towards gay people in this case is completely asinine,' she said.

The police had set a major investigation in motion, she admitted. But since the calculations Rico's program was giving them were completely untested, providing them to the police might just waste their time.

'And they might have their own ideas. Leads we don't know about,' Maggie pointed out.

Paddy hazarded a guess about what those might be.

'I bet they're putting plain-clothes cops in the gay bars. Even if they aren't talking about homophobia publicly, they could still be trying to snag the perpetrators in the bars.'

Deciding what they would try took two hours.

If the killers wanted new victims, they would probably be watching a different gay bar and its patrons already. The Studio couldn't post guards on twenty-three streets – they didn't have enough reliable people at their disposal. Over the years Mari had hired various jobbers to help out with minor tasks, but this assignment was dangerous and they only had until nightfall if they wanted to avoid losing another day.

But they did have cameras they could set up to watch some of the streets. For some previous Studio jobs, Rico had built tiny, inconspicuous cameras that they could set up almost anywhere, designed to provide direct live feeds. Four were ready. He had parts for four more and might have time to assemble them by evening.

'Eight,' Paddy said, shaking his head.

Eight cameras wasn't very many, he said with a sigh. They would only cover one third of Rico's hot spots. Startlingly few if you considered the entire list of 264 places.

But that was all they could do. Money wasn't the issue – Mari would have paid – even though each camera was worth thousands of pounds. But they couldn't simply walk down to the corner shop and buy more. Even parts would be difficult to get.

'And they all have to be placed before nightfall,' Rico reminded them.

While Rico and Berg were assembling the new cameras and verifying that the old ones still worked, Lia, Paddy and Maggie made a round of the places at the top of Rico's list. They were almost all just as expected, quiet side streets near bars popular with a gay clientele. A new multi-storey car park had just opened near one of them, bringing several new CCTV cameras and a busy stream of traffic. That street they dropped from the list but bumped up the next in its place.

Berg and Paddy practised placing the cameras high on walls using telescoping poles. The hardest thing was guessing the right location for the desired angle of view. On the street they wouldn't have much time to spend adjusting camera placements.

'What do we do if we see something on the cameras?' Lia asked Mari.

Mari had already considered this. They would do what they could and organise a few teams of guards. Paddy could hire five or six security professionals he knew to help. They would post teams of two around the city so they could react quickly if anything happened.

And they couldn't forget the police.

'These streets are all in the heart of London. The police can be on the scene pretty quickly if we call in an alarm,' Mari said. 'And yes, in that case I would be willing to call the police.'

Paddy and Berg set out to put out the cameras at eight o'clock. It was already dark. Berg was driving the Studio's grey van, and Paddy was in his dark blue BMW. The victims had always disappeared, and the bodies had always been dumped, at night. Rico guessed they had at least four hours, maybe five. They reckoned getting the cameras in place would take at most two hours with each having four cameras to install.

Lia took Gro for a short evening walk. Park Street had few spots suitable for dogs, the buildings were packed so tightly together. But here and there a sad patch of grass could be found, and they could jog a little along the banks of the Thames.

'Do you think anything will happen tonight?' she asked Mari after returning to the Studio.

'Maybe,' Mari said.

But they had to be prepared for nothing to happen too, she said. They had to be prepared for anything.

16.

Afterwards, when everything is over, Mari has one thing she can cling to. How fast it all was. This is Mari's consolation and defence: the pace of events, how they propelled each other into motion.

They have everything recorded. Their own snuff film where they can see it all second by second.

Berg is in Kensington placing the sixth camera. Paddy is driving towards Clapham.

The Studio has a direct connection to both. In his large office, his hands full of cables, Rico directs the images from the cameras to different displays. Eight displays in a row with six showing real-time feeds, two waiting blankly for the final cameras to be in place.

The streets are peaceful. The cameras show that there are few people out tonight – the cold is keeping them indoors.

Berg is ahead of schedule. He is that good. A loudspeaker in Rico's office crackles into life.

'Is six working?' Berg asks.

'Perfectly,' Rico replies.

On Rich Lane, Berg moves back to the Studio's van. He still has one camera to install, in Stoke Newington.

Mari watches Paddy and Berg's progress on the Topo's display. They are two dots on a map on the computer screen. Her thoughts are entirely on them, on Paddy, who is so reliable, and Berg, who always does everything with such care.

Paddy's car is creeping forward, but Berg's van is still a static point on Rich Lane, and Mari knows why: before Berg starts driving away from camera number six, he has to put his toolbox in its place in the back of the vehicle. He always does that. He isn't the kind of man to have things rattling around in the back of his van.

Something moves on the screen representing camera two, placed on the outskirts of Soho. Mari, Rico, Lia and Maggie watch as a dark car glides into the picture and stops. They wait to see what might happen. No, it's just a car that pauses for a while and then continues on.

And in that moment while their focus is on camera two, something happens on display number six. They don't notice it immediately. They lose the first seconds.

Afterwards, when everything is over, Mari knows that if they had been watching the situation from the beginning, everything might have gone differently. They had the security teams Paddy had enlisted waiting in the city. Maybe they would have had time to ring and stop everything, maybe call in the police. This didn't need to happen.

She will never forgive herself for this.

Camera number six shows a white van park on Rich Lane. A male figure steps out. The man opens the back doors of the van and stretches in to pull something out.

A large, black rubbish sack.

They see from the shape and weight of the sack what is in it, and when the man dumps the sack on the ground and cuts it open with a knife, they see the victim's black trousers and garish shirt. Despite the growing darkness, they can see that one half of the shirt is red.

The camera eye shows the heavy shoes and slim trousers of the man dragging the body. They have seen these legs before, on videos where people are killed.

The victim sprawls as the man drags him away. Then they can only see one leg.

Their camera angle isn't wide enough to see everything that happens. They hear voices, their own voices, startled cries as they try to catch up with the situation.

A moment passes. The victim's leg swings, and they know what the man is doing – he is arranging the body in the alley.

Berg also sees this in his van through the camera he just installed.

And then a sight assaults them that rips their lives apart.

Mari, Lia, Rico and Maggie stand in the Studio surrounded by Rico's computers and stare at the picture transmitted by camera six from a lane in Kensington. Berg has appeared in the picture. Their Berg. It shouldn't be like this. Berg should not be in the picture.

Mari realises why Berg is there. There is only one murderer. The man dragging that body. One man is doing all of this, killing and taping his killing and throwing his victims on the street.

That is why their valiant Berg does not hesitate to intervene. Berg is out of the van to stop the killer. Berg is raising his pistol. He aims his weapon and shouts.

Everything stops. All they can see of the victim lying on the ground is a lifeless leg.

At the Studio they can't hear what Berg yells, but they see how he falls.

Their Berg, their valiant friend, falls like a felled tree.

They can't see the shooter, but they see the bullet hit Berg in the temple. The shooter must be an expert marksman. Otherwise this would not happen. Otherwise all of this would not be taking place right before their eyes.

Mari looks at the camera image, her mind unable to understand everything she is seeing and what she should do. Complete silence. No one can speak.

Berg lies on the street. Then the camera shows his body twitch. They understand what just happened: the killer shot him again. Making sure of his kill.

A sound from the loudspeaker on Rico's desk breaks the silence in the Studio. It's Paddy, asking what is happening and why no one is answering him.

Afterwards, when everything is over, Mari watches their personal snuff film over and over at the Studio. She watches as the body of the victim in the black and red shirt lolls as he is dragged along the alley. Mari watches as Berg arrives in the picture. The assurance in Berg's hands as he aims his pistol at the killer. Then he's hit, and he falls. Their Berg.

A man falls like a tree, and everything crumbles, everything Mari has built her life upon.

She watches the images in the video again and again until she knows every fraction of every second by heart. She repeats them in her mind, and from them comes a word she repeats in her mind. Forgiveness.

There will be none. She will never give forgiveness for this, not to herself, not to the shooter, not to the world.

The time for forgiveness is past.

II

The Laboratory

17.

Some things they could do on autopilot.

Paddy started towards Kensington and Rich Lane. He controlled his shock and sorrow so he could continue to function. There was no time to lose. The killer had disappeared from their camera image immediately, getting away, but someone might find the bodies in the alley any second.

'Get Berg's gun, keys and mobile,' Mari said to Paddy over the phone. 'Remove the camera, and drive the van a little way away.'

Mari's voice sounded mechanical, Lia thought. Herself, she could scarcely speak or even really think.

One thing at a time. Think one thing at a time.

The familiar people around her she saw in slow motion. One thought at a time, she tried to move forward from this moment.

Berg is dead. He's lying there with that other body.

The killer came today hours before he did the last three times.

The victim in the red and black shirt had to be the missing man, Evelyn Morris' friend, Brian Fowler. Probably the killer had a video somewhere of killing him too.

Why did he come so early? Why did he dump the body on Rich Lane?

They were each thinking the same questions. Fowler was kidnapped in Camden, somewhere else entirely.

'The killer knew the police are still combing the area around the Black Cap,' Rico pointed out.

The man had chosen another gay meeting place in Kensington but not to snatch a new victim, to get rid of a previous one. They were on the right track – they could predict where the killer might go – but knowing what he would do there was impossible.

In the feed for camera six they saw Paddy arrive in the alley. He knelt over both bodies, and they could see in his frame the moment the final knowledge came to him: nothing could be done; Berg and Fowler were dead.

Paddy quickly went through Berg's pockets, taking out a set of keys and a phone. From the street he retrieved Berg's gun. His wallet with driving licence, credit cards and money could stay in his trouser pocket.

'The police need to be able to identify him,' Mari instructed Paddy. 'The very second they find him.'

Not only mechanical but almost cold, Lia thought. For some reason, Mari's voice scared her almost more than what she had just seen on the video screen.

Of course she understood why Mari and Paddy were doing this. They were trying to protect the Studio, to minimise their losses.

Lia wouldn't have been able to do that. She knew that if she even tried to do something like that she would start screaming. They had already experienced an irrecoverable loss. They had seen Berg murdered, and after that everything else was stupid and pointless.

Someday I'll probably be thankful that Mari and Paddy are able to do this right now.

Thinking about that was sad but also calming. The thought of things to come, that there would be some kind of future.

For Maggie it wasn't. She just sat sobbing quietly.

When Paddy removed camera number six from the wall on Rich Lane and the picture it was broadcasting to the Studio disappeared from the screen, Rico started crying too.

One of them had to go to Berg's home.

Lia only understood the significance of that when she heard Mari talking about it quietly on the phone with Paddy. When the police found Berg's body, they would search his flat in Barnet soon afterwards, either tonight or tomorrow morning at the latest. They had to remove all evidence that Berg had worked for the Studio.

'He doesn't have anything on his home computer,' Mari told Paddy. 'We talked about that once. He said he kept all of his messages to here online instead of on his hard drive, and it's all encrypted.'

The goal wasn't to remove any indication that Berg had known them. Just everything that might hint at the work the Studio did. 'There won't be much,' Maggie said suddenly. They were startled to hear her speak.

'I've spent some time there,' Maggie continued. 'He told me about his business.'

Looking at his flat, you would just think Berg was an old carpenter doing the sorts of jobs any independent tradesman in that industry might, Maggie said.

'He has some tools and a workbench.'

Lia remembered the workbench concealed behind a curtain. She had been in Berg's flat that very morning before their outing in Woodside Park. Berg had confided in her about how he met Mari. They had shared their silly little jokes.

'We still need to make a visit,' Mari said. 'Just to be sure.'

Paddy headed towards Barnet. He already had Berg's keys. He ended his call to the Studio to ring the security guards he had hired for possible emergencies. They wouldn't be any help now.

Lia sat down next to Maggie, taking her hand and squeezing.

'Are we going to leave him there on the street?' Maggie asked Mari.

Mari took a few moments to answer.

'We have to,' she said. 'As soon as Paddy is far enough away, we'll ring the police.'

Rico made the call. Using a computer program that rerouted the connection and altered his voice, so that there would be no way to trace the call.

At Mari's instruction, Rico also sent the police what their camera had recorded of what happened on Rich Lane. He cut out the beginning with Berg flashing in and out of the picture while he installed the camera, as well as stripping all the metadata that might lead back to the Studio.

'I'm using AnonFiles,' Rico told the others. 'And Tor.'

Talking about practical matters helped him. AnonFiles was an anonymous file sharing site, and sending a link to the file to the police through the Tor network would obfuscate the path the message took.

They all listened to his hacker jargon without hearing it. When Rico left to look for an unprotected WiFi network somewhere else in the city to send the materials, Lia had to hold herself back from stopping him. Her instincts told her that going outside was bad.

Paddy searched Berg's apartment quickly. He didn't dig to the back of every cupboard, he just gave everything a quick once-over. Berg had been as meticulous at home as at the Studio. A place for every-thing and everything in its place.

The most important thing was to look for any papers. Paddy checked the desk drawers and other places there might be stacks of papers or files. There wasn't much that could connect Berg to the Studio's address, mostly just a few taxi receipts, which Paddy collected. None of the documents showed the others' names. A couple of postcards Maggie had sent on holiday could stay mixed in with notes and letters from Berg's relations.

Nothing in the flat indicated that Berg had been in a relationship with anyone. Which they already knew.

By the time Paddy arrived at the Studio, it was past midnight.

They didn't talk much. No one hurried home. Now it was import-ant to be together for a while. But none of them had the strength to work any more. They had any number of things to investigate – they knew that – but just the thought of it felt overwhelming. Before long they couldn't put off going home any longer, though.

'We have to concentrate on surviving,' Mari said.

Paddy offered the others a lift, and Maggie and Rico accepted with relief. Lia intended to go with them, but then she suddenly remem-bered something. She walked from Rico's office to the Den.

Gro. The dog was awake and greeted her with tail wagging. She had been waiting for someone to come.

Lia looked at the dog. There was no way to explain that Berg didn't exist any more. It felt important not to cry.

If I cry, Gro will feel bad. If I don't cry, Gro will be fine.

The thought felt simultaneously ever so logical and ever so childish.

'Will you two be all right?' Mari asked Lia in the corridor.

Lia nodded as she clipped the leash to Gro's collar.

'I'm going to take a taxi,' she said.

'Can you have a dog in your flat?' Mari asked.

Lia could hear from Mari's voice that the mechanicalness was fading. Shock was taking over, even for Mari.

'For now, yes,' Lia said.

Mari handed her something.

Lia looked at the bunch of unmarked keys. She recognised the keys to the front door of the building and the Studio – she already had those – but the ring held several other keys as well.

'For emergencies,' Mari said, turning and walking back to her office.

Lia looked at Gro and knew that she had to leave. She had to move forward, one thing at a time.

18.

They both slept poorly, woman and dog.

The strange, small flat and the loss of everything familiar confused Gro. Lia had a hard time falling asleep thinking about how the police would find Berg.

They had left him on the street. Two bodies, two more in a series of horrific crimes, and they had simply left them on the street. But what would the alternative have been? There wasn't one.

Living with the decision they had made was difficult, but at the same time Lia felt gratitude: Mari and Paddy had settled the matter for all of them.

She slept a few hours simply out of exhaustion. Early in the morning she awoke startled to find someone else sleeping in her room. Soft snoring. That sound had never been there before.

She looked at Gro lying still and drooling in her sleep, and then she started to cry. Now it was possible, with the dog sleeping, safe at home.

The crying brought with it a harsh insight. Berg's death was not only the end of many things that were important to them, it was also the beginning of new, evil things. Everyone at the Studio was out of their minds with disbelief and grief. She was crying for Berg for the first time and knew it wouldn't be the last. This was just a shock reaction.

The real sorrow was yet to come. And they didn't know who the killer was.

In the morning she had to get up because Gro needed to go out. Otherwise Lia would have stayed in bed.

Fuck how I feel. I'm not going to leave a dog in distress.

She walked Gro along Kidderpore Avenue and the neighbouring residential streets. She felt strange. She felt like stopping strangers and telling them: I have a dog. My friend was shot yesterday.

After Gro had her morning pee, Lia hurried back inside so no one in the King's College residence hall would make a fuss about the dog. She didn't want anyone complaining about her keeping a pet.

At home she had everything she needed for her usual morning rituals, but now there were two of them.

'What do you eat in the morning?' she asked Gro.

Gro looked at her hopefully, her tail wagging a couple of times, and Lia nearly burst into tears again because the poor creature still thought life would get back to normal soon. The four-pawed idiot believed the world was good and of course Berg would come back and of course Lia would have a little extra something for a guest.

One of those things was true. There was leftover pizza in the fridge.

Sunday.

Lia went to the Studio before noon. Rico and Paddy were already there, and Maggie had rung to say she was on her way. Everyone looked like they had been crying.

The Rich Lane bodies were all over the TV news and online. They hadn't made it into the papers yet.

A Rich Lane body. That was all Berg was now.

The police had investigated the scene through the night and issued their initial statement at eight in the morning. A fourth person kicked to death, and a fifth victim who had been shot.

Lia and the others noticed what information the police withheld in order to protect their investigation. They didn't say they had received a video recording of events in the alley. Or that Berg had died trying to stop the killer – concealing that felt wrong to Lia since it robbed Berg of his importance.

When she arrived, Maggie was very calm, much more so than the others expected.

'I took a pill,' she stated quickly.

As a group they tried to concentrate on the things that needed doing. They and the police had a video of the previous night's events in Kensington. In it they could see the killer, potentially well enough to identify him.

Did they need to help the police more with Berg's case? The video would show them that he didn't bring Brian Fowler to the street, but it also showed that Berg had a gun. Did they need to convince the police that Berg hadn't been party to the killings in any way?

They had five cameras installed on streets around London.

Paddy hadn't had time to install the last one he had been carrying. Should they leave the cameras in place? Would it be worth trying to set up more?

There was no end of questions, but it was hard to decide things because Mari wasn't at the Studio. None of them wanted to ring her in case she was sleeping. She could have been up all night, so they had to give her time to recover.

They focused on the video. Watching it was oppressive, almost nightmarish, but they had to determine what they could see of the killer. Rico enlarged one image after another, all the ones in which any part of the guy was visible.

No face. They could see what he was wearing, a baseball cap, leather jacket, dark trousers and heavy shoes. But no clear picture of his face, not even in profile.

The killer's vehicle was so blurry that it would be no help identifying him, but Rico did get one detail out of the enlargements. The white van had a two-word advert on the side. They couldn't read it, but just the fact that it existed meant something.

'He might be using a logo from a maintenance or security company,' Paddy suggested. 'Then no one would take any notice of him parking his van on streets at night that don't have parking spaces.'

Now that they thought there might only be one killer, the earlier videos appeared in a different light. It was possible he had just repeatedly spliced together pictures of kicks he had meted out himself.

'We can tell his height from this,' Paddy said.

The police would be able to estimate it precisely because they had the victim's body and the video showed the killer dragging Fowler. They were almost the same height. The killer was also strong. Despite his slender frame, he was able to move his victim relatively easily.

'He works out,' Paddy said. 'That kind of strength takes work.'

They rewound the video over and over, back and forth, every part of it in which they could catch a glimpse of the victim in his red and black shirt. From this they could now be sure it was Brian Fowler. When they compared images from the video with pictures they had found of Fowler, he was recognisable, if only just.

At some point in the afternoon they realised that Mari might not come in to the Studio at all that day. She hadn't made any contact.

Lia looked at the big bunch of keys Mari had given her. 'For emergencies,' Mari had said.

Stealthily Lia tried the keys in the different doors around the Studio. The key ring held keys for all of them, including the large freight doors at the back of the Den. But there were two more keys that didn't seem to belong to the Studio at all.

Had Mari known when she gave Lia these keys that she wouldn't be coming in?

Lia threw a ball for Gro in the Den. The dog was elated: a familiar game and a familiar place with her master's smell everywhere.

'Listen, pup,' Lia said. 'If there's an emergency, what are we going to do then?'

19.

When the sorrow comes, it is a tsunami the size of a building that leaves nothing standing in its wake.

Mari knows the sorrow is coming; she can feel it on her shoulders and in her temples. It makes her put her hands to her head, massaging lightly, preparing for what is to come.

That is why she first gives Paddy instructions for searching Berg's belongings and arranges for Rico to send the video to the police. And this is why she gives the keys to Lia. She has to prevent the worst consequences of Berg's death from hitting them all.

These are things she can do. After the others leave the Studio, she stays behind to watch their very own snuff film. She memorises the images. She looks at them as long as she is able.

In the morning, before dawn, Mari takes a small scrap of paper, scribbles a few words on it, places it on her desk and leaves the Studio. On the street she hails a taxi. She glances at the driver and, as she looks, Mari knows this precaution is only coming from her medulla. She sees nothing. The driver could be anyone, and Mari's brain wouldn't detect it.

She gets out in Hoxton three streets before her flat. Always at least three streets early.

As she walks to her home, no one else is on the street. That much she can still notice. She has to get home, behind locked doors.

Being at home is a relief. Mari stands in the hall. The doors are closed. She sets down her bag, observing her own reactions.

Screaming? Weeping? What physical expression would be right? Right in what sense?

When this sorrow comes, it is the size of a building. Mari almost sees it coming.

She sits on her living room floor, at the edge of the large room, near the large windows. The sorrow comes, and she wraps her arms around her knees and squeezes. She's breaking down in so many places.

Mari curls up under the sorrow. She rocks on the floor.

Their Berg is dead.

She can't think. All her thoughts hurt too much.

This is torment.

20.

Lia opened the front door of the unfamiliar building with one of the keys from the big key ring.

Bridport Place. There were no resident's names listed – this was not one of those buildings where each name was written next to the buzzers or in the hall. The building was old and handsome, and apparently a pub had once operated downstairs. Everything felt so big and strange.

She looked for flat number nineteen. There was no name on the door, only a number.

For a moment she hesitated about ringing the doorbell. It felt wrong for some reason. She glanced at the lock and her keys and then chose one. The door opened easily. Stepping inside, she quickly pulled the door shut behind her.

Mari's home.

On the floor in the hall was Mari's bag. Lia was used to seeing it at the Studio. Seeing it here felt strange. And stepping into the flat at all felt forbidden, as if she were breaking an unspoken rule. Mari had never invited her or the others from the Studio to her home or even told them where she lived.

Lia had spent hours at the Studio thinking. But no word had come from Mari, not even a text to any of them, and when Paddy tried to ring, no one answered.

They didn't have Mari's address, and Lia only knew that she lived in Hoxton. She guessed they wouldn't find the address in any public listings, so spending time looking was pointless.

But the bunch of keys Mari had given her held two keys that didn't belong to the Studio. And Lia remembered Mari's expression the previous night when she handed Lia the keys.

Over the past year Mari had disappeared for a few days on one or two occasions. Just like that, as if somehow ceasing to exist for a moment. She had never explained her disappearances to Lia – suddenly they just didn't see her at the Studio, no one seemed to know where she was and Mari only replied to their messages after several days. She hadn't been sick then. Lia thought she would have noticed that.

Lia suspected Mari had been away from London travelling and didn't want the others to know about her trips. Now this was a new situation though, clearly brought on by Berg's death.

At the Studio they were getting nowhere. Rico had gone through the video from the night before, searching through it frame by frame for any details they could use to identify Berg and Brian Fowler's killer. Maggie and Paddy had scanned the news broadcasts about the Rich Lane victims.

But without Mari, their work lacked purpose. Everything was on hold.

Lia had started prowling the Studio offices. Gro followed her everywhere except into Mari and Rico's offices, so she rarely went in either. That was why she didn't notice the paper on Mari's desk until the afternoon.

Bridsataman paikka. Asunto yhdeksäntoista.

Mari had written the address and flat number all in Finnish so only Lia would understand the cryptic message.

Lia had set out immediately by taxi, leaving Gro in Paddy and Maggie's care.

Mari's home was large, disconcertingly large as far as Lia was concerned.

There were six rooms in addition to an open kitchen. It quickly dawned on Lia that Mari's flat and terrace covered practically the entire top storey of the building.

She walked through the flat carefully, not wanting to barge in or startle Mari, who might be sleeping.

The decoration had a simple beauty. Berg's hand was visible everywhere in the Studio, but here Mari had assembled a world of her own. Lia recognised brand names she had only ever seen in style magazines and expensive boutiques.

The living room alone was at least forty square metres. That was more than twice the size of Lia's entire small flat. There didn't seem to be much in the room: two mismatched sofas – one Missoni and one something expensive and Scandinavian – and some imposing tall windows. Apparently Mari liked that kind of combination since at the Studio she had two different sofas in her office too.

She found Mari in the bedroom, lying on the large bed fully dressed. She appeared to be awake.

'Hi,' Lia said.

Mari looked her in the eye, but only for a fleeting moment.

Lia saw a great deal in that short space of time. This was all Mari could do right now. Mari had been crying, but Lia wasn't sure whether she had slept. Lia sat down on the edge of the bed.

'Should I ring a doctor?' she asked.

'Don't,' Mari said.

Her voice was faint but her thoughts lucid.

'Do you need something?'

No answer.

Mari's face contorted. She pulled her arms up to cover it. Under white clenched knuckles her jaw trembled.

Lia grabbed a blanket from a chair, set it on the bed next to Mari and quietly closed the door behind her.

At the Studio Lia didn't say anything specific about Mari's condition or her home. She just said she had been to see her. Paddy wanted to ring Mari, but Lia encouraged him to wait.

They were all walking wounded because of Berg. Talking about what had happened was hard, but still it was constantly present. Mari's absence made them restless, as did the knowledge that the killer was probably still free.

Maggie went through the information she had found about Berg's relatives. Only two lived in Britain, a half-sister and a cousin. In Sweden there was more family, on Berg's father's side.

Luckily we don't have to tell them the bad news, Lia thought. 'What will the police do with him?' she asked Paddy when the others weren't listening.

'They'll move on two fronts,' Paddy said.

Berg's body had been taken in for forensic analysis. His death had become part of Operation Rhea now and would be assigned its own principal detectives, one of whom would be contacting Berg's relatives and friends, and the others would be digging through all the information they could get about him.

'They'll go to his flat today. They've probably already been there,' Paddy said.

Lia tried to lighten her mood by temporarily concentrating on practical matters: she took Gro outside and then went looking for proper dog food for her.

The six o'clock news announced Berg's name to the entire world, following a police press conference. British and Swedish citizen Bertil Tore Berg, sixty-three, had been shot the previous night in Kensington. The circumstances of the shooting were unclear. His body had been found near another man's, thirty-four-year-old Brian Fowler. They also reported that Fowler had disappeared three days earlier after spending the evening at a nightclub with a previous victim, Evelyn Morris.

The news did not make any special mention of the video the Studio had sent the police, but eventually the police did announce receiving evidence that Berg had tried to stop the man suspected of Fowler's murder. They also asked the public for any information regarding events or movements in the immediate vicinity of Rich Lane the previous evening.

Bertil Tore Berg, sixty-three, citizen of Britain and Sweden.

You couldn't describe Berg like that, Lia thought. He was their wizard of stage design, their friend, their bear in overalls. Gro's master. Berg was laughter, intelligence, attentiveness. The sounds of the Den.

Lia knew why Mari was lying at home incapacitated.

Paddy and Maggie left, but Rico wanted to stay with his machines.

'Can you watch Gro for a little while?' Lia asked.

'Are you going to Hoxton?' Rico asked.

Lia nodded.

'Tell Mari that...' Rico began but trailed off mid-sentence. 'Say that we'll get through this too,' Rico finally said. 'I'll work on my tablet so I can sit with Gro Harlem in the Den.'

Mari's flat was dark and silent.

Lia switched on the hall lights and glanced around. Had Mari been up and around?

Nothing in the flat suggested so. There were no clothes tossed over the back of a chair and no cup left on the table. The large kitchen showed no signs of anyone having eaten there. Lia looked in the fridge, which was almost the same size as her entire kitchenette in Hampstead. An open milk carton, cheeses, and something in the vegetable drawer. Everything arranged in orderly fashion.

Does she have a cleaner?

Was that possible? Mari protected her privacy with almost frightening fastidiousness, but the flat was large and Mari was always at work. And she had money – maybe she did use a maid.

Lia listened quietly at the bedroom door. Nothing came from inside. Lia turned off the hall light so it wouldn't shine into the bedroom and carefully opened the door.

Mari was sleeping, her breathing deep and slow.

Lia inspected the flat more thoroughly. She wanted to see all the rooms, but she had to do it cautiously.

Holy shit I'm curious about her.

That didn't mean voyeurism though. You couldn't go too far into friends' personal areas, especially not with a friend like Mari.

She didn't open any drawers or sniff around in any cupboards. She sat in different places, read the spines of books in the wall of bookcases and looked at the paintings. There were few decorations, although she knew Mari travelled a lot.

She thought for a moment about Mari's office at the Studio. One wall there was dedicated to shelves bearing dozens of neatly arranged binders with information about the Studio's previous jobs, the ones Mari had never been willing to talk about. But Lia couldn't go riffling through the binders without Mari's knowledge. The very thought was impossible, also because a beautiful curtain Berg had made covered the shelves. Not only would Lia have to break Mari's trust, in a way she also would have been insulting Berg.

Glancing around a friend's house stayed within the bounds of propriety though.

I'm not prying. I'm just looking.

She allowed herself a couple of open-faced sandwiches. The bread and other bits and bobs were easily accessible in the kitchen – she didn't need to go snooping too much in the cupboards.

It was almost time for the Channel Four news. But of course there was no normal television in Mari's home, either in the living room or the kitchen.

Lia went into the study. It resembled Mari's office at the Studio: a large room with a long, handsome desk, binders and books on the shelves. An enormous plasma screen covered one wall. Mari must have used that for watching TV.

Lia spent a while searching for a remote but didn't find one. Finally she plucked up the courage to sit in Mari's chair and looked at the desk. The laptop was in sleep mode.

She brushed the touchpad. The machine started reviving, which also woke up the wall display. On the screen Lia saw quick links for television and several other options: apparently Mari watched TV through the computer.

Opening the evening news on the computer, and thereby also on the enormous flat screen, Lia leaned back in Mari's chair and ate. She felt a little guilty. But also relieved.

Guilty because here she was sitting in her friend's inner sanctum, seeing things with Mari's eyes, possibly dropping crumbs in a place where no one was supposed to eat. Relieved because Mari was sleeping. Things might work out and the time for grieving might pass someday.

Berg's and Brian Fowler's deaths weren't even the number one story on the news any more. At its height, Craig Cole's Gropegate scandal had dominated the headlines for a few days, and the letters, phone calls and scrapbooks the Studio had made to help him had spawned their own consequences, but the notice they had attracted was waning as well. The video killings would remain in the news for some time to come, until eventually they had to make room for other things as well.

Publicity was a cold sea governed by no one and in which no one was safe. Lia was wondering whether that was sad or just the way the world dealt with problems and moved forward, but then her thoughts were disturbed when something started ringing.

A soft buzzing, insistently repetitive. Lia frantically searched for its source so that Mari wouldn't wake up, until she spotted a telephone icon pulsing on the computer screen. Opening the app, Lia read the name next to the caller's avatar. Mamia.

Mari's mother? What was her name? Don't they live somewhere in Häme, near Pori?

Before she had time to think it through too carefully, Lia clicked the Answer button. She jumped when a face flashed onto the computer screen and the large wall display.

An elderly woman with dark hair stared from the wall. She couldn't be Mari's mother – she was much too old.

'This is new,' the woman said in Finnish.

'Good evening,' Lia answered when she didn't know what else to say.

'Dear girl, I can't hear you,' the old woman said. 'You need the headphones with the microphone. They're there somewhere. Or turn on the microphone on the computer.'

Lia stared at the old lady who was instructing her how to use Skype on Mari's computer. Looking around, on the edge of the desk Lia found a light pair of headphones with a small mic attached. Quickly she plugged them into the computer. Mari had to sleep, and Lia didn't want Mari to see her messing with her computer.

'You're the Finn,' the old woman said once Lia had the headphones on. 'You're Lia.'

Lia realised that the woman had to be some relation to Mari. She could hear it in her voice and see it in her features, her cheekbones.

'Yeah,' Lia said.

'Where is Mari then?' the woman asked.

'In there – sleeping.'

The woman's eyes sharpened ever so slightly.

'I'm Mari's grandmother,' she said. 'Her father's mother. Mirjami Rautee.'

Lia smiled and nodded. The video connection was a little slow, giving the feeling that you had to exaggerate your gestures and speak more clearly for the other person to understand.

'In the family everyone calls me Mamia,' Mari's grandmother said.

'Mamia,' Lia repeated.

'There's a little story behind the name,' Mamia said.

Lia took a breath and thought for a second. Mari was sleeping off a case of shock so severe she had wanted to give Lia her keys to every door in the Studio and her home. Mari certainly hadn't intended for Lia to end up talking to her grandma, but she could hardly take offence.

'What kind of story?' Lia asked.

'Let's not get into that now,' Mamia said. 'Maybe we can talk about it sometime though.'

The same quickness, the same accuracy in every thought as Mari.

'Now I don't want to be unfriendly, Lia,' Mamia said, 'but since you're answering when I called Mari, it's clear that everything isn't right there. Mari hasn't answered me in days. At all. You are apparently a new visitor to Mari's home, or at least you haven't been there often. You didn't know to use the headset for the phone, and you have a plate under that sandwich that Mari doesn't use for sandwiches. It's too small. You must have taken it out of the cupboard yourself. What's going on there? Is Mari ill?'

Lia had a difficult time balancing what she could and couldn't tell Mari's grandmother. The bluntness of Mamia's questions didn't help the situation.

But in her own way Mamia was also leaving her space not to talk about things, Lia noticed. Mamia wanted to know specifically whether Mari was in some sort of distress, but she wasn't one of those old people who didn't give others space to live their lives.

Lia said that a good friend of theirs had died tragically, and they were all trying to get over the shock.

'It wasn't Paddy, was it?' Mamia asked immediately.

How much does she know? Lia wondered. *Could she know about the Studio?*

'No,' Lia said. 'Not Paddy.'

'Good. I've told Mari over and over that in many ways women may be at their best single, but if a man happens to come along you can fall for, you should give the option serious consideration. Mari doesn't exactly have men lining up outside her door. Men who could keep up with her that is.

'You don't want to tell me any more about this death,' Mamia continued. 'That's fine. Not everything needs to be spread around.'

Lia listened, baffled by the woman's frankness. Mamia relaxed and gave a laugh.

'You're obviously hungry. I don't mind if you eat while we talk.'

Their conversation was strange and stimulating.

Lia didn't remember ever meeting anyone like her – only her first encounter with Mari had made as deep an impression.

Mamia had to be at least eighty years old, she decided. She didn't know how old Mari's parents were, but the wall-sized display revealed the lines in her grandmother's face. Mamia was very thin. She had on a light frock, almost a summer dress, although early spring was cold in Finland, Lia knew.

Good blood circulation. She must exercise a lot or be health conscious otherwise.

Mari hadn't told Lia much of anything about her family. Only that they were from Häme and they were social democrats. Her sister was a teacher somewhere, or at least she had been. And there was a brother who secretly married a Chilean woman without telling anyone.

'You've been at *Level* how long now? Six years?' Mamia asked.

'Yeah, I guess. Why?'

'It's good to get yourself a solid position,' Mamia observed. 'But that's quite a long time to spend at one publication. If you compare it to others your age on the London job market. Don't most people switch places every few years?'

'I haven't needed a change,' Lia said. 'It took me a long time to get used to this job. I'm not much of a… career person.'

'No, you aren't,' Mamia said.

Her expression was so warm Lia couldn't take offence at how direct she was being. Mamia seemed to be well-informed about life in London. Maybe Mari had told her about it.

'You and Mari, neither of you think about your careers,' Mamia said. 'Sometimes I envy you. When I was that age, we had so many more rules. It was rare for someone to go abroad unless they had to in order to make a living. Back then you had to choose what you were going to do and stick with it.'

'What did you do?'

Mamia had been a secretary in a magistrate's court. Her diction told of the meticulousness and diligence she applied to discharging her duties. At times she had been frustrated with the hierarchical institution, but now she was mostly proud of her working years. She had seen people's lives from many different perspectives, she noted, and learned how to manage information.

'You were a little surprised to have an old lady like me calling you over the Internet,' Mamia said.

Lia laughed.

'Yes, it was a bit of a shock,' she admitted. 'My grandparents have got used to mobile phones, but email and the Internet and all that is still a struggle.'

'I can imagine. I do much better than most. On the other hand, one does have plenty of time at this age.'

'Mari doesn't talk much about her parents or other family,' Lia said. 'Where do you all live?'

The furrowed face on the wall turned serious.

'Here and there,' Mamia said. 'Here and there.'

They talked for a long time. Mamia spoke about Finland, the dramatic twists and turns of the recent elections and what was on at the major art museums and theatres.

Lia deduced from their conversation that at least some of Mari's family members lived in Finland but that communication between them was not uncomplicated. Still, how dear Mari was to her grandmother was obvious.

Lia recognised a good number of similarities between the two. Mari had surely inherited some of her sense of justice from her grandmother. They had the same quick wit and the same habit of issuing orders.

'I imagine you're still hungry,' Mamia said. 'You can stop being so polite and picking crumbs off your plate. There's Finnish crisp bread in the kitchen. I know because I sent it.'

Lia obeyed, fetching more bread. She forgot to take care not to drop crumbs in the study as Mamia told the story of her nickname.

'It happened near Pori,' Mamia said. 'I'm sure you don't think someone from Pori could come up with something like this on her own. We're far too serious.'

Mari and her three siblings had been visiting their grandparents.

'It was a rare joy for us,' Mamia said. 'It didn't happen often at all.'

Mari's mother didn't like sleeping in strange houses, she explained, and there were other reasons.

'They had strong childrearing principles. Children weren't allowed to speak rudely. Swearing was punished. They were likely the politest, most obedient children in all of Finland.'

Mamia had taken issue with many aspects of parenting in her son's family. Lia noticed from Mamia's careful choice of words that she was tiptoeing around the topic.

Once when Mari's family was visiting, Mamia was watching the children play inside. Mari's parents were outside, and in the middle of the game Mari's little brother said, 'That's shit.'

'The boy said it without thinking,' Mamia said. 'We had been watching television and there was a comedy show where one of the characters cursed about a Finnish rally racer's car using that word. And the little boy repeated the word, as children are apt to do. My thought was that these overly obedient children felt so free with me that they could say anything that popped into their heads.'

The little boy was frightened when he realised he had said a swear word. He thought he had offended his grandmother and knew if his parents found out they would punish him.

'I told him it was a word just like any other word. A strong word, yes, which should be used with care and consideration. But since their parents didn't want them to use it, they should honour that.'

Then she invented a game for the children. They could choose a nickname for her. The children thought that was ever so exciting, and Mari's big sister chose the name Mamia because when she was little she used to call Grandmother Mirjami that when she was learning to talk.

'So I said that from now on, I'm Mamia. And whenever you say Mamia, it can mean anything you want. And it's also a swear word, but only we know that.'

Lia laughed in surprise.

'I didn't see any harm in it,' Mamia said. 'It was good for the children to learn that swearing could be perfectly acceptable at times and that no one should make such a fuss about it. It was a harmless way to let the children talk like children.'

The name game had become Mamia and the children's shared secret. Saying her nickname amused the children to no end. Sometimes they would chant it. 'Mamia, Mamia, Mamia.'

Mari and her siblings never revealed the game to their parents, Mamia said.

'What does the name mean now?'

Mamia smiled.

'It's simply Mamia. They can swear all they want now. Now they can do as they wish.'

The call had lasted for more than an hour when Lia noticed that night had long since fallen outside. Mamia saw Lia glancing at the clock.

'We should stop now,' Mamia said.

'It would be nice to chat longer,' Lia said. 'But I have a dog I need to take out and some other things to do.'

Mamia looked contemplative.

'You mentioned that Mari doesn't talk about her family there,' she said. 'She doesn't say much to me about her friends. I've heard a little about you. And Paddy, of course.'

'That's how she is,' Lia said.

Neither said anything for a moment.

'Lia, do you know that I've always thought that Mari is one of the last women that life could ever crush. She's experienced so much.'

Lia swallowed, not knowing what to say.

'But then if something ever were to knock her down...' the old woman said, trailing off. 'If you can, take care of her now. She doesn't want to be taken care of. She can't stand anyone watching over her. But no one can survive everything alone.'

Lia thought of Mari lying in her bed nearly incapacitated with grief.

'If something gets through all of Mari's defences, things could go very badly for her,' Mamia said. Lia nodded.

Mamia smiled plaintively.

'Goodnight.'

The old woman's face disappeared from the wall. Lia picked up a few breadcrumbs she had dropped and turned off the computer.

She walked to the door of the room and could sense before she entered the corridor that someone was there.

In the hall she found Mari, swaying, leaning on the wall for support.

What had Mari heard of their phone call? At least the end.

Mari looked at her. The agony was visible in her eyes. Lia knew she couldn't say anything about Berg directly. And this wasn't a woman anyone could nurse.

'Gro is waiting,' Lia said. 'I have to take her out and then get her home.'

Water welled up in Mari's eyes. Cautiously Lia approached and hugged her. They stood in the dark hall without saying anything, holding tight to each other and crying.

21

On her way to the Studio, Lia turned on her smartphone. She had five messages and three calls, all from Rico. Lia's phone had been on silent as Rico tried to contact her all night. The text messages just said, *Ring*.

Has he found something new about the video killer? Lia wondered as she dialled.

'No, nothing new,' Rico answered immediately. 'But we forgot something very important. Berg's call history. The phone company has a record of all his calls.'

They had taken Berg's mobile phone, but the police would be able to investigate his phone traffic by digging into the telephone company's records. At the Studio they knew the calls wouldn't be any help capturing the killer, but they would tie Berg to the Studio.

'I told Mari we should be using crypto-phones with untraceable metadata,' Rico complained.

'How fast can the police get the call data?'

'Paddy thinks they can't do it during the night. They'll need a search warrant, and they'll have to go to the phone company's premises since they don't let anyone into their system remotely. But in a criminal investigation this size – they'll be there first thing in the morning when the phone company opens its doors.'

Lia looked at her phone: almost ten. They had perhaps only eleven hours before the police would be able to connect the Bertil Tore Berg found dead on Rich Lane to the Studio.

'Paddy and Maggie are here,' Rico said.

'I'll be there in a minute,' Lia promised.

Determining whether Rico could mess around with the call information by hacking into the telephone company's system took them nearly an hour. It turned out to be nearly impossible in such a short timeframe.

Rico knew of cases where it had succeeded, things he'd heard from his hacker friends. But Berg's operator was Vodafone, one of the world's largest telecom companies, whose systems had notoriously difficult security.

'Hacking their mobile accounts is pretty easy,' Rico said.

People were doing that all the time all over the world hoping for free calls, but penetrating the information the company kept about its customers was a different proposition altogether.

'And we don't just have to get in to look at it. We have to be able to alter it,' Rico said.

Mari wouldn't have taken this long to realise that the phone operator had the call information too. If she was healthy, Lia thought. *We need Mari.*

The entire existence of the Studio was now under threat.

Rico began breaking the matter down into its essential parts: what things in Berg's calls and messages were dangerous for them? Just that he had kept in such close contact with all of them, for one. Berg had communicated with Mari, Paddy and Rico about Studio business, but most of his messages to Lia and Maggie were more personal.

According to the law, the telecom company was obliged to maintain information about the times of any calls or messages, as well as the numbers of the senders and receivers and the customer's location when they made the call where the customer was in the network. Retaining the content of messages was a more delicate matter.

'There are a lot of crazy rumours about that,' Rico said. 'Some people claim every message anyone ever sends is secretly stored in some kind of permanent archive somewhere.'

In reality practices for saving the content of messages differed widely around the world, and the laws varied too.

But the police might be able to turn up some of the content of Berg's messages and would at least contact them at the Studio, and possibly even look into their backgrounds. Paddy's activities as a private investigator and former cop would be of particular interest. Especially since he had spent some time in prison for his participation in an attempted armoured-car jacking. That was his one and only criminal escapade, but it would arouse suspicion. Rico's background as a hacker would come out too, and since the killer had uploaded his videos using hacked user accounts, they would definitely haul Rico in for questioning.

Because Lia had been in contact with the police a year earlier, their databases might also contain entries about her. Mari certainly wouldn't want to have any sort of contact with the authorities. Maggie was the only one of them that wouldn't be caught in the net.

'We have to remove your information,' Maggie said. 'If they question me, they won't get much. I can just say Berg was my friend and we met through the theatre.'

Could they replace the call information they hoped to delete with new data? Lia suggested. The police would have a harder time picking out Berg's calls to people at the Studio if they were buried in a mass of other data. Rico was an old hand at setting up dummy corporations and creating plausible electronic histories for them. Could he fake phone calls too?

'I've never tried that,' Rico said.

Despite the rush and the pressure, the idea got him excited.

They worked late into the night. As Rico researched how to meddle with phone connection information, Maggie and Paddy collected names and numbers they could place in Berg's phone records as a smokescreen. They concentrated on his carpentry work so it would look like Berg had contacts with customers and firms in the industry. The easiest was to use contact information for the big wholesalers and timber suppliers because no one there would remember whether a certain carpenter had rung at a certain time.

Lia helped the others and took Gro out for occasional walks. The poor dog's schedule was all out of whack, but at least she was used to sleeping in the Den.

When Rico thought he had the process of altering call data under control and they had collected dozens of phone numbers, the biggest question lay ahead: how to get their hands on the Vodafone data.

The company's main offices were in Berkshire, Newbury, more than fifty miles from London. There was an administrative office building in Paddington, but the technical staff were in Berkshire.

'I don't think the police will go all the way to Newbury. And we don't have to either,' Rico said.

All they needed was to break into the company's data system and telecommunications archives. Many employees at the offices in Paddington would also have access to those servers.

'But going there ourselves doesn't necessarily make sense,' Rico said.

Rico showed them a small memory stick. All he needed was to have someone plug this USB drive into a Vodafone computer connected to the internal network.

'After that I'm as good as there. Once the connection to the Vodafone archives is open, I don't think it will take me long to change Berg's metadata. But we have to do it without anyone noticing the memory stick.'

Maggie nodded.

'That sounds like a job for me,' she said.

22

Maggie arrived in Paddington at 9.04 a.m. The Vodafone administrative HQ was located in a large glass office building at One
Kingdom Street. Maggie walked into the towering lobby whose walls
listed the names of the businesses operating in the building only in
small letters. She showed the laminated badge hanging around her
neck to the uniformed guard in reception.

'Good morning.'

The guard glanced at the card, which claimed Maggie was Judith
Bates, a telecommunications official with Ofcom, a British communications regulatory body.

'Good morning, Ms Bates,' the man said warmly. 'Do you have
an appointment?'

'No, we don't announce when we're coming at Ofcom,' Maggie
said. 'I'm on my way to the Vodafone legal department.'

The man immediately turned serious. Ofcom had received a great
deal of attention in the media recently after attacking the tabloids
for phone hacking, and the agency had gained a reputation as an
aggressive watchdog for the powers that be.

The guard ushered Maggie through the electronic security checkpoint to the lifts.

In the Vodafone legal department, she was received by a young
man who did a good job of controlling his expression after seeing her
Ofcom inspector's badge. When Maggie asked to see the department
head, Jon Fordham, the man frowned.

'Mr Fordham is indisposed,' the man said. 'If you had made an
appointment...'

'Dear boy,' Maggie interrupted, 'we have our reasons for not doing
that.'

Maggie quickly sized up the man. One of the younger employees,
possibly only an intern, who didn't necessarily have access to the
company's protected data systems.

Instantly Maggie decided on her next move.

'I have a tip for you,' she said in a more gracious tone. 'It would be
a good idea for you to find me someone in management right now.
And your security chief, Mr Grove, will want to know I'm here.'

'Why?'

Maggie smiled.

'Security chiefs want to know everything.'

'Grove is in Newbury,' the man said. 'Almost all of the security department have their offices there.'

'I know,' Maggie said. 'I've been there too before. Give him a ring anyway. He'll be pleased with you for informing him so quickly that an Ofcom competition regulator is here. He'll probably be here before long anyway.'

From the man's face, Maggie could see how nervous he was. Looking on his laptop computer, he began searching through the department staff calendars.

'Mr Fordham and Mr Lewis are otherwise engaged,' he said. 'Both department heads.'

'So early on a Monday? How diligent of them,' Maggie said.

'A visitor has just arrived,' he replied.

Maggie shrugged. While she waited, she took two papers out of her briefcase and read them. Then she realised what could be happening in the department.

'Is another government official already here?' she asked.

The man lowered his eyes, and Maggie read volumes in his expression.

'I'll find someone else,' the man said, snapping his computer shut and leaving.

Maggie glanced around to make sure no one was within earshot and rang Rico.

'The police are already here,' she said. 'They arrived in the legal department just before me. We could already be too late.'

At the Studio a heated debate broke out in Rico's office.

If the police had already presented their search warrant to Vodafone and gained access to the phone records, should Maggie continue her mission? Or should she get out of there as quick as she could?

'Stay there,' Rico told her. 'Stay on course unless you hear different from us.'

He rang off and looked at Paddy.

'Do we have any way to delay the police at the Vodafone office?'

Lia shook her head as she watched Paddy and Rico confer. They were exhausted after a sleepless night, but none of them could go to sleep even after Maggie had left on her assignment.

Maggie's back story had come from Paddy, who had heard about Ofcom making surprise inspections. It didn't take long to design an identity for Maggie in keeping with the agency's style, but creating the necessary identity documents took time.

Those kinds of jobs had been Berg's territory, since he was the expert. But as a graphic designer, Lia had been up to the task of creating an ID card, and Paddy printed test specimens on the specialised printers in the Den. They knew Berg always did that. They went through several drafts, honing every detail so the final card would stand up to scrutiny at Vodafone. Paddy and Lia had also made up a thin stack of papers with the Ofcom logo and official-looking text. If necessary, this would add to the impression that Maggie was indeed an inspector on a surprise visit.

She had handled her outfit herself: a stylish but unremarkable two-piece suit, wig and glasses changed her appearance sufficiently.

'And what if Vodafone contacts Ofcom asking about what the inspection is about?' Lia had asked Paddy during the night.

'That's possible but highly unlikely,' Paddy said. 'Under no circumstances does a telecom company want to irritate Ofcom. And they'll know that getting personal data on inspectors like this isn't that simple since the agency wants to protect their work.'

No detail had been left to chance. Maggie had thoroughly thought through her role, and they had done a string of test runs. Now they had to change their plans on the go.

In the Vodafone legal department, Maggie was directed to a smiling man in his fifties.

'Good morning, Ms Bates,' Kenneth Laing said, shaking her hand. 'How can we be of assistance to Ofcom?'

Maggie handed him the memory stick.

'Thank you, Mr Laing. You can start by opening this on your computer.'

Bewildered, Laing stared at the blue stick adorned with the Ofcom logo.

'You must know that isn't possible.'

'How so?'

'We have very strict rules about what outside devices we can attach to our work computers. No memory sticks. Unless they have been carefully inspected first.'

'Smart rule,' Maggie said. 'That's standard procedure anywhere. But unfortunately I had to send my own laptop in for service on Friday and I haven't got it back yet. Of course I can stop by our office at Riverside House and bring back another computer.'

The man saw on her face what intense irritation the idea aroused in her.

'How long would that take?' Laing asked.

'At least an hour. Perhaps an hour and a half, depending on traffic,' Maggie said.

Laing hesitated.

'This is highly irregular,' he said.

Maggie looked at Laing, evaluating whether she should apply any more pressure. She decided not to say anything and waited.

'What's on the memory stick?' Laing asked.

Maggie knew that everything depended on her answer right now. They had rehearsed it ahead of time.

'That's precisely what I want to hear from you. An explanation for what is on this memory stick.'

Laing was taken aback. Maggie noticed how the man continued shifting his weight from one leg to the other in agitation. Laing probably didn't realise he was doing it.

And even before the man said it out loud, Maggie knew she was through.

'Please follow me,' Laing said. 'Would you like coffee or tea?'

As Maggie was walking into a small office decorated in Vodafone red and white, Paddy was calling the company's central telephone exchange.

'This is Detective Chief Inspector Martin Beresford,' Paddy said, introducing himself to the operator and asking to be connected to

Jon Fordham in the legal department.

A moment later the woman replied that Fordham wasn't answering. He was on the premises but wasn't picking up his phone.

'I'm calling on police business. This is very important,' Paddy explained. 'I need to get in touch with the inspector meeting with Mr Fordham immediately.'

The woman tried ringing again, to no effect.

'I'm sorry, but Mr Fordham still isn't answering. You'll have to ring your colleague at his own number.'

'But my colleague isn't answering his phone either. Otherwise I wouldn't be talking to you,' Paddy pointed out.

'I can try someone near Mr Fordham if that would help,' the operator suggested.

'Yes, if you would be so kind!'

A small red light flashed on the memory stick as Kenneth Laing's computer loaded it.

'Can you please now tell me what this is all about?' Laing asked.

'Of course,' Maggie said pleasantly. 'Or let me open this file. It's easier to show it.'

She leaned over the keyboard and double-clicked a file on the memory stick named 'Vodafone3.xlsx'. On screen a table of numbers and alphabetical codes opened up. At the same time programs on the memory stick were also opening a connection from Laing's computer to somewhere else entirely: to Rico, at the studio.

Laing looked at the Vodafone3 spreadsheet and then turned to Maggie.

'I'm sorry, but I don't recognise this, Ms Bates.'

'You really don't?' Maggie asked.

She let the innocent question hang in the air between them. Kenneth Laing had experience and talent, which was why the young man had directed the inspector to him. But Laing's ability to tolerate silence was just as weak as most people's. Long, pregnant pauses made him uneasy. Calmly Maggie looked at Laing, whose face was illuminated by the light filtering through the large windows. The blue-tinted glass panels of One Kingdom Street created an unreal feeling as if everything were happening in a dream world.

Laing searched the table for details he could recognise.

'This isn't about taxation or finance, which are what I specialise in,' he said.

'No,' Maggie said.

She watched the red light flashing on Rico's memory stick. At first it had been quick, but now it was just a steady blinking.

'I could do with a coffee with milk,' Maggie said. 'No sugar. And skimmed milk, if you have any.'

'No one in that department is answering right now,' the woman at the Vodafone switchboard said to Paddy with regret. 'They're all off somewhere. Some of them aren't even at work yet at this hour. A lot of them don't come in until ten.'

'Isn't there any way to contact them?' Paddy asked insistently. 'What do they do if an emergency happens where people's lives are in danger?'

'I'm sorry,' the operator said. 'You'll need to ring back a little later. Or I can take a ring-back request.'

'No, I'm the one who is sorry,' Paddy said. 'I'm sure you've already tried everything possible. What was your name, by the way?'

'Martha,' the woman said uncertainly.

'Martha,' Paddy repeated. 'Nice to meet you, Martha.'

The woman laughed.

'So first thing Monday morning you have a rude policeman calling you,' Paddy said. 'Not the best way to start off a week.'

'You haven't been rude at all, just demanding,' Martha said. 'There just isn't anyone answering over there right now. Unfortunately.'

'It is unfortunate,' Paddy said. 'You probably aren't even in the London office. The phone centre isn't here, is it?'

'No, we're in Newbury these days.'

'What would you do, Martha, if there were an emergency and you had to make contact with someone in the legal department but no one was answering their phones?'

The line went silent. Finally a second laugh came.

'I'd make an announcement over the PA system,' Martha said. 'We have a connection to that too.'

Paddy closed his eyes and waited.

'I can't do that now though,' Martha said.

'Why not?' Paddy asked.

'Well because we're only allowed to do that in special circumstances. We've only ever really used it during fire drills,' Martha explained. 'And once they played music over it and read greetings from all the companies at the anniversary of the building's opening. But it's really only there for emergencies. It broadcasts everywhere in the building, to the conference rooms and loos and everywhere.'

'Martha, this is an emergency,' Paddy said. 'No one is dying, but believe me, this is about big things. We're going to spend weeks cleaning up the mess if I can't talk to that police officer right now.'

A long silence.

'If we do make an announcement over the loudspeakers, what would you want it to say?' Martha asked.

Maggie sipped the coffee Kenneth Laing had brought and looked at the man and his computer screen.

'Listen, you probably don't have any reason to worry,' Maggie said. 'That table contains your monthly mobile traffic figures, a comparison to the other major operators in Britain and the number of service disruptions for each of you. I'm here to find out how your own figures match up with the information that has come to us.'

She cast a friendly glance at Laing.

'This hard approach is intended to test how you handle information transparency requests,' Maggie pointed out.

Laing visibly relaxed and mimed wiping sweat from his brow.

'Whew,' he said. 'I was thinking we had a problem.'

'That depends on how your numbers compare to ours.'

She knew her role. During the night she and Lia and Paddy had determined what she needed to know about the Vodafone legal department's work.

Maggie was just about to continue when an announcement rang through the office.

'Mr Fordham,' a female voice said from a small loudspeaker situated above the door. 'Mr Jon Fordham, this announcement is for you. Please ring the switchboard immediately.'

Laing stared at the loudspeaker in surprise. They heard as the same message was repeated, also echoing in the corridor.

'Excuse me,' Laing said. 'That request is for one of my colleagues. Highly irregular.'

He stood up, stepping into the corridor and glancing around. When he apologised for the interruption and left for a moment, Maggie leaned back in her chair in satisfaction and watched Rico's memory stick. The light had started flashing faster again.

Rico's fingers flew over the tablet's virtual keyboard at a speed Lia and Paddy found unreal.

Most people can't type that fast on a real keyboard, Lia thought.

On the Topo's display, commands, lines of code and long streams of data flashed past.

Rico had gained access to Berg's phone records and was currently removing any information about calls and messages that would connect Berg to the Studio. At the same time he was adding new entries for conversations and texts that never really happened.

Lia and Paddy didn't breathe a word. This was Rico's job; they couldn't help with this.

'Time?' Rico called out, making the others jump.

'Two thirty-four,' Paddy said.

Rico was into his third minute working with the phone data. They had guessed they would have three, maybe four minutes in the metadata archives. Maggie would do her best to delay the person at Vodafone and keep the memory stick in his machine as long as necessary, but the police were also in the legal department.

Thanks to the office building's public address system and the helpfulness of Martha at the switchboard, Paddy had managed to contact the inspector who had come to the legal department to review Berg's customer data. But now the police officer was calling his station. He had received a message that someone urgently needed to speak with him, but it would only take a few more seconds before he realised the alert was wrong. Before long he would return to his task and be given the phone records to look over.

'Tell me when we hit three minutes!' Rico yelled to Paddy and continued his furious work.

Lia saw Gro in the corridor. The door to Rico's large office was open, but Gro didn't presume to enter. She was lonely and needed them, but no one had time right now.

I'll take you out in just a minute. In just a minute when this is over.

'Two fifty-five,' Paddy announced.

Rico stopped. His fingers came up from the keyboard, but his eyes continued sifting through the data visible on the screen. Lia saw the effort on his face – Rico was frozen in place staring: had he done everything?

Rico's breath caught.

'I still haven't changed the log,' he said in agony. 'They might notice that someone was just in the file. Changing that will take time. At least half a minute. Maybe a minute. Should I do it?'

Paddy cast Lia a quick look. They didn't have a clue.

Rico's fingers attacked the keyboard again. Lia and Paddy watched as he barrelled forward not knowing whether they had succeeded, whether they still had time – whether changing the archive log information was the one thing everything else hinged on.

The time was three minutes and forty-nine seconds when Rico cut the connection between the Topo and the Vodafone server. Bouncing out of his chair, he marched to the door, startling Gro in the corridor.

'Get Maggie out of there,' Rico said to Lia and Paddy.

He knelt down to pet Gro. His hands were shaking.

When Kenneth Laing returned to his office, Maggie had already received the text message from the Studio: *All done. Get out.*

'Something irregular is going on out there,' Laing said apologetically. 'The police are visiting with some of my other colleagues. And that address system is never used for summoning people like that.'

'The announcement did feel a bit odd,' Maggie said.

'The police are probably here about those video killings,' Laing said, lowering his voice.

He waited for this confidence to make an impression, but Maggie remained silent.

Laing looked at his computer screen. Maggie had removed the blue memory stick, and the spreadsheet was gone.

'We're going to have to return to this at a later date,' Maggie said.

She explained that she had just received a message on her phone about an urgent question regarding a legal matter going before the court that morning.

'And you seem to be busy here too,' Maggie said. 'We'll get back to this later. And we may end up handling it in Newbury after all. People from our office do travel out there quite frequently.'

The man nodded absentmindedly.

'A very irregular morning indeed,' he said. 'Ofcom and the police here in our department at the same time. You would think we'd done something... well... illegal.'

'Indeed,' Maggie said with a sigh.

Thanking him for the coffee, she picked up her briefcase and strode to the door. 'Two official visits on the same morning,' she said. 'One really might get the idea you had done something.'

23.

The fourth video showed up online on Monday night.

Sitting at home on Kidderpore Avenue, Lia saw excerpts from it on the morning news. Again the video had been uploaded by hacking another YouTube account. The account owner never even saw the video herself since it attracted so much attention and was ordered removed by the police almost immediately.

The video showed Brian Fowler being kicked to death.

It was like the killer wanted to send a personal message to the whole world, Lia thought. In terms of its imagery, the new video was similar to the previous ones, but the effect was different. Now the police had begun their search to catch the killer, and someone had tried to stop him on a street in Kensington.

He wants to show that he's invincible. He plucks one victim after another off the street, does to them what he wants and then leaves the bodies in the streets. And spreads sick pictures of it around.

Anything could be coming. And he wants people to know it.

Gro sensed Lia's mood and huddled at her feet as if preventing her from disappearing too.

Leaving the dog in her small flat during the day was difficult, but she couldn't think of any alternative. She didn't have time to go to the Studio, and because she had spent part of the previous morning there, she would have to concentrate hard all day at *Level*.

She comforted herself with the knowledge that she had been able to devote at least some time to Gro the previous evening. When Maggie had returned from her visit to Vodafone, Lia had hurried to work dead tired and then dropped by Mari's flat in Hoxton in the early evening. She had seen Mari sleeping, and there were dirty plates in the kitchen – at least Mari had been on her feet and eaten some-thing. From Hoxton Lia returned to the Studio to pick up Gro and managed to get home to collapse in her bed before dark.

The amount of work and shuttling from place to place was starting to tax her, especially since the knowledge that somewhere a man who had killed five people was probably walking free was lurking in the back of her mind the whole time.

When she returned home after work, Gro was overjoyed.

'I don't know how I can keep you,' she said to the dog as she took her out.

Just saying that thought out loud felt bad. Gro was a stray saved from difficult conditions. It wasn't fair for her to have to get used to another new home and new people again.

Caring for Gro meant something else to Lia too. The dog was a living, breathing bond to Berg.

'*Min snälla, underbara hund,*' she said to Gro in Swedish.

Did Berg ever talk to her in Swedish? A dog couldn't recognise languages, but maybe something she knew would get through.

Lia didn't know whether she could keep a dog in the King's College residence hall. What she knew was that giving up Gro wasn't an option. The name Berg had given the dog was a clear sign of his respect for her, and caring for Gro was a matter of honour for Lia.

The fourth video unleashed a tidal wave of criticism in the media. The Metropolitan Police Service commissioner was condemned for the fruitlessness of the investigation, and the video-sharing websites were censured for their irresponsibility. Criticism came from politicians, interest groups and members of the public alike, and the tabloids practically excoriated the authorities.

Hey, guys, this killer is taking the mick out of you, blared the *Sun*.

They also poked fun at the name Operation Rhea. The police had a habit of choosing names for their big operations from a list compiled of more or less random, sometimes rare words. This made it unlikely that the name would clash with anything concrete referred to in the case at hand. A rhea was a flightless bird from South America reminiscent of an ostrich.

'This rhea can't seem to get off the ground either,' the *Sun* wrote maliciously in their lead article.

Some of the staff at *Level* seemed more interested in the police investigation's lack of results than in the murders themselves. Although the *Sun*'s headlines were a detestable attempt to garner newspaper sales from a tragedy, the paper did manage to channel people's feeling of helplessness in the face of these crimes, editor-in-chief Timothy Phelps suggested in a meeting.

The police leadership responded to the criticism by holding two press conferences during the day. In the first they released two stills from the video they had received from Rich Lane. They showed the killer dragging Brian Fowler out of a van.

Did anyone recognise this man, the police asked the public. Or the vehicle the man was using?

At the same time, the police claimed that the general public in the city were not in danger. Additional police resources had been called in from other areas for Operation Rhea, and street patrols were increased. But the public was asked to support the investigation in any way they could, and anyone out in the city at night was encouraged to stay aware of their environment.

Although the pictures of the killer were blurry, their publication caused an enormous stir. The pictures spread quickly online, which also made new copies of the previous videos crop up.

See the Monster of the Decade, proclaimed the *Mirror.*

Lia and the rest of the *Level* team shook their heads at the sensationalism.

'First, the pictures don't show how he looks,' said Sam. 'And second, *the monster of the decade* almost sounds like a title of distinction.'

In the second news conference of the day, the police began to shift blame to the video sharing services and their users. YouTube, MySpace and the other companies were helping the police in their investigation, but the heart of the problem was that the police or the government didn't have any way to stop the spread of content online.

'This killer gets part of his gratification from making these shocking videos,' the police inspector said. 'And some of the public are humouring him by sharing the videos.'

The law did give the authorities the option of intervening when materials threatened general safety, even to the point of exercising extraordinary measures.

'But we have no way of completely deleting the videos if people keep copying them,' he said. 'And if we can't capture the perpetrator, we can only punish the people who disseminate these materials.'

Those methods of punishment were slow and too lenient to help in this situation, the inspector pointed out.

'Today in the press we saw claims that this killer is making a mockery of the police. What he is doing is making a mockery of absolutely everything, of all of society, and that is why everyone is responsible for stopping him.'

That evening on the way to Hoxton, Lia was messaging Paddy. He was at the Studio, he had spent the whole day there with Maggie and Rico. They were considering what to do next. Rico had reviewed the fourth video frame by frame but hadn't found anything new.

Arriving in Hoxton, Lia again noticed small changes in Mari's flat. The handbag had disappeared from the hall. Perhaps that was a good sign, that Mari had grabbed her bag. The dirty plates in the kitchen had been loaded into the dishwasher, but Mari hadn't started it yet because there were so few.

Of course it was possible that a cleaner had come, but Lia didn't believe that. In this state Mari wasn't going to let anyone in here, this close.

The bedroom door was open a crack. Lia listened at the door for a long time without opening it. Not a sound. She could just about make out Mari's shape on the bed. Either Mari was sleeping or just wanted to rest.

Lia believed Mari knew that she was visiting, and that this knowledge helped Mari.

She went to sit in the study. The laptop was in sleep mode. Lia hesitated for a moment and then woke it up. She saw from the browser history the websites last visited on the machine. Mari had been online during the day, reading the news. She had also watched the fourth kicking video.

She knows where this is going. That the killer is still free.

She knows that the Studio can't operate fully without her.

Suddenly the room filled with a familiar ringtone. Lia guessed whose name would pop up on the screen.

Mamia's concerned face flashed onto the big wall display.

This time Mamia waited silently for Lia to find the headphones and microphone. Once Lia had them on, the talking-to began.

'It's been a week!' Mamia said. 'Do you understand what kinds of things an old person can start dreaming up in that much time?'

Lia had to smile despite Mamia's indignation.

'I'm sorry,' she said. 'But we did speak the night before last.'

'Yes, but it's been a week since I've been able to catch Mari. Yes, I know that isn't your fault. But you could ask Mari to answer every once in a while. I've been standing guard at my computer waiting for one of you to condescend to logging on so I could ring.'

'Is something the matter there?' Lia asked.

'No. But there is where you are.'

This time avoiding telling how things really were was harder for Lia. Mamia wanted to know what condition Mari was in.

'Since you know Mari, you must know that she always wants to keep some things to herself,' Lia said.

Mamia suddenly turned deadly serious. Lia was surprised by the reaction, as if she had just insulted her.

'I have known Mari since the day she was born,' Mamia said slowly. Her voice held a new, harder edge. 'I have known Mari her entire life,' Mamia continued. 'I think I know her better than any of her friends in London. Including you.'

Lia felt simultaneously sheepish and obstinate. Mari's grandmother wanted the best for her and concealing from her that her granddaughter was in some sort of grief-induced depression was absurd. But Lia knew that Mari had left her home country in her early twenties, founding the Studio years later after moving to London – it was unlikely Mamia knew everything she had done or that Mari wanted her grandmother knowing.

Mamia realised the situation. Her expression softened.

'Listen,' Mamia said. 'I have perhaps five years left to live. I'm about to turn eighty-three, I'm half blind, I have sciatica and my mobility is starting to be so-so even on my good days. I certainly don't have more than ten years ahead of me. At this point I only have one thing I really care about any more. Mari and her siblings.'

Lia listened, abashed.

'I am the only person in Mari's family she keeps in regular contact with,' Mamia said. 'She only rings her siblings very infrequently. Have you ever heard Mari talk about her parents?'

No, Lia had never heard that.

'Tell me how Mari is doing,' Mamia said. 'Maybe I can help.'

Lia nodded. Mamia had a lot in common with Mari. You couldn't argue with people like this for long. It was futile.

Lia didn't tell the whole truth. Not how Berg died, not anything about the snuff videos or the Studio.

When Mamia heard that Mari had been keeping to her flat for several days now, she was visibly concerned.

'She isn't talking to you?' Mamia asked.

'Not much. This is very unusual, but we're all feeling horrible.'

'But the rest of you aren't feeling as horrible as Mari? Why?'

'It could be she blames herself for what happened. That she should have been able to stop his death somehow.'

'Could she have?'

Lia hesitated. It was an appalling question. You couldn't answer something like that.

'No, I don't think so,' she managed to say.

'This is very bad,' Mamia said. 'It sounds worse than ever.'

'Has this happened before?' Lia asked.

She could read the answer on Mamia's face.

'Has Mari talked about her childhood?' Mamia asked.

'No.'

'I thought not.'

Mamia was mulling something over. Her hesitation lasted a long time.

'Will you promise me one thing?' she finally asked.

The woman's face was warm but melancholy. During this very moment Mamia was deciding to confide in her, to trust her.

'Promise me that sometime later when Mari is better you'll tell her that you know. That you know what I'm going to tell you.'

Mamia moved closer to her computer's camera, as if trying to get closer to her. Lia nodded.

When Mari was small, her family lived a very unusual life.

Her father, Mamia's son, was a biologist named Mikael Rautee, his parents' only child and the head of his class as a teenager. From the beginning it had been clear that Mikael would excel as a researcher and achieve a good position. On a conference trip to

Helsinki, Mikael met Auni Nurmi, a teacher and educational psychologist. They fell in love, and things progressed quickly. Ultimately they would have four children.

'And they came rather quickly,' Mamia said, and Lia understood the emphasis.

'At first I wondered why they were running a baby factory. But Auni wanted it that way.'

At first everything went well. The family kept in contact with the children's grandparents. Auni didn't like it when Mikael's parents asked about how childcare was going. Looking after everything herself was important for her.

'Auni was never a gentle or warm person,' Mamia said. 'She still isn't.'

Mari and her siblings never went to school. Their mother taught them at home. That was possible in Finland as long as the parents notified the county school board and the children completed the proficiency tests required for compulsory education.

Auni was an educator who wanted to develop her own teaching model. She started designing it with Johann Gerber, a German, in the late seventies and early eighties. Gerber had been Auni's teacher at a German university, and they became research partners.

'At the time everyone seemed to be talking about education and childrearing.'

There were Summerhillism and Waldorf Schools and all sorts of other philosophies of education, Mamia recalled. The waves of 'free' educational movements in the sixties and seventies had caused a backlash, demands for a return to discipline. The large schools and classes that before had represented equality began to be seen as harmful to students. Everyone was searching for new directions in education, and most believed the best results would come through small groups and special programmes.

Auni Nurmi and Johann Gerber were especially interested in the education of exceptionally gifted children. In particular in the findings that gifted children often became bored in large classes when forced to adapt to the pace of slower students, which could lead to the brightest turning into underperformers who hid their talent to avoid arousing jealousy in their peers.

'Auni and Johann believed in home schooling. They thought it allowed them to train children as elite individuals from the beginning. Their intent was good, in a way, although the idea that almost anyone could be groomed into a top performer was somewhat... foolish. It set such demanding goals for the children.'

Mari's mother tried the method at home, on her own children. There were two main principles: perfect focus on continuous education and the elimination of all activities that were too emotional or distracted from learning.

The experiment got out of hand, Mamia said.

'It wasn't a family. It was a laboratory test.'

Lia listened in shock to the events Mamia described.

Mari was the family's third child. When she was born the experiment was already well underway and family life had adapted to it. Her father went to work, supporting the family financially and participating in teaching at home in the evenings. The mother was responsible for the children's education during the day and kept precise diaries of her research.

'At first they called it Dedication,' Mamia said. 'Dedicated education.'

'I've never heard of it,' Lia said.

'Neither has anyone else. My husband and I only heard the term years later when everything came out. They had different names for it and were always coming up with new ones. I guess the idea was that if it had the right name somehow it would gain more respect.'

The children weren't allowed to stay in contact with people outside the family. All their energy was focused on acquiring knowledge. They didn't watch television because it was too entertaining. Sometimes they listened to radio programmes if they related to topics they were learning about. At that time, in the 1980s, they didn't have the Internet, Mamia reminded Lia.

Every day they studied for ten hours, although Sunday was shorter. Schedules and subjects were planned based on pedagogical research: Finnish, foreign languages, lots of maths, science. Not much art, mostly just listening to music and sometimes a little drawing. They memorised information at a tremendous pace from books and encyclopaedic summaries their parents went to libraries to write up.

Lia devoured every strange detail of Mamia's tale as it shed new light on sides of Mari she had never known and explained the ones she did. Mari's loneliness. Her desire for control, her overwhelming need to master her environment. Her constant assimilation of information. And her ability to recognise other people's thoughts.

At the same time in Germany, Johann Gerber's family's three children were going through the same thing. The experiment was meant to demonstrate that children raised exactly the same way in two different countries would all become geniuses. Mari's mother and Gerber had agreed that if she had better educational outcomes in Finland, they would publish their findings under the names Nurmi and Gerber. If Germany did better, it would be Gerber and Nurmi.

'There was something attractive in the idea that anyone could become exceptional. In a way it was splendid. Very democratic,' Mamia said.

Their family had always been for equality, she said. Lia nodded, remembering what Mari had said about her extended family. She had been tight-lipped, only speaking about her father's side, never about her mother or childhood.

'We called it the Laboratory,' Mamia said. 'What they had to endure.'

The children were unequalled in the masses of facts they could recite, but socially they were very reserved.

'And serious. So much so it was hard to understand,' Mamia said. 'They were physically healthy, but it was like something was missing from them.'

The children always attended to their basic daily chores, as if they had grown up in a young offender institution.

'But even in reform schools the children are always surrounded by other children,' Mamia pointed out. 'Mari's family lived in their own little world. The children were so hungry for the companionship of other people.'

In order to maintain even the weak connection they had with their grandchildren, Mamia and her husband never reported them to the authorities. At her workplace in the magistrate's court, Mamia did investigate the legality of this sort of childrearing: the country's constitution and primary education laws at the time gave parents the right to decide how their children would be educated.

Whenever Mamia saw the children, she tried to give them a glimpse of a more normal life. At their grandparents' house the children could try things that were forbidden at home: using the telephone, reading picture books, watching television.

'Mari suffered the most,' Mamia said. 'She was the quietest and most withdrawn. She was also the best in her studies and always had the best exam scores. Auni expected Mari to be her shining piece of evidence that would bring notoriety to her research.'

Their mother frequently told the family that the results of the study would reward all their hard work. They just had to work hard enough.

'Sometimes when Auni and Mikael weren't around to hear, I would tell Mari that one day she would get out of it. That someday it would end and they could live like other people.'

Mari never replied to that. She didn't dare, Mamia said.

Lia felt so sick she could barely speak.

Mari spent her childhood thinking of escape.

Nurmi and Gerber's experiment failed horribly.

The children in both families started showing maladaptive symptoms. Mamia had heard that one of the Gerber boys in particular rebelled aggressively. Gerber had treated his children much more harshly than the Rautees and sometimes disciplined them physically. Mari and her siblings became fearful and hypersensitive. They were always watching other people's reactions, Mamia said.

And Mari started focusing on interpreting other people. As a child she had to struggle to know what her parents and siblings and other people were thinking and feeling, and that became her means of survival.

But that didn't completely explain her ability. There had to be something else to it.

Auni Nurmi and Johann Gerber wrote one report on their study. In it they included the children's learning outcomes but didn't deal with their development in other areas. When Gerber presented the report to experts in his faculty in Germany, the reception was one of dismay. Germany looked with suspicion on any educational programme that trained elite groups. The burden of National Socialist education was still too close, and after the war any theories that stressed discipline and leadership tended to be rebuffed.

In Finland the whole experiment was never addressed in any university or by the educational authorities. Officially it didn't even exist.

'Mikael also suffered from it,' Mamia said. 'He still hasn't recovered, just like the children.'

Mari's parents divorced when she was a teenager. Up until that point the family had soldiered on together. It was no coincidence what professions the children ended up in, Mamia said.

'I think they've always been trying to fix what happened to them.'

Mari left Finland immediately after graduating in record time with a degree in psychology. Her big sister became a teacher whose philosophy was completely the opposite of her parents'. Mari's little brother had cut off all contact with his parents.

Mamia had lost contact with Mari for years. She didn't even know precisely where she had been living. After settling in London, Mari had started calling Mamia now and then, but she only heard from the other siblings occasionally.

'They meet sometimes,' Mamia said. 'No one talks about the past. Theirs is a family without memories. The children grew up very fragile in a way. Which is why I've always feared something would happen to one of them. Especially to Mari.'

Mamia fell silent. Everything had been said.

Lia weighed what she had heard. Inside her, pity and indignation roiled. How could anyone have done this in 1980s Finland, which was so proud of its democratic education system, one of the best in the world? What trials and tribulations had Mari endured as she grew up?

Dedication. The Laboratory.

In a way her mother's goal had been realised, Lia thought: Mari was exceptionally gifted. But not just at the things her mother had intended, also in her strange, sometimes painful tendency to observe others and see what they were thinking. How could she ever talk about all this with Mari?

'You said Mari is lying at home alone now barely able to speak,' Mamia said.

This had happened before. At the time of her parents' divorce and when Mamia's husband, Mari's grandfather, died.

'I suppose Mari thought she should have been able to prevent what happened.'

The children had been raised to think that they were chosen to live an exceptional life where they were personally responsible not only for their own success but for how everything played out in the world.

Once Mari went mute at a Rautee family reunion, Mamia said.

'It was one of the rare times when Mari and her sister were allowed to see that many people at one time when they were children.'

Lia was surprised.

'At Vanajanlinna Estate? Near Hämeenlinna?' she asked.

'Has Mari talked about it?' Mamia asked in amazement. 'It's been so long. It was a rather unpleasant situation. After the party she had to stay in bed for several days.'

Once Mari had confided in Lia how at the age of eight, at this very party, she had first understood her ability to read people. But in Mari's version of events, the reunion had sounded different, not at all dark.

'Tell me about it,' Lia said.

Mamia looked away.

'It's a long story,' she said. 'We'll have to talk about it another time.' Fatigue shadowed the old woman's face.

'We've been talking a long time. It's almost night here,' she said. 'Are the nights very different in England than in Finland? It's been ever so long since I've visited.'

Lia thought.

'They are a little different.'

The night felt different since there were more people around, she said.

'Yes, you're right,' Mamia said. 'You're right. The world always feels different depending on how many people you think you're sharing it with. Goodnight. Please ask Mari to ring.'

24.

They had to go to the police.

Lia was the first to say so out loud, in a meeting at the Studio. Rico, Maggie and Paddy's expressions showed that the same thought had been running through their minds.

It was afternoon. After doing a short work day at *Level*, Lia had rushed to the Studio. The previous night she had heard Mamia's bewildering tale of Mari's childhood. The rest of the evening she had spent at home pondering how to lure Mari back to the land of the living. And the whole time her grief over Berg flickered in the background.

Everything that had happened since had clouded the fact that the man who killed Berg and four other people was still free. The police certainly would have announced if the man had been captured – even the tiniest details about the video killings were being endlessly rehashed in the news media. More and more politicians had taken up the issue too. The actions of the police were still under harsh scrutiny, and some were calling for them to be given more resources and leeway.

Apparently, the pictures of the killer dragging Brian Fowler's body hadn't led to any detentions or arrests. But at the Studio they still had Rico's calculations of the places the man might strike next.

'I can't give my program to the police,' Rico said.

In it he had used so much information acquired illegally from official and private databases that the police would realise immediately that the programmer was a hacker. And Rico couldn't risk police interviews: he broke British and international law every day. But he agreed with the rest of them about the goal in general. They had to use every expedient, and they had already tried all of their resources.

Receiving the results of Rico's program wouldn't help the police much if they couldn't also know how the calculations were made, Paddy pointed out. 'They might have information they could add to improve the results.'

'We could maybe give them the variables. In theory they could dig that up themselves. And the results of the calculation,' Rico said. 'But not the program or any information about who made it or how.'

'I could ring Gerrish,' Lia said.

She had been thinking about this all morning, delaying the obvious solution. Lia never wanted to see Detective Chief Inspector Peter Gerrish of the City of London Police ever again given the doubts he must harbour about her based on their previous meetings. But she had once supplied Gerrish with information and he had done the same in return. The DCI would probably at least answer her call.

Rico, Paddy and Maggie considered the idea possible. If any of them wondered at the least experienced member of the Studio taking the initiative, it didn't show.

'It could work,' Rico said. 'But how are you going to get the police to believe that you did the calculations yourself?'

'Maybe I don't have to,' Lia said.

The previous time Detective Chief Inspector Gerrish had grudgingly accepted that Lia wasn't going to reveal all of her sources. He had tried to look into Lia's background, but when nothing suspicious came up, he concentrated on the main issue, solving the crime.

'Five dead, the killer free and the media waging open war on the police,' Paddy said. 'I'm thinking that in this situation the police are going to appreciate any kind of help they can get.'

Lia had prepared herself to meet DCI Gerrish. She was not expecting a warm reception.

Gerrish walked down the steps of the City of London Police headquarters on Wood Street and looked at Lia curiously. After they shook hands, he told her why.

'It was high time for us to meet again.'

One year earlier they had met three times. Each had heard things from the other that helped them investigate a crime. But in Gerrish's eyes Lia had to be a strange case: a civilian who intervened in police business, and in only the most shocking crimes no less. Still he had agreed to the meeting without hesitation.

Gerrish led her to the Major Investigations Team offices. Lia remembered the narrow corridors, and the piles of paper on Gerrish's desk had not grown shorter since her last visit. As she was sitting down, Gerrish motioned to one of the piles.

'That case from last year,' he explained. 'It isn't over.'

Because several things about the case remained unsolved, the police had not completely given up their investigation. All unfinished cases in the police division were taken up for evaluation once a year. They reviewed the evidence, seeing if anything new had come to light about the parties or facts involved.

'We don't reopen them completely, but someone approaches them with fresh eyes,' Gerrish said. 'We've been meaning to get in touch with you.'

Lia shook her head.

'I don't have anything new about that case.'

'You didn't come because of that?'

'No. I came because of the video killings.'

The police detective's gaze turned penetrating.

'Are you serious?'

Lia ignored the question.

'I have information that might help you.'

'Then I have to tape this conversation,' Gerrish said quickly, leaning towards the digital recorder at the edge of his desk and turning it on.

'Is that necessary?'

'Apparently it is.'

The recording made Lia more nervous, but she couldn't take time thinking about it.

'I have a sort of calculation for you,' she began, spreading out a map of London marked with the places indicated by Rico's program.

She explained how a computer program had been tasked with analysing probable future locations for more killings in the video series.

Gerrish listened to her account in silence.

'We came up with twenty-three places. One of them is where the latest murder, the one with the two victims, Brian Fowler and Bertil Tore Berg, happened,' Lia said in conclusion.

She had memorised what to say. She used Berg's full name, as a stranger might.

'We?' Gerrish asked.

Lia was prepared for this. With Paddy she had practised responding to the questions Gerrish might present.

'I did the calculations with a friend. He knows computer programming.'

'And your friend's name is…?'

'That I'm not going to say.'

Gerrish stared at the map.

'You got one right,' he said.

Lia nodded. Quickly he snapped up his mobile and made a call.

'This is Gerrish,' he said when someone answered. 'I have a civilian here who claims her computer program guessed Rich Lane right. In advance. Before the shooting there.'

Lia didn't hear the answer, but she could tell its tenor from Gerrish's face.

'I don't know how it's possible. But the results are right here in front of me,' Gerrish continued.

He clearly didn't like the instructions he received, but he didn't start arguing.

'Let's go,' he said to Lia after ringing off.

'Where?'

'You want to get mixed up in a police investigation?' he said coolly. 'Well, you are now. My colleague wants to see you. His calculations didn't get any streets right.'

The drive was only five kilometres but the afternoon traffic made it feel much longer.

Sitting in DCI Gerrish's car, next to him, she tried to keep calm in a situation that was out of her control. She glanced around the car. Gerrish's office was cluttered, but the car was spotless, without a single paper or drink can. Either he loved his car or one of his subordinates cleaned it regularly.

'Why are you drawn to cases like this?' Gerrish asked.

'That thing a year ago was mostly a coincidence,' Lia said. 'It just… came into my life. This one I wanted to intervene in myself.'

'Why?'

'Because I can. And because I don't think the police are completely handling it the way they ought to be.'

'What do you mean by that?'

'Well, that you're concealing the fact that this is anti-gay violence.'

Gerrish fell silent for a moment.

'We are investigating the gay aspect,' he finally said. 'We have a lot of resources on that. What we say in public is a different matter.'

'Why?'

Gerrish suddenly turned the wheel and overtook two cars by veering into the oncoming lane.

'That's a pretty big question,' he said.

When Gerrish pulled out onto Victoria Street, and Lia saw that they were approaching New Scotland Yard, her breathing quickened. The headquarters of the entire Metropolitan Police Service.

Gerrish noticed her gaze.

'We aren't going there,' he said.

New Scotland Yard was an administrative centre, and that was where Operation Rhea had begun, he said. The investigation quickly moved into another space when it became clear how big the case would be. Such large investigations required dozens of rooms, which the police rented in buildings where they could proceed unnoticed.

They passed the tall, shining mirrored towers of New Scotland Yard. Gerrish changed lanes and turned onto Artillery Row. A couple of corners more, and on Francis Street he pulled into the underground car park of a large, red brick building.

Gerrish flashed his badge at the security guard and stopped the car where the ramp widened. As they hurried to the lift, Lia saw one of the guards climb into the car and drive it off somewhere into the bowels of the car park.

Second level, entrance checkpoint. Gerrish swiped himself through the electronic gates with his ID. To the officer at the reception desk he said, 'We're going to the incident room. She's with me.'

Gerrish only paused for a moment to write a name on the guest register lying on the counter: Lia Pajala. Lia noticed that he spelled it right from memory. The officer behind the desk handed Lia a visitor pass, and Gerrish hurried her on through the network of corridors.

Their arrival silenced several small groups of police investigators, who stopped working to stare at Gerrish and Lia. This was the room from which the operation was run around the clock. Next door Lia could see into a windowless hall where twenty or so police officers sat answering phone calls in hushed tones.

'Brewster,' Gerrish said, nodding to the head of the investigation. 'Here she is.'

Keith Brewster was a tall, impatient seeming man, who eyed Lia closely.

Lia ignored his look. She glanced around nervously at the large space. The incident room was full of tables, chairs, computers and information. Here and there stood tall notice boards with lists of things, place names and small pictures. Even in the age of computers they wanted to keep all of this out where the investigators could see it. Some items on a side table were completely foreign to Lia: electronic devices, small glass bottles and strange words written on a whiteboard.

Enlargements of images from the video killings dominated the walls of the entire space. They made the place creepy. The pictures were all too familiar to Lia. Rico had enlarged many of the same ones at the Studio for them to look at, but here their dreadfulness was eye catching.

Two pictures showed Berg. Something ripped inside Lia. Crime scene photos of their Berg. Blood, so much blood. Berg's position unnatural. The other picture showed how the force of the shot had ripped his head apart. Berg was a broken, mangled, dead creature.

Lia couldn't scream. She couldn't cry. All she could do was stand and stare. Her throat hurt, and she had to swallow. In these pictures was all the sorrow of the world, but she couldn't let it loose.

'Who is she?' Brewster asked Gerrish, nodding towards Lia.

A Finnish graphic designer, he replied. A civilian who had provided information about a previous criminal case and now possibly about the video killings.

'She says she got Rich Lane right,' Gerrish said.

'Not possible,' a young male police officer said from the side of the room. 'How the fuck is that possible!'

At Gerrish's signal, Lia spread her map out on one of the tables. The ten or so officers in the room regarded her with conspicuous suspicion, but when they saw the map, the entire mood in the room changed.

The lead investigator, Brewster, quickly scanned the bits of street marked on the map.

'Twelve of the same places we had,' he counted. 'All the other entries are in entirely different places. How did you come up with these?'

Lia listed the same variables she had to Gerrish earlier. The young officer was dumbfounded when he heard that Lia had precise information about the businesses at specific properties and the location of CCTV cameras at her disposal. The police had more comprehensive records than any other official agency, but the details in them were often out of date or otherwise deficient.

'How can you get even partially accurate information about so many properties?' the man demanded.

'We combined several different databases,' Lia said. 'Including commercial business directories.'

Brewster straightened up from the map.

'Yes, you must have, since this information is impossible to get from any one source,' Brewster said. 'We have SCAS to help us, but even they haven't been able to get all this.'

Gerrish noticed Lia's questioning look. The Serious Crime Analysis Section was a service of the National Crime Agency that specialised in identifying serial rapists and killers, he explained. Its analysts and databases were located in Bramshill, in Hampshire, but it helped out police forces across the country on request. They had been involved in Operation Rhea from the beginning.

What information did the police have in their program? Lia asked.

Gerrish conducted a short, hushed negotiation with his colleagues. As the product of this discussion, Brewster called Lia over to look at a printed table on the wall.

'Here is a list,' Brewster said.

The information in the table was mostly familiar to Lia: Underground stations, the proximity of bars...

'How did you choose the clubs?' Lia asked.

They had to be known gay gathering places that had been open for a while, Brewster explained. The name of the club could have changed over the years, but it needed to have been in business for more than two. Before Rich Lane, each kidnapping and discovery of a body had happened near an old, established bar.

'We didn't limit them that way,' Lia said. 'Newer gay bars were fine too.'

'If we combine your information with our calculations, the result could be very precise,' Gerrish said. 'Twelve places.'

Twelve possibilities, Lia thought, knowing the others were thinking the same thing.

If the killer still intends to snatch more victims, it will have to happen at one of these twelve places.

'In the course of this investigation we've already received another unusual tip-off,' a female inspector said to Lia. 'Did it come from you?'

'I don't know anything about any other tips,' Lia said quickly.

'It was from Rich Lane. I think you're bluffing and want us to believe you weren't behind it.'

Lia knew well enough that the woman meant the video of Berg's death on Rich Lane. But she hadn't mentioned that it was a video. She was trying to make Lia slip.

'I don't know what you're talking about,' Lia said.

Gerrish gave Brewster and his female colleague a narrow look.

'We can put these twelve locations under heightened surveillance tonight,' he said.

'It'll be tight,' Brewster said.

'Call everyone in,' Gerrish said.

Brewster glanced at Lia.

'We'll make you a civilian consultant on the case.'

Gerrish stepped in immediately.

'No. I don't recommend that.'

Lia saw that Brewster was forced to tamp down his irritation, but he didn't want an open dispute with Gerrish.

'Very well,' Brewster said. 'But she has to stay reachable. And I want the source material used to make these calculations now.'

Gerrish pulled Lia aside as the other investigators studied Lia's map.

'You need to leave now,' Gerrish said. 'Unless you have more information.'

'No, I don't. What is a civilian consultant?'

Sometimes the police used experts in various fields in their investigations, such as medical, telecommunications or financial professionals, Gerrish explained. The police tried to tell them only the details of the crimes they absolutely needed to know, and they were bound by confidentiality.

'Why couldn't I be a consultant in this case?'

'Because I don't think it would be the slightest bit practical.'

Gerrish extended a card with his mobile number.

'All the source material used to make the calculations,' he said. 'Immediately.'

He saw Lia starting to object and hurried to prevent her.

'This isn't something you can refuse,' Gerrish said.

The police commissioner was going to call in significant back-up for the evening. The Metropolitan Police's Homicide and Serious Crime Command was responsible for investigations of this nature. Hundreds of inspectors operated under the unit across every borough in the Greater London area. Most of them could be called in quickly, and it was possible to call in help from other departments too. A lot of reserves were already connected to Operation Rhea, and plain-clothes investigators were trawling the London gay bars every night searching for clues about the killer. This turn of events would transform Rhea into one of the biggest police operations the city had ever seen.

Lia promised to deliver Rico's background material quickly, despite knowing that Rico might still resist. But there weren't any alternatives.

'I've had two civilians like you before,' Gerrish said. 'Two civilians who became part of a murder investigation. Who got involved of their own free will.' A young man years ago and a middle-aged woman, Gerrish said. Different investigations, different people. 'The thing you all have in common is that you imagine you can choose what you do,' he continued. 'That there is information you can tell and information you can keep to yourself. It doesn't work that way.'

In major crimes, the investigators had to have all the information, immediately and without reservation. If not, someone always suffered.

'If you get mixed up in an investigation, part of the moral responsibility for solving it lands on you,' Gerrish said. 'No court of law would hold you to it, but still it's there.'

Lia didn't have a response to that.

'You're pulling out of this now,' Gerrish said. 'Completely. You send us that information and then leave this behind you.'

Lia stared at Gerrish, indignant. She had just helped the police in their investigation, but now Gerrish was ordering her away.

'A civilian can't have a role in a serial killer investigation,' Gerrish said. 'There isn't any safe way to be involved. Don't even think about it.'

It was typical for a civilian who became part of a police inquiry to fall under a sort of euphoria at first, Gerrish said. Everything was deadly serious, everything was exciting and every detail felt significant. But before long reality would hit, and when you were dealing with a serial killer, the situation could be life-threatening. Keeping Lia involved any longer than absolutely necessary was irresponsible.

'Your colleagues seemed to want to include me,' Lia pointed out. 'And if you're downplaying the fact that gay people are being targeted –'

Gerrish silenced her mid-sentence by shaking his head. This wasn't the time or the place to thrash out these questions, Lia understood.

'Stay away,' DCI Gerrish said. 'I didn't want to bring you to the incident room, and I don't want to bring you here again.'

The police could also arrest her if necessary, he added.

'On what grounds?' Lia asked, astonished.

'Suspicion of interfering with official police business. For questioning. I can come up with a pretty long list of reasons for an arrest warrant.'

'I'm sure you could,' Lia said. 'And the moment you do, you lose the information used to make these location calculations.'

Gerrish took her into the corridor, found another officer and asked him to escort Lia back to the lobby.

'What did those other two civilians do?' Lia asked Gerrish as she left. 'Were they any help to you?'

'They were. A little,' he said. 'I've kept in touch with them a bit. The woman is doing quite well. The man not so much. He's in a wheelchair.'

'What happened to him?'

'He got too involved.'

Rico didn't resist when Lia announced that they had to deliver his databases to the police.

'I'll just clean them,' Rico said.

He altered the files he had used so the original sources couldn't be traced. He stripped the original formatting, making the text and numbers a raw mass of data he could reformat. In order to ensure secrecy he ran the files through a series of conversion programs so nothing exactly like them would exist anywhere.

'Of course the police will eventually get their hands on my sources, but now they won't know who collected the data. They'll still have all the addresses and other details available immediately though,' Rico said.

Paddy wanted to know everything Lia had to report about the operation the police were planning, but that wasn't much.

'Twelve places,' Paddy said, thoughtful. 'In London.'

'We landed on the right place with eight cameras,' Lia said.

'Still. Twelve places under surveillance is... outrageously few.'

As Lia was leaving the Studio, Paddy asked how Mari was.

That was hard to answer. What could she say to that, she couldn't say that Mari was probably just lying in bed? She couldn't tell about Mamia or the Laboratory.

'I don't really know,' Lia said truthfully. 'She needs time.'

How was Mari really doing? Lia wondered that night in Hampstead. She knew that Mari would get in touch if she needed urgent help. But how long could she keep to her flat, sheltered from the world? Was hiding at home good or bad for her? Might Mari disappear some-where as she had done before?

With Gro by her side, Lia set out on a run. The dog was excited to get out, but she was also clearly nervous. She wasn't used to spending the day alone in a small flat, and she didn't understand where her previous life had gone. She constantly tried to stay close to Lia.

Lia felt like the best thing she could do for her was tire her out, so they ran late into the evening.

We're quite the pair. A frightened dog and a frightened woman.

The paths of Hampstead Heath were quiet. At the same time around the city hundreds of police officers were preparing for an enormous manhunt.

Somewhere in London, at a gay bar, someone might become the next victim.

Lia ran with Gro until she couldn't go any further herself. She had to go home and sleep. Her body was giving way although her mind was occupied with difficult questions.

Will they catch him tonight? What will come of all of this?

And how is Mari doing, really?

25.

Mari lies at home in Hoxton, in her own bed, awake but eyes shut tight. She dreams of Berg.

Berg is in her dream with her. They walk cobblestoned streets, they walk asphalt streets. What is this place? Sweden, the land of Berg's ancestors and where his family still lives.

Mari smiles at Berg, and Berg smiles back.

Mari has never been to Sweden with Berg, but in this state between dreaming and waking they are there. Dear old man, Mari thinks.

'Would you like to meet my relatives?' Berg asks. Berg's placid voice that always says how much he respects others.

'No,' Mari says. 'I can't.'

'Why not?'

'You're dead.'

The peaceful old man in the overalls turns serious.

'Yes, I am.'

Mari knows her dream is absurd. She knows she is in some sort of stupor, but she can't force herself out of the state.

She sees Berg's relatives arriving. They gather around him. Are you dead? they ask him. Women and men and teenagers and children. Berg has many relatives, and they are amazed to find that he has died.

'I did it,' Mari tells them.

Some of them turn to look at her. Finally they are all quiet, looking at her.

A strange dream, an evil torpor, Mari thinks, and the dream continues even though she knows she's dreaming.

This is the moment of her confession. Mari doesn't say anything, and no one else in the dream says anything else any more either, but everyone knows what happened.

Berg is dead. Berg is dead because years ago Mari approached him, befriended him and asked him to join the Studio.

Mari did Berg a favour. She tied him to herself with kindness.

The Miracle Girl. That was what Berg called her then. Mari offered Berg a job that was a dream come true, but there had been much more to it than that. A deep respect had grown between them.

An unassuming, convivial regard, and a shared satisfaction with the things they created.

It is an indisputable fact that Mari used kindness to draw Berg to herself and that he wanted to come. It is just as indisputable a fact that by founding the Studio, planning its dangerous work and using that to change the world without regard for the risk, Mari has been playing God. She wanted to feel powerful. She imagined she could create her own little world.

And here are the results.

Mari weeps. In her daydreams Berg's family comes to her, their skin pale and faces twitching. They accuse her. How could you? they say. They are right. How could she?

Mari weeps with eyes closed and swollen, hurting from crying. She thinks of the man she brought into the Studio, the man she has now let fall.

She thinks of all the people Berg has been taken from. Who have been robbed of his intimacy. Berg was happy at the Studio, but it wasn't his whole life, unlike Mari. Berg had a family he kept in touch with, and friends. The events of Rich Lane will spread in slow waves of loss touching more and more people's lives.

And when Mari thinks of the small street in Kensington and the man who dragged the body of his fourth victim there, the weeping stops. Her weeping stops, breaking off like a dry branch.

Snap.

This man. The video killer. Who is he?

Mari asks the silent question. Who are you?

At home in Hoxton, in her bed, Mari opens her eyes.

Suddenly she knows something about this man.

26

The morning news didn't report anything about the police surveillance operation the previous night.

Lia flipped through all of the main channels and searched online. Nothing.

Not a word about an increased police presence at gay bars, nothing about investigators patrolling near them. There were still several stories about the video killings, mostly dealing with the grief of the victims' loved ones and their friends and colleagues' memories.

One channel interviewed Annie Bayhurst-Davies from Gallant. She summed up the situation: after Brian Fowler's death, four out of five victims were snatched from gay bars and three of them were gay men. The fifth victim seemed like a heroic bystander who failed trying to intervene. 'We're waiting for an immediate police inquiry into why an attack is being waged against the entire LGBTI community,' Bayhurst-Davies said. 'If the investigation ignores the special characteristics of hate crimes, it may prevent solving these terrible crimes and increase the suffering of those touched by this tragedy.'

Gallant had received reports of possible leads. They had directed these reports to the police but were not convinced the information would be investigated immediately and thoroughly.

Lia took Gro outside. She could sense Lia's intense concentration on something else. She ran around Lia's legs a couple of times, but when Lia wasn't interested in playing, she sniffed at the corners of the statue garden.

She wasn't particularly interested in Poundy, the canine statue Lia held so dear. Most likely to Gro the statue just looked like a block of stone, lifeless and insignificant, instead of a frozen dog.

In the courtyard of the residence hall, Mr Vong approached them.

'I do not believe we have been properly introduced,' Mr Vong said, indicating Gro.

Lia wondered whether Mr Vong was pleased or irritated at the appearance of a dog in the building, but deducing anything from his face was difficult. Fortunately he bent down to scratch Gro behind the ear, and fortunately Gro graciously allowed herself to be scratched.

'Beautiful dog,' Mr Vong said. 'She must be rather lonely when you are at work, Ms Pajala.'

'Has she been making a noise?' Lia asked, worried.

Mr Vong shrugged. 'Only a little, when I walk past your door.'

'I could...' Mr Vong continued, 'I could have use for an assistant of this kind during the day.'

The offer took Lia by surprise.

'That would be marvellous,' she said quickly.

'She could accompany me when I do my rounds fixing things. And if I need to visit somewhere else during the day, she could stay in my flat, which is somewhat larger than your otherwise charming abode.'

Lia nodded. Mr Vong spoke with such sinuous courtesy. How could such a small, everyday offer of help cause such a deep sense of relief?

'What is her name?' Mr Vong asked.

Gro, Lia said, after a famous Norwegian politician, Gro Harlem Brundtland.

'I have never heard of her,' Mr Vong said.

Brundtland was an influential woman and winner of many awards for public service. Even after she retired she continued doing good. A wonderful person, Lia assured Mr Vong.

'I have never heard of her,' Mr Vong said apologetically.

'Just as wonderful as the man Gro used to belong to,' Lia said but then realised she was sharing too much.

Mr Vong's sensitivity and tact did not fail for even a moment. If Lia had ever doubted it, here was evidence. She almost felt like hugging Mr Vong.

The old gentleman did not say anything. He took the dog with both hands and scratched and patted, listening to her small growls of pleasure.

'Naturally such a lovely dog would belong to a lovely person,' Mr Vong said.

Out of consideration he did not even glance at Lia, who had to look away to control her surge of emotion.

The whole day was busy at *Level*, and when Paddy rang in the afternoon, it took Lia a moment to understand what he was really asking.

'Do you want to learn to shoot?' Paddy asked.

The idea felt disagreeable. They had talked about it before, and Paddy had promised to teach her if she wanted, but Lia hadn't really considered it seriously.

'Why?' she asked.

'It's a useful skill,' Paddy said.

There wasn't anything special about it, Paddy explained. Shooting was a skill with a frightening reputation, but when you tried it, the emotions surrounding it started to fall away.

'Or, actually, they change. A lot of people fear shooting, but learning how to do it lessens the fear. Instead you have a new experience, the feeling of overcoming fears.'

'Why right now?' Lia asked.

'It's a skill you need for your own safety,' Paddy said. 'At least the basics of handling a weapon. If you want we can continue beyond that later.'

Of course Lia grasped the underlying reason: what had happened to Berg. And the idea could have come from Mari originally. Paddy certainly wasn't ringing at Mari's behest right now, but they had probably talked the issue over previously at the Studio.

Lia was tired, and the thought of handling a weapon aroused difficult emotions. But Paddy and Mari considered it important, and Lia knew they were right in a way.

If I need to learn to shoot someday, then why not now?

After work and after checking with Mr Vong that he could keep Gro through the evening, she went to the address in Harrow Paddy had given her.

She was surprised when she arrived. Lia had expected to see other people practising at the firing range, but Paddy took her into a basement that turned out to be almost completely deserted.

At the Harrow Rifle & Pistol Club only the dark-eyebrowed proprietor, Bob Pell, was on the premises. Pell greeted Paddy as an old customer.

'First we need to establish our own rules,' Paddy explained.

Britain's weapons laws were among the strictest in Europe, and for all practical purposes handguns had been outlawed since the 1990s. Behind the ban was a series of dreadful mass shootings, and strict regulations had been imposed even for target shooting. The Harrow range usually operated completely legally, but Pell also ran a side business: secret unauthorised practice with handguns.

'Everything else happens according to the same safety regulations as legal practice sessions,' Paddy assured Lia.

No new members had been allowed into the shooting club for years, and their activities were limited as well. Pell had known everyone who came for years and could offer certain trusted customers turns on the range when they could be more flexible about the legal issues. At any other range Lia never would have got anywhere near a gun this quickly without membership and a careful police background check.

Paddy taught the basics of weapon handling with precision and so calmly that Lia immediately forgot they were doing anything illegal. It was almost as if she were learning to play a musical instrument. Paddy told her that he remembered teaching all of the Studio's employees the same way.

'Including Maggie?' Lia asked, astonished. 'And Mari?'

'Yes, them too.'

Maggie hadn't been particularly interested, but Mari was quite a good shot, Paddy said. Mari didn't like guns, but Paddy had never met anyone who approached learning as efficiently as her.

'I think she can learn just about anything in a matter of minutes,' Paddy said.

The thought of Mari as a quick learner gave Lia chills. Just a couple of days earlier she had heard from Mamia about the Laboratory and Mari's strange childhood.

'And Berg?' Lia asked.

Berg was an excellent marksman.

'That wasn't why Kensington happened,' Paddy said seriously. 'He could have hit that bastard from any distance. The killer was just faster. The thought of shooting a person was so foreign to Berg that he probably couldn't believe the man would really shoot him.'

Lia was impressed by the strict rules followed even at a range like this. There were specific commands that ensured safety: you couldn't fire a single shot until the range master declared *Commence fire*. Weapons always had to be carried muzzle-down, breech open and ammunition clip removed.

Paddy had Lia practise a relaxed but completely controlled firing stance for a long time before letting her even touch a gun. The first shots were with a light air pistol like many beginners all over the country used.

When Paddy brought Lia a Heckler & Koch P7 pistol, the mood changed. Just taking it in her hands, Lia felt her senses sharpen. Paddy had chosen this weapon specifically for her because it was relatively small and had an unusual safety mechanism, a lever that prevented the weapon from discharging unintentionally when the shooter released her grip on the gun.

'Easy,' Paddy said. 'This one is going to kick more.'

The first shots with a real pistol were like jumping into cold water, Lia thought. Everything tingled, and she felt like running away. She ordered herself to keep going.

Since the shooting itself happened so fast, she had to struggle to keep up with the situation. Her arms began to fatigue, but she shook them between practice rounds.

She liked that the gun felt like a precision instrument and that she had to learn a completely new way of gripping something. A grip you did with your whole body. Paddy watched her stance and eyes the entire time.

'Very good,' he said, praising her aim.

Aiming was difficult for a lot of people at first, he said. Often it was difficult to get used to finding the right trajectory for the bullet. But Lia did it naturally.

Bob Pell dropped in from time to time to check on their progress. He eyed Lia, clearly interested, but Lia ignored his glances. He looked like he was nearing fifty after all.

'There isn't any hurry for you to learn this,' Paddy reminded Lia between firing sessions. 'It's important you go at your own pace.'

And in time, if Lia wanted to keep practising, Paddy would show her how to shoot at something other than a round target on the back wall of a firing range.

Lia considered Paddy's words.

'You mean human-shaped targets,' she said.

Paddy nodded.

'I'm never going to shoot a person,' Lia said. 'I'm never going to be in a situation like that.'

As she said it she comprehended the reality of the situation.

Here I am imagining I'm not really shooting an illegal weapon. That this isn't even a real gun.

Berg was shot. If I'm working for the Studio, even I could end up needing a gun.

'Show me now,' Lia said.

Paddy started spoonfeeding her.

There were different places on a person you could shoot for different objectives, Paddy said. Hitting the hands was difficult, but that was a way to prevent someone from injuring you or another person. The chest had the most surface area to target, but shooting there was always a big risk because it was often fatal.

'If you're in a really bad spot and there isn't any other way, then you shoot at the head. That kills your enemy the fastest.'

But the most practical thing was to shoot the person in a place that wouldn't end their life but would hurt them enough that they couldn't move properly any more or retaliate because of the pain.

'What place is that?'

Paddy indicated precise locations on the outside thighs.

'There are several centimetres of tissue here before you hit the big veins,' he said, pointing to his own legs. 'If you hit the side of the thigh here, you get maximum effect. The shot won't kill, but the pain will stop anyone.'

Another option was to try to aim for the knees, but then you had a bigger chance of hitting a major blood vessel.

'But the hands would still be usable,' Lia said.

'Yes. But shooting for the legs almost always works. Except in the worst cases.'

Lia imagined a human pelvis on the round target at the back of the firing range. She raised her weapon. Breathe out, squeeze.

After the explosions had ceased, Paddy removed his ear protection and looked at how she had done. He knew what she had been trying for.

'Pretty good,' he said. 'One went straight into the thigh where it should. A couple went wide. One hit more in the testicles. But there are blokes who need to be prevented from reproducing.'

Lia grinned, not feeling the slightest bit guilty.

'First time?' Bob Pell asked Lia as he followed them out.

Lia nodded.

'Pretty good for a beginner,' Pell said to Paddy. 'Where do you keep finding them?'

This earned Pell enough points in Lia's mind that as she left she threw him a quick wink.

As they climbed the stairs out of the basement back onto the street, everything felt a little new and different. It took Lia a few seconds to realise where the feeling was coming from. She had stepped over another threshold. She knew what using a gun was like and that theoretically anyone she met could be carrying a weapon.

Lia's initiation into a group of people previously foreign to her had begun.

There were people who could draw a gun and shoot it. There were people who could take another person's life.

27.

'Crazy,' Theo said.

He said it as carefully as he could, pronouncing the English as precisely as he knew how. *C-r-a-z-y.*

No answer came. But just now Theo Durand didn't feel like he had much to lose. He had to say it out loud.

Crazy. The man who had brought him here was stark raving mad. He didn't look mentally disturbed in the beginning, but there was no doubt now.

Maybe Theo had noticed something in the man's eyes, a flash of some frightening *otherness*, because at first he had hesitated to go with him. Then that *otherness* had come out later, in his eyes.

Theo was thirsty. The heat made him sweat. He could feel how his entire body was struggling to retain moisture, but the penetrating heat was winning. He perspired constantly, even when he was lying on the floor motionless.

This constant, terrible thirst. The man had given Theo water once. Theo wasn't sure how much time had passed. He had slept a couple of hours, maybe three, but a day might have already passed since the man brought him here.

Theo had inspected his cell. At first he didn't even dare move around, but as time passed and no one came, he began roaming the cell. He tried the bars, attempting to bend them, but they didn't budge.

The worst was the silence. And the darkness. No sound came from anywhere, which meant that the walls of the building were thick, and the only light shone dimly from somewhere behind the bars.

And then there was the camera flashing high on the wall. Theo looked at the camera. With his lips he mouthed the silent word at it.

'Crazy.'

The man had to be there, on the other side of the camera. If not constantly, then some of the time. He had to see. He had to be there watching, because the only thing Theo could imagine to explain all this was that it aroused the man.

He had taken almost all of Theo's clothing at gunpoint, along with his shoulder bag, phone, everything. All he had left was his underwear.

Theo's chest glistened with sweat. He could just barely see in the dark room. The man had to be there somewhere looking at his half-naked body through the camera.

Because if the man wasn't there watching, what did he want?

That was too frightening to contemplate.

What did he want? Thinking about that made his gut clench.

Theo hadn't recognised the danger immediately, not after that first flash in his eyes. The man had behaved so calmly. Spoken so easily. Chatted like anyone might. What brought Theo here? the man had asked. Where was he from? Just think, the man knew the 17th Arrondissement of Paris, had walked the streets where Theo lived. What was Theo looking for here? Maybe a specific building, one of the town's many attractions?

They had smiled together at the situation. Theo at his confession, knowing he seemed simpler than he was, part of the stream of tourists that poured through this place every day. But the man had said he came here for the same reason, to go to the same place.

Theo had still been smiling when the man brought him to this dreary building and urged him to step inside. What a squalid place. Could this be where everyone talked about? Theo had thought in confusion. And Theo had smiled, because he knew the man had also brought him here to offer sex. He didn't intend to agree, not so easily. Theo didn't do that – but it was exciting if someone suggested it.

The proposition never came. The man took out a gun. Theo hadn't smiled now in more than a day.

Theo jumped at a noise. Someone was close. Had he fallen asleep again? Who was it?

He saw the man behind the bars. In his hands he carried nothing. Thank God he didn't have a gun.

What did he want? Did he want sex now, after subjugating him, after wanting him, after holding him prisoner? Was this what turned him on? What did he want?

From the darkness a small paper bag appeared. Theo heard a soft rustling as the man opened the mouth of the bag and set it on the floor where Theo could reach it through the bars.

'What's in it?' Theo asked.

He had to get the man talking. You had to get crazy people like this communicating with you. Otherwise things could go badly.

'Eat,' said the man.

Swallowing, Theo stepped closer to the bag. In the darkness he tried to see what was in it.

Something powdered, like slightly damp sand. A little lumpy.

A syrupy smell came from the bag, and a sound escaped Theo's mouth. It wasn't a word, it was a release. Theo let out a yelp, evidence to both of them that he was completely at the man's mercy.

'Crazy,' Theo said, moving away from the bag, as far away as he could get from the man.

'Eat,' the man said. 'You aren't getting anything else.'

'What's in it?' Theo asked.

The man looked at him. Dear God what eyes.

'Eat,' the man said.

Theo pulled back against the wall, pressing against its filthy surface. His legs started giving way. The man was a lunatic, keeping him here as a prisoner, only giving him some powder for food.

Then the man left. Theo heard quick steps, and then somewhere a door opened.

Theo screamed. No words came out, but sound did. He screamed his horror out.

The door closed, and he was alone again. Crazy.

28.

Everything had changed in Mari's flat.

When Lia stepped into the hall, she saw immediately that the lady of the house was on her feet and had been for some time. The lights were on in every room, and the bedroom door was open. Music echoed from somewhere. Hard rock, familiar sounding.

Suddenly it was switched off. Mari had noticed her arrival.

'Hi.'

Mari looked different as she entered the hall. Not completely different from before, but something had happened. Mari's gaze moved quickly, and she avoided looking directly at Lia.

'Good to see you up and around,' Lia said.

'I'm halfway better,' Mari said.

Nothing more needed to be said. Lia understood the rest.

Leaving her jacket in the hall, she followed Mari into the living room. Everywhere were stacks of books, printed papers, opened newspapers and magazines. Mari was researching something.

Mari sat on one of the wide windowsills. It was like a long bench, with space for Lia too.

Lia pulled her legs up under herself Indian style and looked at Mari, who had a pen and notebook next to her. Mari had been listing words, with lines drawn in between.

'Paddy taught me to shoot,' Lia said.

'Good.'

Lia had expected a little more, a more interested reaction. Nothing came.

'What are you thinking about?' she asked.

A moment passed before Mari replied.

'Mark Chapman.'

Mark Chapman. The man who killed John Lennon.

'The day Chapman shot Lennon, he had been waiting for him a long time,' Mari said.

She continued talking for a long time, and as she did, Lia's blood went cold. Mari spoke of strange, frightening things. Things it was hard to understand existed and about which she didn't really want to hear.

In 1980 Mark Chapman was twenty-five years old, a kid from Texas who had set out to see the world, an insecure drop-out and part-timer with mental health issues. He had attempted suicide. Since he was a boy he had entertained all sorts of fantasies, including talking to imaginary people. For years he had been obsessing over things, for example Dorothy from the film *The Wizard of Oz*, *The Catcher in the Rye* and John Lennon.

On 8th December 1980, Chapman spent hours waiting outside Lennon's New York City flat. For some time he had been hinting to acquaintances that he felt like his life was out of balance and he might do something alarming. He was bitter at Lennon, whom he idolised, for what he saw as hypocrisy: in public the star talked about the poor and unfortunate of the world but he lived in the lap of luxury himself.

Chapman shot Lennon four times in the back on the street. After the murder, Chapman gave several interviews. In them he repeated thinking he was the protagonist from *The Catcher in the Rye*, Holden Caulfield, who hated hypocrisy. One passage in particular from the book touched Chapman: Caulfield imagines himself as a saviour who has to catch children to protect them – to save their innocent souls from the hypocritical future of the world.

'People have always wanted to believe Chapman,' Mari said.

People wanted to believe the murderer's explanation for killing Lennon, that Chapman was mentally disturbed and thought he was someone else.

But the facts said something else, Mari said. Chapman had thought about killing several other celebrities. He had visited New York earlier the same fall, intending to kill Lennon then too. He told a lady friend about his dark fantasy before he acted it out, although he claimed he was giving it up. On the day before the killing, he assaulted another famous musician, James Taylor, and talked to him about Lennon.

In addition to a pistol, Chapman prepared for the murder and set the stage for it by purchasing a copy of *The Catcher in the Rye*. After the murder he remained at the crime scene reading the book, which he also quoted to the police.

'He wasn't a madman with no idea what he was doing,' Mari said.

Chapman was an extremely distressed person who wanted to do something big to alleviate his distress and get famous. He used Lennon and *The Catcher in the Rye* to do that, forevermore linking himself to their fame.

'Actually Chapman's goal wasn't just to kill Lennon. He reported thinking that day outside Lennon's building that what he was doing was wrong and wanting to leave. Killing Lennon was just a tool for him to destroy something big, to make himself great.'

'Why have you been researching John Lennon's killer?' Lia asked.

'Because this guy is doing something similar,' Mari said. 'He's just doing it on a larger scale. Those ten black videos – I realised yesterday that we've overlooked a crucial fact.'

The killer had gone to great pains planning his actions. The black videos, the places he snatched his victims, the taping of the killings, the precise editing of the videos. Everything had been done with planning and precision.

'For people like that, every detail matters. And not just the things we notice. He probably has reasons for all sorts of things we don't even realise we're seeing.'

The killer started by posting ten videos online with no sound or picture. This wasn't just a scare tactic or a practice for breaking into people's accounts. For this man, they meant something.

'He's so careful about details that he must have thought out everything about these videos. That there are ten of them. And how long they are.'

That was why Mari had rung Rico and asked him to research whether the videos' lengths matched any other videos on the Internet. Rico had made a program that crawled the major music and video sites to find clips that were the same length down to the second.

'We found a lot of them. Hundreds of thousands.'

Checking each result one by one would have taken weeks. But Mari asked Rico to further crosscheck the results for any single common factor.

'We found something. This is a top ten list. The videos are songs. They're part of a ritual, a fetish. He's a fan. Not a fan in the sense people usually are though, a fan in the sense of a fanatic. For him liking an artist means creating an entire world, a twisted religion only he follows.'

Lia shook her head. Keeping up with all of this was a challenge.

'There isn't anything in it that will make sense to us,' Mari said. 'He lives in his own world. To us things look one way and to him a completely different way. He can operate in our world as effectively as anyone, but everything he does is driven by a kind of religious fanaticism. To him his victims aren't even people. To him they're just... pieces to manipulate. Hateful things he can use to his ends. Like Chapman used Lennon.'

This man, the person who killed Berg and four others, had his own *The Catcher in the Rye* and John Lennon, Mari said.

'Who is he?' Lia asked.

'Queen. The band. And Freddie Mercury.'

The phenomenon even had its own word, Mari said. *Celebrity obsession syndrome.*

'Chapman was an extreme case,' Mari admitted. 'And so is this man. But they have several different overlapping obsessions.'

Admiration had its dark side too. Idols aroused strong feelings in their fans. Some of them, the unbalanced ones, developed fantasies around their idols that could lead in dangerous directions.

'But the idol is never the underlying reason for the admirer's actions.'

All ten black videos matched the length of a Queen song. That was the connecting factor that Rico's program had found.

'It can't be a coincidence,' Mari said.

'That's... crazy,' Lia said.

'Precisely.'

'Why Queen?'

Even as she said it, Lia realised how obvious the answer was. Freddie Mercury, the lead vocalist of Queen, was one of the most famous gay men in the world and one of the most famous victims of AIDS. Their murderer was killing people he grabbed from gay bars.

'I think Queen and Mercury and gay people are just parts of a larger picture here. They don't completely explain what he's doing,' Mari said. 'But we can use them to try to figure out who the killer is.'

They sat and talked for a long time.

Mari poured them some white wine, and even though what they were talking about was strange and dark, there were moments when Lia felt as though Mari was recovering. Some things in their lives were returning to normal.

This killer didn't have anything in common with normal people who admired celebrities, Mari said. You had to separate what most people experienced from morbid obsessions.

'For us it's no big deal if someone likes a musician. Everyone's a fan of something. It's a good thing. But for people like this man, it becomes an alternate reality into which they channel all of their bad feelings and aggression.'

Mari grabbed her laptop and started looking for something. After a moment, music started playing from speakers hidden around the room. Lia recognised Queen instantly even though she had only ever listened to a couple of their albums.

'I'd know that sound anywhere,' she said.

'Me too,' Mari said.

It sounded at once beautiful and bombastic, Mari thought. A rock band who named themselves Queen were instantly flaunting any number of things: irony, arrogance, daring.

Mari took a large sip of wine.

'I have to show you something that's going to make this even more repulsive,' she said.

Lia blanched. What could make this any worse?

Mari turned off the music and searched for something else on her computer. Then she turned the display towards Lia so she could see.

Lia recognised the video immediately. It was the first kicking video, the one she had seen more than a week before at *Level* with her colleagues.

But now music played to its rhythm. Queen's old hit 'We Will Rock You'. Lia knew it well since it was a staple of sports stadiums around the world.

The killer had edited the video to make the pictures flow to the music. Lia watched until she had to look away. Mari stopped the video, and a perfect hush fell over them.

'How did you notice that?' Lia asked.

'It was pretty obvious as soon as I realised that the videos were the same length as specific songs,' Mari said.

Combining the music with the video only took Rico a few seconds, after which he hadn't been able to watch the video at all any more.

Lia grimaced. She knew exactly how Rico must feel.

Mari showed her what songs the killer had used so far. 'We Will Rock You,' 'Now I'm Here,' 'We Are the Champions,' 'Another One Bites the Dust.'

The songs weren't from the same record originally, Mari pointed out.

'I think he's making his own greatest hits album,' she added. 'These are his ten favourite songs.'

The Internet was full of homemade video clips set to people's favourite songs: they danced; they lip-synced; they taped their pets moving to the music. Some could be quite complex video compositions.

'If that's true, these are the sickest fan videos ever,' Lia said.

Mari nodded.

'He's combining snuff films and music videos. The purpose is to reach as broad an audience as possible. And change people's experience of what they watch online.'

Why didn't he publish the videos with the music from the start? Lia wondered.

'I don't know,' Mari said thoughtfully. 'It probably has some significance. Maybe it's his way of showing defiance. *Figure out what's going on and you'll find me.*'

'He wants to be found?'

'He knows he'll get caught. But he wants recognition for the greatness of his actions.'

It was starting to get late, already after ten o'clock.

As she realised how much time had passed, Lia immediately thought of Gro. Then she remembered that the dog was in good hands with Mr Vong, who had promised that she could stay the night if necessary.

How could they pass on Mari's information to the police? Lia asked.

'I don't know,' Mari said.

The videos were still running on the screen, one after another. Lia could see how the rhythm of each synced perfectly with the music playing in the room.

The combined effect was terrifying. Lia had never been a particular fan of Queen – the band had seen its heyday so long ago – but with the videos their music started feeling almost revolting.

'I think that's exactly what he wants,' Mari said seriously.

'Even though he loves the band?'

'Even so. This man wants to take things away from people. He wants to change them, pervert them.'

They had to ring the police, Lia said. They had to pass on this information.

'Gerrish said they have to get any information immediately. Whenever anyone conceals information, someone suffers,' she explained.

'Oh, Gerrish said that, did he?' Mari said, looked at Lia long and hard before continuing, 'OK.'

She looked for her mobile and dialled a number.

'Rico? Send them to the police. Right now.'

Then she immediately rang off. She and Rico had already been considering sending the videos to the police, Lia realised.

'When the police release them, good won't be the only thing that comes of it by any means,' Mari said.

'What do you mean?'

The celebrity connection to the slayings would turn the media's interest white hot.

'The front pages of the papers won't have room for anything else after this,' Mari said.

They both had the same thought: Berg's death was going to become even more public. Beyond a source of trauma and grief for the entire nation, the killings would become an even larger media event, which meant that some in the media would have scant concern for the suffering of the bereaved and would start focusing only on the sensational aspects of the crimes.

'Still,' Lia said. 'Maybe the videos will move the police investigation forward. Maybe the fact they were made to Queen songs will fit with one of their profiles. That might help them catch him.'

Mari nodded.

'Let's hope so.'

They had gone through a bottle of wine. Mari fixed them a bite to eat, cheese and bread and fruit.

Sitting by the tall window with her best friend, Lia felt as though she knew too much about things it wasn't good to know anything about, and she thought that the only thing in this situation that might help was for Mari's strength to return.

We need her.

Mari looked at her, a warm memory in her eyes.

'When you came to the Studio the first time, you were so confused,' Mari said. 'I felt like saying, calm down, girl, I'm about to show you things you've never even dreamed of before. But I couldn't say anything like that. You were so panicked.'

'Well, you did show me things I'd never dreamed of,' Lia said.

'Yes, I did.'

Mari's eyes began to water, and she choked up.

Lia knew what Mari was crying for, for what they had had at the Studio. And Berg.

When she had cried that out, she poured them more wine and said one of their Finnish words, the words that English couldn't quite match.

'*Perkele.*' Yes, it was the name of the Devil, yes it was an expletive, but it was also so much more.

Mari was coming back.

By eleven o'clock they were seriously tipsy. Mari had turned off the music, which was too fraught for them now.

Lia could feel it was time for a small confession.

'I've been talking to your grandmother,' she said. 'Online.'

'Yes, I know,' Mari said. 'I saw on the computer that she had called.'

'She told me... about your childhood,' Lia said.

'Ah.'

Upon hearing this, Mari looked aside.

'She told me about the Laboratory,' Lia said.

Mari sipped her wine. Her expression revealed absolutely nothing.

'That means you're the only one outside my family who knows,' Mari said.

That was enough. A desire to protect the woman in front of her filled Lia, a need to show she was worthy of trust.

'Mamia just asked me to tell you that I know,' Lia explained.

'Mamia is a dear old lady who always thinks she knows what's right for other people,' Mari said. 'In that sense I take after my family perfectly.'

An awkward silence fell. In order to fill it, Lia started talking about *Level*, little things that were happening at work. Mari wasn't listening.

'We were like caged animals,' she suddenly said.

Mari and her three siblings had believed that life was supposed to be as limited and regulated as it was in their childhood home. Their mother convinced them they were different from other children because they got to have school at home and they had their own special way of learning. When they saw pictures of big school classes, it felt strange: did everyone else really have to sit and read in such big groups?

Mari's big sister was the only one of them who sensed that something was wrong with the way the family lived. But even her sister didn't know how many things in their severe upbringing were so unusual. Over the years of visiting their grandparents they began to understand.

'We could see it in their expressions. When our own grandmother looked at us that way. Shocked at how we were. Caged animals.'

The neighbours thought the family must belong to a strange religious sect, Mari later learned. Intense religiosity was typical of families who home schooled.

'There was also something very Finnish about the way our neighbours let us isolate ourselves,' Mari said.

Lia understood. In Finland people didn't assume everyone had to be social all the time. Keeping at a distance a family who had chosen an idiosyncratic way of life was just as well.

Over time the four siblings developed a strong sense of community. Even though they didn't keep in touch as adults, trust was always their bedrock. Their relationships had already been tried so thoroughly in their childhood. It was as if they owed each other something – what, Mari wasn't sure.

'All we had was each other. And Mom, in the beginning. Mom, who wanted us to be quiet and sit still and concentrate on our studies all the time every day. We tried to be the best at knowing things.'

The days of home school melted together. The schedule was always the same. Up at seven, morning chores and then studying by eight. Breaks only for eating and once a day for time outside. On outings they avoided meeting other people. Instead, while they walked their mother quizzed them on what they had been reading.

'Sometimes when people stared at us outside, I thought it was because they were jealous. That other people knew we were special.'

There was always the feeling that they were supposed to be. A feeling of constant, absolute necessity to be better than others.

They studied enormous amounts of material. Speed reading was one of the first things their parents trained them in. And constant testing: their mother was always assessing how well they were learning what they were reading.

'Information was our escape. If we knew things, we felt safe.'

Afterwards, as an adult, Mari thought that her mother had really been incapable of treating children like children. Perhaps Auni Nurmi had started her research project partially so her children would grow up to be like her as quickly as possible.

Lia could hear from Mari's voice how hard this was on her. Lia felt like interrupting the story, but she didn't have the nerve. She had always sensed something almost manic in Mari's appetite for information. Now she knew why.

Mari's parents ended up having a series of serious rows with the children's grandparents, who at one point threatened to go to the authorities, to report the family to the district child protection officers. Mari's mother threatened to move the family out of the county and cut off all contact with the grandparents. She also pointed to the children's exceptional test results.

Twice a year the headmaster from the local secondary school visited them. They didn't tell him exactly what kind of pedagogical experiment the family was running, but the headmaster was very impressed with the children's knowledge and their mother's focus on discipline.

'I always made up these complicated imaginary stories about that old man,' Mari said. 'About him and everyone else we met.'

Of course the children wanted their mother's approval. They did everything, and sometimes their mother was satisfied.

'Whenever one of us got good marks in a test, she always said the goal wasn't here in this moment and place. The goal was always somewhere ahead of us.'

The most important thing was always the research, Nurmi and Gerber's experiment, and the whole family was responsible for making it a success. They were the Nurmi and Gerber experiment.

In a way they never terminated the experiment, it just sputtered out as the family broke up. Mari's parents were fighting more and more, and the children began to realise how odd their lifestyle was and became ashamed of it. When their parents split, their mother moved to Germany to continue her research. None of the children went with her.

'Then Mamia let it all out at once, years later. She said our family was a laboratory. That was the moment I started hating my child-hood. And Doctor Auni Nurmi.'

Lia swallowed her discomfort at the words Mari used to describe her mother.

'I don't want anyone knowing anything about this,' Mari added.

Lia nodded.

They talked for a while longer. Mari asked about Lia's meeting with Detective Chief Inspector Gerrish, but Lia noticed Mari wasn't concentrating on their conversation.

In the end they just sat quietly, sipping their wine and looking out. Only a few lights were on in the neighbouring windows. The street stayed mostly deserted, with only the occasional pedestrian this late at night. Really there was nothing to look at. It was peaceful. It felt sufficient.

When Lia left for home in the small hours of the morning, she looked out of the taxi window at London, Islington, Chalk Farm, and Belsize Park. She thought of the killer who somehow had become even stranger now. She thought of the stacks of books and papers in Mari's flat and the moment during the evening when Mari had sworn.

Mari was still living in the Laboratory. But she was coming out.

29.

The police didn't announce the connection between the snuff videos and Queen.

Lia waited for it to appear in the news at any moment, and all day at *Level* she kept an eye on the wires. Not a word.

She texted Mari about it. Why were the police concealing it?

The police were probably researching their violent crime databases for anything related to Queen, Mari guessed. The investigators were combing the Queen forums online, sifting through Queen fan videos, interviewing people who knew the subject.

'The police don't want to let it out because as long as only they have it, the murderer might make a mistake and do something on one of these forums,' Mari wrote.

During the day it occurred to Lia that maybe *Level* should write about it. The strange connection between the killings and the band would be an amazing scoop for any news outlet. The print run would sell out, and the website would probably crash under the traffic. They would be the envy of everyone in the media.

But the thought of leaking something to her own magazine was too difficult. Lia would have a hard time doing it without revealing she knew something about it, and, above all, the news could hurt the police investigation. The whole idea made her more and more ashamed as the day wore on. How could she even have considered something like that, treating it like news to sell?

She spent the last two hours of the day plugging away harder than usual, assuaging her conscience by agreeing to some extra work for the next week and making a couple of calls to arrange something for the evening.

Before her appointment in Hoxton, she stopped in Harrow at the shooting range. Paddy had arranged for Bob Pell to take over supervising Lia so that she could come and practise if Pell had space on the range. Pell tried to offer additional instruction, but Lia declined.

She shot for an hour. She was getting better all the time. Her Heckler & Koch P7 did get hot quite quickly, but that forced her to take breaks and focus more on her performance.

At the end of the hour, she rang Mari to announce she was coming soon. This time she didn't use her key to Mari's flat, she rang the bell. Mari came to open immediately.

'Let's go out,' Lia said.

Mari's guard went up instantly.

'I don't want to go to the Studio right now,' she said.

'Who said anything about the Studio?' Lia asked and made Mari grab her coat.

Lia had found an appropriate place within walking distance of Mari's home. Not right in the neighbourhood, because she guessed Mari wouldn't want that.

When Mari saw the name on the door, Anga Yoga, she stopped.

'I don't want to do yoga,' she said.

'Of course you don't,' Lia said and dragged her in.

She had reserved them their own small room where an instructor was waiting, a woman with strong Caribbean features.

Although the serenity of the yoga studio was in complete contrast to the noise of the half illegal shooting range Lia had just left, the places also had an absurd similarity. Both demanded perfect focus. Both had strong effects on the mind and body.

The instructor looked at Mari's reluctant stance for a moment and then pulled Lia aside.

'Your friend doesn't want to do yoga, and she isn't really in the right shape for it now anyway,' the woman said.

'She's in fine shape. And she needs something like this,' Lia said.

'I don't mean physical shape,' the woman said quietly. 'If a person is spiritually weak, yoga can be too much effort. It can trigger too strong emotions.'

'Let's take it easy then,' Lia said. 'And stop immediately if she starts feeling bad.'

Mari agreed to come into the dressing room, where they changed into the loose clothing Lia had brought. She agreed to sit on the floor in the small practice room.

When the instructor asked them to slowly lower themselves into a supine position, tears began running down Mari's face.

The hour was an intense experience for all of them. The instructor and Lia guided Mari through a gentle series of movements, watching as she cried and feeling their own eyes water as well. It was as if they were watching someone close to them lying down on a hospital bed for a frightening test no one could know the results of.

But at the end of the hour, Mari stood up and, after hopping in the shower and some cold water, she could talk again without getting emotional.

'That was good,' she said to Lia. 'That was really good.'

They grabbed food on the way back to Mari's flat.

Lia noted that apparently Mari wasn't in the habit of chatting with the staff at the Co-op down the street.

She wondered to herself why Mari lived here in particular. Hoxton had long been one of the more threadbare areas of East London, but it was changing rapidly. Especially at the southern end, more creative people and IT professionals had moved in, and some blocks were already among the most stylish in the city. But Mari lived in the part of Hoxton bordering on Islington still dominated by old housing estates populated by families of humble means. Tiny grocery shops gave the streets their colour, and languages other than English were common. Mari's building was on the edge of Shoreditch Park and a few other similarly handsome buildings stood around, but otherwise the area was rather shabby. Although restaurants that looked insignificant from the outside might have the praises of big-time food critics pasted in their windows, Lia noticed: maybe looks were deceiving.

Mari sensed Lia's meditations.

'I like these streets,' she said.

If you looked closely you could see signs of wealth and need, like nests of different cultures living side-by-side. The Hoxton Square area a little further south was already quite smart, but here a person could still be themselves.

Upstairs in the flat, Mari locked the door behind them and sighed. 'Alcohol.'

Lia opened a bottle of wine, and, while Mari sorted out the food in the kitchen, made two quick calls. First she checked with Rico that all was well at the Studio and nothing new had come out in the news about the police investigation. Then she talked to Mr Vong to make sure he wouldn't mind Gro staying with him again.

'Not at all,' Mr Vong said.

They got along very well, he assured her. They had even seen a hare on their walk on Hampstead Heath that day. That had been very exciting for Gro, Mr Vong related enthusiastically.

Lia and Mari didn't talk about difficult things. Not a word about the video murders or Berg. Lia could see from the stacks of books spread around the flat that Mari was continuing her investigation, but they didn't talk about that.

Mari did ask whether the Studio had heard anything from Craig Cole, but so far as Lia knew, Cole hadn't been in contact.

They ate the supper Mari had made and then sat in the same place as the previous night. Lia talked about *Level*. She had the feeling that the others at work had started evaluating her more closely, as a possible future Art Director. Mari talked about things she wanted to change about her flat some day. She had been thinking about building a sauna, but that would require quite a battle of papers and planning permission, not to mention the renovation itself.

Mari had her computer next to her, which gave Lia an idea.

'Have you been in touch with your grandmother?'

Mari shook her head.

'Not yet. All in good time.'

'Let's ring her now,' Lia suggested.

She could see from Mari's face that at first she meant to refuse but then changed her mind.

'I've never rung her with anyone else,' Mari said.

They moved to sit side-by-side. They were a little crowded on the windowsill. Lia had to lean on the windowpane, and Mari set the computer on a bench in front of them. But once they got the VoIP program open and saw themselves in the picture onscreen, the situation amused them both.

'Should we hide our wine glasses?' Lia wondered.

'From Mamia?' Mari snorted. 'Hardly.'

Mamia answered after just a few rings. They saw concern on her face. Her breathing was raspy over the audio connection as she squinted at their picture.

'Well now,' Mamia said.

She was clearly delighted to see Mari after so long.

'Hi Grandma,' Mari said.

'Hi you two,' Mamia said.

She asked after Mari's health and wouldn't believe a bit of it when Mari assured her she was fine.

'Even an old lady like me can see you aren't,' Mamia snapped.

But if Mari was up to sipping wine with a friend, she had a good enough grip on life that her grandmother didn't need to worry about her, Mamia said.

'Have you watched the news from Finland? We're having demonstrations here, in three cities. Young people protesting over growing income inequality. One of the marches is happening in Turku!'

Mamia thought Turku was a lethargic, sleepy place where nothing real ever happened, Mari explained to Lia.

'In that city it's impossible to have an opinion,' Mamia huffed.

'And that galls you,' Mari said, laughing. 'But you want to join in.'

'I might even,' Mamia said.

As they chatted, the evening darkened around them. The glow of Mari's computer screen lit up her and Lia's faces. They looked white and unreal and hopeful.

No one talked about Mari's other family members. Lia felt like she wasn't supposed to ask about them or Mari's background in general. They had plenty to talk about anyway. A couple of thousand kilometres separated them from Mamia, along with about fifty years, but she still felt like one of them.

At some point Lia realised that she had never had such long phone conversations with her own relatives. Not even her parents. Lia rang them maybe once a month. Usually she didn't use the computer so she wouldn't have had video. Although it was nice seeing her parents, video calls were often a bit irritating when you thought about it: it was so easy to see when the other person's thoughts started to wander and the novelty of seeing you wore off.

When Mamia announced she was going to bed, they wished her goodnight several times, and after the call ended, Lia moved over to face Mari again.

They sat there in silence for a long time.

After opening another bottle, Mari asked how the others were holding up at the Studio.

Maggie was doing well, Lia said. She had been in contact with Berg's relatives in England, saying she was his friend and wanted to help with the funeral arrangements if they needed assistance. She hadn't been coming to the Studio every day. She needed to take a little distance.

'Rico – Rico is still Rico,' Lia said with a smile.

Rico was always doing something. Out of all of them, staying busy was easiest for him. His machines and programs always needed updating and tweaking. Only recently had it dawned on Lia how deeply Rico was mourning for the other victims besides Berg. Rico had only known Mike Cottle distantly, but even a distant personal connection made him more sensitive to what was going on.

'And Paddy misses you,' Lia said.

This was a cheap shot, she knew. But Lia wanted Mari back at the Studio soon, and Paddy did too, for his own reasons.

'Did he say something?' Mari asked.

'No, nothing in particular. But I can tell.'

'I've been thinking about ringing him.'

Lia didn't understand what she meant until Mari's face eased into a smile.

'You want to ask him out?'

Mari nodded.

'You want to ask him out now when you're both...' Lia said, searching for the words.

'Out of our minds with grief,' Mari said.

She looked at her phone.

'This doesn't have much to do with logic.'

Berg wasn't even buried yet. Mari had been huddled at home in a state of near paralysis and only just set foot outside for the first time in days. Paddy probably blamed himself for everything that had happened just like all the rest of them.

'This is the worst moment to be thinking about anything like this. But I'm still basically a coin toss away from ringing him.'

Lying on her bed at home, Mari had worked through a lot of things. Such as the fact that none of them had unlimited time.

'You forget that at the Studio,' Mari said.

Lia knew what she meant. At the Studio their work always demanded commitment. You felt like you always had to be on your toes to manage such important things. They often rode the high that came from a feeling of power. That was why it was easy to put off things like thoughts of dating, since you could never be sure what would come of it.

Mari and Paddy had known each other for several years. The whole time they had both known that one of them would make a move at some point. Waiting had been fun in some ways too, Mari noted. It had been a sort of long-term flirtation.

Paddy had been with other women. Mari had seen a couple of men during that time too.

'Pretty short-term stuff though,' she admitted. 'But this Mr Moore – I've always known something more could happen with him.'

Lia smiled. 'Ring.'

'Now?' Mari asked, surprised.

'Now.'

A smirk spread across Mari's face again.

'That would serve him right.'

Lia poured them both more wine and handed Mari her glass.

'I want to listen.'

Mari laughed. They drank. The temptation to shrug off the anguish of the past days by acting silly was overwhelming in their drunken state. Instead of living in the shadow of grief and fear, it felt good to be light-hearted and irresponsible for a while.

'This is almost like being a kid,' Lia said. 'A teenager. Daring each other to ring a boy.'

'It wasn't like that for me,' Mari said. 'My childhood was a fucking freak show.'

She took a swig of wine and started looking for the number in her phone. Paddy answered after three rings.

'Mari?'

'All right, Paddy?' Mari said.

Lia leaned in, almost placing her ear to Mari's to hear every word. The situation was at once extremely comical and extremely serious. They felt reckless. Anything could happen.

'Yeah, fine,' Paddy said, confused by the late night call.

'Did I wake you?' Mari asked.

The phone went silent. Mari's voice was a little too loud, a little too revealing.

'You're drunk,' Paddy said. He sounded drowsy and amused in a grumpy sort of way.

'Yes,' Mari said. 'You nailed it.'

Silence again.

'I want to ask you out to eat. To Pied à Terre,' Mari said.

Paddy sighed.

'You're drunk,' he repeated.

'Pied à Terre. It is a French place I've wanted to go to with you for a long time,' Mari said.

'Sounds expensive.'

'I can afford it.'

Such a fancy restaurant, Paddy said, feigning hesitation. And what if he just wanted fish and chips?

'They know how to fry fish and chips. Would you check your calendar to see when you're free?'

Paddy laughed.

'Are you serious?'

'I am.'

'It would be like... a date?'

'And fish and chips,' Mari said.

Paddy let her wait for her answer.

'Yes, that's fine then.'

Lia didn't mean to cry out, but a little yelp still escaped. She was so happy for Mari. And jealous – jealous because something was happening between Paddy and Mari.

'Jesus Christ,' Paddy blurted out. 'Is Lia there too?'

Mari and Lia couldn't answer they were laughing so hard.

'Jesus Christ,' Paddy repeated. 'Two drunk Finnish women.'

'I'll drink to that,' Mari said, raising her glass to Lia.

'Go to sleep already,' Paddy said. 'Goodnight.'

They could hear as he rung off that Paddy wasn't sorry about the call though.

They couldn't go to sleep now. They had to sit and talk. Lia started talking about the thing that kept running through her head whenever she was in Mari's flat: why had she lived so long in such a small flat in the basement of a student residence hall?

'It's a pretty building,' Lia said. 'Old and lovely in a plain sort of way. It's convenient and awfully cheap. I've liked living there because I can control it. But it is small and rather bare. Maybe I should move some day. When it starts feeling necessary.'

'You have to let things happen in their own time,' Mari said. 'Not everyone has to live up in an eyrie.'

They both smiled at that thought: the expansive view from Mari's windows was gorgeous in the dark. A cityscape you could only get with money.

'You're always wondering how I pay for all of this,' Mari said.

Lia nodded. This was one of many things she had wondered to herself about Mari and the Studio.

'How do you have money for the Studio and this flat?'

'You know a lot already,' Mari said. 'But there's more I can tell you now.'

She had entrusted her money to four portfolio managers in different parts of the world. Profits from her Frankfurt investments were the steadiest, but Hong Kong was where she made the quickest money. New York and London produced quite well at times too.

Everything had started in Hong Kong though. While she was there, Mari had helped a British equity banker with some personal issues. In exchange, he suggested investment opportunities, and once Mari had made her initial money, he also found her three other colleagues in different countries to do the same thing.

'They give me somewhat different advice to that which they give other people,' Mari said. 'It isn't illegal, but it isn't exactly legal either. It violates their fiduciary obligations.'

To their investor clients, the men recommended opportunities that the financial management companies that employed them had chosen. But Mari they told about the ones they believed in personally. The strategy had paid off well. For the previous month, the total value of her portfolio had been 11.4 million pounds sterling.

'And the best thing is that it's invested in so many different places that there's no way to lose it all.'

Lia snorted. Hearing such a large number was at turns strange and amusing.

'That's so much money I can't even wrap my head around it,' she said.

Mari nodded towards the dark buildings looming in the night on the other side of the park.

'It is a lot, but it also isn't very much at all. For example, you couldn't buy a single one of those buildings with it. The value of money always depends on what you use it for. I mostly just need it for the Studio though.'

As Lia returned for the second night in a row from Hoxton to her home on Kidderpore Avenue, to her tiny room on the basement level of the King's College residence hall, she thought of time and its passing.

She was almost thirty years old. She had been working full-time for more than six years now. She had about £10,000 invested.

Seems like this would be a good point to know what I want. To decide what things are important to me.

Mamia was ready to hit the streets with protesters sixty years younger than herself. Mari had just found the courage to rejoin the world and take a decisive step forward with Paddy.

Lia had them, and Rico and Maggie, her colleagues at *Level* and her parents in Finland. She had seen various men from time to time, and there were a few people she didn't want to think about.

And in the flat above her she had Gro and Mr Vong.

They'll do just fine.

It was early Saturday morning. Before lying down to sleep, she checked the news for any new information about the video killer. No police reports, nothing. Several days had passed now since anything new had hit the press about the case.

She didn't know whether the silence signified something good or something evil.

30.

The media's handling of the killings changed instantly once the police announced their macabre connection to Queen on Saturday. The Video Killer became the Queen Killer, the papers rushed out special editions and the TV channels interrupted regular programming.

'This is the unfortunate result of the constant growth of celebrity worship and the entertainment business,' said Christopher Holywell, a criminal psychologist and profiler, during the Metropolitan Police press conference, which three British channels and CNN broadcast live.

Singers and movie stars were constantly being ranked by popularity: there were the A-listers, the B-listers and then all the rest, Holywell continued. But getting on the A list also meant trouble for a star, things like death threats and stalkers. Frequently celebrities had to request restraining orders against fans, and some tended to meet quite a lot of fans who were willing to break the law. Unbalanced people even gravitated towards lesser-known stars – often the fan's enthusiasm had less to do with the actual reputation of their idol than how important he or she was to them personally.

'We often applaud celebrities for living like normal people. But for many of them that's impossible nowadays, or it means taking unacceptable risks. Becoming a big star means your life changes and you have to start thinking about security arrangements, including for your family,' Holywell said.

'Are there a lot of these stalkers?' the *Daily Mail*'s reporter asked.

No one could know how many there were, Holywell said. Examples cropped up constantly, but most of them managed to stay out of public view. The celebrities didn't want to draw attention to the problem to avoid encouraging other crackpots. Private firms usually handled celebrity security, so many threats never came to the authorities' knowledge.

One thing united fanatic admirers: they tried to get attention from their idols in dramatic, outrageous ways. Often there was a sexual or violent aspect to it. A woman who stalked Michael Douglas and Catherine Zeta-Jones threatened to cut the actress up in pieces like a roast and feed her to her dogs. The evidence against the accused included a letter from Zeta-Jones in which she described her complete loss of peace of mind as a result of the harassment. She feared the anxiety would be with her for the rest of her life.

'The wider public may sometimes have a difficult time taking these cases seriously because so much of pop culture feels unreal,' Holywell said to the reporter. 'But these are very real crimes. Frequently the harassment goes on for years getting worse and worse before anyone takes action.'

Serial killings generally lacked a clear external motive, at least one a normal person could comprehend. Usually the killers point to irrational, seemingly random facts for their reasons.

'Tracking these killers by trying to identify their goals or motivations is difficult. But identifying victims can help catch them.'

Serial killers usually selected their victims from five groups of people: the elderly, children, prostitutes, homeless teenagers, or gay men.

'The social standing of the victims is critical,' Holywell said. 'These groups are easier to kill because their safety networks are weaker.'

Serial killers killed because it had a powerful psychological effect on them. Holywell believed that celebrity was becoming increasingly important for murderers.

'Fantasy and reality become confused. According to one theory, all serial killers are connected by an addiction to their own fantasies: they feel a compulsion to live them out that exceeds all normal inhibitions related to killing. Celebrity and fulfilling one's fantasies are very addictive things.'

Nowadays killing was an easier way to achieve fame than ever before. That was why fame had started playing into the acts themselves. Criminologists had discovered that if a serial killer received a nickname in the press and the media provided detailed descriptions of his killings, the pace of attacks tended to increase. Details would also start coming through in the murders meant to influence the public in certain ways.

This killer had now linked himself with one of the most famous rock bands in the world to ensure his own future fame. He knew by now that everything about him would become just as interesting in the public's eyes as anything a pop star did. And that's what he wanted – pop stardom through murder.

'Online auction sites sell memorabilia connected to famous serial killings. You can buy objects and clothing a murderer once owned. We've seen locks of Charles Manson's hair for sale. And if someone wanted, they could go online right now and buy a pouch of sand from the foundations of John Wayne Gacy's house where he buried twenty-six of his victims,' Holywell said.

'Is there some particular significance in the killings to the music used in the videos?' a reporter asked.

Queen did have a song named 'Killer Queen'. Based on its length it didn't seem to belong to any of the black videos, but could the songs themselves have some symbolic part in the overall picture?

'It would seem that everything is significant in these crimes,' Holywell said. 'Every single tiny detail.'

That was why the police had made this information public. They appealed to everyone listening or reading – did the Queen connection mean anything to anyone? The police tip-off lines would be open twenty-four hours a day, seven days a week.

Holywell had one other plea for the public.

'Don't distribute these videos. Don't increase their popularity. Control the curiosity we all naturally feel.'

Serial killers typically took trophies from their victims, something to serve as a symbol of their accomplishment and a memento. The trophy could be a piece of clothing belonging to the victim, or sometimes even a part of the victim himself. In the video murders, the video served as a trophy.

'Every time someone watches one of these videos online, the trophy becomes more valuable to him. It becomes even stronger evidence of his power.'

Holywell was the first person in the police who seemed to have any idea what was going on in the case, Mari observed to Lia over the phone.

'But we may learn much more about these killings, perhaps unexpected things,' she said. 'Hopefully not.'

In the press conference, the police only showed short clips of the kicking videos set to Queen's music. Even these brief excerpts deeply disturbed some viewers, but the TV news immediately rebroadcast them all over Britain. Then they started spreading online, despite official pleas.

And within a couple of hours another meme started spreading online. People synced the snuff videos with the entire songs so everyone could watch the videos straight through with the accompanying music, seeing how every blow really was edited in time with the beat.

That same night the police released a statement reminding the public that distributing the videos could interfere with the police investigation. Still the pace kept picking up. Curious viewers linked to them over and over, yielding hundreds of thousands of hits within the day. Most of the comments online registered dismay, but jokes started to appear in amongst the condemnation too.

'I detest people,' Lia said to Mari over the phone. 'Really and truly.'

'I know,' Mari said.

'For some people this goes straight to the very basest parts of them. The vultures.'

'Best to prepare for more of this to come.'

Mari still didn't want to return to the Studio on Sunday, but she asked Rico to meet her at a coffee shop.

They hugged in greeting. They didn't always do that, but now it felt necessary.

'I stopped crying a few days ago,' Rico said.

'Good,' Mari said. 'For me it still comes back from time to time. Sometimes I can go half a day without doing so though.'

They had work to do, lots of work. They had to investigate everything the connection to Queen might reveal, Mari said.

'I've already been doing that,' Rico said.

Because of the black videos they knew all ten songs the killer had chosen. That list still wasn't any help identifying him: the same songs showed up on thousands of playlists Queen fans had posted online.

'But they are all pretty old,' Mari pointed out.

The songs were from the 1970s, one from the very early 80s.

'He would be in his fifties,' Mari guessed.

The man was from the generation that lived through the rise of the music video.

'He's probably had some involvement in film or video production,' Rico added. 'You don't learn editing like that overnight.'

Rico also had some important new information. He had started investigating the people whose user accounts the killer had hacked to upload his videos. They were mostly young people with no obvious connection to each other.

'Then I looked at what else they had done online,' Rico said.

Digging that up had been extremely time consuming. Rico had needed to find each user's IP address and then search what else had been done from those locations. He had found lots of network traffic, along with dozens of passwords to different sites like online retailers, discussion forums and gaming servers. The normal things young people did online.

'And they had all poked fun at Queen,' Rico said.

Every one of them had written something negative about Queen on some website or another.

'One of them was an outright troll. He just roamed sites making fun of artists and their fans at random. He obviously enjoys the negativity,' Rico said.

How easy would it be for the police to find the connection between these users and Queen fans? Mari asked.

'They can do it,' Rico said. 'If they think to look. It takes time, but they do have plenty of manpower.'

'I don't imagine you can track the killer from these teenagers' user accounts?'

No, that was too hard, Rico said.

A profile was forming though, he pointed out. A white man, in his fifties, in good physical shape, with experience making videos, working with computers and marksmanship, and a regular visitor to Queen fansites. Not a very specific profile but something at least. Maybe the police had more.

'And then the most important thing,' Mari said.

'What?'

'He hates gay people.'

The next morning the staff at *Level* discussed the violent Queen videos spreading online with just as much disbelief as everywhere else.

'What does this mean for us?' editor-in-chief Timothy Phelps asked. 'Someone tell me what our angle should be.'

The subject wasn't fans or celebrity worship, he added immediately. That was generally benign in most people's lives.

'But is the subject desensitisation to violence? Or the kind of little shits who get a kick out of sharing a real killer's sick pictures?'

No one in the office had an answer. Timothy Phelps shook his head wearily.

'If only someone could say why this is happening.'

'Maybe that's the subject,' said Sam Levinson. 'The bewilderment. The confusion about how something like this can exist and whether we should start thinking about drawing new boundaries online.'

'Too difficult. Too strange,' Phelps said.

'Sam's right,' Lia said. 'If we only choose one of these perspectives, it feels like we're treating the topic too coldly. None of these is going to be enough on its own. Either we deal with the videos broadly or not at all.'

The AD, Martyn Taylor, cast her an approving glance.

'We can't not address it,' Phelps said. 'That option has been taken off the table, sad to say.'

Fortunately they had a week before their next issue, so they had time to think.

Lia tried to focus on her layouts, but she knew her head wasn't really in the game. Not thinking about the video killings, Queen and the pure evil spreading online was impossible.

That afternoon she decided to take up a task she had been putting off for days. Martyn Taylor had asked her to develop something new for the magazine's online edition. The whole issue of digital versioning was a bit sticky for Lia: every publisher expected their staff to produce electronic versions of their existing publications but usually without additional expense and within the same deadlines as before.

Taylor had asked Lia to come up with new ways to use moving images in *Level*'s electronic version. They just had to be either free or cheap and of course fit with the visual image of the magazine. Practically speaking the job was nearly impossible.

'Sam, help,' Lia exclaimed.

And help did come from the neighbouring desk, as it had frequently before. Over the years Sam and Lia had collaborated closely on a variety of new article series and frequently gave each other feedback. Working together was easy.

Lia told Sam what she had already done in terms of researching compatible features for their digital platform and looking at what the competition was doing. She had seen a lot of videos. Music, speeches, adverts. All of the electronic publications had them, including *Level*, but they had to come up with a way to do it better.

The brainstorming session with Sam yielded increasingly absurd ideas. What if they asked people they interviewed to choose three videos to link to from the article? The Prime Minister's favourite YouTube clips, film stars' favourite film trailers of all time.

'I already know what Martyn will say,' Lia said. 'He'll say great, because it would be free material, but why do we want to guide readers to some other website, away from *Level* content?'

What if the digital edition had a competition? A link that would always show up in a different place in the magazine. Sometimes it could be hidden in a headline or a picture – wherever. On one page there could always be a hint about the link's location.

'A little like a crossword, but this would be a visual puzzle,' Lia said.

Sam liked the idea, although he did see problems with it. Why would the reader want to play with the magazine in the first place? But maybe they could develop the idea in some other direction. They could offer prizes – some readers always went for that. A magazine that didn't offer opportunities to win things was a rarity these days, but *Level* had tried to keep its kitsch marketing in check.

Sam looked online for ads that might spawn more ideas. As Lia watched one more startlingly expensive-looking commercial, she suddenly sat up. She had just seen something she didn't understand.

'Show me that again,' she said.

Sam clicked back to the beginning of the video. In the picture a man walked along a pavement drinking a smoothie through a straw. The man then saw a lorry on the road bearing down on a woman crossing the street. The woman was pushing a pram and didn't notice the lorry. Lia knew the advertisement; she'd seen it before on TV. Next the man would rush to the woman, snatch her and the pram up and catapult into the air. The idea was that the smoothie could make anyone a do-gooding superman.

Lia watched the part where the woman stood in the middle of the street not glancing to either side. What a stupid woman. Why was she just gawping and not acting like normal people did. Why was she being portrayed as stupid?

'Why do they always need a man saving a woman?' Lia asked Sam.

Sam grinned.

'No man could give a right answer to that question.'

Something in the advert bothered Lia. And she knew that was what the people who made it wanted. The simplicity of characters in commercials could irritate you as much as you wanted just as long as you remembered the product.

Then the images moving on the screen gave rise to another idea, a serious, real one. It was so frightening Lia couldn't continue working.

She apologised to Sam for the interruption and made up an excuse about a meeting she had forgotten. Then she fled the building.

Luckily Mari picked up instantly.

Lia didn't have time to explain her idea before Mari asked, 'Can you come to the Studio right now?'

Something jumped inside Lia.

'Are you coming too?'

'Yes.'

31

When Mari arrived at the Studio, everyone else was already there. She hugged Maggie, and smiled at Paddy and Rico and Lia. Mari sat down at her desk as if she had never been gone.

They all made a silent promise not to think that one of the group was missing. They had to investigate the video killings. They had to concentrate.

'On Craig Cole too,' Mari said.

The others were surprised.

'You want to return to the Cole case?' Rico asked in surprise.

They had been able to put Cole's issue on the backburner, but Mari didn't think they could leave it unfinished.

'He isn't in the clear yet, and we can't leave him on his own.'

Lia believed she knew why Mari wanted them to stay on Craig Cole. Mari wanted to give them all something good. A feeling that they could accomplish something, help someone.

Maybe Mari also felt some sort of connection to Cole. Craig Cole had fallen from a position that looked unassailable from the outside. Cole's popularity was based on genuine warmth and talent. Losing that had been unfair.

The same thing had happened to them – the Studio's wings had been clipped mid-flight, sending them crashing to the ground. A cold, brutal act had shattered their world. Perhaps after falling from so high, Mari wanted to do what she had always done, setting herself aside and focusing on the needs of others.

Mari had received information that Cole's agent would no longer even meet with his former star client.

'They haven't seen each other for weeks,' Mari said.

That was bad news. Just a little while ago a radio personality like Cole would have been an important client for any PR agency. Now the agent wanted surreptitiously to dump him.

'I can't believe no one wants to hire Craig Cole,' Mari said.

Popularity like that didn't disappear that fast. One radio station had offered him a short-term hosting job, although he turned it down.

But Cole needed something new. 'Maggie, could you look into it?' Mari asked.

'My pleasure,' Maggie said.

Cole needed the right-sized opportunity, Mari suggested. Not a return to the past, not to the centre of attention. But something where he could feel needed and liked.

'I have a few ideas of where to start,' Maggie said.

They talked about the video murders for the next hour. As they conversed, strange aspects of the killings that had come out over the past few days started to click into place for Lia.

From his previous work in the police and the private security industry, Paddy knew the magnitude of the celebrity stalking problem. The police kept files on the biggest stars, with records of criminal complaints, reports of threats and any other details. Companies that offered security services made constant risk assessments for their star clients about events at which they were to appear. These firms also investigated fan forums and hate sites where people discussed celebrities, looking for signs of threats.

Paddy had been turning the Queen and Freddie Mercury fansites inside out. Of course most of them were innocent, full of normal, harmless chatter.

'But it sometimes goes beyond that.'

The elapsed time since Mercury's death had done nothing to dampen the fervour of his cult following. Some sites offered extensive analyses of each and every picture and morsel of information ever made public about his life. And some tributes an outsider would hardly consider flattering.

'Some of them are really strange,' Paddy said.

For example, someone had written a veritable tome trying to prove that Mercury wasn't gay and hadn't died of AIDS. The singer's homosexuality was still such a difficult thing for some fans that they fought against it tooth and nail. As a young man, Mercury had had one long relationship with a woman, who had become his closest friend, but he also had plenty of male partners over the years.

Lia shared with the others the idea that had just startled her so much at *Level*.

'Maybe this is nothing,' she said. 'I don't know much about these things. But I started wondering why the victims don't move. Why do they lie on the ground ready to be kicked?'

The question surprised the others.

'Why don't they try to get away?' Lia asked. 'Wouldn't a person who knows they're in mortal danger try to get out of there?'

Mari looked at Lia silently for a long time.

'That's true,' she finally said. 'You're right.'

A person being kicked to death would use all their strength to try to escape. Or at least avoid the kicks. But the victims on the videos mostly just lay there. They raised their arms to shield their heads and rolled a bit. But none of them tried to resist or even grab their attacker's legs. None of them tried to get up. It was unnatural.

'Why didn't we think about this?' Mari asked.

'I don't know,' Paddy said. 'Maybe because we've only been looking at what everyone else is. We haven't been thinking about the situation from the victims' perspective.'

In distress like that, a person would do anything to get away, Mari said. The killer had to have done something to them before killing them.

Maybe he slipped something in their drinks at the bars, Maggie suggested. Ruffies.

'That's a possibility,' Mari said. 'Or maybe he did something to them outside the bars. There are so many eyes in these clubs.'

Whatever he did to them, this discovery was important.

'In any case,' Mari said, 'we've just found one more way to narrow down possible suspects.'

The man probably knew a little about drugs or medications and knew where to get them. That would give the police one more lead to chase down.

'Do the police know about this?' Lia wondered.

'Of course,' Paddy said. 'It's their job to think about attacks from the victims' perspective.'

And they had the bodies, Paddy added. In crimes like these they always did thorough autopsies and ran toxicology screenings.

'The police know that he's killing gay people. The police know he drugs them with something. They know all of this but they're keeping schtum,' Rico said.

They could all hear the suppressed anger in his voice.

'Often they have to hold back details like this,' Paddy said. 'Sometimes for weeks or months to protect the investigation.'

Mari turned to Lia.

'Didn't you say you saw a table with bottles and machines in the police incident room?'

Lia said she had. She was embarrassed to realise that she remembered almost nothing about the table and its contents. It hadn't felt important then. The gruesome images of the victims posted on the walls had dominated her attention. For a fleeting moment she had wondered whether the devices and bottles were for collecting some kind of evidence but had shut the thought out of her mind.

Did it matter that much? Maggie asked.

'Isn't the most important thing that the police know? That the police can investigate whether the victims were drugged?'

'That's critical,' Mari said. 'But so far nothing indicates the police are really investigating anything about these crimes the way they should.'

Mari looked them all in the eye, one by one.

'I don't think the police are going to catch him,' she said. 'But we can.'

32.

Detective Chief Inspector Keith Brewster was waiting for Lia in the large building on Francis Street – the one that looked lifeless on the outside but which housed within it an Operation Rhea in full swing.

He let Lia write her name in the visitor log and take her pass from the guard. Brewster eyed Lia closely, but Lia didn't say anything. She had a clear goal for her visit: to get back into the incident room.

When she rang and asked Brewster for a meeting, at first he declined.

'You're a bystander,' was Brewster's curt reply. 'We'll get in touch if we find it necessary.'

But half an hour later while Lia was still contemplating how to overcome the lead investigator's reluctance, he suddenly rang back.

'I'm not sure this is a good idea,' Brewster said. 'But Holywell wants to meet you.'

'Really?'

Before Lia had brought them the Studio's projections of future crime scenes. Brewster's second-in-command in the investigation, criminal psychologist and profiler Christopher Holywell, was interested to hear what else Lia might have to report. And Lia seemed to sense that Brewster was privately pleased that DCI Gerrish didn't have anything to do with it this time.

'Peter Gerrish doesn't know you're coming?' Brewster had asked.

'No.'

'We'll notify him of your visit, of course,' Brewster said. 'Sooner or later.'

'As you wish,' Lia had replied. 'But I understood you were in charge of the investigation, not him.'

They had planned out her meeting with the police the previous night at the Studio. Over and over Mari and Paddy ran her through what she was supposed to do.

'At first don't say anything,' Mari said. 'If they try to talk to you in the lobby, say that this is the kind of thing that needs to be discussed elsewhere. If they try to take you to an interrogation room, say you want to talk about it with other investigators present. Don't give them any other option. Don't mention the incident room. Wait for Brewster to decide that for himself.'

Lia didn't need to lead Brewster along though. He took her straight to the incident room.

It was early evening, and only a few police detectives were around besides Brewster and Christopher Holywell. A handful of investigators manned the telephones in the adjacent room.

'Most of them are sleeping,' Brewster said. 'People have been pulling sixteen-hour days. Pretty soon they're going to start dropping like flies from exhaustion. These people never stop unless someone orders them to rest.'

The pictures on the walls of the large room were still the same. The sunlight revealed their every detail, but Lia wasn't shocked to see them any more. They were just tragic and depressing. Gloomy fragments of reality.

Christopher Holywell came to introduce himself as soon as he saw Lia. A rather small man, he was dressed less formally than his police comrades, in jeans and polo shirt.

'Why are you involved with this case?' Holywell asked, managing to make the question sound friendly despite its directness. 'Gerrish and Brewster say you're a complete outsider. Gerrish also urged you to stay out of it.'

'I have my reasons,' Lia said. 'Just like Gerrish and you have your own ways of leading investigations. So do you want to talk about that or the information I have?'

Any other policeman would have moved on to Lia's information, but not Holywell. The forensic psychologist looked at Lia very closely.

'I was a psychologist, years ago,' Holywell said. 'Then I got roped into assisting in a police investigation.'

He recounted being at turns shocked and intensely interested by everything he saw and experienced.

'For some of us, understanding crime changes us. We're still afraid of it, but at the same time the experience wakes us up. It makes you feel more capable,' he said.

He had started studying forensic psychology and, within a few years, had risen to teaching at Portsmouth University and joined the ranks of Scotland Yard's Murder/Major Investigation Teams as a profiler. He trained SCAS crime analysts in Hampshire and represented Britain at international events in the field.

'As an investigator I always get the really repellent, weird cases,' Holywell said.

'And you're still satisfied with your choice of profession?' Lia asked.

Holywell laughed.

'I specialise in crimes against sexual and gender minorities,' he added.

Lia nodded. At least someone on the investigation knew what was going on.

'Well, what do you have?' asked Brewster, who had been waiting impatiently.

Lia hadn't said over the phone when she proposed their meeting. They had planned that at the Studio too: Lia had to get into the incident room.

'These,' Lia said, pulling a stack of papers out of her bag.

They were printouts of online conversations from the people whose accounts the killer hacked to upload his videos. These were the ones who had each mocked Queen or Freddie Mercury in some way.

Clearly Brewster and Holywell weren't expecting anything like this.

Lia explained the progress of the discussion threads. As she talked, she glanced around, trying not to let on what she was searching for.

Overhearing the conversation, the other investigators came to listen in. Lia realised she was stuck in the wrong part of the room. She was too far away from the table that interested her.

'Let me show you something,' she said, walking over to a table next to her target.

She spread the papers out on the empty table so they were all visible at once.

'Look at the dates and times,' Lia said.

The men bent over to examine the printouts.

'What's significant about them?' Holywell asked.

The killer had chosen users out of the long discussion threads who poked fun at Queen, but the discussions were all from different times. The oldest was from more than a year before.

'Couldn't the different times indicate that he's been planning this for at least that long?' Lia asked. 'Maybe the killer participates in these discussions himself.'

At the Studio Rico had been trying to track down contact information for everyone in the threads, but that was slow. It would be easier for the police because they could get information directly from the service providers.

The investigators read the sheets of paper one by one and then pondered.

Lia stood behind them, calmly looking at the next table, which was full of unfamiliar machines and small glass bottles. On the whiteboard above the table were words and abbreviations written in marker.

Two syringes also lay on the table. Lia hadn't noticed them on her first visit when she had been further away from the table. The syringes were small and thin. They had long needles.

Drug syringes?

She quickly tried to memorise the words on the whiteboard. At first remembering them felt easy as she focused all of her powers of concentration. But when she turned away for a second, she realised she couldn't even remember half of it. There was too much.

'Is this all?' Brewster asked.

Lia shrugged.

'Isn't this enough?'

Brewster cast a stern glance at Holywell.

'How did you get these?' Holywell asked Lia.

'The same way as the information about Rich Lane,' Lia said. 'Using computer programs to sift through a lot of different things.'

'What things?' Holywell asked calmly.

'What had been done online from their IP addresses, what websites they hung out on.'

'Where did you get the IP addresses?'

'The same place you did,' Lia said.

'The ISPs?'

'Yes,' Lia said. 'You just did it by the book. If our killer did visit those pages, he probably masked his connection. But there's still something there to investigate.'

Brewster interrupted their conversation.

'If this is everything, then we don't have any reason to detain you here any further.'

'Sure there is,' Lia said. 'I want something in exchange.'

Holywell shrugged lightly. 'We knew all these kids were Internet trolls to one degree or another. And that at least one of them had mocked Queen,' he said.

But the police hadn't realised that all of them had done so, Holywell admitted. Lia's information would help their investigation.

Lia saw how Holywell's gaze quickly paused on Brewster, and when the lead investigator immediately moved away to shuffle through some papers on his desk, she realised the police had planned the meeting out ahead of time too. Holywell wanted to talk to her alone.

He wants to figure me out, and I want to remember that list of words on the wall.

'Do you think you know why this man is committing these crimes?' Holywell asked.

'No,' Lia admitted. 'I understand it has something to do with *celebrity obsession syndrome*. That's what you call it, right?'

Holywell nodded.

'It isn't an officially recognised diagnosis,' he said. 'And it doesn't completely explain what's going on here. But it's an apt name for how some people's imbalance presents. This man follows serial killer logic. They all have fetishes, details they worship. Usually they're sexual or violent. This man's fetishes relate to obsessive admiration and violence.'

Freddie Mercury died in 1991, before the rise of the Internet, so he escaped much of the hate speech and aggression so common online. But a figure like Mercury, who lived with such flourish, was in a class of his own when it came to engendering abnormally strong feelings in his admirers even after his death, Holywell said.

'It's as if the star's death creates a space for his admirers that they fill with their fantasies,' he said. 'And this sort of idolisation can be much more powerful for people than you might believe. Because of the Internet more and more people have the ability to create their own reality and only associate with people like themselves.'

Lia had a hard time concentrating on what the profiler was saying and simultaneously trying to commit to memory the list on the wall behind him without being noticed.

Henssge. Anect. Subdural haematoma. Nearly twenty words and abbreviations, some with numbers following. The words didn't describe anything Lia was familiar with. She guessed it was a list of drugs and chemical compounds, but also realised that impression was influenced by the flasks and syringes and strange devices on the table.

What was in the flasks? Why were they here – the police had to have separate laboratories, right?

Some of the flasks were empty. Two had liquid, one clear, one yellowish.

Maybe it doesn't mean anything. They could just be sampling tools.

As Holywell continued his analysis of Freddie Mercury fans, Lia grasped just how much he had researched the topic.

Anything related to the star they admired could become a fetish for some fans. Just recently a woman in the United States had been issued a restraining order. She was a Queen fan who had become obsessed with an actor who resembled Freddie Mercury. He played Mercury in a musical tribute to the band, and this fan began sending him and his wife strange messages.

A major homicide had been blamed on Mercury worship before in Britain, Holywell pointed out.

'What was it?' Lia asked.

The murder happened in 1999, Holywell explained. A television presenter named Jill Dando was shot down in cold blood on her doorstep in Fulham. The man convicted of her murder was Barry George.

Lia knew the name from the year of appeals following the conviction.

'George was also a fan, in his own way,' Holywell said.

Over the years Barry George had been convicted of various sex crimes, and he suffered from personality disorders. He worshipped a wide range of celebrities, especially Princess Diana. He collected thousands of pictures of women, both celebrities and people he met himself. For some of them he had contact information. George had an interest in guns, dressed in uniforms and sometimes impersonated a police officer, a soldier or sports stars. He even managed to wiggle his way into newspaper articles using celebrities' names as his own. Once troops guarding the royal family detained George for hiding near Kensington Palace with a rope, a large hunting knife and a poem dedicated to Prince Charles.

At the time of Dando's murder, George had been using the name Barry Bulsara. Bulsara was Freddie Mercury's real surname.

Lia nodded at Holywell's account while feverishly repeating the names of the drugs on the board behind him.

George had represented himself as Mercury's cousin and tried to get into the singer's former Kensington flat so often and disruptively that the police were forced to remove him physically. George had even tried to have surgery to make himself look as much like Freddie Mercury as possible.

'Some fans do things like that,' Holywell said. 'Or rather, they aren't really fans, they're a sort of über-fan who think they can get closer to their idols by becoming more like them. Or that they're special people so that should show in their appearance.'

George's only stint of employment had been a short gig as a runner for the BBC, but the network hadn't kept him on. Apparently George had taken exception to the way the BBC dealt with Mercury's death. No one knew why George would have wanted to kill Jill Dando, but there were different theories. Dando resembled Princess Diana. Dando had worked in a prominent position at the BBC, with which George had a conflicted relationship. And his whole life Barry George had behaved aggressively towards women and wanted to be famous.

'Barry Bulsara,' Lia repeated.

Of course she recognised what the criminal psychologist was doing, trying to create a connection with her without revealing too much. All of Britain knew the Dando case, and everyone had followed the continuing saga of Barry George. After seven years in prison,

George was freed. No one else was ever accused of Dando's murder, but serious doubts had arisen about the evidence used to convict him. In part because of his troubled upbringing, numerous experts had supported George's release, and a popular campaign ensued.

But many in the police still believed in George's guilt, Holywell added.

'Do you believe this man is like Barry George... or Bulsara?' Lia asked.

'No,' Holywell said. 'This man and George have the same obsessive admiration in common, but otherwise this one is a much more dangerous case. Our killer is exceptionally strong and intelligent.'

Lia read the names, words and figures on the board behind Holywell.

Henssge. Anect. 4.512. Alphabet – why did it say 'alphabet'?

'Our perpetrator would kill anyway,' Holywell said. 'You could compare it to building a house. For this man killing is like building. He's good at it, and he wants to do it. He's been waiting a long time for the chance to build what he's been planning. The way he videotapes his killings and makes them into Queen fetish objects is the macabre exterior of the house.'

Lia's heart pounded. She stared at the list of words and abbreviations on the whiteboard. She thought she could remember them, at least most of them. She thought she could describe the things on the table.

'It would be best for you to give this up,' Holywell said quietly. 'It would be best for you to tell us what you know and let us take it from there.'

'Is that the stuff used to drug the victims?' Lia asked, pointing to the glass bottle behind Holywell.

This question took Holywell completely by surprise. Quickly he glanced at DCI Brewster, who had also heard the question. Lia could see from Brewster's expression that she had gone too far.

'We're done now,' Brewster said curtly.

He wasn't speaking to Lia but rather to Holywell.

'I came to bring you information that could help you,' Lia said to them both. 'And to ask why you aren't publicly treating these as anti-gay hate crimes.'

Brewster stepped towards Lia angrily, but she stayed calm. Mari had made her instructions clear: When you ask it, don't get angry. Don't yell. Don't give them any reason to react. Just pay attention to what they say.

'I'm leading this investigation with the full support of my superiors,' Brewster said. 'Which, by the way, is none of your business.'

Holywell lowered his eyes, which revealed everything to Lia.

Brewster. Brewster is responsible.

'I think she could help us,' Holywell quickly said to his superior.

'Rolfe,' Brewster said to one of the detectives following the situation from the sidelines. 'Please show Ms Pajala out.'

33

That night new videos showed up online.

Lia, Mari and the others watched them together at the Studio as they went through the information gathered from the police incident room.

The videos used Queen music timed to fit with clips from violent films, reportage from war zones and anything else that showed people dying or being abused.

When the videos started appearing, it was unclear who was making them for a while. But from the usernames used to upload them it soon became obvious that their creators were just trouble-makers who wanted to get a rise out of people by showing them unpleasant images. Some of the videos were just clumsy excerpts from B-movies, but some of them had required a good deal of effort to make the shootings, stabbings or explosions match the rhythm of the music.

Many of the creators wanted credit for their work. Seeing the reactions the videos elicited, they started advertising them on social media with links to more of the same kind of content.

Queen's most popular song, 'Bohemian Rhapsody', inspired the most knock-offs. It was so long that some of the film makers didn't have the patience to edit imagery for the whole song, but they had no inhibitions when it came to the brutality of the pictures.

'I detest people,' Lia said.

She would come to repeat that more than once during the day.

The videos attracted a lot of views. Within two days of the tabloids starting to call the murderer the Queen Killer, several dozen of these videos had been uploaded. They made the news on several channels, which quickly multiplied their viewership.

'Just when you think you've seen humanity sink as low as possible, something new comes along,' Mari said.

The Times pointed to the frightening social aspect of the videos. On its website it reminded its readers that this was no different from happy slapping, the random acts of violence young people committed to catch on camera and post online. Usually it was an assault on another youth.

Happy slapping and these new videos were a difficult subject for the media, *The Times* observed. They had to tell people about the phenomenon even though the publicity was precisely what fed it.

'The police don't have time to respond,' wrote one commentator. 'Videos can be restricted but not completely deleted. The real question is about the wellbeing of families, support and training for teachers and the limits we each set on acceptable behaviour in our interactions each and every day. This is not a problem we can erase or ignore, but we can prevent it. If you know that your children are watching these videos, intervene. All freedoms have limits. Despite our commitment to democracy, as a society we do not sanction demonstrations that devolve into riots and hooliganism. Likewise, we can ill afford to allow happy slapping to spread, and these videos are beyond the pale.'

When a video entitled *Bohemian Whipsody* started circulating online, a line had been crossed. The video, uploaded by a user named 'dethcalls', became a hot topic because the author claimed to have assembled it from video clips of actual deaths, mostly brutal beatings that ended up being fatal. In the longest one a man whipped a motionless, naked woman.

'A snuff film made into a music video,' Paddy said. 'And the person who created it could easily be a minor.'

Most of dethcalls' previous uploads had been removed due to complaints. The music he used was extreme heavy metal, and the images usually depicted the subjugation of women.

'Can you find out who dethcalls is?' Mari asked Rico.

The job took Rico a couple of hours.

The boy was seventeen years old and lived in Nottingham. His name was Ian, and he had a long record of involvement with social services and the Youth Crime Unit.

'Poor kid,' Paddy said.

Mari shook her head.

'That video isn't the work of any "poor kid",' she said. 'That boy is going to grow up to be a big problem.'

But the Studio wasn't going to get involved, Mari said. *Bohemian Whipsody* was deleted before long, but it would live on in the darker corners of the Internet and become a hit in its own little gruesome subgenre. But it wasn't a pressing problem for them.

Henssge. Anect. Subdural haematoma. Alphabet.

Lia remembered almost all of the words, abbreviations and numbers she had seen in the incident room. She tried to duplicate the list as well as she could by writing the words on the whiteboard in Mari's office at the Studio in the same order she had seen them.

She wasn't sure of two of the numbers, but everything else was etched in her mind.

'This is part of a forensic pathology investigation,' Paddy said immediately upon seeing the list.

The forensic analysis was happening elsewhere than in the Operation Rhea offices, and the police would only be receiving specific information about the results of the analysis. But it was possible that the detectives had wanted to see with their own eyes something that had been found in the bodies.

Paddy recognised a few of the terms in the list. Subdural haematoma meant intracranial bleeding. Henssge had to do with Henssge nomograms, a method for calculating time of death based on body temperature.

'The Alphabet is MPDV and other drugs like that,' Paddy said.

Murder victims were tested for possible drugs in their systems, and many of the modern designer drugs were known by abbreviations, the 'alphabet' in common police parlance.

One of the abbreviations had been circled: Anect.

'I've never heard of that,' Paddy said.

Rico only took a few seconds tracking it down on the Topo. The drug in question was Anectine. In hospitals its active ingredient was known as SUCCS. Succinylcholine.

'What does it do?' Paddy asked.

'Paralyses muscles. It paralyses a person's muscles but keeps them conscious.'

Anectine was used especially in emergency situations, for example when victims of an accident were being transported in an ambulance. If there was an urgent need to intubate, succinylcholine relaxed the patient's muscles instantly so the tube could be inserted.

The drug's advantages in medical treatment were almost immediate effectiveness and short duration, ten minutes at most. The downside was that the patient couldn't communicate after receiving it.

'If the killer is injecting his victims with Anectine, they wouldn't be able to scream or fight back at all. But they would stay conscious; they would know what was happening to them and stumble along as he forced them to wherever he was going to kill them,' Mari said.

Lia couldn't say anything. She was nauseated by the thought that the killer could do something like this. Paddy stared at Mari in shock.

'Do the victims know what's being done to them?' Mari asked. 'Do they feel pain?'

Rico scanned the web pages he had open on the Topo.

'It seems like it,' he said quietly.

The instructions for administering Anectine warned health professionals specifically that it did not render the patient unconscious or remove feeling. That was why its use was so specific.

'It's really strong,' Rico said, still reading online. 'The muscles start relaxing almost instantly. The first ones are the throat muscles, which is why you can't talk.'

He did a cross-search with Anectine and the other words Lia had memorised at the incident room. One of them came back with results: furosemide.

'It's a drug they usually use for something else completely,' Rico said. 'But it can also be used to prolong the effect of Anectine.'

Mari stood up from her desk and walked to the windows.

'He injects them with drugs so they can't call for help or fight for their lives. Then he keeps them like that as long as he wants,' Mari said.

For a moment there was perfect silence. Rico's low voice was the first to break it.

'If you give a large enough dose of Anectine, it can also kill,' he said.

'I don't think this man would make a mistake like that,' Mari said. 'I don't think he would let them die before he's finished doing what he wants.'

In the middle of an evening that felt as if it would go on forever, Mari suddenly suggested that Maggie and Lia go home.

'No, I can stick it out for a while longer,' Maggie protested. 'If nothing else, I can think about Craig Cole.'

But Maggie did leave, and a little later Lia gave in too.

'Go and take Gro for a walk,' Mari said. 'Try not to think about anything.'

It didn't work. When Lia arrived in Hampstead, Mr Vong had apparently already left for Gro's evening walk because he didn't answer his doorbell.

For a fleeting moment Lia considered the bars where she used to go looking for male companionship. Right now that felt impossible though, if only because all she would be able to think about would be people getting snatched from gay bars.

She couldn't go online. The news sites and discussion boards would just be full of talk about the Queen Killer.

She couldn't drink alone. Too depressing.

Lia still had her copy of the old travel guide Mr Vong had given her once, *Good for You, London!* Thumbing through it often helped her in lonely moments. For all its frivolity, it portrayed the city around her with an unreal beauty. She couldn't go there though, not now.

She went out, walking to the small sculpture garden next to the hall of residence and waiting for the silent peace of the statues in the light of the street lamps to do its work.

What was Mari doing right now? What did she want to talk to Rico and Paddy about? What could be the reason for keeping Lia and Maggie out of a discussion?

Right now hundreds of police officers were trying to investigate this terrifying series of murders. At the same time, dozens, perhaps hundreds of people around Britain were sitting at their computers making perverse videos to Queen songs for other people to watch.

And somewhere there was a man who had killed five people and meant to kill more.

Hampstead, Lia's timeless, placid village was not what she needed now. It was late, but she decided to ring Bob Pell and see whether the shooting range was still open.

'Are we at that point in our relationship already? Late-night calls and all?' he said.

'Can I still come in?'

'Of course.'

No one but Pell was at the range. Lia knew she might be giving him ideas with her late arrival, and Pell did try to initiate some mild flirtation. But after seeing that Lia really did want to concentrate on shooting, he left her in peace.

In half an hour Lia's nervous exhaustion disappeared. Pell noticed the break in the gunfire and came to look at her results.

'Not bad,' Pell said.

'I think working as a graphic designer helps,' Lia said.

She was used to seeing things as precise lines and measurements. She felt like she could instinctively estimate where to aim.

Pell snorted. 'I didn't know they taught shooting at art school.'

Lia was actually so promising that trying shooting at a moving target would be worth her time too, he said.

Lia seized the opportunity instantly. Pell turned on the range's machinery and large, round targets hanging from tracks began moving at the rear of the hall. Lia spent nearly an hour shooting at the moving targets, and as one after another went swinging, she knew her aim was progressively getting better.

'More tomorrow?' she finally asked Pell.

'Why not?' he said. 'Fancy a drink to celebrate your progress? I have a bottle of good red wine out in the office.'

'No, thank you.'

'Suit yourself,' Pell replied quickly. 'Come tomorrow before nine if you want. You're one of the fastest learners I've ever seen.'

Lia thought she knew at least one person who learned faster than her.

34.

Mari sits in her office at the Studio.

The others have left, including Paddy and Rico once night fell. She gave them assignments, deciding to try to bring an end of this evil.

The others at the Studio know she isn't strong yet, but she is almost there.

And sitting here makes her stronger. The rooms Mari has worked for so long, the space and the machines, the strength of the place. She has been building the Studio for too long – no one is going to take it away from her.

They took Berg. They aren't going to take anything else.

Mari is now focusing all her resolve on one thought: the man who did all of this will not walk around free much longer.

Whoever you are, I'm going to bring you down. I'm going to throw you like a tiny pebble into a ravine, Mari thinks.

She smiles at this feeling, how good it feels to think of catching him.

Is it revenge? Or executing justice? Her feeling contains both, noble and base. Sometimes the two intertwine.

But that doesn't matter. Those are moral distinctions; their time will come when the goal has been reached. First they have to figure this man out. They have to know why he acts the way he acts.

They have to understand their adversary. And they must know and understand this man better than anyone else can know him.

'You are one sick fuck,' Mari says.

Swearing at him out loud heightens her senses. She listens to her voice. She hears the power of her resolve.

It is no coincidence this man is killing gay people. Nor that he makes videos of his killings using songs from a band led by a gay man.

Mari closes her eyes and thinks of Queen and Freddie Mercury.

She has spent hours over the past days watching videos of concert recordings and interviews with the band, almost through the night. She knows their history by heart. She knows how all the members of Queen talk and move; she knows their facial expressions. She knows by heart the light, shrugging serenity with which the emaciated Freddie Mercury said his farewells to the world in his final days.

This Mari knows: how to take control. She learned it as a child, in a way that warped her entire life, and everything that has happened since then has pointed towards setting straight that twisting in one sense or another.

Mari cannot endure the feeling of powerlessness. After a childhood like hers she is unable to accept submission, not after realising she was living in the Laboratory.

She knows how to collect information and assimilate its essence, with a speed others find astonishing. She understands people with a sensitivity without compare, and right now she is trying to understand a man who wants to kill gay people and turn their murders into a tribute to the band he worships.

Really he doesn't worship only the band. He worships the gift, the ability to touch others deeply, an ability no one else can duplicate. Queen touched this man. Maybe that has been the most powerful experience in his life.

A brief reading of this killer would be: sociopath. Loner, manic, attention-seeking. A homophobe moved by simple instincts.

The police profiler, Holywell, probably looks at him this way.

And the killer probably is all that but much, much more.

Mari listens to Queen. She looks the songs up online, clicking one after another. Many of them are familiar, some new. She isn't trying to think of what they do for this man. She wants to experience them powerfully herself.

The man seeks out his victims, lures them within reach, pumps them full of paralytics and puts them in front of a camera for execution. He kills, because for him, killing is art.

He kills, because he is the next logical step from happy slapping and celebrity worship, an unholy union of the two, a nightmare no one wants to contemplate.

Who is he making his art for? Everyone who clicks on his videos. His audience is the whole world. He worships power and fame.

This killer wants clicks. He wants a million clicks online. He is going to reach his goal.

And suddenly Mari realises that simply waiting for this man to make a mistake will not lead to his capture. He is ahead of the police and ahead of the Studio. He has done all of this so precisely, patiently revealing each grotesque detail to the world.

There will be more victims if the police or they at the Studio don't dare to think further ahead. They have to find the courage to make assumptions and move towards their fears.

Mari sits in her office at the Studio and tries to understand a man who cannot be understood.

Sorrow fills Mari to her core. Not just for her own loss or for the loss of the victims' loved ones. What she mourns is that she has lived a life that has made it possible to understand such a sick person.

35.

His throat hurt.

Theo Durand lay on the floor of his cell, trying to control the twitching of his arms and hold himself together.

More symptoms kept appearing. He had never experienced anything similar before, as if his whole body was surrendering to pain and compulsion.

Something in his throat was swollen, badly. How was that possible, when his whole body cried out for water? Theo didn't know.

He hadn't had anything to drink in hours, possibly days. The passage of time was a mystery – the light visible in the cell was always the same strange yellow one.

The crazy man who brought him here hadn't shown his face. Theo didn't know whether the man's absence was good or bad.

Sometimes his throat hurt so badly that his eyes watered. Whatever was so swollen felt like it was blocking his whole throat. He had cautiously tried to touch it, first with his tongue, then with his fingers. The pain was so intense he had to give up.

Did the throat pain come from the spice?

Theo had eaten the contents of the bag the man left. The lunatic's dirty paper bag was the only thing he had. The powder in the bag was so disgustingly strong that just a few pinches of it made him gag, but if he hadn't eaten anything he would have lost consciousness. The lumpy powder's burning bite preserved his grip on this world.

The powder must be some sort of spice, Theo decided, but eating it frightened him. He didn't really know what was in it, and every time Theo took a little helping of it from the bag with his fingers and painfully swallowed it, he felt the thirst in him surge.

And what a thirst it was.

Crazy man.

Steps outside the cell. He was coming.

This time Theo had to get the man to talk. He had locked Theo in here, and he was the only one who could let him out.

Eyes stared at Theo through the bars.

'Tell me what you want,' Theo said. 'Do you want something? We can talk about it.'

He heard the hoarseness of his voice, and every word hurt like a slash at his throat.

The man didn't say anything.

'Maybe I can give you something you want,' Theo suggested.

If he wanted sex, let him have sex. Anything so Theo could get out of this place.

'Eat,' the man said, pointing at the paper bag on the floor.

He talked, Theo thought. At last he talked.

'I have been,' he said. 'It's too strong. It makes me so thirsty.'

'If you eat, I'll give you water later,' the man said. 'Eat.'

'Why?'

'It will prepare you.'

Theo didn't understand. What did the lunatic mean?

'Prepare me for what?' he repeated.

His voice was higher. They both heard it.

'It's preparing you to burn,' the man said.

Theo felt the nausea in him grow.

'Fucking lunatic,' he said.

It was a knee-jerk reaction, and it was wrong. But it was out now. He couldn't take it back.

The lunatic went quiet. He stood motionless, nothing in his face moving at all.

Suddenly Theo understood why the man was standing right where he was. He was staying out of the camera picture. The camera was sending images somewhere, and he didn't want to be seen. Maybe someone else could see the picture. As soon as the man left, Theo would try to talk to the camera, try to call for help.

Before that he had to get this lunatic to talk more.

'What is it?' Theo asked, pointing to the bag.

'Coriander,' the man said.

Theo stared at him, speechless. This was all going over his head.

'It will prepare you,' the man said.

Theo squeezed his eyes tight shut. Feeling his arms twitching, he pulled them around him. The blood pounded in his head. He was trying to understand what the man said. Was there anything he could say to this… *creature?*

There wasn't.

When Theo opened his eyes, the man was gone again.

36.

The fifth video differed from the earlier ones.

In it there was no kicking, and no one lying on the ground. It was mysterious and slow. The images were so dark and grainy it was difficult to tell what they showed.

When Lia, Mari and the rest of the Studio saw it, their first reaction was a strange relief. If they could conclude anything from the video, it was that another mangled body wasn't lying somewhere waiting to be found. Although the images were unpleasant, there was still the feeling that they had to watch them. They were evidence that the killer was free and continuing his work.

That the video was the work of the same man, of this they were sure.

'It's him,' Mari said. 'That's as sure as sure can be.'

The killer had just changed his mode of operation.

Perhaps he was frightened, Paddy guessed. Having Berg show up on Rich Lane in Kensington had disturbed his plan. He had executed Berg, brushing him out of the way, but maybe the possibility of getting caught had made him re-evaluate the sense in his brutal attacks.

'Or maybe this was the plan all along,' Mari said. 'This video isn't the work of an afternoon.'

The song was Queen's 'Somebody to Love', one of the ones that matched exactly the length of the black videos. That was why they were among the first to detect it. Rico had written a program that crawled the Internet's most popular music services and sent alerts whenever one of the six possible remaining Queen songs appeared in a new video.

Rico was also convinced this one was from the killer after inspecting it more closely. Although the images were cut to match a slower rhythm than before, he believed he could tell the maker from his work.

'You can just tell,' he said.

He could see it in the change of focus, the camera angles, the great skill with which the killer used footage that otherwise looked like the product of an amateur.

The clearest evidence was what the images showed. The camera, which remained still the entire time, showed a dark room with a man locked in.

'There is light there,' Rico said. 'There's just so little that it looks dark.'

On the bottom half of the screen now and then they could see the man trudge back and forth slowly. He paced like a prisoner in a cell.

Two scenes showed him screaming. He stared straight at the camera and screamed at it. Not out of pain but distress.

'He sees the camera. He knows he's being filmed,' Paddy said.

The prisoner in the video was begging the camera for help. Watching it was horrific. There was no doubt the situation was genuine.

'That isn't acting,' Maggie said.

Near the end they could see him more clearly in the centre of the darkness. When his half-naked body hit the light, it glistened. He was sweating, profusely.

'It's hot in there,' Paddy said.

In some of the pictures it looked as though the man had something in his mouth.

'Is he eating sand?' Lia asked.

Deducing anything from the pictures was impossible. Rico ran still after still through his image processing programs, ultimately deciding that the substance was lighter than sand.

The final images were the most shocking. The man stood up straight in the middle of the room, looked at the camera and drew something on his bare chest with his forefinger. He did it with the same light brown substance he was eating. When his hand moved out of the way, the picture showed that on his chest in block capitals he had written the word HELP.

'He's pitting his hopes on someone else seeing the camera image other than whoever locked him in there,' Paddy said.

His hope was not in vain. When word of the video started circulating, it was viewed more than one hundred thousand times on YouTube alone before the site admins took it down. There was plenty of time for it to be copied to other sites and continue spreading.

The police kept schtum. The media asked DCI Brewster and the other leaders of the investigation, but they weren't willing to comment on the video or even say whether they were looking into it.

The police wanted to keep open the possibility that the fifth video didn't belong to the same series as the previous four, Paddy guessed. And they wanted to prevent the phenomenon from growing even larger.

'That's possibly true,' Mari said. 'It's still a stupid attitude to take though.'

The police might be preventing serious study of the video elsewhere. The Studio certainly weren't the only people besides the police who could look into it. This was precisely the sort of problem crowdsourcing could help with, which was exactly what Rico used in his research of the videos. If the video was being analysed all over the world, by every means possible, someone would see something new in it, Mari was sure.

But for the police the homosexual aspect of the case was just a little too much.

How do we know the man in the fifth video is gay? Lia asked.

'We don't, but we do,' Mari answered.

The man was slim and in his thirties. He didn't look particularly fit. In the pictures he didn't appear to have any tattoos, and there were no recognisable details on his underpants. Nothing pointed to his background.

But there was something special in his features Lia recognised. It was hard to define. Maybe it was mostly about the expression of emotion, a sort of sensitivity. Sensitive didn't completely describe his face, but it was close.

'Gay men show their feelings,' Rico said. 'Often that's the only identifiable difference.'

Seeing the emotions of the man on the video wasn't hard. He was filled with an immense dread.

'He doesn't know what's happening to him,' Mari said.

Lia could hear from Mari's voice that she had just about had enough of the situation and waiting for the police to act.

In the middle of all this, work at *Level* had become stressful. Most of Lia's time was spent thinking about everything but design layouts, and she was always just killing time, waiting for the moment she could get to the Studio and then home in the evening.

On the night the fifth video appeared, she found Gro and Mr Vong in Hampstead outside the residence hall. They were headed out for a stroll.

How were they getting along? Lia asked when she saw the dog.

Very well, Mr Vong said. Gro was a good assistant. When Mr Vong was out doing his caretaker work, Gro always came with him and was never afraid of noises or strange places.

Of course not, Lia thought. Gro was used to Berg's equipment in the Den, occasional loud noises and all sorts of different projects. It was probably all very comforting and homely for her.

'Hopefully Gro can still stay with me,' Mr Vong said. 'For a while longer?'

Lia nodded. The dog and the elderly gentleman had quickly adopted one another. Mr Vong had plenty of time for her, and perhaps she recognised that Mr Vong was the closest thing to Berg the world had to offer now.

Lia wasn't needed here.

When man and dog had disappeared on their walk, Lia went and dropped through Mr Vong's letterbox a small present she had bought for him. It was a book with interviews from some of the world's greatest political leaders about their life experiences and visions for the future. The only woman in the group was Gro Harlem Brundtland. Lia didn't send a card with it. Mr Vong would know who was thanking him.

She rang Bob Pell to see if he had space on the range in Harrow.

'For Paddy Moore's students, always,' Pell said.

Paddy paid him so well for the use of the firing range that it was in his best interests to cancel any other appointments that clashed, he told her. Lia spent the rest of the evening practising shooting stationary targets.

Just before heading off to bed, she rang Mari at home in Hampstead.

'How did it go at the shooting range?' Mari asked.

Well, Lia reported. She wasn't sure how long she wanted to practise shooting, but she thought she wanted to learn to do it well.

'Is there any point in it?' she asked.

'Of course there is,' Mari said. 'Maybe it's just what you need right now.'

'How's yoga?' Lia asked.

She liked that they asked after each other as if nothing out of the ordinary were going on. They had known each other for fewer than two years but had gone through so much in that time. Here they were as friends – the things they talked about were anything but casual, but between them was a special warmth. They watched over each other like an old married couple.

They needed that. They needed normal life.

Yoga was going well and doing her good, Mari said. Before going to any more classes she had checked whether Anga was the sort of studio she wanted. Lia had done excellent work choosing it. The instructor was among the best in the city, and the studio was genuinely dedicated to yoga, not a place you came to show off expensive outfits. Mari had also looked into the different styles of yoga and what kinds of effects they had on people. Lia grinned hearing that Mari had read about hot yoga, Christian yoga, Ashtanga, and all the others and still found that the one Lia had chosen for her was just right. Regular, straightforward yoga, effective but simple.

Ending the telephone call was difficult. Their chat was so close to what they'd had before all this, before Berg's death.

'Our life is never going to go back to the way it was,' Lia said.

'No,' Mari said. 'But it can go back to being good.'

'I feel sort of… *kaiho*, you know,' Lia said. 'Sort of nostalgic but more in a sad way.'

'I know,' Mari said.

37

Craig Cole was surprised to meet Lia on his doorstep, accompanied by Maggie, whom he had never met before.

'This is my colleague Margaret,' Lia said. 'She knows a lot of people in the media.'

Cole asked them in, and they sat in the kitchen.

'I thought your work was done,' he said. 'The work you did for me. It went beautifully.'

The nasty stories about Cole had stopped quickly after the programmes and opinion pieces defending him came out. Bryony Wade's family hadn't appeared in public again.

'The parents probably realised they didn't have anything more to gain out of this,' Cole said.

Looking at him, they could see he still wasn't sleeping well.

'We have a proposition,' Maggie said. 'A job offer, actually.'

At the Studio they had decided that Maggie would visit Cole this time because she had found a job opportunity for him, and Mari's thoughts were elsewhere.

Cole looked aside upon hearing the word 'job'.

'I haven't actually been looking for work.'

'I know,' Maggie said. 'But maybe you should be.'

Maggie kept her eyes locked on Cole as she presented the opportunity she had found. He was sitting diagonally across from them, a little hunched over, as if communicating that he didn't want to see anyone, ready to fly out of the room. When he heard Maggie's thoughts, his posture began to straighten.

In Bradford, there was a radio station named The Pulse. It was very small, not the sort of place he would have ever considered before even for a moment. The station's programmes mostly dealt with regional issues, but it had established a foothold in the press of national pop stations.

'They're looking for a host for their music programmes,' Maggie said.

A small sort of smile crept onto Cole's face. He had done music broadcasting when he was young, long before he became a star of talk radio.

'A fifty-year-old man hosting a top-of-the-pops programme?' Cole said.

'They don't just want new music,' Maggie said.

The majority of their listenership was adults, and now they were looking for a host for their programmes directed at the over-forty crowd.

'That wouldn't make any sense,' Cole objected. 'I'd have to move to Bradford.'

'Yes, you would,' Maggie admitted.

She knew Cole was familiar with Bradford. Early in his career Cole had worked as a reporter in the county and he knew what a peaceful place it was.

It would be a fresh start, Maggie explained. Cole could do work he liked for a reasonably large audience. Hosting a music show would still be sufficiently different from the work he had been doing in recent years though.

'The best thing is you can't fail at it,' Maggie said. 'If it doesn't work out, not all that many people will hear about it. If it does work, soon you'll have a faithful audience.'

'I don't know,' Cole said hesitantly.

He made them tea. Lia remained an observer in the conversation since Maggie had the situation well in hand.

Maggie talked to Cole about the latest shake-ups at the BBC and ITV. Chatting about this and that, she kept the conversation light and focused on the entertainment industry. Cole poured the tea and offered them their cups.

'They won't want me in Bradford,' he said.

Maggie and Lia exchanged a quick glance.

'Yes they do,' Maggie said. 'I've already asked.'

'You talked to them about me?' Cole asked, confused. 'Before you talked to me?'

'Settle down,' Maggie said. 'I didn't promise you were coming. I simply asked what they would pay if I could get someone like Craig Cole for them.'

'And?'

Cole's expression made it clear how much this answer would mean to him.

'The station director said that if I could get them someone like Craig Cole, he would pay them the same amount he's earning and maybe a little more. Then he asked whether I knew you and what you were doing nowadays. He asked how much he would have to pay me to tell you about their station and find out if you were interested.'

By the time Maggie and Lia left, Cole had agreed to think about visiting Bradford. He could do that much without any commitment, Maggie assured him.

'If you don't like the place, just tell me and that will be that. We can look for something else or just drop it if you want.'

'He'll probably go to Bradford at least to have a look around,' Maggie told Mari at the Studio.

'We can't be sure of that,' Lia said, trying to put a dampener on their expectations.

But Maggie thought she knew how entertainment stars thought, and she had researched Cole specifically.

'It's a place Cole can feel safe. He'll go for a visit at least.'

Mari thanked Maggie for her effort, but it was easy to tell that her mind was mostly elsewhere.

That night Lia visited the shooting range again. Holding a weapon was beginning to feel routine. She knew how her Heckler & Koch P7 worked and what it demanded of its handler.

'We usually just say HK, not Heckler & Koch,' Bob Pell pointed out. 'You can tell an amateur by the way they talk.'

'I am an amateur,' Lia said.

Pell looked at his score record and nodded knowingly.

'You won't be for long,' he said. 'Mr Moore can make a passable shooter out of anyone.'

Lia frowned at his slightly dismissive tone, but couldn't help asking what it would take to become better than passable.

'Dinner with me,' Pell replied.

'I don't think I want to learn that much about shooting.'

Pell burst out laughing.

'You're going to be much better than passable if you keep it up like this,' he said. 'You want to shoot, and that determination is what will mean you'll be good. That can't be taught.'

The thought made Lia reflective.

'Why do you want to shoot?' Pell asked.

Lia didn't have an answer to that. She thanked him and left for home.

Pell's question wouldn't leave her in peace though.

Why do I want to shoot?

She felt sick when she saw the violent videos spreading online. Just a little while ago the idea of even holding a gun had felt uncomfortable. Her close friend had been shot. By rights Lia should have felt more distrustful of guns now, especially since she was practising in secret.

But holding a weapon and learning how to use it brought her a feeling of security. The difficult relationship she'd left behind in Finland so many years ago had made her fear for her safety, and in London she had been involved with several crimes. Whether her life held real or imagined dangers, shooting helped her face them.

I want to learn to shoot because I want to be the kind of person who moves towards the difficult things in this world.

38.

The police didn't release any information about the fifth video. Not even a statement about the possible actions they might take in response.

The silence of the police affected Mari. Lia noticed that her determination was taking on an increasingly hard edge, as if she knew something unavoidable was coming.

They were constantly waiting for something that would change everything again. That something didn't come. Lia always left for the Studio immediately after working as short a day as possible at *Level*. She walked her familiar route from Fetter Lane, behind her the buzzing streets of the City and the dome of St Paul's reaching towards the heavens, before her Bankside and its industrial buildings, office blocks and shrine to the arts, Tate Modern, but the transition didn't work the way it used to: before it had been a journey from the rest of the world to the protection of the Studio, but now the world always travelled with her.

They all gathered in Mari's office. Mari often looked exhausted these days. She was hardly sleeping at all.

'Time is running out,' Mari said, not for the first time. 'Time is running out for the man in that video.'

At times she kept a freeze frame from the most recent video on the large display on her office wall. It was a close-up of the imprisoned man's face. Lia couldn't look at the picture for long.

'I'm sure the police are doing their best,' Paddy said. 'But that isn't enough. We have to do what we can.'

Paddy reckoned that at that very moment the police were continuing their investigation in the gay bars of London, interviewing customers and sifting through possible sightings. He heard occasional details about the investigation from his friends in the police force. Brewster and his group had looked into the availability of Anectine: unfortunately it was a common drug for use in emergency medical treatment. Because it wasn't a narcotic and wasn't terribly expensive, getting it wouldn't be difficult. The police were looking into whether any had been stolen, whether anyone had purchased an unusually large amount, whether there was evidence of Anectine's misuse elsewhere.

The police were also looking into similarities in the killer's MO with other previous crimes and whether anyone had ever been arrested in Britain whose crimes resembled these.

'They're doing all that and investigating the kids whose accounts the killer used to upload the videos,' Mari said.

But maybe the police didn't realise what was most important to him.

'They aren't thinking about Queen,' Mari said. 'It seems too strange for them, as it does for everyone. The profiler, Holywell, might be the only one thinking about it. They all naturally think that there have to be logical reasons for killing, like money or revenge. Or war. But sometimes people kill for reasons that don't make sense when you look at them from outside. It's hard to tell how crucial Freddie Mercury and celebrity are in what this man is doing.'

That was why the Studio had to have the courage to think these thoughts.

Two days later Mari and Rico were ready to show the others the results of their work. On the big screen in Mari's office they showed a map with two kinds of marks on it, black and red. Lia immediately recognised the locations marked with red: they were the streets where victims had been found.

What were the black marks? Maggie asked.

Places in London with special significance for Queen and Freddie Mercury, Mari explained. They were important sites for the band's hardcore fans: buildings where band members had lived, concert halls where they had performed, studios where they had recorded, nightclubs where they had partied. The school where Mercury had once studied and the antique auction house where he'd often purchased expensive rarities.

Lia breathed in deeply as she realised what the patterns on the map showed. The red locations where bodies had been found matched up with the black marks.

'He's choosing his victims from gay bars with connections to places that are important to him,' Mari said.

All four places had specific connections to Freddie Mercury's life. The singer used to visit the Royal Vauxhall Tavern sometimes, and Heaven had been one of his regular haunts. Near Rich Lane, where

Berg had been killed and Brian Fowler's body dumped on the street, there were both a new gay club and a pub where Mercury had been seen from time to time. They didn't know for sure whether he had ever visited the Black Cap in Camden, but Roundhouse Studios, where Queen recorded, was nearby.

'How could Freddie Mercury have visited so many clubs?' Lia asked, astonished. 'A person that famous?'

Mercury had been well known on London's gay scene, Mari said, but no one talked about it in the media. The star usually went to bars in a group, with a personal assistant and several friends. He chose places where he could see the other patrons without being the centre of attention himself.

'Of course people always noticed him. They would try not to stare, but everyone knew when he was there,' Mari said.

If Mercury wanted to talk to someone, an assistant would surreptitiously go and invite them over. The singer was generous buying drinks for other people but never partied very hard himself. However, the parties he hosted in his own home were the stuff of legend.

Freddie Mercury visited clubs in London and many other cities around the world. Sometimes he hit on men, and he used drugs with his friends. All of it stayed mostly hidden from the public because they were living in an era before camera phones and the Internet.

'And because people wanted to give him space,' Maggie pointed out.

Times were different then. Although some papers did pay for rumours, the scandal business had yet to escalate to the modern paparazzi war where more and more people were constantly being recruited to provide information and pictures.

'It was a much more gentle time,' Maggie said. 'Not in the attitude towards gay people but in the attitude towards celebrities.'

The four places on their map were important to the killer.

'He's visited all of them, at least at some point. It may be that he lives near some place connected to Mercury or Queen,' Mari said.

That was why they had to look for information about the buildings in these locations, including their tenants and the businesses that operated there.

'It's a shot in the dark,' Mari admitted. 'But we have to try something.'

The work was slow.

Sometimes Lia would flee the slow pace and rigour of the work and go to the shooting range in Harrow. There she felt as if she was making progress even if everything else was at a standstill. And Bob Pell's antics weren't unwelcome either, given everything that was going on. Pell was too old for her, and Lia couldn't imagine ever being interested in the proprietor of a slightly shady shooting range, but there was something in his rough manner. It was fun to have someone to flirt with. Mari had Paddy, and they were going to progress from a collegial relationship to dating sooner or later.

Maggie was the one who ended the wait.

One evening they had been sitting for hours sifting through residential registries and data about London buildings. Mari had started to doubt whether there was any sense in the whole enterprise.

'What if he's keeping him prisoner somewhere else entirely?' she asked. 'It is possible.'

They had assumed the location was in London because all of the previous victims had been grabbed there. But that assumption could be dead wrong.

'Then this would just be even more difficult. The number of possibilities is endless,' Mari said.

In addition to London, Freddie Mercury had lived in New York, Munich and Montreux. Queen had toured concert halls and stadiums all over the world for years. If all of those cities were possibilities, that was too much to investigate.

Maggie listened to what Mari was saying and shook her head. They had to focus on what they had, Maggie said. Mari fell silent.

'What do we have?' Maggie asked. 'What do we know about that video?'

She stared at the still frame on the wall of the half-naked prisoner from the fifth video. For a moment there was perfect silence.

'We see a man who is afraid he is going to die,' Rico said.

Maggie nodded.

'True. What else?'

The man was nearly nude. But still he was hot and probably having a hard time breathing, Paddy added.

'He's in a locked room without shoes. Almost everything has been taken from him. He's isolated,' Paddy continued.

'Locked in what kind of room?' Maggie asked.

'We can't see anything,' Rico said quickly. He had been through the images in the video dozens of times searching for things that might help them identify a location. There simply wasn't anything.

What material were the walls and floor made of? Maggie asked.

'Concrete,' Rico replied.

The floor was concrete, and the enlargements showed how rough the flatwork was. The walls had been treated somehow. They looked like concrete too, but they also had a tinted surface coating.

'What kind?' Maggie asked, keeping her voice unfalteringly clear.

It was impossible to tell for sure, Rico said, because the images were so dim and the background was out of focus.

'And the colour of the walls?' Maggie continued.

They all stared at the picture. In the darkness behind the man they could make out a yellowish wall.

Brownish yellow, Paddy said. Maybe beige. A colour you could find anywhere.

'And what if it isn't just anywhere,' Maggie said. 'What if it's a common colour in that building? Or in that place? In that city?'

A new sharpness appeared in Mari's eyes.

'Ochre,' she said. 'That colour is ochre. People use it all over the world, but in some countries more than others.'

Rico snorted. The sound came at once from frustration and a newly kindled spark of enthusiasm.

'It's impossible to delimit a colour geographically,' he said, but he immediately started looking for the place in his enlargements where the colour of the walls was shown to best advantage.

The others gathered behind him and watched as he manipulated the images on the Topo. After finding the sharpest one, he quickly cropped a piece of it and started running it through other applications.

'I don't have the right tools for this,' he said after a minute. 'But other people might.'

On his display, Rico switched to a chat window where a conversation was going on in a closed forum. The others looked curiously at the usernames. One was Errol, another biTer.

Guys, Rico wrote, starting a new thread, *who can find where in the world this wall paint is. right answer earns you a phat botnet, 100k machines, open-ended. full admin rights of course.*

To the message he attached two pictures of the concrete wall and one of the floor. Only twenty seconds passed before someone took up the thread.

That's the colour of your imaginary girlfriend's knickers, replied Errol, one of the group's smart-alecks.

So you're a painter now or what? biTer said.

What botnet? asked deverec.

This is serious, Rico wrote. *I could use some help. The botnet is Lycia.*

That heated up the conversation.

Lycia holy shit! deverec exclaimed.

Race you, biTer said.

What were Lycia and bots? Lia asked Rico as they watched the hackers on the forum start competing to track down the colour's location.

Lycia was one of many botnets, an illegal computer control system hackers used. A botnet was made up of bots, malware that took over thousands of computers around the world. The computers' real users didn't know that whoever controlled the botnet was using their computers. Lycia was a sought-after botnet in hacking circles, and rights to it were precious.

'You can buy rights to a botnet from Russia for a week for a few hundred pounds,' Rico said. 'But not one like Lycia.'

Lycia's artificial intelligence was so refined that it was almost alive, he explained. The basis of the network was a polymorphic virus that could alter itself on every machine it connected to. The botnet could constantly adapt to its environment to remain hidden.

When the hackers' answers started coming in, the mood at the Studio electrified.

That ochre colour is all over africa and south america at least, announced biTer. *but that wall aint.*

What do you mean? Rico asked.

The cement has pieces of rock in it, biTer replied. *porous rock. could be coral rock, dead hard coral*

Rico smiled nervously. *Where from?* he continued.

Dunno, biTer wrote. *my source says the tropics, maybe africa but definitely the tropics*

What's your source? Rico asked. The answer made him smile again.

I tell you in your dreams, biTer replied. *Lycia is mine.*

'Coral,' Mari said, looking at the freeze frame from the video on the wall.

'Where was Freddie Mercury born?' Maggie asked.

She asked it quickly, without thinking it through, but the idea made the others turn to her in surprise.

'Zanzibar,' Mari said.

Standing up from her desk, she extracted a book about Mercury from a pile.

'There are pictures of his house in here,' she said, showing the others the book. The old, light-coloured stone building in the picture seemed ordinary enough. Perhaps a bit austere.

'Where is Zanzibar exactly?' Lia asked.

'Off the coast of Tanzania,' Rico said quickly.

'That might not be underwear,' Mari said, pointing to the man on the video. 'They could be swimming trunks.'

They all looked at the image as if seeing it for the first time.

'It's possible,' Rico said, flipping through enlargements on the Topo, looking for a better detail shot of the man's shorts. The fabric didn't tell them anything, and no brand names or patterns were visible, but their length suddenly seemed significant.

'If he's wearing shorts, Zanzibar would explain that,' Maggie said. 'And fans are always gaga over the places stars were born. Just think how many childhood homes have been turned into museums.'

Mari's eyes flashed.

Determining that the websites of the Tanzanian police and media didn't have any information that could connect to these crimes took them under an hour. According to the Tanzanian police, nothing worthy of reporting had happened in Zanzibar recently.

'What about other countries' embassies and newspapers?' Mari asked. 'The man doesn't look African. If he's from a western country and he's being held prisoner, there should be something about him somewhere. A report of a disappearance or something.'

'Should we divide up the countries?' Paddy asked.

Coming up with the right search phrases in all the major languages would be faster, Rico said. That way they could cover multiple countries with the same queries. He and Maggie chose the keywords: man, missing, Zanzibar, Tanzania. They translated the list into dozens of languages and limited the searches so they would only cover the previous year.

The searches immediately returned three results.

'My God,' Maggie said as she glanced through them.

One hit was from Germany, the second from Kenya, the third from France. One person from each country had disappeared in Zanzibar within the previous year.

The names of the missing persons required a little extra digging, but they turned up too. When Rico fed them into an image search and the results flashed up on the screen, everyone went silent. In one of the pictures, the man they had been staring at for days as a half-naked prisoner in the fifth video looked back at them.

Only a little information was available about Theo Durand and even less about his disappearance in Zanzibar. He was a Parisian accountant who had been on holiday on the island alone and disappeared without a trace a few days earlier.

His relatives in France had posted a notice about his disappearance on the website of the Manu Association, a support group for the missing and their families. The news hadn't reached the French media since the disappearance of a single tourist wasn't going to drive traffic or subscriptions. Even using Durand's name they couldn't find anything on the Tanzanian police website.

Maybe Tanzania wasn't keen on reporting information about lost travellers, Paddy said. It wouldn't exactly increase tourism.

There was no doubt the man in the video was Theo Durand. The likeness was obvious.

'We have to tell the police about this immediately,' Paddy said.

'Not yet,' Mari replied. 'Durand has been a prisoner for days now. If he's even alive any more. I'll be ready to give this to the police soon, but first I want to talk it through with all of you.'

'If he's a prisoner in Zanzibar, the British police aren't just going to pop over there to investigate,' Paddy said. 'The Tanzanian authorities and Interpol will handle it. And possibly the French authorities.'

'Do you trust the Tanzanian police to handle the case?' Mari asked.

Paddy shook his head.

'We'll give the police here one day,' Mari said. 'If nothing happens in that time, I'm going there myself.'

The others took a second to realise what Mari really meant.

'To Zanzibar?' Lia asked.

'That's crazy,' Paddy said sternly.

'It's dangerous,' Mari said. 'Maybe more dangerous than anything we've ever done. But I think it's going to be our only option.'

Paddy had a hard time keeping his temper.

'I don't understand why we're even talking about this,' he snapped. 'The whole idea is completely daft.'

'I didn't say I was going alone,' Mari said. 'I'll take other people with me.'

Lia silently watched their debate. She knew Mari's idea was anything but stupid. Going to Zanzibar would be reckless and maybe dangerous. But if time was short, someone like Mari and the Studio might be able to help.

Suddenly Lia understood that Mari had been emotionally prepared to start chasing this killer for some time now.

She already knew this might be the only way to catch Berg's killer.

Paddy marched out of the room. They heard him walk straight to the front door and out of the Studio.

Lia looked at Mari and thought she understood her more than ever before.

Mari has decided to face this man herself. She just has to find him.

39.

The pavement outside the Operation Rhea HQ was deserted when Lia arrived on Sunday a little after nine in the morning. Instead of going inside, she glanced down the ramp leading into the car park and at the windows, most of which were covered by Venetian blinds.

The police profiler, Christopher Holywell, quickly appeared from a side door. He had been expecting her.

Holywell rubbed his hands together. Lia understood it had nothing to do with the chilly wind blowing down on the street. Holywell was on guard because Lia had surprised him by requesting an urgent meeting. At the Studio they had decided that the profiler was their best chance, partly because he had treated Lia so warmly. Finding his personal phone number had required Paddy's contacts in the police force, and fortunately Holywell agreed to the meeting despite knowing that his superiors would frown upon it.

'What do you have?' Holywell asked.

Lia took out her phone and showed him the picture on the display. 'This.'

For a moment Holywell stared at the picture of Theo Durand taken from the French missing persons organisation before realising what was going on.

'Christ almighty,' he said. 'Let's go inside.'

'No.'

'Come on –' Holywell started to say.

'No,' Lia interrupted. 'We're talking about this here. On my terms.'

Holywell shut up. His gaze flicked between the small phone display and Lia's face.

'Where did you get that?' he asked.

Lia recounted how much work had gone into finding it and turned over what she knew about Theo Durand. Reeling off the details only took a few seconds: Theo Durand, accountant from Paris, age thirty-two. Disappeared without a trace on vacation in Zanzibar.

'Zanzibar?' Holywell repeated.

'The island in Africa. Fifty kilometres off the coast of Tanzania,' Lia explained.

'I know where Zanzibar is,' Holywell said quickly. 'Why was he grabbed there?'

'Because the man you're looking for is there.'

The profiler took a moment to digest this information.

'Freddie Mercury was born in Zanzibar,' he said.

'You have a good memory,' Lia said.

Holywell stared at Lia, and Lia realised that the power relationship between them was turning in her favour. The police investigator had to react to the information she was giving.

Lia remembered Mari's instructions. *Don't let him take you inside. Don't let him record your conversation. Stay outside, and be fast.*

'That would fit the killer's profile,' Holywell said. 'Zanzibar. A change of place. This bloke is doing a lot of things differently.'

The change in the videos from kicking to the dimly lit images of a starving prisoner was a clear tactical shift, Holywell said.

'It's unusual. Not rare, but unusual.'

Serial killers almost always had their own peculiar MO. These things brought them satisfaction and became a major part of the killings for them. But the Queen Killer was altering things, adding new dimensions. First came the black videos, then the kicking. Now the fifth video was different from the others, and he had shifted from London elsewhere.

'We have some comparable cases, killers who changed their MO and locations,' Holywell said.

The police's Serious Crime Analysis Section had their own database, named ViCSAL. In it they had collected thousands of detailed pieces of information about the perpetrators of serious crimes, especially murderers and rapists. By combining and cross-referencing this information they had often been able to move forward previously unsolved cases.

Serial killers who modified their methods were more common now than before, Holywell said. One thing united them all: they were all seeking fame. All of them became fascinated by famous serial killers and tracked their activities before starting on their own deadly careers.

'He wants to keep shocking people,' Lia said.

'His audience,' Holywell agreed. 'He knows that if he had just kept on with the kicking videos, gradually he would have lost his influence. He wants to give them something new to look at, always new details. And now Zanzibar, a completely new place.'

'He can't know that we've tracked down his location,' Lia pointed out.

'No,' Holywell said. 'He probably thought that would stay secret for a while longer. That it would only come out when he was finished with what he means to do there.'

'I want to know two things,' Lia said quickly.

She could tell from looking at Holywell that he wasn't comfortable with the position he was in.

'What?' he asked.

'Tell me how you intend to start the investigation in Zanzibar. How long will it take?' Lia said, pressing him. 'And I want to know why you're avoiding admitting publicly that these are gay hate crimes.'

Holywell controlled himself well, Lia had to admit. His voice remained calm.

'Since this is a French citizen missing in Zanzibar, the operation will fall to the local police,' Holywell said.

The Metropolitan Police would immediately contact Interpol and the French and Tanzanian authorities. There was a priority classification for things like this that pushed them ahead of everything else. Interpol had teams of experts at its disposal who could get anywhere in the world in under a day, but they were called upon infrequently.

'Whether Interpol wants to send one of those teams will be up to them,' Holywell said. 'We can send investigators to Zanzibar too, but that would be done in cooperation with Interpol as well. And everything would require the blessing of the local authorities. We don't even know yet whether anything has actually happened in Zanzibar itself other than the disappearance of a tourist. How seriously do you think the Tanzanian police are going to take this when the whole basis for suspecting a crime has occurred is an online video of a man in dark room?'

'You've seen that video,' Lia said.

'Yes, I have.'

239

The way Holywell averted his gaze revealed he knew exactly what the Studio did. The police probably wouldn't be able to act quickly enough to save Theo Durand.

'How long will this take?' Lia asked.

'To get the investigation going there? Or to open a new investigation if the local police have already searched for him?' Holywell snorted and took a few nervous steps.

'A few days,' he guessed. 'Maybe even a week. First we'll have to see how sure we are the man in the video is in Zanzibar.'

'A week!' Lia exclaimed in astonishment. 'You said this would be classified as urgent.'

'We can't just up and send someone there. It doesn't work like that. We don't even know what's there.'

Lia had received her answer. Mari wasn't going to wait around for the police.

'And my other question.'

Holywell weighed the situation.

'I'm not in charge of this investigation,' he said.

'I know.'

'I don't decide what information we release.'

'I know that.'

'If I were in charge, it might be handled somewhat differently,' he said, lowering his voice.

He was trying to win Lia's confidence. Lia realised he was about to tell her something the police didn't usually discuss with outsiders.

'The police have done a lot in the past few years to fight homophobia,' Holywell began, proceeding to list measures already familiar to Lia. Every police division had officers appointed to handle LGBTI issues. They ran campaigns to encourage the public to intervene in hate crimes.

'But this time no one wants to talk about gay people out loud,' Lia said.

'We talk about it as much as the officer in charge of the investigation sees fit. He doesn't want to fuel a panic.'

Several years before, the police top brass had decided not to address the sexual orientation or gender of victims of crime in public unless it was absolutely necessary, Holywell said. The media had a tendency to dig up salacious details about victims' pasts and frequently spread incorrect information about their sexuality.

'You don't understand everything that's going on here,' Holywell continued.

For some in the police force, any attention directed at minority issues always felt as if it was being taken from somewhere else, he explained. More manpower had been dedicated to Operation Rhea than to any other case in years. In London alone detectives had interviewed more than a thousand people.

The police knew these looked like gay hate crimes. How much they wanted to treat those crimes like their own special thing was another matter. Some police officers had a hard time digesting the constant recognition of new minority groups.

'It always means new committees. Organisational restructuring where the latest pet project of the political correctness crowd runs roughshod over everything else.'

Not long ago positions had been created for inspectors to focus on football hooliganism. When the media filled with news of child sexual abuse, special investigators were named for those crimes too. There were units dedicated to human trafficking, to preventing kidnapping and searching for missing people.

'All of these are necessary,' Holywell pointed out, making his own position clear to Lia.

When an officer specialised in the latest matter in focus, he received a promotion. When a case involved minority issues, the investigation received more manpower and more money.

'That's always what this is about,' Holywell said. 'Manpower and money. How much of each there is. What they're used for.'

'Manpower and money,' Lia repeated. 'And those shouldn't be focused on gay issues?'

Holywell's eyes were tired.

'You don't know what this is like,' he said. 'There are men inside this building who would be ready to go through hell to save someone, no matter who they are. They wouldn't even hesitate. But some of them also wonder about all the other jobs left undone while the focus is on gay people. They also can't stand that these issues can mean an easy ascent up the chain of command.'

His tone of voice communicated that this last thought was the central issue.

'You have some sort of reorganisation coming?' Lia thought out loud. 'And it's going to determine who is in charge and where the manpower and money go.'

Procedures were usually reviewed and updated at three-year intervals, Holywell said.

'There's a review report coming up soon,' he said. 'And there are a lot of different camps who want more money for their areas of expertise.'

'You have one of the biggest hate crime cases in the country's history going on under your nose but you're thinking about new positions and promotions,' Lia said.

'I'm not in charge of this investigation,' Holywell said again. 'If I were, things would be handled differently.'

'It's hard to believe the police are wasting time on power struggles when people's lives are at risk,' Lia said.

'Lots of things happen in this world that are hard to believe – some are even harder to accept,' Holywell said.

Lia nodded. A bitter feeling of powerlessness was spreading through her. The options were dwindling.

Grabbing her mobile, she sent Theo Durand's picture to Holywell's number.

'You'll receive a message in a second with a link to a page about that missing man,' Lia said. 'But you can find it yourself by searching his name. It's spelt T-h-e-o D-u-r-a-n-d. The D at the end is silent.'

'I'd like you to come with me now to tell the investigators every-thing you know,' Holywell said.

'No deal,' Lia replied. 'I'm not coming unless you arrest me. And if you intend to do that, my lawyer will be here before you manage it.'

A text message alert came from Holywell's pocket. The picture Lia sent had arrived.

'You've been warned to stay away from this,' he said.

'Lots of things happen in this world that are hard to believe and even harder to accept,' Lia said and left.

40.

Sitting in the window seat of row fifteen on the aeroplane, Mari leans back and breathes deeply. Now she can let go and just let everything be.

So much has happened in such a short time. They have been struggling to keep up.

When Lia returned from meeting with profiler, Holywell, Mari understood immediately what was ahead. They had to leave, to do what the police couldn't.

Lia was afraid. Mari could see that. The others at the Studio could see it too.

Mari looks at Lia sitting next to her on British Airways flight 0065 to Nairobi. Lia isn't afraid any more. In little more than twenty-four hours she has begun to adjust to the idea of going to confront a man who has killed so many.

Mari offered Lia the option of staying in London. Lia was torn, hesitant about leaving but feeling such a strong pull as she watched the others prepare for the journey.

'I think this is going to be hard,' Mari said. 'And that this will change us.'

After that everything was settled. When you give a person a chance to choose a new, stronger self, just the option can help them get a grip. The only reason to cling to the past is fear, and Lia has already learned to surpass herself.

Courage is not just a character trait, Mari thinks. It is also a skill. You can learn it and practise it. The hardest thing is to combine it with knowledge: to know what is coming and still move forward.

Lia had needed to ask for time off from *Level* for the trip. That hadn't been easy, she had told Mari. The AD position moved further away in Lia's eyes, beyond the horizon, the moment she notified her boss Martyn Taylor that she was suddenly going on a trip without any specific return date.

Mari knows Martyn – they've met several times – actually, they are quite well acquainted – but Mari didn't help Lia with this. If Lia wants to become the artistic director at *Level*, she will have to earn the place herself.

Taylor was confused and then irritated. Finally he gave in though. Mari knows why: Lia is that good. Martyn Taylor has recognised it. He knows that this is a woman he has to hold onto, a woman who can sometimes be stubborn and impossible to restrain, which is exactly why she is so promising.

Taylor agreed to find some cover, he agreed to having Lia notify him of her return date when it suited her, he agreed to everything. When Lia saw that, her doubts about the journey melted away. She understood that something very unusual was happening but that it must be done.

Lia got her time off, dropped by to see Gro at Mr Vong's flat and rang her parents in Finland.

They have all packed for a trip of unknown duration. With Rico and Paddy's help they are taking all the tools they might need and a good deal they can't imagine ever needing. Three large cases full of technology, all with import documentation. Weapons transport has been entrusted to a reliable courier firm that will deliver them in such a way as to prevent any connection to the Studio.

Rico's programs haven't been given to anyone or declared on any customs form. At some borders they would be considered weapons, entire weapons systems, which was what they actually are.

All of this supports them as they set off, along with the reason that they have to go.

Mari is not afraid now. She has met men and even women who have killed people. The others at the Studio know some of these cases, but none of them knows everything, and Mari intends to make sure it stays that way.

Leaving the Studio was hard. Away from the Studio she feels more vulnerable.

But this man is too evil. These deeds cannot be overlooked.

Is he calling to them? Could he know they are tracking him?

No. His videos have challenged anyone to stand up to him. He believes he is invincible, worshipping his idol with acts and images no one could stop, ascending to the level of his idol and beyond.

Mari intends to drop him like a tiny pebble into a ravine. Like an insect, without mercy, without warning, in mid-flight. The man who took Berg from them will not continue his grotesque slayings. Not if it depends on Mari.

Berg.

Mari looks at Lia sitting next to her. With them on the same row of seats, across the aisle, sit Paddy and Rico. They are preparing for a strange task. That is why Mari wanted Lia, the least experienced of them all, next to her.

'I've written something,' Mari says.

Lia looks at her with bright eyes.

Maggie is travelling to Stockholm. The whole Studio is on the move, and life as they know it is changing. Maggie is going to Berg's memorial, to represent all of them.

When Maggie goes to the service, she will see a chapel full of strangers. She will move amongst those strangers, into a room where everyone sitting is connected only by having known Berg at different stages of his life. For Maggie it will be an honour to be Berg's friend in that company.

Maggie asked Mari to write the eulogy she will give at the service.

'If I write it myself, I'll cry like a baby,' she explained.

Mari understood. When someone else writes the words, they are easier to speak. Maggie and her roles. She is so used to learning speeches someone else has written and making them her own. Conveying only the emotion meant to be conveyed.

'I wrote this for Maggie at the service,' Mari tells Lia and hands her a folded piece of white paper.

Lia opens the paper and silently reads the words Maggie will soon read in a small chapel in Stockholm.

I remember his way of arranging his work tools. A place for every-thing and everything in its place. We reveal ourselves to others in these little things.

I remember his way of closing doors.

His look when we talked about someone whose life was full of hidden trials.

How quickly he calmed himself after an argument.

And how once he had realised that he touched people too infre-quently – and decided that to avoid becoming a grumpy old man he had to start patting people on the shoulder and hugging his friends more.

We think we show ourselves to others in grand gestures, in our accomplishments, but it is in these everyday things we see the reality. What we are, not just what we pretend to be.

For many he was a beloved relative or friend. Or set designer or master carpenter.

To me he was a miracle man.

What I saw of him in everyday things – in his way of arranging tools, closing doors, looking at those close to him – that was beautiful. He loved the things he made. He loved people.

I can't do that. I can't love anyone. Not now. My grief is too much.

I grieve so much for him.

Someday I may be able to think differently, but now I think: a human being is a falling tree. We have only the time it takes a tree to fall to the ground. We hold each other up, but in the end all trees fall.

Miracle man. I don't know if I was strong enough to hold you up.

I remember you.

Mari watches Lia fold the piece of paper and place it in her pocket. Lia looks away and Mari turns as well to avoid intruding on her grief.

Leaving on an aeroplane, high in the sky, there is a feeling of disconnection from everything. For a moment, nothing can break.

III
Killer Queen

41.

Immediately upon arrival, in the taxi on the way from the small Kisauni Airport towards Stone Town, two things became clear.

First, it was hot. A heat that washed over them and came closer and penetrated deeper than any heatwave in England. In the early evening air was a promise of the cooling breeze that would rise from the ocean, but it hadn't started yet. Their clothing stuck to their skin.

And, secondly, there was no electricity.

Rico laughed out loud when he realised. The entire Zanzibari main island of Unguja had no mains power.

Kisauni Airport had lights, which was why they didn't notice immediately, but when the taxi driver started talking about how hard life was without electric lights and they saw in the waning daylight that no lamps glimmered within the houses, the situation was clear.

'How did we not know this?' Rico said, grinning at Mari.

The power outage made Mari solemn.

'This could be a problem,' she said. 'I don't know why we didn't know about it.'

She and Paddy had spent hours reading the Zanzibari news. Rico had found out everything he could about the level of technical equipment available on the island. None of them had grasped that the island wouldn't have power.

Once they arrived in Stone Town, they discovered why they hadn't easily discerned the problem from London. No electricity was already everyday life here. Because it had been going on for months and the telephone network still worked, the problem was no longer news, or at least no one was going to talk about it on the travel websites.

The issue lay with the cable coming from the mainland, along the floor of the ocean, the desk clerk at the Cinnamon Hotel told them. The cable was broken, probably snapped by a ship carrying out maintenance work. No one knew who the guilty party was because apparently no one was investigating. Or repairing it.

'Maybe they'll do it on the mainland,' the receptionist said. 'Yes, they should do it.'

The receptionist at the Cinnamon was an older man used to foreign travellers. The hotel was beautiful, an old renovated white building.

It took its name from the local spice tradition: Zanzibar had once been a notable centre of the spice trade.

They had chosen their accommodation carefully so they would have space for all of Rico's equipment and adequate privacy. The whole hotel had only six rooms, of which they occupied four.

'We heard that a tourist disappeared on the island recently,' Mari said to the receptionist. 'A Frenchman.'

'No,' the receptionist replied. 'That is not possible.'

'Why not?'

Zanzibar – or the main island of Unguja, which is generally just called by the name of the whole island group – was generally a very safe place. There were around 600,000 residents, but other than the capital, the other population centres were mostly villages. Between those buzzed mopeds and *dala dala* – beaten-up vans that operated as minibuses. A few passenger aeroplanes came to the island each day, and a ferry ran to the mainland, but mostly people just lived day-to-day lives.

'This is a very peaceful place,' the man assured them.

Mari did not believe him. For Lia these suspicions and a power outage affecting the entire island were downright bewildering. If they hadn't realised it at the Studio, how could they prepare for what was ahead of them? But Mari and Rico's way of handling the issue quieted any concerns.

Everyone on Unguja used generators, the man at the desk had said. They always turned them on at dusk. The hotel guests could charge their phones and use other electrical devices for several hours each night, and the generator could be available at other times as necessary.

'Not good enough,' Rico said.

Several of his devices had such sensitive batteries that the potential voltage spikes coming from a generator could damage them. And under no circumstances was Rico going to allow the Topo anywhere near a dirty power source like that. Immediately he rang a company in Nairobi and ordered a charger that would store power from the generator and then charge their batteries with a more even current. It would arrive on the next plane.

Rico had arranged Internet access in advance. The Topo had its own satellite connection, and they also had a separate satphone. The case that contained the small base station was a bother to carry, but it ensured them uninterrupted, secure access any time they wanted.

The power outage might also benefit them, Mari said.

'How?' Lia asked.

The island's phone network was unlikely to function without issues, and they were almost certainly the only ones with twenty-four hour access to an IT arsenal and good network connections, Mari explained.

'Not even he could have all this. At least not as protected from disturbances like ours are.'

He, Lia thought.

He was also here somewhere. Maybe close.

It was already dark by the time they had moved into their rooms. Thick candles illuminated the rooms – despite the receptionist's promises, the hotel was saving the generator. They were lodging right in the heart of Stone Town, in the centre of a rambling collection of narrow lanes. When they gathered in the lobby to go out, Rico handed each a small torch. They were so light that you could hang one from a buttonhole but bright enough to be useful.

The colour of Stone Town was the bleached white of sand. The buildings were whitewashed, and those that were painted properly were still white. Here and there they noticed that familiar dirty yellow ochre – the colour they had used Rico's hacker friends to identify just a short time previously. Between the old buildings were some smaller structures, some made of concrete. By looking closely, in places one could see that stones and even coral were sometimes mixed with the cement. Mari had worked out why: to save on construction costs.

As they walked the streets, they listened as one generator after another growled into life. Still light only flickered from within the buildings and outside a few small shops. Mostly it was dark.

In this labyrinth they would have easily lost their way, but Lia and Paddy quickly pieced together their route. The important thing was to know the main thoroughfares and your own position relative to them. In the darkness of the evening and in amongst the buildings, landmarks were difficult to see, but they committed the street corners to memory as they went.

Stone Town was an entirely new kind of experience for Lia, a mixture of African and Middle Eastern characteristics, Islamic culture and the ever-intrusive commercial brands of the West. Barefoot children roamed the streets, with the sound of a bicycle bell ringing here and there. In front of the buildings sat men in colourful tunics and small hats. The women were less visible – they had to be in the kitchens of the city watching boiling pots.

White-skinned foreign travellers were easy to pick out here, but, on the other hand, there were a lot of them in Stone Town. Lia thought she could also see a few foreigners in the mass of people who had taken up more permanent residence. These navigated the winding, bumpy streets more comfortably, and their clothing was a combination of western and Zanzibari.

Was one of them *him*?

Paddy had set the rules for moving about in the city. They always had to go in pairs if possible. Never without weapons, but only Paddy and Rico carried them constantly. Lia still didn't feel completely confident with a weapon, and Mari didn't want one.

They also had other tools, Mari said. Lia wasn't sure she wanted to know what that meant, but Mari's confidence was reassuring.

They ate dinner at a small Indian restaurant located in the centre on the first floor of an old building. The place filled quickly. The reason was the tandoor: the restaurant was not dependent upon the generators because it had an old-fashioned wood-fired oven out of which poured dark, sweet, slightly smoky aromas.

By day the restaurant must offer a good view of Stone Town's busy main street, Kenyatta Road. Now, in the darkness, they could only see dim lamps and flickering candle flames.

They had to be like any other tourists, Mari said. They had to behave like tourists while they investigated where Theo Durand disappeared. First thing in the morning they would have to meet with the local police and look into any leads.

Wanting to show off his language skills, the waiter at the restaurant churned out English and French as he presented the food, along with a brief lesson in the local Swahili. When he had taken their orders, Mari asked whether he had heard about the disappearance of a French tourist on the island.

No, the waiter assured them, no one had disappeared in years.

'He's lying,' Mari said quickly after the man had left.

According to the news, there had been numerous hold-ups in Zanzibar over the years, and travellers had got in other trouble as well in the archipelago. Because someone didn't always investigate what happened to tourists, and many of them might just have left the area on their own, disappearances weren't necessarily reported to anyone.

Lia was exhausted from the journey, the heat and the whole situation. The conversation was scanty. They were all just waiting to get to bed and start work in the morning.

After dinner, Paddy and Lia led them back to the hotel through the warrens of Stone Town without a moment's hesitation. Minus the constant feeling of danger, strolling here might be nice some day, Lia thought.

She sneaked a glance at Mari. She seemed calm, as if arriving on the island had removed all uncertainty and set a clear goal in front of her.

As if she knows what's ahead.

42.

The sixth video was the most savage of all.

Watching it made them ill, and its appearance online was an upsetting omen. How could this killer be stopped when all they could do was watch as a person was tortured?

Rico woke the others early after logging on to the Topo and seeing what the night had brought. They gathered to watch the video in Mari's room.

In the picture was a young man, western, light skinned. His age was difficult to determine precisely because he was in such bad shape. All he was wearing was a pair of shorts.

Mostly the video showed him sitting slumped against a wall. He shook, his body jerking. He was emaciated, but the worst thing was that his skin was covered in grotesque sores. Blackened, swollen, bloody wounds. He looked like a person who had been tortured so long he had given up any hope of staying alive.

'The only way to put a person in that state is time,' Paddy said.

He guessed that most of the marks were burns. The man had been burned with something. He had been starved, probably for many days.

'If that's true, he was grabbed a while ago,' Rico said.

The video clearly combined images from several days. Occasionally the man was seen agonisingly scratching the dark wall with his fingers. In a few close-ups his face was distorted in a scream. He screamed, but the video had no sound.

The Queen song the video was made to was called 'You Take My Breath Away'.

At the end of the video, the man tried to stand. His legs wouldn't support him, but he forced himself up. He stared past the camera, his eyes fixed on something beyond. His eyes shone with untold dread.

Maybe that was what made the video so awful, Lia thought. The first videos had been full of intensity and aggression, and the fifth a strange, chilling expectation. Here a man, who knew he was going to die, was being held prisoner and tortured brutally.

Rico asked out loud the question that weighed on them all. Could the killer know about their arrival in Zanzibar? Had the video been uploaded during the night because of that?

'I don't think so,' Mari said.

Hundreds of thousands of tourists visited the main island of Unguja alone every year. They included people from dozens of different countries, and Stone Town was abuzz with visitors. How could the killer have detected them in that mass of humanity?

'I don't think he knows anything about us,' Mari said.

The only thing that connected them to the killer was Berg. The police hadn't been able to trace Berg's connection to the Studio, so how would a man who was doing all this at the same time have been able to do it?

But they were running out of time.

The man in the fifth video had appeared to be wasting away slowly. This new one would die from his injuries at any moment, if he hadn't already.

Of course it was possible that the killer had filmed these two men some time ago. Maybe they were already dead. But the kicking videos had always come fresh, with the bodies dumped in public places relatively soon after the killings – Mari believed that this was how the killer wanted to work. He wanted them all watching these victims as they suffered.

New copies of the previous video were still spreading online. Rico estimated that within the space of a few days it had been watched around the world hundreds of thousands of times, maybe over a million. The newest video had only garnered several thousand views so far because it had only been online a few hours.

'Can we see whether it's being watched in Zanzibar?' Paddy asked.

Rico shook his head.

'That won't help. Even if we could tell, we wouldn't be able to see the IP address it was being watched from. He's sure to have anonymised his computer and network connection.'

They divvied up tasks. Rico stayed at the hotel to go through the images from the sixth video frame by frame. He guessed that the shots had been processed more than the previous videos – the space behind the man had been obscured from view.

Lia and Paddy would talk to the local police. Mari wanted to tour the city, to get a feel for the area. In daylight and with other people around, she felt confident enough to go out for a while on her own.

As she left Mari's room, Lia noticed that both pillows of the wide bed had been used. In this heat there was no need for a duvet. Apparently Mari hadn't spent the night alone – perhaps Paddy had been with her. Lia didn't ask.

43.

The first thing you notice in the Darajani Market are the smells. The smell of frying food, raw meat kept in the open air, exhaust fumes. And the sweet enticingness of incense.

Mari walks among the booths and tables, making her way through the press. She has not been this vulnerable in years.

She is ready to abandon her complex security measures for a moment and expose herself to come-what-may because in this job they are going deep into the most painful and important things in her life. The whole endeavour is reckless, perhaps megalomaniacal. But Mari has taken it upon herself, and the others at the Studio have decided to come along.

Or perhaps the killer made the decision for them by firing the shot that felled Berg and then by walking up to him and executing him where he lay. After something like that they had only two choices: hide and lick their wounds for the rest of their lives or make this man pay for his crimes.

The Darajani Market is full of sounds. It is a clamorous maelstrom covering a large square and a squat, dirty market hall in the middle of the old town. Here they sell everything with bright colours or tentacles or spines, alive, fried or dried. This is a place where the multitude of people and merchandise might conceal anything. This kind of place Mari would normally avoid or at least take someone along to as backup, but now she wanted to come alone.

The man comes here too sometimes. Everyone in Zanzibar does. Tourists, locals, small children – every single person on the island has been right here at some point in time.

Mari looks at the crowd and senses the intentions of those walking around her.

A woman buying ingredients for dinner. She doesn't really know how to cook, not the way that would make her husband praise her food, and every night when she sets the evening meal before the family she feels inferior. She selects herbs, feels the aubergines with her hand, but really she doesn't want to be here. She wants to be somewhere else entirely, living a different life.

That man in the dark glasses is looking for customers. He sells everything, from tiny to enormous, legal to illegal, but mostly he stocks the illegal because those give him the greatest profits. In the Darajani Market on the island of Unguja in Zanzibar the lines between legal and illegal still exist – they are monitored, but in nearby lanes they disappear, and goods and services and drugs and perhaps even people become only objects of trade. Everything is on offer; with this man in the dark glasses anything can be bought or sold.

Mari walks between the stands. The space is confined; she can feel the throng on her skin. And Mari comes ever closer to this man who kills. He is here somewhere, maybe not in the market right now but here on the island.

Mari feels as if every moment is bringing her closer. She knows that if the killer passes by, she will recognise him. Maybe not from his clothing – he won't necessarily be wearing the trousers and shoes people around the world have seen in the kicking videos. But Mari will recognise him from his eyes, from what lies behind them.

In London this man killed five people, four meticulously planned and one as a by-product. He performed those deaths theatrically, ferociously.

Now he is torturing. This man is here somewhere and has chosen wasting away as his method of killing. As if as he comes closer to what he wants he is slowing things down, biding his time. Perhaps on the island there is something that is making him act this way.

For this man, killing is a form of self-expression, just as music is for a musician. His creation is death.

Mari looks at the stall in front of her from which rises a light, yellowish wisp of smoke. A stick of incense burns away the evil as it worships the good, and suddenly everything Mari has read about the objects of the murderer's devotion falls into place.

Mari knows why he is here, and she knows why he has decided to wear his victims down.

Even in the heat of the blazing sun, Mari shivers as if from a cold draught, almost as though the killer is near.

Almost as if she has got inside him.

44.

At the Malindi Police Station, Paddy didn't waste any time on pleasantries. The two old policemen behind the desks were used to many kinds of customers, but not large western men who marched in displaying irresistible authority.

'Who is the officer in charge of this shift?' Paddy asked.

One of the policemen spoke monosyllabic English.

'Who are you?' he asked.

Paddy pulled out his passport and ID card which said he was a professional private investigator.

'What you want?' the policeman asked, begrudgingly glancing at the card.

'You have two missing person cases here,' Paddy said. 'The people missing are in danger. I need to see your superior.'

The commanding officer was young. On his belt he carried a heavy pistol, and he spoke more fluent English than his subordinates, but he didn't look like a man who led large investigations.

'We don't give out any information unless the families ask,' the commander said. 'Or unless the request comes through the official channels.'

His eyes moved restlessly between Paddy and Lia. Lia hadn't introduced herself, but apparently that didn't matter. As the man, Paddy was assumed to be directing the encounter.

The commander's office was a small cubby hole hidden at the back of the station. The computer squatting on the table was old and clunky. Criminal investigation here was not at the cutting edge of international policing.

'We know that one of the missing people is a Frenchman named Theo Durand,' Paddy said. 'Who is the other one?'

The commander was reluctant to cooperate, but he didn't have the nerve not to answer Paddy's question.

'We have carried out the proper notifications,' the man said. 'To the people concerned. If you aren't a member of the family or a government official, we have nothing we can share with you.'

'Where are these notifications of yours?' Paddy asked.

'With the appropriate authorities.'

'Who are they?'

'The embassies,' the commander said.

He instantly realised he had revealed something: the other missing person was not from the same country as Theo Durand. The commander looked at Paddy in irritation.

'What do you want here?'

'To capture a dangerous person.'

'Who?'

Paddy froze, looking at the commander.

'You don't have a clue what's going on,' Paddy said tiredly. 'You don't have a clue what's happening on your island right under your nose.'

The police commander shrugged. This clearly wasn't the first time some foreigner had criticised the local police, and he wasn't interested in accepting complaints.

'Let's go,' Paddy said to Lia. 'There's nothing for us here.'

Rico quickly found a news story about a missing Italian man once he knew what to look for. The information was on the website of an Italian newspaper.

His name was Aldo Zambrano. The date of his disappearance was unclear, but the news story had only been published the day before. Online they found a few pictures of Zambrano, who was from Cosenza. He was the same man as in the newest video.

Mari calculated the dates. Some time must have separated the disappearances of the two newest victims, but both had been at the killer's mercy for several days. Who knew what had been done to them after shooting the videos. Or whether either of them was even alive any more.

They roamed the city all day.

Stone Town was ramshackle but still beautiful. Lia quickly grasped the layout of the small city, but the totality of it was impossible to comprehend in a moment. Despite the heat and the oppressive atmosphere, she found herself here and there staring at street corners bleached with dust behind which nearly anything could be hiding, or the beautiful wooden doors of the old buildings with their thick iron locks.

No one in the city was talking about the missing men. That they discovered quickly. They asked about Durand and Zambrano around the hotels: even in the backpacker hostels no rumours were circulating, as if the missing men simply did not exist.

They found the hotels where the men had stayed. The staff at each had clearly been ordered to keep quiet. Small banknotes convinced them to open up a little.

They didn't know any details about the disappearances. All over the island, tourists tended to leave their hotels early in the morning, returning to rest during the hottest period of the day and then going out again in the evening. Hotels didn't keep track of their patrons' comings and goings, only making sure that intruders didn't come into the rooms. Tracking foreigners' movements would have been difficult anyway: sometimes someone suddenly decided to go off on a tour of the island or scuba diving without telling anyone at the hotel.

The police had collected the missing men's things. The Frenchman had been travelling alone and had only been missed once his relatives in France started asking after him. The Italian had been with a group of friends, who after waiting a while had started making noise about his disappearance.

'The police silenced them,' one of the waiters in the hotel told Paddy. 'The Italians threatened to go to the international press, but the police said that since the man had disappeared under mysterious circumstances, they would do best to be quiet.'

'Mysterious circumstances?' Paddy asked.

The man was *shoga,* the waiter said, using a vulgar Swahili term for gay. Sometimes it meant a close friend, he said, but there was no confusion about the sense in which the police had used it about Aldo Zambrano.

'Most of his friends were probably *shoga* too,' the waiter said.

The friends had left a couple of days before having waited for Zambrano in vain.

'They weren't close friends,' the waiter said. 'Not couples. They were just having fun.'

Lia and Paddy couldn't get the Italian man's travelling companions' information from the hotel, but Paddy thought they would turn up. At the very latest when the Italian news began reporting the case more widely.

As day turned to evening, they still hadn't made much progress in their search. The police station closed and the city began preparing for another night without electricity.

They all gathered in Mari's room at the hotel. Lia checked her voicemail. She had kept her phone with her all day, but at some point a message had appeared without her hearing it ring. It was from Detective Chief Inspector Peter Gerrish.

'Ring me,' Gerrish said tersely.

The police profiler, Christopher Holywell, wanted to talk to Lia, and so did Gerrish.

'Ring now,' Gerrish demanded.

It was only a matter of time until foreign police started showing up in Stone Town to join the investigation for the missing men.

'What investigation?' Mari asked. 'My impression is that the police here haven't done anything about it.'

But Mari and the others knew they were in the right place. And although they hadn't found out much from the locals, they had to press on.

Mari had also received a message from London. It was from Maggie, who had returned from Berg's memorial service in Stockholm. Maggie said she was at the Studio ready to help with anything, and she had a question.

'What do we do about Craig Cole?' Maggie asked in her message.

Cole had visited Bradford and talked to the director of The Pulse, and the new job and prospective colleagues seemed pleasant. But now he was telling Maggie that he was hesitating.

'Something is weighing on his mind,' Maggie said.

This was probably the same problem Mari had seen him struggling with before.

'He doesn't dare to act. He won't defend himself,' Mari said.

But right now they didn't have time to concentrate on Cole. Mari suggested that Maggie meet him again on her own.

Ask why he hadn't filed a complaint about Bryony Wade with the police, Mari suggested in her own message. 'Chat with him. Try to find out what is preventing him from getting over this.'

In Mari's room, Lia felt an almost palpable pressure. She had never seen her companions so uncompromising, shutting out other matters so they could discover what they had come to Zanzibar to discover. Surrounding them was an old city that would not easily give up its secrets. Interpol and detectives from Tanzania would be coming – perhaps, eventually – but in the meantime anything could happen on the island.

So many days have passed. Maybe Durand and Zambrano are already dead.

'I want to go out,' Lia told the others. 'Anywhere, just so long as I don't have to sit here.'

Lia and Paddy jogged through the centre of Stone Town to the sea and Shangani Street, which ran along the shore.

Only a hint of light remained. They had their small torches, but they didn't need to turn them on quite yet. By the side of the road, the sand was compacted by foot traffic, making it good for jogging.

On their run, they circled the whole city, resorting to using their torches once darkness fell in earnest. Children yelled greetings to them. The last fishing vessels were returning to shore, their catches being carried off in baskets.

If the situation hadn't been so bad, it would have been beautiful, Lia thought. The scene was nearly as atmospheric as her evening route at home in Hampstead.

In London, Maggie waited for Craig Cole outside his house.

'You lot like surprising people,' Cole said when he saw her on the street.

Maggie smiled thinking how their visits must seem to Cole. Women from a PR firm who appeared without an appointment wanting to talk to him, bearing strange propositions.

'This time I'm not here to suggest anything new,' Maggie said. 'I just came to chat, if you have some time.'

Cole asked Maggie in and sat her in the kitchen, which was familiar from her previous visit.

Maggie talked about the radio station in Bradford and what was going on with their programmes. Small independent stations like The Pulse had the luxury of doing things the way they wanted, but not everything had to focus on Yorkshire issues.

'It isn't how small they are that's the issue,' Cole said. 'Going to a small station feels fine.'

'What doesn't feel good about it then?' Maggie asked.

Cole cast her a hesitant glance. Maggie knew she was more approachable for him than Mari and Lia had been. Being more or less his age, he could more easily imagine Maggie having similar life experiences to him.

'I've been wondering whether the best thing wouldn't be to withdraw from public life entirely,' Cole said.

Maggie nodded. She understood that impulse well. All famous artists and media personalities considered it as they aged. Once you had experienced the rush and elevated sense of self brought by popularity, at some point wanting to get away from its negative aspects was natural. Everyone always assumed celebrities would be constantly available to the media, willing to open up about their lives and keeping themselves in peak physical condition – before long the whole thing became a burden.

But Cole also had his own reasons for wanting his privacy.

'I've done some things I'm not proud of,' he told Maggie.

Maggie understood that this confession was difficult. He wanted to open up because he knew he had a difficult choice ahead of him.

Craig Cole had been unfaithful. Over the years he had cheated on his wife, Gill, three times.

'They never meant anything to me,' Cole said, not looking at Maggie. 'They only mattered afterwards, when the shame hit me.'

They had always been young women Cole met on business trips. He had had dozens of opportunities for affairs but only slipped these three times.

'Some people in this business wouldn't think anything of three dalliances,' he said. 'But for me they have always been horrible failures. Afterwards. When they were happening, I wasn't thinking anything, but afterwards that made it even worse.'

His infidelity and the feelings of shame that came along with it had become such a big issue for Cole that Bryony Wade's accusations had simply felt like the universe passing judgement on him. Cole had done wrong, not towards a teenage girl, but towards his wife.

'For most people cheating is just hedonism or narcissism. They use it to prove something to themselves, not others,' Cole said. 'In my life I've had plenty of evidence that people like me. But that wasn't enough.'

Cole had strayed three times but thought about his betrayals thousands of times, making them a central part of his identity.

'It probably says something that I've never liked remembering those three women, what the sex was like. They were very attractive. In their twenties. But I don't fantasise about them or dream about doing it again. I've learned what a man who does those things is like – despite everything he already has. I fantasise about what life would be like if I hadn't done it. Or what it would be like if I got caught publicly.'

Cole realised that he was the one who had made his mistakes so important. As if he wanted to have some flaw, some imperfection to condemn him.

'What kind of person wants that?' Cole asked Maggie.

Maggie didn't have an answer.

Cole had confessed his affairs to his wife. The first two he had admitted when he was drunk, both at once, and the situation had led them to a crisis in their marriage. Gill had considered divorce, but after seeing Cole's contrition, she had decided to stay with him.

'When I had to tell her about the third time, something between Gill and me changed,' Cole said.

Looking at him, his wife had seemed to understand. He wasn't just looking for sex, he was looking for the storm of emotion that followed being unfaithful.

That was why Cole hadn't filed a complaint about Bryony Wade. He had been afraid that one of those young women with whom he had cheated on his wife would go public. To the point of paranoia he had suspected that one of the three had told Bryony Wade about what had happened and was just waiting to get an opportunity to blackmail him.

Cole had money, lots of it. His and Gill's finances were secure and would be for the rest of their lives. He didn't necessarily need to look for work, but the money also left him open to possible blackmail.

Maggie could see that this admission had taken a major emotional effort for him. Cole searched Maggie's expression for disapproval. When he didn't see any repudiation, talking about it became a liberating experience.

After their meeting, Maggie sent Mari a brief message about Cole's admission and the situation. The approval of his audience and his good-guy role were so important for Cole that they had also become an emotional compulsion.

'He isn't worried about going to Bradford because he's afraid of failing. What he's thinking about is whether he wants his old life back at all,' Maggie wrote.

'Let's wait,' Mari replied. 'Wait and keep in touch with him. And be ready for anything to happen here. We're getting closer.'

When Lia received a text from Rico, she and Paddy immediately turned back towards the centre of Stone Town.

He was waiting for them on Kenyatta Road near an old building. Some time ago a grey paint had been applied, but the stone walls beneath could have been at least a hundred years old.

Before them stood the Zanzibar Gallery, a shop selling books, decorations and tourist trinkets. The main streets of Stone Town were home to any number of similar shops. Stepping inside them was not a good idea unless you were willing to listen to fevered sales pitches and haggle over wildly inflated tourist prices. During the course of the day, Lia had gone looking for water in a few of these shops and learned why some customers practically fled after getting a taste of the aggressive sales tactics.

Lia and Paddy could see from the door that Mari was inside the shop.

Rico pointed to a small sign on the wall with a glass case below. Mercury House, the sign read, below it in the case two small posters with pictures of Freddie Mercury and a few paragraphs about his life and musical career.

'They don't know anything,' Mari announced when she came out of the shop.

The salespeople weren't interested in talking to a tourist who wasn't buying. They didn't even know the precise history of the building – they just kept repeating that Mercury lived here, Mari said.

She had been thinking about Freddie Mercury since they arrived on the island. The man they were tracking was in Zanzibar in order to be close to one thing: Freddie Mercury. If you wanted to get close to a person who had died so long ago, where would you go?

Slowly they walked up the street.

Maybe investigating the building itself more closely would tell them something, Mari suggested. That would take resourcefulness though, since the shopkeepers were so negative.

'But it may be that the solution is something else entirely,' Mari said.

She looked at the entrance to the adjacent hotel. After thinking for a second, she asked the others to wait and entered the building.

She was only gone a couple of minutes.

'I guessed as much,' she said. 'This isn't the only place.'

The hotel receptionist had told her that some of Mercury's family had lived in the Zanzibar Gallery's building at one time, but it wasn't Freddie Mercury's home.

'They just marked a house on a main street with a connection to the Bulsara family so tourists would find it,' Mari said.

'They can't do that,' Lia huffed.

This was Africa, Paddy reminded her. 'That sort of thing is perfectly normal here. It's just a way of making sales. And they probably think they're doing the tourists a favour by not making them have to wander around looking for some out-of-the-way place.'

Lia was shocked. Travellers were constantly coming to the island and taking pictures of this building as if it were Freddie Mercury's childhood home. They had just seen people with cameras in front of the shop. Tourists took these pictures home and told their friends about the find they had made. Thousands of pictures were floating around of the birthplace of Freddie Mercury that wasn't genuine.

'Where is his house really?' Lia asked.

Following the directions she had received from the hotel, Mari led them away from Kenyatta Road. Here again was an old building, but the windows were closed. A sign hung on the main door: Camlur's Restaurant.

They couldn't get into the restaurant to look around since it appeared to be closed, but one side door was open, and housed some sort of bar. Mari wanted to go in alone again. Lia thought this was strange until she grasped the reason.

Mari thinks she's going to recognise him. If the man is in there, Mari will notice him.

'What do we do if he's in there?' Lia asked Paddy. Paddy's gaze was steady and his voice was quiet.

'Everything has been planned,' he said. 'Don't be afraid. He doesn't have any way of knowing who we are.'

Mari returned and described the building. Of course after so many years and so many renovations, no signs remained of the building's former residents. The bar staff were sick of hearing questions about Freddie Mercury. That was strange once you took into consideration that the building's history was its only selling point and everyone sitting at the tables was a tourist. But they had brushed aside enquiries about the Mercury family's connections with little more than shrugs.

Rico thought he knew the reason why.

'They don't want to call attention to Mercury because Zanzibar is a Muslim area.'

Having a famous gay artist's fans constantly running around their city was a serious embarrassment for the island's Islamic powers that be.

'That's why you hardly see anything about Mercury living here.'

It was true, Lia realised. They had only seen that one sign on the wall of that one shop. The Camlur's Restaurant building didn't announce the fact even though the locals all knew the history. Down near the ferry terminal was a tourist bar named Mercury's with pictures of the singer on the walls, but that building didn't have anything to do with the Bulsara family.

They walked to the shore and found a restaurant where they could sit outside in the muggy evening air. After a quick meal, they moved back to the hotel, finding their way by the beams of their small torches.

Mari asked Lia to join her in her room for a moment before going to bed. Mari's room was on the first floor. They sat near the wide-open window, the shutters turned out towards the night.

If they had been in London, this would have been time for a nightcap, Lia thought. Alcohol wasn't offered casually on the island though – the locals sold drinks to tourists but weren't constantly forcing them on you.

Interpol and the British police would come before long, but they didn't know precisely when, Mari said, thinking out loud.

'It could still be a while,' she said. 'They have to work their way through the bureaucracy.'

Time was running out. More than a day had passed since they had arrived on the island.

'Now we have to try to sleep,' Mari said. 'Tomorrow something is going to happen. It has to.'

Mari had sensed Lia's concern.

'We're prepared for lots of possibilities,' Mari assured her. 'And the police are coming.'

They listened to the silence of the old stone city. Nights were so dark here they needed their own word, Lia thought.

'*Sysipimeä*,' she said.

Mari nodded. 'It's too beautiful a word for this though,' she said.

Coal black so thick the circles of light cast by candles and lamps seemed infinitesimal. A black moment with the feeling that an explosion could happen anywhere at any moment.

'This place needs fire now,' Mari said. Burning bonfires. The island needed enough fire to do away with the dark.

45.

No position was painless.

Aldo Zambrano lay on the ground and let the pain be. He had to try to think of something else. He couldn't think of this because if he thought of how much pain he was in, he would start to cry and his face would hurt.

The conditions for human existence were simple. That was what his professor at home in Cosenza had taught. List the conditions for human existence, the professor had demanded, and they had listed them: oxygen, food, water.

Those are not the conditions for your existence, the professor said. Two things make human life possible: civilisation and debate. Without these, man becomes an animal.

He was wrong.

The condition for survival was the lack of pain. There was nothing else but that, Aldo now knew. There was life without pain and life with pain, and talking about anything else was pointless as long as this kind of pain existed.

Aldo stank of pain. He could smell it himself. The festering burns on his body reeked. The penetrating heat made the parts of his skin that could still be called skin sweat. The burned places swelled.

If Aldo ever got out of here, if he ever got back home, he would teach his professor the true boundary conditions of existence. They depended on the amount of pain. There were two kinds: just bearable and excruciating. As long as The Man was not here, the pain was just bearable.

But when The Man wanted to cause Aldo pain, *mio Dio*, the pain was excruciating and consumed him.

No one could know that kind of pain existed. When The Man first chained him in place in his cell and brought the fire near, Aldo had stared at it in shock, horrified but at the same time strangely, fiercely curious. What would the fire do to him? How could The Man do that? How long could he do that? Would the man really burn him, or was he only threatening? What was going on?

The Man held the fire near Aldo's skin. The chains stopped Aldo from fleeing. He struggled but could not get away. The flame warmed a piece of Aldo's skin. He felt the burning begin and the pain rising.

Aldo broke into screams. He was a grown man who had screamed so long he almost went mad from the screaming alone. And when The Man took up the torch again, Aldo thought that now it would be over, and then he saw the man moving the flame to another spot on his body. Aldo began to shriek.

The first time, The Man had burned him in five places. The fire scorched five holes in him. From then on Aldo was no longer able to understand how many times it happened. As his skin burned, he momentarily lost consciousness only to revive each time in the middle of that horrible agony. Sometimes The Man gave him water – Aldo didn't understand why, why he didn't just end it all. Maybe The Man wanted to keep him alive despite the torture.

In his cell alone, Aldo looked at his burns. He had them on his thighs, his shins, his sides, his arms. He couldn't see his back, but he had them there too. They looked smaller than he had imagined. The blackened, open, ragged burns were smaller than they felt.

They hurt constantly. In every position Aldo tried.

The area around the wounds was swollen, stretched and shrivelled skin, and in some places Aldo saw a thin foam. The moisture in his skin was welling out, red and yellow, a bloody froth that looked as if things inside him were trying to get out through the holes torn in his flesh. Aldo no longer felt human. He was only matter, incomprehensible pain and burned meat.

The conditions for existence. That had been a course at the University of Calabria in Cosenza, during which a grey, slightly dishevelled professor talked for hour after hour on subjects he had spent years reading about. But the professor didn't know anything about the subject. Aldo would go there and walk into the lecture hall in the middle of the class, interrupting everything. Everyone would stare. 'Look what man can do to man,' Aldo would say. 'Look what the real necessary conditions for human existence are.'

A sound came from somewhere.

Aldo realised he was hearing a voice, several voices. The door opened. Steps. No words. Someone made a sound. Was it The Man?

There were more than one of them. Aldo realised that The Man was talking to someone. The talking stopped. Aldo had definitely heard The Man talking, but now it was quiet.

A flopping sound. A fall. What fell?

The pain made Aldo's hearing more sensitive. For a fleeting moment he thought about screaming. Should he scream for help? But The Man was there. The Man would bring the flame again.

Aldo listened to something heavy being dragged across the floor. Squeaks. Something opening. A door? A cell door? Small sounds he couldn't understand.

And then: a groan. Someone made sounds of pain.

The Man was torturing someone else. Aldo had heard that before.

Aldo heard a faint sound from somewhere, and he realised it was his own raspy breathing. Instinctively he had been holding his breath trying to hear what was happening.

What was happening nearby was over quickly. He heard a door close. The Man was near.

Aldo caught movement out of the corner of his eye, a fluctuation of light and shadow. A flame. It was moving again.

Was it coming towards him? It was.

Aldo closed his eyes so he wouldn't see.

He heard the man's footsteps. Although he squeezed his eyes shut, he could sense the flame of the torch The Man was holding. The smell of smoke. Again.

'Don't,' he pleaded.

He knew it was pointless, but still he pleaded. He had to look. He couldn't not.

The Man opened the door and came to him.

'Your turn,' The Man said.

'No,' Aldo begged. 'Don't... Let me –'

The man grabbed him, and Aldo howled in pain.

The Man grabbed him and dragged him to the chains and shackled him to the wall. Again.

Aldo looked at The Man. Aldo hurt so much he couldn't think any more. Everything was spinning, but he looked at The Man.

At least he looked for a moment.

'If you try to talk to the other one, I'll kill you instantly,' The Man said.

Aldo couldn't make a sound. Everything went blank inside. The Man went to the door and took up the torch. Then he returned to Aldo.

'Soon you will be ready,' The Man said.

Aldo stared at the burning torch in the man's hand.

'Ready?' he asked. 'For what?'

'For the pictures,' The Man said and pushed the torch so it almost touched Aldo's foot.

As he began to scream, Aldo knew that another prisoner was close who was hearing all of this. The Man wanted them both to hear what he did to them but not be able to speak to each other. The Man wanted Aldo to scream and the other victim to hear.

46.

The text message came sometime after five in the morning. Lia woke up to the alert sound. She had been having a hard time sleeping.

The text was from Peter Gerrish.

'Ring me. I heard from your work that you're travelling. Ring me now.'

The time difference from London was three hours. Gerrish had sent the message in the middle of the night. The police in London were working the case around the clock.

Lia didn't ring. She stood up, quickly showered and went to knock on Mari's and Rico's doors. She didn't bother with Paddy's door – she imagined he had spent the night in Mari's room.

'It's good you haven't rung Gerrish,' Mari said when they met in the breakfast room. 'There isn't any reason to let the police know you're in Zanzibar,' she carried on, keeping her voice low enough that the waiter wouldn't hear.

He was a little surly at having them wake up so early, but he still made coffee and tea and then went to get fresh bread.

Lia looked at Mari.

'Did you sleep at all?' she asked.

'A little,' Mari said.

During the night she had had an idea. Several, actually, she said. The most important one was that they might have a way to find out where the killer was staying.

'If he came here to be close to his idol, he might be staying somewhere near where Mercury used to live,' Mari said.

'In the Camlur's Restaurant building?' Lia asked.

The previous evening the building had looked rundown and rambling. But maybe there were flats there – the restaurant and bar only made up part of the space.

Lia, Mari and Paddy set out early. Rico stayed at the hotel: he was having problems with battery charging. The charger from the mainland seemed to be working, but the Topo and a couple of other machines' batteries still didn't seem to be charging.

'I don't know what's wrong,' Rico said.

It was almost as if the refined machines didn't want to work, in protest at being brought to the hot, damp island, he mused. Batteries were often the weak link in machines. Maybe the problem was in the uneven current. As his last resort, Rico had a power inverter they could plug into the cigarette lighter of a car.

'They aren't very efficient, but nearly every car in the world has a lighter plug. It's the only universal power outlet.'

As they were touring the city, Mari had seen a street-level office advertising flats. The office hadn't opened yet when they returned to it, but in the window, next to the letting photographs, was a phone number.

Omar Ngowi arrived ten minutes later, very quickly considering they were in Zanzibar. Ngowi was a slender man approaching sixty whose face always bore a fascinating, odd expression, a combination of a forbearing smile and a dreamy distance from the here and now.

Ngowi opened his office door, asking them in and encouraging them to sit around a small table. He didn't have many brochures or the like. His was a small company.

'If I wanted to buy a flat here, what should I do?' Mari asked immediately after the introductions.

Curiosity flitted across Ngowi's eyes.

'You want to buy a flat here at eight in the morning?'

'Possibly,' Mari said. 'How would I go about it?'

'Do you have a specific place in mind? A specific flat?' he asked.

Not yet, Mari replied. First she wanted to know how to buy or rent a flat on the island.

'Your agency is the only one I've seen here,' Mari noted. 'Where are all the others?'

Ngowi shrugged.

'There aren't many. Only two really, foreign owned, big ones.'

Selling properties and buildings in Tanzania was a veritable jungle of red tape that cut foreigners off from some rights. In Zanzibar the markets were regulated with even more care because the authorities realised how attractive the sandy beaches of the archipelago were to foreign investors.

Foreigners couldn't buy any land or homes in Zanzibar without a local go-between. Frequently people had to found entire corporations with Zanzibari owners to do it. These would serve as a front for the foreign owner and handle all the bureaucracy. Renting had its rules too, but getting around them didn't require as much creativity.

'This is a place where almost anything is possible,' Omar Ngowi said.

'Are foreign owners' names recorded somewhere though?'

'Names?' Ngowi said, leaning back in his chair in amusement. 'Sometimes the names are known, sometimes they aren't. Names are relative. If necessary they become commodities as well.'

Mari smiled back.

'Your real name isn't Omar,' she said.

'No,' he admitted openly.

'You use it because it's easier for foreign business partners to remember and say,' Mari continued.

Ngowi nodded. 'Because they don't care what my parents thought when they were naming me a lifetime ago. Here in Zanzibar we have many cultures: African and Zanzibari. Then Islamic culture brings its own dimension. And then the strange, rich world of the tourists. Endless excitement. Like a nature programme you can watch hour after hour.'

Mari laughed.

'Where are you from?' Ngowi asked.

When they introduced themselves they had only told him their names and hadn't mentioned their nationalities.

'Britain,' Paddy said.

'You are,' Ngowi said to Paddy. 'But these ladies, them I would have placed somewhere else. In Europe, yes. Germany? No, not Germany. Scandinavia.'

'We are all from London,' Mari said, settling the matter. 'Omar,' she continued, leaning forward. 'What would you say if I wanted to buy a flat on Kenyatta Road, in the building with Camlur's Restaurant?'

Ngowi did not bat an eyelash.

'I would say you aren't the first person to ask. People ask occasionally. Maybe once a year. A person will come in who wants to buy Freddie Mercury's boyhood home and make money on it.'

Who owns the building, Mari asked.

Ngowi did not know for certain. He had never found out because there were no flats for sale in the building. Everyone who lived there was local, most of them renting. They weren't much interested in who used to live there a long time ago. Ngowi only investigated the ownership arrangements of the buildings where flats came on sale. Otherwise doing so was just extra work.

'But on this island no property is sold to a foreigner without me hearing about it. Me and the two big agencies. We hear about almost all of the bigger lettings to outsiders as well,' he added.

Despite its hundreds of thousands of residents, in practice Zanzibar was just a small village spread out across a big island, Ngowi said.

'So you would know if a foreigner had bought a flat in Freddie Mercury's building, even if it happened through a local intermediary,' Mari said.

It had become apparent to Ngowi that Mari was looking for information, not a flat.

'Absolutely,' he said. 'But there aren't any foreigners living in the Camlur's building.'

Mari nodded. They had probably found all the information they would get from this office. She stood up, thanking Omar Ngowi and walking to the door with Lia and Paddy following after.

'Where are you off to in such a hurry?' Ngowi asked.

'We have a lot of things we need to look into,' Paddy said congenially.

'You tourists,' Ngowi sighed. 'It *is* like watching a nature programme. Always rushing from one thing to the next.'

They were already on their way out the door when they heard Ngowi speak again.

'The Camlur's building doesn't have any foreign owners,' Ngowi said. 'But that isn't Freddie Mercury's family's real home. They only lived there some of the time, and Freddie almost not at all. You probably don't have time to hear about where the Bulsara family's real house is located though.'

Freddie Mercury's extended family had lived in several buildings in Stone Town. It was no wonder the information about them was confused and that it was misused to lure tourists in.

Once they were all sitting around his small table again, Omar Ngowi told them about all of the places. Taking out a well-worn map, he showed the location of each building as he described it.

There were a couple of places where Freddie Mercury had lived with his parents, when he was still little Farrokh Bulsara. There were several buildings where other family members had lived. At least one aunt had lived in the Zanzibar Gallery building, and right next to the square near the old post office was another similar building.

Further out of town, on Nyerere Road, was the Zoroastrian temple the family had attended. The Bulsara family was from India and were adherents of the teachings of the Prophet Zarathustra. The temple had deteriorated to the point of uselessness, but in its day it had been beautiful.

'They say Freddie went there too,' Ngowi said. 'But there aren't many who would really know, and their memories are beginning to be frail.'

The island was full of places with connections to the Bulsara family. Ngowi pointed out a place in Stone Town along the shore: the Shangani Street swimming beach where Freddie swam as a child with his friends. Outside the city was another similar place at a small cove.

'Achatina Beach,' Ngowi said.

That was a new name. Before it had never really had a name. For a long time it had been a popular swimming spot, and Freddie was known to have gone there often. The boys roamed the island, and of course only men and boys could swim freely with others watching, Ngowi pointed out. Nowadays swimming was not allowed on Achatina Beach because the whole area was protected. Nearby there were some caves where a rare mollusc named *Achatina reticulata* lived.

'There aren't any of the snails on the beach,' Ngowi said. 'But they still call it Achatina Beach. People think it is good that at least some of the beaches can't have expensive hotels built on them even if it is for the sake of a snail that no one ever sees.'

The Bulsara family had been upstanding members of the community, and many older people remembered them well. But what little

Farrokh had turned into was a more difficult matter to swallow. For Muslims, Freddie Mercury's homosexuality was a complicated issue, and although the island no longer boasted a strong Zoroastrian religious community, Mercury's entire public persona was at stark variance with that tradition as well.

People had tried running Freddie Mercury tours of Stone Town to give visiting foreigners a chance to walk in the singer's footsteps. There were plenty of interested tourists, but the efforts tended to sputter because the more conservative locals frowned upon the idea. Once there had even been talk of a Freddie Mercury statue, just for the tourists, but the idea disappeared with a whimper rather than a bang.

'I don't understand what the big problem is,' Ngowi said. 'You wouldn't believe the tourists we see around here all the time. Women wearing almost nothing and men holding hands. But we also have our Tanzanian traditions. And Muslim traditions.'

Freddie Mercury's actual childhood home was located in the more rambling part of Stone Town, Shangani. The area was made up of tumbledown buildings, some of them more than a hundred years old, and the alleys that snaked between them. Mercury's home was simple, a white, two-storey building with dark front doors made of thick timbers. The beautiful old doors were the only thing that differentiated it from all the others.

'The building is not for sale,' Ngowi rushed to point out. 'I've checked many times.'

But the neighbouring building had been sold recently. Two years previously a foreign-owned company had purchased it.

'Does the owner live in the building?' Paddy asked.

Ngowi didn't know. He didn't know anything about the owner, but at the time of purchase he had heard rumours that the sale happened because it was next to the Bulsara family's old house.

Zanzibar was like a small village, the agent repeated, but one could do almost anything to the buildings of Stone Town, any kind of renovation you wanted, without attracting any attention. If the owner stayed on the right side of the authorities, no one came snooping behind the thick walls of the houses to see what was going on inside.

'Can you find out who owns the building?' Mari asked.

Ngowi glanced to the side and thought. Even before he had his mouth open, Mari had the banknotes ready in her hand.

'Of course we will compensate you for your trouble,' Mari said.

'That isn't necessary,' Ngowi said.

With his eyes he counted the total Mari was holding.

'But it is true that I will need a little help to get this information,' he said. 'A little more help.'

Mari added a couple more notes from her wallet. The agent gave no indication he had seen any of this.

'I need to make a few phone calls,' he said. 'It will take time. Here you can't always get people on the phone instantly, unlike me.'

An hour later they had one address and two telephone numbers.

Lia stared at the piece of paper in Mari's hand. When Omar Ngowi had rung his contacts, none of them had understood the Swahili conversations or even realised he had found the numbers until he started writing them on the paper before their eyes.

One of the phone numbers belonged to a man who had killed five people and maybe more. The other belonged to the local man who served as the intermediary for the purchase of the building.

'Why are these numbers important to you?' Ngowi asked.

There was no suspicion in his eyes. He was not looking for more money, Lia realised. He was interested because three foreigners had appeared in his office asking strange questions. A temporary bond of secrecy had developed between them and Ngowi, and he wanted to help them achieve their goal, whatever it was.

Paddy looked at Mari without answering Ngowi's question. Lia didn't know what to say.

'You know that most people in the world are good and decent,' Mari said to Ngowi. 'And then there are those who aren't. And a small number of them are truly sick.'

Ngowi froze. He looked at Mari silently and then nodded almost imperceptibly.

'This address,' Mari said, looking at the piece of paper. 'Next to Tippu Tib's house in Shangani?'

That was how the addresses of the old buildings went sometimes, Ngowi explained – relative to known landmarks.

'In Stone Town there are many alleys with no names. Or if they have a name, it is only Swahili and not written anywhere.'

Tippu Tib was an important person in the history of the island, a notorious slave trader who lived in the 1800s. His beautiful house was on the verge of collapse. No one kept it up, although some families did live in it. Next to it, on an unnamed side street, was the Bulsara family's old home.

Mari asked Lia and Paddy to follow her outside for a moment.

'We can't ring these numbers directly,' Mari said once they were out of the office.

The killer would realise instantly that something strange was going on if he received a call from a foreigner. They had to contrive some way of approaching him, of luring him out of the house in such a way that he wouldn't have time to suspect anything.

'Do you still want me to look for a flat for you?' Omar Ngowi asked from the door.

'No,' Mari said. But she did still have one more request.

'If I want to make contact with this foreign owner through his local intermediary, how would I go about it? What could be an urgent reason for the intermediary to ring the owner?'

The question surprised Ngowi.

'Do you mean something like a problem with the plumbing?'

Nothing so directly tied to the structure itself, Mari said. Something more like red tape, a permit issue requiring immediate attention.

The agent thought for a moment.

Recently a huge property hullabaloo had taken place in Stone Town, he said. A state official had come from the mainland demanding a census of all residents living in buildings older than the 1980s.

'The lists are never right,' Ngowi said. 'They're always missing all manner of information. Someone in Dar es Salaam got it into his head that old buildings have to be protected and so all of the resident lists had to be checked. No one in the government wants to put a shilling into restoring the buildings, but they had to pretend to do something.'

The government representative had demanded that the Zanzibari property officials immediately visit all of the old buildings, list the residents and take their signatures for the archive. A terrible row ensued, mainly because people were afraid of getting caught for under-the-table lease arrangements and because most regulations from the mainland were viewed as unwelcome fiats as a matter of course.

'But people obeyed. Everyone was listed,' Ngowi said. 'And a week later the lists were behind the times again. No one reports anything to the authorities here that they can get away without reporting.'

Mari thanked Ngowi for his help.

'What would it cost for you to forget we were ever here?' Mari asked.

Ngowi picked a wood block up off the ground next to the building and wedged the door to his office open for easy customer access.

'I've already forgotten,' he said. 'I watch you tourists like a nature programme, and then forget you when it is done.'

47.

They had to keep moving as long as they had daylight, Mari said.

They were gathered in her room at the hotel again. The generator was chugging away somewhere – they had asked the hotel to turn it on even though it was daytime because they had to have the ceiling fan. It was still hot though.

Lia stared at the piece of paper on Mari's desk. It burned in her mind. The killer's address and telephone number.

Of course even people like that have flats and phone numbers. They have parents, maybe jobs, maybe friends.

Although probably not this man. At least not any more.

Knowing the man's address and telephone number felt frightening. The thought of ringing the number was even more frightening.

They had to prepare quickly. While Mari was polishing her plan, Rico and Paddy went and used a fake identity to hire them a van. Then they rechecked their gear. All Lia needed was for Paddy to bring along a weapon she could use if the need arose. She didn't want to think any further ahead than that.

Planning the phone calls took the most time. Mari and Lia tried to learn what they could online about Tanzanian housing officials and regulations – the task would have been easier, but almost everything available was in Swahili.

They looked up information about the two phone numbers they had. They quickly found the second man, the go-between in the house purchase, in several different registries and business records. Audax Mkapinga was what the Zanzibari called *papasi*, a tick. One of those small-time businessmen and hustlers who were always trying to sell all sorts of services to anyone who came to the city and who were hard to get rid of.

The other number didn't turn up any public information. Not the name of the killer, not any other contact information.

They spent time weighing the risks associated with the task ahead.

'There could be anything in that building,' Mari said. 'Other people. Traps. Explosives.'

But Mari and Paddy were working on the assumption that the killer was acting alone. They would have to look for possible traps when they went in.

Lia realised they weren't talking about what else they might find in the building. The bodies of two men, Theo Durand and Aldo Zambrano.

They went through the plan over and over again.

How they would travel. Which of them would do what. What things they couldn't let the killer do no matter what.

The plan was to get him out of the house momentarily, overpower him and take the building. They didn't know who was in the house, and he might have help.

During these hours and conversations, Lia learned some new things. The Studio had never just been the exciting bunch of do-gooders she had thought. It was a strike team. When necessary, their skills and determination could combine in dangerous displays of power. The Studio was Mari's weapon. All of their abilities were at Mari's disposal against the enemies she chose.

Mari, Paddy and Rico spoke of what was ahead of them in a way that told Lia volumes. They had faced frightening adversaries before.

When a knock came at the door and a strange man appeared, Lia wasn't even surprised. Broad-shouldered and silent, Ron was only introduced to her. The others already knew him.

Ron was one of Paddy's most experienced associates, a former bodyguard whom Paddy had trained as a private investigator.

'You didn't think I was going to let you run around this island without any security, did you?' Mari asked Lia when the others weren't listening.

Lia didn't have any answer for that. Yes, that was what she had thought, but now that Ron stepped into the light, having a body-guard felt natural. Mari had hired Ron to protect them from a distance. He had been with them the whole time, keeping an eye on the hotel's security, watching whether anyone was following them.

Ron knew what kind of man they were looking for. What he hadn't known was that the plan was actually to catch him, but the thought didn't faze him.

'There aren't very many of us,' he said, glancing at Paddy and Rico.

'Mari knows quite a bit,' Paddy said. 'And so does Lia.'

'Still,' Ron said.

They went over the plan one more time with him. That was enough for Ron.

'You don't know what's going to happen there once you have him,' was his only comment for Mari. He knew who was in charge of the operation.

'No, we don't know,' Mari admitted.

'It doesn't matter much though,' Ron said. 'We have to take this maggot out. Let's get to work.'

They located Audax Mkapinga simply by ringing him. Rico routed the call through an online service so Mkapinga wouldn't be able to tell where it was coming from. He picked up immediately.

'Hello,' Paddy said. 'I'm looking for Audax Mkapinga.'

'I'm him!'

'Where are you right now?'

Near the House of Wonders, Mkapinga said in surprise.

'Thanks,' Paddy said and rang off.

'Won't he be suspicious since the call ended so abruptly?' Lia asked.

'We aren't going to give him time for that,' Mari said.

Everyone in Stone Town knew the House of Wonders, Beit al Ajaib. It was one of the most famous buildings in the city, a palace built in the 1880s. It was the first building in Zanzibar to get electricity, the first building in East Africa with a lift, and once it had been inhabited by a sultan who kept wild animals chained in the courtyard. Its unusual history had given the building its name. Once it had also functioned as a government building with British officials working there – including Freddie Mercury's father, Bomi Bulsara. Some time ago it had been turned into a cultural museum.

Although the building was decaying and a herd of *papasi* on the prowl for tourists roamed outside instead of the wild animals, there was still something special about the building, Lia thought as they arrived.

The House of Wonders Past.

A noisy surge quickly surrounded them. The peddlers could easily provide anything from taxi rides to drugs.

Where was Audax Mkapinga? Paddy quietly asked one of them. The man motioned towards the building.

Mkapinga did not have a reputation on the island as an actual criminal. They had checked that much, but they had no way of knowing what kind of man he was beyond that. That was why they didn't go straight inside to find him, instead waiting until they came across him leading a group of three tourists.

Mkapinga did whatever jobs he could find in Zanzibar. Which included feeding made-up stories to visitors in the House of Wonders.

'The Sultan would ride into the building on an elephant,' they heard him telling the travellers. 'That was why the main doors were built so wide.'

Lia and Rico followed Mkapinga and his tour group from a distance. Mari and Paddy just made sure they got a good look at him and then went to wait outside.

Ron was inside but hidden, ready at his post.

Lia felt her breathing quicken as they walked slowly, tracking Mkapinga's movements but also remaining unnoticed. If Lia hadn't practised tailing with Paddy, she would have had a hard time controlling herself.

Most of the building's sights, beaten-up artefacts and old pictures in showcases, were on the bottom floor. When Mkapinga and his guests ascended to the first floor, Lia and Rico could see that no one else was up there. The upper floors of the building had handsome prospects over the whole city, but many of the exhibition halls were bare.

Mkapinga's group soon grew bored since there was so little to see. Lia glanced at Rico but didn't need to say anything. They were both thinking the same thing: they had to get Mkapinga further away from the entrance lobby.

Occasionally they had to let him out of sight for a moment so he wouldn't wonder about the foreigners following him.

What if he disappears? What if he notices us and makes a run for it?

But Mkapinga's soft voice continued echoing through the halls. Lia looked at the empty exhibition room he was walking through with his group. Large, wooden louvres clacked against the enormous window frames in the light breeze. Although outside the sun was shining, inside was surprisingly dim. There were no lights, since the museum didn't have the resources to keep a generator running during the day.

That was just fine for Rico and Lia. They wandered around the building. Minutes passed. Mkapinga was in no hurry. He knew the tourists he was leading would pay more the more time passed.

In the heat of the afternoon, Lia felt as if she could have stayed in this moment forever. Soon a lot of things were going to happen, including things they wouldn't be able to control. They were following a man who could be hiding anything. The heat created a deceptively calm, sluggish feeling.

Voices came from the adjacent hall again. Rico nodded, and a shudder rippled across Lia's skin. The group of three tourists was leaving, and Mkapinga was wrapping up the tour and collecting his fee. He did it skilfully, without mentioning money at all.

The tourists disappeared to walk around the outer terraces. Mkapinga was all theirs.

He was surprised when they walked up to him in the large exhibition hall at the back of the building and greeted him. But Mari had planned how to dispel his suspicions.

'I'm looking to make some purchases,' Rico said to Mkapinga.

'What kind of purchases?' he asked, looking at them carefully.

'Different kinds. For me and my bride,' Rico said, motioning to Lia standing next to him.

Audax Mkapinga quickly understood where this was heading. A young, foreign couple, interested in Zanzibari antiquities. Maybe also in things that lay in legal grey areas.

Mkapinga's expression said that he was ready to negotiate about anything.

'Who did you hear about me from?' he asked.

'Friends,' Rico said. 'We met a couple in London who had been thinking about buying a flat here.'

'Yes. Indeed.'

All that was in the hall were a few modest posters that no one was guarding. If the building had camera surveillance, it wasn't going to be working now without electricity.

Rico gave Lia a signal with a little squeeze of her hand.

'I'm tired,' Lia said. 'This endless heat.' Lia went and sat on a bench at the side of the hall. 'You men can talk business while I just sit down here for a second.'

Mkapinga looked satisfied as Rico led him to the other end of the room.

'I want to buy some of these old, ornate doorframes you have on the island. But not just ones that look old. Genuine antiques,' Lia heard Rico say.

She saw Mkapinga agreeing – he was pleased to have such an eager buyer. Then Lia saw Ron step into view behind Mkapinga. Something black arced through the air.

The sound knocking out Mkapinga made was negligible. It was drowned out in the complaints of the old, creaky building, the squeaks of the floorboards on the other levels. There was no danger any of the other visitors had heard the sound.

Lia waited for a moment and then went closer.

Mkapinga lay on the floor unconscious. Ron had acted quickly and carefully. Lia saw him holding the small weapon he had used: a Monkey Fist, a round metal ball covered in rope to soften the blow. He had finished up his attack by flinging a black fabric bag over his target's head.

Rico searched their unconscious victim's pockets for a phone. He checked for weapons but didn't find any. Ron stayed to bind his hands and gag him while Lia and Rico took Mkapinga's mobile phone to Mari and Paddy waiting outside.

In the phone they recognised the killer's number. And now they had a name. Filip Dillon.

They stared at the name for a moment. Rico started searching it on the Topo. Hardly any results came back, and none of them offered anything interesting.

'Try Philip with a ph,' Mari suggested.

Maybe Mkapinga had written the name wrong not knowing its modern English spelling.

There were a lot of Philip Dillons, but none of the top hits seemed like the man they suspected of homicide.

'This doesn't tell us anything yet,' Mari said. 'This guy knows how these things work. We aren't going to catch him with just a name.'

Still, the name was important. It changed things: they knew something about him now that he didn't want the world to know. At least about the name he was using, whether it was real or not.

Rico sent a message to Maggie in London and asked her to find out everything she could about the name Philip Dillon.

Mkapinga's mobile turned out to be a goldmine. The memory contained dozens of old text messages, some of which were from Philip Dillon. They communicated in English, but the texts showed that Mkapinga wrote English much worse than he spoke it.

Mari read Mkapinga and Dillon's messages for a while and then wrote a draft of a new message.

Hurry to meet. Tanzaniah govment man come tomorrow morning check house.

She didn't send the message, instead standing and staring at it for a while.

'Too correct,' Mari said.

She added a couple more misspellings and sloppy words. *Huree meet now. Tanzaniyah man comin tomoro mornin check hows.* She sent the message.

A couple of minutes passed and then Philip Dillon rang the phone. Mari let it ring instead of answering. A few seconds later she sent another text to Dillon:

Fone top up gawn. Come here tanx Audax.

Dillon replied quickly.

Where should I come?

Darajani market 15 minuts. Need money govment man, Mari wrote.

On my way, Dillon answered.

Ron returned from the House of Wonders. He had hidden Mkapinga, carefully bound, in a cupboard he found in the remotest corner of the dozen rooms on the top floor.

'No one is going to find him there until we want them to,' Ron assured them.

Quickly they set off for Shangani.

How did Mari know that Philip Dillon wouldn't invite Audax Mkapinga to meet him at his own house? Lia asked.

Mari had sized up Mkapinga in the House of Wonders.

'I don't think he knows what's happening in Dillon's house,' she said. 'Dillon doesn't want anyone coming in. He wants to be alone there in the kingdom he has created for himself.'

They only had a few minutes to prepare to meet the killer in his own world.

48.

They left the van two streets away, partially as a precaution and partially because many of the alleys in Shangani were too narrow for car traffic.

It was almost four o'clock. They still had a good two hours of light. In Zanzibar, sunset was always after six, year round.

If the men hadn't been with them, Lia would have been so terrified she couldn't have moved. Now she was just able to keep it together. Knowing that Paddy, Rico and Ron were there helped, and knowing that they had guns.

Mari also had to have other safety measures she wasn't talking about. She had to.

Lia and Mari walked together, slowly. Step by step they approached the house. The streets were so narrow here, just small lanes surrounded by high building walls. It felt as if someone could have just reached out from one of the houses and touched them at any moment.

They saw the crumbling walls of Tippu Tib's great house and the gaping windows of the upper floors. A bad smell wafted from the large, once beautiful door, like the stench of a mouldy cellar. They circled the building, approaching its corner and the side alley with no name.

Philip Dillon was there.

They recognised him immediately, the man whose legs they had seen on the videos, the man who had killed Berg on their own snuff film.

Dillon almost had his back to them, stopped in front of his house staring at his phone. They saw his strong back and that he was punching buttons on the device.

They just had to go, Lia knew.

Mari walked ahead, a large tourist map held poorly folded in her hands. Dillon heard them coming and turned to look. For a quick moment Lia gazed at the man who had killed five people, a man the likes of whom should not even exist and who did not deserve to walk free in the same world as real people. And yet, here he was.

Lia lowered her eyes. She couldn't stare. Dillon looked surprisingly small and strange. His hair was cropped unusually short. He was a puzzle piece that didn't fit any puzzle, and yet his bearing exuded a focused power.

God help me. Get me away from here.

Lia felt Mari's grip on her arm. Mari went first and Lia had to follow. Mari's will carried them forward. Lia felt her legs faltering.

How would they look to him? Dressed for the heat, sunglasses, the woman in the front carrying a big wrinkled tourist map.

Does he realise who we are? Has he seen us in the city? Does he suspect something?

'Excuse me,' Mari called to him.

Lia froze. Mari dragged her along, encouraging her to continue walking, and Lia thought she had never seen anyone be so brave. Her head was pounding, echoing warning cries of danger.

They walked forward slowly. Dillon was only ten metres away now, staring at them.

They could see his face properly now. A narrow, expressionless face, as if chiselled with a knife. The man whose videos of murder were like personal messages from the Devil.

'Excuse me,' Mari said, 'is Freddie Mercury's house around here?'

Lia walked towards the man in a complete fog. She registered his movements, saw the distance to him growing shorter but didn't know how Mari could continue forward.

Lia couldn't any more. She couldn't even breathe.

Then Dillon took a long step towards them. They saw his strength, his body pure pent-up power. He moved lightly, his phone still in his hand. He didn't say anything.

Dillon looked at them intensely, with something in his eyes Lia didn't recognise. She had never seen eyes like that before.

Was it possible that eyes like that existed in this world, eyes that showed both intelligence and some unnatural presence?

Dillon extended his hand with the phone, pointing with it at their map, the big pile of paper in Mari's hands.

Then Ron appeared behind Dillon, something black flew through the air, the same black arc as in the House of Wonders.

This is a miracle, Lia thought.

Dillon was already on his way to the ground when he shouted and lashed out. The black hood blinded him, but he flailed back furiously with something sharp and shiny that had appeared in his hand. Lia gave a yelp, and Mari jerked backwards, but Ron was prepared for the attack.

Ron dodged and with a quick, calm motion of his arm knocked the knife from Dillon's hand. A shiny silver switchblade fell to the ground. Ron grabbed Dillon by the neck and forced him down to the street.

They heard Paddy coming, running up behind them and jumping on Dillon.

The three men wrestled. Hooded, Dillon was like a bellowing, nearly uncontrollable animal. He pulled and kicked, struggling with his whole muscular body. And then Ron pressed his pistol against Dillon's metatarsus and fired a shot through the silencer. Dillon twisted in pain, and as he collapsed to the ground, it occurred to Lia that she had never seen anything like that happen to a person. It was as if the plug powering him had simply been pulled out of the socket.

49.

Paddy and Ron carried the killer in.

Philip Dillon was still wearing the black hood Ron had put on. It was made of a light fabric that wouldn't suffocate him but kept him from seeing and muffled his voice. As the first order of business, they tied his hands behind his back and bound his feet at the ankles.

The front door of the house wasn't locked, so getting in was easier than they had dared to hope. As they stepped through the dark, low wooden door set in the thick, white stone walls, Lia noticed that she could breathe again.

The order of tasks was clear to everyone. This was what they had been going over all day. They had to find out what was in the building and make sure they were safe. They had to put Dillon somewhere he couldn't get out of and then immediately determine whether his prisoners were in the house and alive.

Ron locked the front door after them and, weapon in hand, checked that no one was in the inner courtyard. Paddy and Rico dragged Dillon, and Mari and Lia followed.

Lia had a hard time taking her eyes off Dillon, even though staring at him was strangely taxing. Here was the killer who had taken so many lives. Even sprawled on the floor unconscious he was frightening. It was as if he might power back up at any second and attack them.

Dillon was wearing heavy, black shoes – the ones they had seen in the videos. His trousers were a lighter, thinner fabric than the jeans in the video images. His shirt was thin with short sleeves.

This man who kills almost for fun wears lighter clothing in hot climates. Just like everyone else.

The thought felt absurd but also helped her snap back to reality. Philip Dillon was a man, dangerous but stoppable.

Suddenly Lia was back in the situation and in control of herself.

The house was big, the rooms connected by narrow, winding corridors. Ron listened at each door for a moment, pistol at the ready, waiting for sounds inside.

One by one the rooms turned out empty.

No one. Neither of the prisoners they had seen on the videos.

Finding that Dillon didn't seem to have any accomplices was a relief, but they immediately moved on to other matters. It was much more important that the prisoners weren't there.

'There must be a cellar,' Mari said.

An old building like this was almost guaranteed to have a cellar. Rico went to look for it.

Paddy and Ron were lifting Dillon off the floor when the kick came.

Lia saw it but didn't have time to cry out. All they heard was Ron's terse grunt when Dillon's legs shoved him in the temple.

Suddenly revived, Dillon had strained his body to the limit, but the kick didn't land hard. Dillon couldn't see where to aim through the bag, and his legs were tied at the ankles, so his effort was imprecise. Ron only staggered backwards.

'Shit!' Paddy yelled, grabbing Dillon by the legs.

He tried to kick Paddy, but Paddy's grip held and then Ron was back in charge of the situation.

'Stop,' he said and pressed his gun against Dillon's head.

The kicking stopped.

'His shoes,' Mari said.

Paddy took off Dillon's shoes. Feeling the touch of Ron's weapon, Dillon didn't try to resist any more.

Paddy and Ron dragged Dillon into the next room and dumped him in a chair. Paddy checked the cords on Dillon's hands and ankles while Ron stood guard.

None of them could speak. Surprising the killer, getting into the house, sweeping the rooms and getting him tied up had been a huge effort. Now the strain began releasing bit by bit.

Only Dillon remained tense. Lia could see his muscles flexing as he tested the strength of the ties on his hands.

When Rico returned and asked Mari and Paddy to come with him into the cellar he had found, there was a moment of confusion.

Paddy didn't want to leave Dillon, but Ron claimed he could guard him alone.

'Lia, can you stay here with Ron?' Mari asked.

Lia blanched.

'Yes... Yes.'

Everyone heard the uncertainty in Lia's voice.

'Take this,' Paddy said, handing her the familiar Heckler & Koch P7.

Holding the pistol helped. Lia immediately felt surer with it in her hands, as if all those hours she had spent practising shooting were concentrated in this moment. No matter what kind of creature Philip Dillon was, he wasn't going to be able to get up and out of that chair without Ron and Lia having time to stop him.

Mari, Rico and Paddy left for the cellar. Lia and Ron waited quietly, both of them staring at Dillon bound to the chair. The only sound in the room was Dillon's breathing. He seemed to be gasping for breath under the hood, but Lia didn't want to take it off. If someone asked her to remove the hood, she didn't know if she would have the courage.

They each took a turn inspecting the cellar. Rico soon returned to ask Lia and Ron to come with him once Paddy was back to guard Dillon.

'Bastard,' Paddy hissed at Dillon when he walked into the room, and in the cellar Lia saw why.

There were three small rooms. Windowless chambers. In the first there were only shelves on the walls with containers, boxes and paper files. In the middle one there were metal buckets filled with something festering with a dark, saccharine smell. Lia had no desire to linger, and didn't dare look at the contents of the buckets.

In the rear room was a desk with computers and a tangle of wires on the floor nearby leading to devices Lia didn't recognise. Somewhere beyond the walls a generator hummed.

All of the computers were on, and Lia could see that Rico had used one of them. On the screen were images. The machine had a camera connection to somewhere. In the small windows they could see movement, people just barely visible in the darkness.

Just barely alive, Lia thought. Theo Durand and Aldo Zambrano.

Dillon's prisoners were alive, but the cameras were connected to an unknown location.

Mari's ability to lead in difficult situations came to the fore again.

'Look at the camera connections to see if you can find out anything,' she said to Rico.

On the stairs leading back up, she told the others what would happen next. They would set up a command post in one of the rooms and hold Dillon there. Rico would concentrate on the computers in the cellar and try to track the prisoners that way. Mari would talk to Dillon.

'The men will be there in the next room. It would be better if Paddy and Ron weren't visible,' Mari said.

'Why?' Lia asked.

'Because Dillon feels uncertain around women.'

Lia knew Mari was expecting something of her too, but she didn't dare think what.

While Ron rejoined Paddy to guard Dillon, Mari and Lia held back for a while to walk through the empty living quarters of the upper floors. Mari wanted to see what was in the rooms.

The furnishings were scant and all well-worn. The kitchen looked downright crude. Half rusted pipes ran along the walls, and the table and shelves were full of used dishes.

A strange sight waited in two other rooms. When they stepped into them, at first they just had to stop and stare. Everywhere there were photographs, framed and unframed. Mixed in were boards plastered with newspaper clippings, but most of the area was covered with small photographs.

All of them showed Freddie Mercury. Other members of Queen appeared in some of them, but as she walked from wall to wall Lia realised there wasn't a single picture without Mercury.

Some of the pictures were familiar, the same pictures from album covers and concert placards used everywhere. But soon they noticed something strange: most of the pictures looked like anything but professional, touched-up advertising images. Freddie Mercury laughing with his eyes shut surrounded by friends. Freddie Mercury sitting on the steps of a building smoking. Freddie Mercury walking down the street so fast all you could make out was a blur.

Philip Dillon had collected hundreds, perhaps thousands of pictures of Freddie Mercury's private life.

'Some fans do this,' Mari said.

Fans could pay considerable sums for pictures that let them feel in touch with a star's everyday life. Friends, domestic servants and people who just happened to meet a star on the street were constantly selling them.

Some of the pictures were already yellowing from age, and they spanned the singer's entire life. Lia noticed a strange effect from the old photographs. Looking at them you started to feel that Mercury was almost present. Philip Dillon must have felt like a part of his idol's life.

'We don't have time to look at these any more closely now,' Mari said.

Lia nodded.

'I need you for something, if you can handle it.'

'What?'

'Come with me to talk to Dillon.'

Paddy didn't like Mari's plan but agreed to it when he heard that he and Ron could monitor the situation from the next room.

'It's enough for one of you to be there the whole time,' Mari said. 'The other can search the cellar and upstairs rooms.'

'What are we looking for?' Ron asked.

'Anything,' Mari said. 'Anything could be hiding in a house like this.'

The door to the next room was open, and Lia could see Dillon on his chair, tied with cords. The cords didn't look as tight as Lia had hoped.

Mari pulled Paddy aside for a second, and they whispered so the others couldn't hear. Lia wiped her brow. The house was hot. In the cellar, Rico was studying camera images of prisoners who had been tortured and might be languishing anywhere. Now they had to concentrate on that, no matter what happened.

Mari returned. Taking Lia by the hand, she squeezed. Without a word, Mari walked into the room where Philip Dillon was sitting, and Lia followed.

That was when she noticed she was still holding the pistol in her other hand.

50.

Mari only left the door of the room slightly ajar.

Dillon sat stock-still, but Lia thought she could see him register the sound of the door. It was hard to say how she could tell, perhaps from an almost imperceptible movement of his head.

The room was completely silent.

Can Paddy and Ron hear us?

Lia heard one of the men clear his throat in the adjacent room. That had to be Ron. Did Dillon react to the sound? She couldn't see under the hood.

Mari looked at Dillon. As the silence hung around them, it was like she was gathering strength.

Finally Mari stepped close to him and yanked the hood off his head.

When Lia saw his face, she gave a cry. She had never seen a person whose cheeks looked so grotesque.

Dillon was chewing his own cheeks. His jaw was grinding feverishly, and his cheeks were sucked in. Rings of blanched white flesh had formed on his face around the places where his molars clenched the skin.

Dillon stared at Mari with eyes wide. He was expecting the person who had removed the hood to attack him.

When that didn't happen, he moved his gaze to Lia.

For a second they stared at each other. There was a mania in his eyes that penetrated her.

Lia squeezed her gun. She felt its weight, and for a fleeting moment considered raising it and emptying her clip into his chest, but then he turned his eyes away again and looked at Mari.

And suddenly his cheeks changed. His pale, red and white mottled face returned somewhat to its normal shape. His jaw was still grinding, but with smaller motions.

He isn't chewing his cheeks any more. He knows he isn't going to die right now.

By the time Mari finally spoke, the silence had been going on for minutes.

'Why did you keep Brian Fowler prisoner for two days before you killed him?' Mari asked.

Lia looked at her in surprise. She hadn't expected a question like that.

Neither had Dillon. The motion of his jaw stopped. He did not reply. A moment later the motion continued.

Dillon had transported Fowler and Evelyn Morris from the Black Cap bar and killed Morris soon after but kept Fowler prisoner for a couple of days before murdering him. Paddy had seen Fowler's body on Rich Lane and noticed that Fowler's bruises were fresher than the other victims'.

'Prisoners are difficult,' Mari continued. 'In the city, keeping Fowler was a risk, even drugged. There's always the possibility someone will notice a prisoner. Why did you do it?'

Lia was trying to keep up with Mari's train of thought.

'Evelyn Morris came as a surprise to you,' Mari thought out loud. 'You were only prepared to take one victim from the Black Cap, but suddenly you had two. She was a woman, but she hung around in gay bars and saw you, so she became a target just like the gay men you took.'

Dillon was now staring at a spot on the wall behind them. Lia glanced at it. His incessant staring at the same spot unnerved her. There was nothing on the wall, only stains.

'Fowler had to wait because you wanted to make the videos at your own pace,' Mari said to Dillon. 'You had planned the kicking and the filming and how and when the videos would spread. It was important for you that the videos were just as you had planned. That's why you don't count Berg as one of your victims, the man you shot in the street. You didn't even get a video of him. He was just an extra obstacle in the way of your work.'

Faint footsteps came from the next room. Ron was going to the cellar, Lia realised. Paddy was still with them, she told herself, trying to calm her nerves. And they had their guns.

Mari's voice was steady as if she wasn't having any trouble staying calm.

'I know what you've done,' she said to Dillon. 'And I know why.'

How could Mari do this? Lia wondered. Mari, who could almost feel other people's emotions within them, almost see what they wanted and even what they thought.

'I know why,' Mari repeated to Dillon. 'You want to use people's disgust towards your killings. You want to use it to make yourself as big as you can. And that's why there have to be victims. There always has to be something new to catch people's attention.'

Dillon's eyes moved, so imperceptibly that Lia wasn't sure she had really seen it. Then he turned his gaze from the wall to Mari. He looked at Mari with unblinking eyes, and Lia sensed that something had changed.

Some part of Philip Dillon that had been gone had just arrived in the room.

After getting her target to react, Mari didn't stop for a second.

'You chose bars Freddie Mercury used to visit,' she said.

Dillon stared at her.

'And you only went inside bars yourself where they don't have security cameras filming their patrons,' Mari continued. 'I only realised that a little while ago. Even some gay bars have CCTV. Some don't want them because their customers prefer more privacy. You knew which ones had cameras. You know a lot about cameras. You probably know everything there is to know about cameras.'

Mari's talking made Lia breathe a little easier. Dillon wasn't trying to attack them – he was listening. Looking at his eyes was still difficult, and the idea that he might look at her again terrified Lia. But everything was moving quickly. Mari was talking. Paddy was monitoring them from the next room. Ron was searching the house. Rico was working on the computers and cameras. Maybe this would end some day.

'What I still don't understand is why you decided to kick to death David Wynn, Evelyn Morris, Mike Cottle and Brian Fowler. I understand harnessing the disgust of your audience but not why it had to be by kicking,' Mari said.

Again a change in Dillon's face. Saying the victims' names out loud made him react. Gradually his jaw set, and the grinding stopped. They only saw a small, slow movement that repeated, like a swallow.

Maybe he was swallowing blood, Lia thought. Maybe Dillon had bitten his cheeks so they would bleed.

'What does kicking have to do with Freddie Mercury?' Mari asked. 'Everything you've done connects to him, but I don't understand the kicking connection.'

A new sound entered the room. Lia flinched, and when she realised the sound belonged to Philip Dillon, it was like an alarm started going off.

He hummed. His lips parted only a little. Out came a low confused, cursing sound.

Dillon was trying to talk. Lia was sure he was trying to swear, but his mouth was full of blood. His voice wasn't working properly, and he couldn't form the words.

Thin streams of red welled out of Dillon's mouth onto his chin. He coughed and swallowed.

Finally his mouth was emptied.

'...rrr,' he managed to say.

Is he swearing?

Finally Dillon got out the slander he wanted to use to abuse Mari. 'Whore.'

Mari continued her series of questions without a moment's hesitation.

Dillon continued his blaspheming. *Dirty fucking whore.*

After recovering from her shock that Dillon had started speaking, Lia quickly realised the track his words were following. He couldn't stand that a woman was talking to him. Languishing bound and helpless in front of two women offended him.

'The kicking,' Mari reminded him.

'Whore,' Dillon snapped.

'The kicking is hard to understand,' Mari continued. 'Kicking doesn't have anything to do with Freddie Mercury.'

'Don't say his name,' Dillon demanded. 'You dirty whore.'

'You don't want me to say Freddie Mercury's name?' Mari asked.

Mari wanted to irritate him by talking, Lia realised.

She wants to take advantage of the fact that he can't stand being subordinate to women.

Dillon's jaw motion started again as Mari repeated Mercury's name. Sometimes he made noises and let out curses, sometimes he just closed up and chewed silently.

'Six videos,' Mari said. 'You have six of them out. Four are left unmade, or at least not released.'

He didn't react in any way.

'Where are Theo Durand and Aldo Zambrano?' Mari asked.

No reaction. Dillon's jaw moved, but he didn't even look at Mari.

'Not in this building,' Mari said. 'But not far from here. You want to keep them close. They're somewhere here in an important place.'

No reaction.

'That means an important place for Freddie Mercury,' Mari said. 'Except Freddie didn't like this island.'

The jaw stopped.

'Freddie never denied coming from here, but he had a strong need to live down his childhood,' Mari said. 'His family was so different from him. He kept in contact with them but at a safe distance from his actual life.'

'Whore,' Dillon said. 'Fucking whore.'

Freddie Mercury had bought gifts for his parents and relatives. He threw family parties. He cared for them and wasn't afraid of showing it. But mostly he lived a completely separate life that didn't include his family. It was impossible to be a world famous pop star and a gay man and simultaneously follow the traditions of a restrained, dignified Indian family.

'That was why he almost never talked about Zanzibar,' Mari said.

'That isn't true,' Dillon growled.

'Everyone close to Mercury knew it wasn't a good idea to talk about this place,' Mari continued.

'That isn't true, you whore.'

'You aren't going to finish what you've been doing to Theo Durand and Aldo Zambrano,' Mari said. 'Or your ten videos.'

Dillon raised his head. He wasn't grinding his teeth any more. He stared at Mari openly.

'You have two alternatives,' Mari said. 'Either you die here or you spend the rest of your life in prison. I'll give you those two options.'

Without waiting for an answer, Mari walked out. Going into the neighbouring room, she started talking to Paddy in hushed tones again. Lia stared at Philip Dillon in confusion.

Momentarily he shifted his gaze to Lia. Then he quickly turned away, and Lia knew he had categorised her as a woman of no consequence.

As she returned, Mari brought Dillon's heavy, boot-like shoes, which Paddy had taken from him. Mari tossed the shoes in a corner, far out of Dillon's reach.

'You aren't walking out of here unless I decide so,' Mari said.

Mari's hard-nosed approach seemed to be working. Dillon's eyes smouldered.

'The order – first the black videos and then just images without any sound,' Mari continued.

Dillon said nothing.

'You were expecting that the people who saw the videos would make the connection before long and add the sound. You hear the songs in your head even without the music playing though. You know them by heart,' Mari said.

'No one knows them,' Dillon said.

Even he seemed surprised he had given Mari anything but more abuse.

'No one knows them?' Mari repeated. 'You mean no one else knows them as well as you do.'

Thus the black videos, Mari deduced.

'You wanted to show everyone that something new was starting. You wanted them to come to understand you one step at a time. And to make the biggest impression you could, to keep capturing people's attention. First all you revealed was the empty darkness inside you. And then your pictures of the killings, without any sound. You knew every new element would increase the media coverage. Every detail you exposed spawned new news stories.'

'Whore,' Dillon growled.

Mari took a paper out of her pocket and eyed it. Lia couldn't see what the paper said.

'That was the elegant explanation,' Mari said. 'The symbolic explanation. You want everything to look like a symbol of something else. But there was something else in that darkness.'

Show Time, Picture Perfect, Reel, Mari read from the paper. Dillon's expression froze when he heard the names, and Lia realised where the paper must be from. In London, Maggie had succeeded in digging up something about Dillon's background and sent it to Rico. Mari had just received it.

As a young man in England, Dillon had worked for a series of film and video companies. He had never stayed at any of them longer than a year though. Maggie had discovered that Dillon had been fired from at least seven firms in the industry.

'You stole from them,' Mari said, still reading. 'You took equipment and used the companies' property so much that it didn't just bother people, it astonished them. The head of Picture Perfect remembers the thing that puzzled everyone the most though was that you spent so much time alone in the darkroom developing old-fashioned film and pictures. You like the dark.'

Mari looked at Dillon expectantly, but he sat silently.

People were usually afraid of the dark, Mari said, but there is also safety in the dark. In the dark you can be who you want to be. You can use the dark.

'Then at work there was the problem that whenever they didn't want to take you along on a job, you turned aggressive. Once you hit a script supervisor because she barred you from coming to a music video shoot. And whenever there were problems in your work, you retreated. You ran away into the darkness.'

Dillon's eyes stayed fixed on the ground.

'You never even got close to Queen,' Mari said.

'Yes, I did,' he said instantly.

'When?'

'At concerts,' Dillon said.

'Those are pretty distant meetings,' Mari said. 'You never got close to them.'

Dillon's mouth shut tight.

When Dillon couldn't hold down a job in the AV industry, he tried something else. First he trained as a paramedic, Mari reported from the information she was looking at on the paper. But that career was cut short too. He passed the tests, but the school's records had a note about his repeated bad behaviour, leading to his dismissal.

'What was it?' Mari asked. 'Did you have a go at some of the female students?'

Dillon's jaw started its nervous motion again.

'No, I doubt it was anything like that,' Mari said. 'You were probably just stealing again. Part of the training was going out with an ambulance crew as an assistant. That was where you saw how to use Anectine.'

Stealing some wouldn't have been difficult for Dillon later on, Mari ventured. 'That was probably the easiest thing in all of this.'

'And I know why you're starving Durand and Zambrano,' she continued quickly. 'You want to make them waste away like Freddie Mercury did before his death. But I still don't understand the kicking.'

Kicking was an ineffective way to kill, but Dillon had made the result certain using Anectine, Mari stated. 'A coward's way to over-power a victim.'

Dillon's jaw was moving more intensely than ever.

'I can only come up with one explanation for the kicking,' Mari said.

Religiously motivated gang killings sometimes involved kicking. When a crowd in an extremist Islamic country stoned someone for breaking Sharia Law, sometimes they also kicked them. Kicking means shame – crushing someone into the muck strips them of their honour in an open display of contempt.

'But you probably also wanted to kick them because it looks so horrifying in the pictures. You wanted to do something disgusting you could do to them alone. Something that would put your videos in a class of their own.'

Lia looked at Dillon's feet. How could he endure the pain of being shot through his instep without even grimacing?

As she looked at the small, clean hole the bullet had left in Dillon's foot, she understood.

Ron knew how and where to shoot. Like Paddy had taught her: if you shoot the edge of the instep, there won't be much blood. The bullet goes through without any risk to life.

Lia felt a chill as she thought that Ron and Paddy knew what shooting people in different places caused.

And so does Philip Dillon.

'You've been planning this for a long time. Years,' Mari said to him. 'Anyone who crossed your path could qualify as a victim, but all of the circumstances were planned: the bars, the kicking, the filming, the disposal of the bodies. And snatching tourists here on this island and torturing them.'

'It isn't just torture,' Dillon grunted.

'If it isn't torture, what is it?' Mari asked instantly.

Dillon closed his eyes.

'Marking them,' he said.

Mari only took a second to understand what he meant.

'The marks on their bodies? The marks burning and kicking makes.'

Dillon remained silent.

'You wanted to make marks on their bodies. Marks like the ones on Freddie Mercury's body when he was dying of AIDS,' Mari concluded.

Especially before modern medical treatments, it was typical for people suffering with AIDS to develop sores, discolouration, and swollen lesions as the disease approached its terminal phase. Dillon had marked his victims with bruises and burns and the last two by keeping them without food and water.

'What is Theo Durand eating in his cell? What's the dark substance you give him?' Mari asked.

'Spices,' Dillon growled.

'Why?'

'So he smells right.'

Mari nodded.

'Freddie liked smells,' she said.

Freddie Mercury loved scents and would often spend large amounts of money on them. The people close to him remembered how careful he always was about his perfumes.

'It's preparing his flesh,' Dillon said.

Lia felt a sudden nausea so strong she had a hard time staying in her place.

'Durand's flesh?' Mari asked. 'Preparing it for what?'

Dillon's eyes shone.

'The fire.'

Lia felt herself go completely cold even though lines of sweat still ran down her face in the afternoon heat. The only thing that stopped the tears from coming was the thought that she couldn't cry.

'It makes the smoke sweet,' Dillon said.

He was feeding Theo Durand a spice so his body would smell a certain way as it burned.

'You sick bastard,' Mari said.

Dillon didn't answer.

'Why gay people?' Mari asked. 'You aren't gay.'

The London police probably assumed the killer had some sort of issue with his own homosexuality.

'That would probably fit the profile they have of you,' Mari said. 'But you don't fit their profiles.'

'No, I don't,' Dillon said.

'You spend a lot of time thinking about what the police have found out about you and what they assume,' Mari continued. 'And you've spent a lot of time trying to get closer than almost anyone else to Freddie Mercury. Is that how it feels since you've had this house? Is that what you get from following his footsteps on this island and collecting pictures only meant for his friends? Getting inside the childhood and private life of the person you worship – it's like learning what was inside of him.'

'I'm not closer to him than *almost* anyone else. I *am* closer to him than anyone else,' Dillon spat.

'But you can't accept that he was gay,' Mari said. 'Everything else is fine for you, but not that.'

'He was led astray,' Dillon said. 'He became... weak.'

Mari stopped. Lia saw how she collected herself.

'*Weak*,' Mari said. 'You mean he became like a woman.'

Dillon fell silent.

'Melina,' Mari said. 'You know who Melina is.'

Dillon's face froze with a cold anger.

Freddie Mercury had sometimes called himself Melina. It was a way of poking fun at himself and his public persona. It was a term of endearment among his close friends.

'You don't like that,' Mari continued quickly. 'It offends you.'

What kind of sex they had wasn't really what bothered people about gay men, Mari said. Most straight people didn't actually think about that since it was too complicated and distant a thing. If homosexuality bothered them, the irritant was something much simpler – the feeling that gays broke gender boundaries. In gay men they perceived a man mixed with a woman.

'That's what they always look for in gay men, the weak side, the woman. And when they think they've found it, they think they've found what's gay in the man,' Mari said. 'Actually it doesn't bother you that he was gay. What bothers you is that you saw a woman in him. A weak woman.'

Dillon stared ahead, not answering, but Lia could see how intense his breathing was.

'You hate gay people because you hate that part of Freddie,' Mari said to Dillon. 'And because you believe that Freddie passed a death sentence on himself in those clubs and bars. You're showing Freddie and the gays and the whole world how much you hate.'

Mari stepped closer to Dillon and stared him in the eyes.

'You don't just kill because you hate gay people,' Mari said. 'You kill because you want to kill and you want to be famous for it. If Freddie Mercury were alive, you wouldn't care about any of these other men. You'd say to hell with all this symbolism. You would try to kill Freddie himself.'

Dillon's scream was so loud that just the sound pierced them through.

Lia closed her eyes so she wouldn't see him screaming at Mari. He wasn't screaming recognisable words. It was an animal roar, rage at being held at their mercy, rage about what Mari had said.

Mari didn't hesitate for a second.

'Where are Durand and Zambrano?' Mari asked. 'Tell me where and you get out.'

Dillon tried to spit on Mari. The bloody saliva didn't make it far enough though.

'Where are they?' Mari asked again.

Dillon stopped screaming. Collapsing back in his chair, he turned his attention away from Mari.

'Bad choice,' Mari said.

Moving to the door, Mari motioned to Lia to follow her with a nod. When Lia stepped into the next room, only Paddy was waiting there. Ron and Rico were still gone.

'What's going on?' Lia started asking, but Mari silenced her with a gesture.

Mari closed the door separating the rooms. Lia watched in wonder as Mari backed up a few metres to the middle of the room, the whole time watching the door.

Paddy handed Mari a gun.

'Get behind me,' Paddy said to Lia.

Lia obeyed.

Paddy and Mari raised their pistols towards the door behind which Philip Dillon sat.

'He's going to try to get out soon,' Mari said.

51.

Dillon got out of the house, out into the dark city, without making a sound. It was inconceivable to Lia. She and Mari and Paddy were in the next room the whole time. They only heard about Dillon's escape when Rico rang Mari.

He had managed to get out of a room whose only exits were the closed door they were guarding and a window with iron bars outside.

Mari talked to Rico for a few seconds and then walked into the room where their raging prisoner was supposed to be. On the floor lay the pieces of cord that had been binding Dillon's hands and feet. His heavy shoes were gone.

The window was open, not broken. Upon closer inspection they could see that the window bars weren't set in the walls. They were attached to the old metal window frame. Opening the window from the inside, you could also push out the iron grating, which they found lowered to the alley below the window.

To Lia's surprise, Mari and Paddy weren't at all alarmed by Dillon's escape.

'We wanted this to happen,' Mari explained.

When Dillon wouldn't tell them where he was keeping Theo Durand and Aldo Zambrano prisoner, the only way to find out was to let him go.

'He'll go to them.'

That was why Ron and Rico were ready outside. They had been through the house and collected all of the weapons they could find. Afterwards they waited outside, ready to follow him.

'And we have another way of following him too,' Mari said as they left.

Mari led them to the van, where Rico was waiting.

'He went south,' Rico reported immediately.

Rico had his tablet open next to him. On the display was a map with a bright, red dot moving on it. On it was the number one, and near it was another, blue dot with a number three. A group of other dots, each with its own colour and number, were grouped to the side of the screen.

'That's Dillon.' Rico pointed to dot number one.

Number three going after Dillon was Ron.

Paddy started the van, and they began driving towards the beach. Lia could see from the Topo's tracking app that they were only a few hundred metres behind the red and blue dots.

'He's carrying a micro transmitter,' Rico said.

The same kind they all were, Mari said. They had been carrying them for security the whole time they had been on the island.

'If something happened, we would be able to see our locations on the Topo at any time.'

Rico had installed the transmitter in one of Dillon's shoes while they were in their possession, out of Dillon's sight.

Rico, Mari, Paddy and Ron had their transmitters attached to their underwear. The transmitter was small, smaller than a fingertip, and you didn't notice it if you attached it under the fabric. It had its own microscopic battery and was in constant contact with a satellite system that passed on location information to the Topo in real time.

'Where is my transmitter?' Lia asked.

In your shoe, Mari said. They hadn't wanted to attach it to Lia's underwear in case she changed clothing at the wrong moment.

'I didn't tell you about it before because I hoped we wouldn't need them,' Mari explained. 'But we had to have something in case one of us was taken.'

Lia understood. Paddy was number two on the Topo app, Mari was four, Lia was five, and Rico was six. It was logical and cautious, but even so, the necessity for such precautions was chilling.

Lia looked out the windows of the van at the dark buildings. Candlelight flickered from some, generator-powered lamps from others.

On the tablet, their small, numbered dots moved in a tight group, with ahead of them Ron and Philip Dillon's dots.

Ron was following Dillon on foot, Paddy said. One of them had to keep Dillon in sight at all times. Ron had volunteered.

Dillon's dot moved slowly but with determination ever further out of the old town.

'He's on his way out of the city, but his foot is slowing him down,' Paddy said.

Dillon's route was following a side road that ran along Nyerere Road, one of the main thoroughfares.

When they arrived at the edge of a large park area, darkness surrounded them on every side.

'The cricket ground,' Mari said. 'All of these places are important for Dillon.'

Freddie Mercury's father had once played cricket on the Mnazi Mmoja Garden pitches, sometimes bringing the whole family along.

Suddenly the Topo's screen flashed. All of the dots disappeared for an instant, along with the map they were moving on. Rico, Lia and Mari stared speechlessly at the machine. Paddy noticed from their silence that something was wrong.

'What now?' he asked.

'A glitch,' Rico said.

Carefully he brushed the screen, and the display came back to life. He breathed a sigh of relief before the display started flickering again.

'Battery,' Rico snapped.

He had charged the Topo's battery, but it had used so much power in the past hours that it was almost on its last legs. The location tracking program was resource intensive because the satellite connection came straight from the tablet. The battery still had power but was significantly degraded.

Rico had a backup, but during the time it took to switch it, they would lose the connection to the satellite completely as the Topo rebooted. Altogether it would take several minutes.

'And there isn't another option?' Mari asked seriously.

'There is,' Rico said. 'The car charger.'

As a last resort, they had the power inverter they could plug into the van's lighter socket. The downside was that the vehicle had to be kept running, and power surges were possible.

'It could cause problems,' Rico said.

'Don't change yet,' Mari replied. 'Not quite yet.'

Paddy slightly increased speed. They were driving about 300 metres behind Ron, who was maybe 150 metres from Philip Dillon as he steadily advanced.

On the dark island, these distances almost felt like kilometres.

When the dots on the screen disappeared again as the screen acted up, Lia thought it would have been easier if she could pray. Not a religious prayer, not words to a single god, but if there were some other place to turn to ask for help.

Mari noticed her anxiety.

'We're going to get him,' Mari said.

Lia nodded but didn't say what she thought.

I don't doubt we'll find Dillon. But what do we do with him then?

Mari rang Ron's phone. That had its risks, they knew. It was always possible that Dillon might be close to Ron and notice him. But as long as the Topo's satellite connection was cutting in and out, they had to know where Dillon was.

'Straight ahead of me,' Ron said in a muffled voice. 'Takes a stubborn bloke to walk with a bullet hole in his foot.'

Ron could only see Dillon as a dark shadow in the gloom, but he was in his field of vision the whole time.

'I can't see you behind me,' Ron warned them.

Mari explained that they were driving without lights, very slowly. They had to follow the road carefully since the street lights were out. They were already a good distance out of the city centre. Here and there around them they saw houses, but no people were about. Along the sides of the road, they mostly saw dense trees.

Mari and Ron broke off their phone connection when the satellite program was working again. They were all visible as tiny moving dots. Dillon's red dot continued on in the same direction.

'What's out this way?' Lia asked Rico and Mari, pointing to the area Dillon appeared to be bound for. Rico couldn't say.

Mari knew one place located in precisely this direction though. The island's old Zoroastrian temple.

52.

A large garden surrounded the ramshackle temple. A fence with iron gates surrounded the garden.

They stopped the van a generous hundred metres away, just in sight of the fence and the old, white edifice behind it.

In the dark, discerning what condition the temple was in was difficult, but the estate agent, Ngowi, had called it a ruin, and everything in the area indicated that it hadn't been used in decades.

'Hard to believe,' Mari said quietly, shaking her head.

She didn't think it was likely Philip Dillon could have been able to use the temple without anyone noticing. Although the temple was large enough, a lot of people walked through the area each day. Using a famous building would be a huge risk.

But Dillon had come here, straight away. They saw his red dot on the Topo, number one, moving only slightly.

'He's listening,' Paddy said quietly. 'And watching to see if anyone is following him.'

Dillon's dot slowly circled the temple grounds, staying outside the fence. Ron followed behind, at precisely the same speed as his quarry.

Mari whispered instructions to the others. Rico and Lia would stay in the car. Mari would go out with Paddy to follow Ron. When Dillon approached the temple itself, they had to be right behind. They couldn't let him reach his prisoners.

Paddy and Mari were extremely careful as they exited the van. They left the doors slightly ajar so closing them wouldn't cause any noise.

Rico held the Topo so the light from the display wouldn't show outside. He and Lia didn't speak. Just watching the dots on the screen moving after each other was oppressive enough.

Dillon was going to the back of the temple grounds, Lia thought. He had to be almost behind the temple now, in a place that wouldn't be visible from the street even during the day. Maybe there was another entrance to the fenced area there.

Then the red dot stopped. It stayed motionless for second after second.

Lia stared at the computer screen.

What if he takes his shoes off for some reason?

The thought gave her chills. She glanced at Rico, who was clearly thinking the same thing.

'Without shoes on that terrain?' Rico whispered. 'No way. He isn't going to take them off.'

The little they could see of the temple garden looked littered and uneven, ground where anything could end up under foot. Why would Dillon go there barefoot?

Ron, Paddy and Mari had noticed Dillon's pause. Lia and Rico saw on the screen how their dots waited for what would happen next.

Suddenly a light flashed on the screen of Lia's phone. Mari was ringing.

'He's just standing still,' Mari said quietly.

'Yes,' Lia confirmed from the satellite locations.

'We can see him,' Mari said. 'He's waiting for something. Maybe he's watching to see if someone is following him. Hard to say where he's going. Somewhere here is an old cemetery, but I don't know what he would want there. I'm getting off the phone.'

'Keep the line open though,' Lia asked.

'OK.'

When Philip Dillon started out again, things happened quickly.

He didn't go to the Zoroastrian temple, he headed off somewhere behind the temple grounds. Lia heard Mari cursing quietly.

'What now?' Lia asked.

'There's another building. A new one that isn't on the map!'

Lia and Rico watched on the Topo as Mari, Paddy and Ron started moving after Dillon at the same time.

'Concrete,' Mari narrated to the team in the car as she moved slowly, almost at a crawling pace. 'It looks like a bunker. The window openings are covered.'

Lia glanced at the darkness surrounding the van. Maybe she could just make out the building behind the temple when she really squinted. Her eyes had to adjust to the darkness first since she had been staring at the Topo for so long.

'Do you see him?' Mari asked.

'Yes,' Lia reported immediately.

Dillon's red number one blinked on the computer screen but he had made good progress now and his tails were falling behind.

'It's like he's going somewhere behind the concrete building,' Rico said.

Then the screen flashed and the satellite tracking program disappeared.

'Shit,' Rico said.

'Bad news,' Lia breathed into the phone.

'The Topo?' Mari guessed.

'Yeah.'

Rico pressed on the machine lightly trying to get more power out of the battery, but the computer was almost done for.

'We can get along without it,' Mari said. 'We can see him again.'

Rico quickly shut down everything else running on the Topo, trying to save the battery. It didn't help.

'What do we do?' Lia asked.

Rico was already getting the car charger out of his bag. Lia started explaining the situation to Mari, but she clearly wasn't listening.

'We keep catching glimpses of him,' Mari repeated. 'He's going somewhere behind the building.'

Lia heard Mari conversing quietly with Paddy.

'We think he's going to get something,' Mari said into the phone. 'Maybe a weapon.'

Rico got the inverter set up and connected to the Topo. When he started the van, wavy lines flashed on the tablet screen and then the display brightened. Gradually the applications came back to life as the power started flowing smoothly.

After a painful wait, the map of the satellite program returned to the screen. Then the blinking dots reappeared.

Lia and Rico stared in surprise at Philip Dillon's red number one.

'He's getting away from you!' Lia hissed into the phone.

Dillon had progressed past the bunker, several hundred metres away.

'He keeps getting further away,' Lia reported.

Mari and Paddy held a hushed consultation.

'I don't think there are any buildings there,' Mari said.

Rico and Lia could see the same thing on the map, which was marked as empty in that area.

'I think the prisoners could be in that bunker,' Mari said.

Lia stared at the dots on the screen. Dillon's dot was far away, hundreds of metres on.

Then Mari and the others were at the door of the concrete building.

'Locked,' Mari said into the phone. 'We have to go in there now. I'm ringing off. Tell me if Dillon comes.'

Lia stared in growing terror at the few small dots blinking on the computer screen. As it stood Philip Dillon was still moving away from them.

53.

When the door opens, heat flares out at them.

Mari follows Ron and Paddy, whose picks have made short work of the concrete bunker's lock. The men go into the building first, securing the entrance.

They have to go in no matter what is there. They know it will be bad, but their time is running out.

And Mari wants to go in because this killer isn't going to finish what he intends to do, not if it depends on her.

Her body is throbbing. She has met evil people in her life but never anything like this.

Before them is a stained plastered wall. The building is strange. Inside it is something odd. It's as if a second building has been built inside it, walls that almost reach the ceiling. And bars.

A weak light flickers over everything. Somewhere there must be a generator. From the ceiling hangs a single darkened lamp. But there is a different shade to the light in the building, and suddenly Mari realises what it is. Fire. Somewhere in here a fire is burning. That is where the stifling heat and smell of smoke are coming from.

They didn't see smoke outside the building. It must be piped somewhere further off or perhaps they just couldn't see it in the dark.

Philip Dillon and darkness. Philip Dillon and fire.

Mari's heart is pounding. Pounding so hard her head is thumping, but she doesn't stop. Somewhere here are two men on the verge of death.

They move further in, and it becomes almost hard to breathe, but they go deeper into the building anyway. Paddy goes left, Ron goes right. Mari follows Paddy, moving along a large, dirty wall. The men have their weapons ready. Mari has hers in her hand but has not yet removed the safety.

Mari looks at the strange, darkened walls, the bars, the small rooms built inside the building. Why would someone build a building with small windowless rooms inside? Then she understands. Cells. Dillon has built cells here, several of them.

How many prisoners does Dillon have? How many people are here dying?

Paddy motions for Mari to stop and moves forward himself. He peeks around a corner. Then he disappears. Ron is out of sight.

Mari waits. Seconds pass, dozens of seconds. A minute. No sign of the men.

Mari waits longer. Her heart pounds, but she does not move. No sign of the men.

Mari removes the safety on her pistol. She steps up to the corner and cautiously looks around it.

First she sees the fire. The flickering flame and the trail of smoke rising from the back of the large room. In the stinging darkness her eyes gravitate towards the light, hard to look at for its brightness, but in the dark, human eyes always move towards the light.

Fire. The painful sight reminds her of something, one detail among the countless Mari has learned about Freddie Mercury. The Bulsara family were Zoroastrians. Zoroastrians keep an eternal fire in their temples, a symbol of divinity and purification.

And then Mari sees Paddy next to the flame. Paddy has fallen to his knees. He is staring at something, staring through the bars of one of the cells. Dear Paddy is just frozen, looking, his hand pressed to his mouth so he doesn't scream.

The sound inside Mari swells. Her ears begin to hum. She moves closer to Paddy and sees Ron to her right. Ron has stopped to stare at the same sight as Paddy. He is leaning against the wall, not out of exhaustion, not taking cover, but just in shock.

Mari can hear the coursing of her own blood, her heart struggling to keep up with what is happening.

When men like this are paralysed, when they are so terrified their legs fail them, it is as though the world has lost its foundation. Everything starts to fall.

Mari goes closer and sees what they see. The sound inside Mari stops. Time stops.

Dear God.

Behind the bars, on the floor of the cell lies a person – the tortured, brutalised remains of a man. A man looking at them.

Aldo Zambrano cannot speak. He is alive but unable to move or make any sound. His whole body is full of burn marks, weeping wounds of scorched flesh.

Mari walks towards Aldo Zambrano. He sees her. They look at each other.

Everything is too much. Man was not made to endure sights the likes of this. Mari makes a sound, not even speech. She sees too much in his eyes. Mari turns away, tries to get away, and then she sees into the other cell. There lies another man. Theo Durand.

His chest is heaving. Durand is breathing painfully, not looking at them. He hears their footsteps but does not dare look at them. He is only waiting to die.

The cells are constructed so the men cannot see each other, but they have heard each other's agony. These men have been kept prisoner, helplessly hearing each other, knowing that the only thing they can expect is death.

A voice inside Mari screams. Someone in her head is screaming. She turns away, from Paddy fallen to his knees and Ron frozen in terror and two men who no longer have anything.

Theo Durand and Aldo Zambrano will never recover from this. There is no treatment, no therapy, no community of family and loved ones that could heal them completely.

They might survive. But Mari knows that no one will be able to remove how they have screamed here and listened to each other's screams.

Mari knows what it is to be subjugated so thoroughly that recovery is impossible.

Mari feels the weapon in her hand. What if she saw Philip Dillon now?

Forgiveness. There will be none. Its time has passed.

She has to get out, if only for a moment. She walks past the cells, turning at the corner of the final cell, without waiting or looking at what might be there.

A table. On the table a mess of papers and pens and filth. Cables. Near the table is a small stool. Philip Dillon sits here sometimes. Here he sits listening to the sounds his victims make.

Mari steps over to the table. On the floor on the other side of the table she sees a pile of clothes, someone's clothing. Zambrano's or Durand's.

Her eyes pick out a drawing in the chaos of the table. Dillon has sat here drawing pictures. And then Mari sees a large book in amongst the papers.

She opens the heavy book with dark covers. A sketchbook. Dillon sketched his videos in advance, making storyboards for them. Mari sees pictures of kicking legs, familiar images from the videos the whole world has seen. She turns the large, thick pages of the book. Close-ups of men who have been burned. Dillon planned it. He planned how to burn Zambrano. He planned everything for filming, plotting out his acts in advance.

Even before she reaches the final pages, Mari knows what is there. The future videos.

Men tortured with fire. And then burned alive. Dillon intends to put them in the fire one by one. Philip Dillon and fire.

The men in the final videos will see what is ahead of them. The victims will see as they are forced into the flames one by one. How they are burned in the dark of the night.

Mari's grip on the book fails.

She reels. She has to get out of here.

54.

The red dot stood motionless.

Lia and Rico saw on the screen as Philip Dillon stopped perhaps five hundred metres from the concrete building. They saw Mari, Paddy and Ron's dots, almost motionless in the building.

How long have they been in there?

Telling time was difficult. From the clock on the display they could see that Mari and the others had only been in the building a few minutes, but even that felt like forever.

What is Dillon looking for? And what have they found in the building?

Lia was holding her mobile ready the whole time. Phone in one hand, pistol in the other.

When the red dot suddenly started moving again, Lia and Rico jumped. Dillon had turned back towards the concrete building and the temple.

Suddenly the wavy lines oscillated on the screen again. The map and dots disappeared for a second.

'No!' Lia shouted. 'What's wrong?'

'It's the charger,' Rico said. 'We must have had a surge when we started the engine.'

The map on the screen wavered again, and the dots trembled. Then the image focused.

Dillon's red dot number one was still moving towards the concrete building. Slowly but steadily.

Lia dialled Mari's number on the phone and then noticed on the screen that green dot number four was moving. Mari was coming out of the building. Paddy and Ron's dots were still motionless.

The phone rang. Mari didn't answer.

Lia and Rico stared in growing panic as Dillon's dot approached inexorably.

When Mari's number four was still moving and Lia saw on the screen that Dillon was going straight towards her, she opened the van door.

'Call Paddy,' Rico suggested. 'Or Ron.'

Rico's face was completely pale. He stared at Lia as she got out of the van.

Then the map on the Topo's display disappeared completely. Lia didn't hang around to listen to the cursing that came from the vehicle as Rico tried to get the program running again.

Lia set off around the temple grounds, towards the concrete building, pistol ready in her hand. She let her mobile ring. Mari didn't answer.

In the thick darkness, the outlines of things disappeared. After staring at the Topo, Lia was having a hard time making out what she was seeing in the night.

If she hadn't been able to slowly start recognising the shapes of buildings and trees, the sandy clearing stretching in front of her would have been like a strange planet shrouded in darkness.

Silently she walked across the sand, glancing at her phone and selecting Mari's number again. Nothing.

When the cloud cover thinned for a moment and the misty light of the moon shone through, Lia noticed a strange spectacle whirling in the air. A moving black swirl was visible against the sky. It fluttered restlessly like an enormous version of the black hood Lia had seen sweep over the heads of two men today.

A flock of birds was whirling in the sky. Or were they bats? Lia wondered. Or maybe they were birds returning from feeding out at sea. She was in a place where she didn't recognise or control anything.

Reaching the back of the temple she immediately saw Mari's dark figure against the light flickering from the door of the concrete building. Mari stepped out of the building slowly, struggling to stay standing.

She had to make a decision, Lia knew. Dillon would come around the building at any moment and see Mari. Mari had a gun, but there was a chance she might not notice him.

Who knew what the killer had gone to get. Maybe he had a weapon again.

Lia couldn't yell to Mari. Dillon was too close. Would Lia have time to get Mari back in the building? Paddy and Ron would be there, and they would be four against Dillon's one. But it was already a matter of seconds. Lia took off running.

Mari barely reacted to her arrival.

Lia grabbed her by the shoulder, trying to get her moving, but Mari just stood there holding her pistol pointed at the ground.

'Don't go in there,' Mari said.

'Dillon is coming!' Lia yelped.

She saw the message get through, but Mari was too numb to react.

Lia dragged her to the ground. Together they pressed themselves into the sand.

They both had guns. Mari wasn't at full capacity, but maybe they would be able to surprise Dillon, Lia thought.

Mari lay next to her. Lia saw the light glimmering from the open door.

The light will tell Dillon that people have gone inside.

They waited for any sound.

Lia didn't dare look up any higher, but she tried to watch the sides of the building. Could she see motion there? Was that where Dillon would appear?

A voice echoed from the building. Someone screamed. It might have been Paddy, Lia thought. It sounded like Paddy. Was he shouting in warning, or just saying something to Ron?

Time passed. Lia was sure that Dillon had arrived at the building and was evaluating the situation. But was he able to see them? It was so dark he wouldn't be able to see them without getting close. They were lying so close to the ground that they could feel a hint of the warmth of the day in the sand.

A sound from the road surprised them completely. Someone was shouting from the van. It was Rico. Lia heard naked fear in his voice.

Rico had been attacked.

The scream stopped. The door of the van slammed shut.

Lia rose up on her elbows. She had to take the risk of looking. Far away on the road their van drove away.

Philip Dillon didn't turn on the lights, he just drove off into the darkness.

Lia didn't go into the concrete building.

She made her decision there, lying next to Mari. Mari, who was completely paralysed by something she had seen in the building and the desperation they had heard in Rico's voice.

What had the estate agent, Omar Ngowi, said? He had showed them the places on the island with connections to Freddie Mercury's family. Most of them were in Stone Town. But a few were a little further from the city. Like the ruins of the Zoroastrian temple here next to her.

Lia always remembered maps. She could always tell directions and distances.

'Achatina Beach,' she said.

Mari heard and understood. Philip Dillon was going in the direction of Achatina Beach.

'Send Paddy or Ron after me. Or both of them,' Lia said.

Before Mari could try to stop her, Lia started running.

55.

The beach was a little more than two kilometres away, Lia estimated. That kind of distance didn't usually take her long, but now she was running on sand and in the dark.

And she constantly had to keep an eye on her environment, searching for signs that might indicate danger.

Right now the darkness also felt like a companion. Lia couldn't see very far ahead, but it would also be hard for anyone to see her.

She held her pistol lightly, constantly at the ready.

Philip Dillon was somewhere ahead of her. He had Rico. Maybe he had already killed Rico.

Mari would have said that this was a job for Paddy and Ron. Mari wouldn't have let her if she had stayed to ask, but Lia knew that this job was made for her. She might be able to get to the place Dillon was going in time.

When a person has run her whole life, her body develops a runner's memory. She knows how long different distances require, and at what points to sprint without really feeling it. Now Lia was going fast. Maybe it helped that she was getting away from the sombre concrete building. Just going inside had shocked Mari out of her senses. Or maybe since she had arrived in Zanzibar, Lia had known that the moment would come when she would have to be stronger than she had ever been.

The night was warm, but the air along the seashore was moving. Running was easy.

Lia sped up. If she didn't think of anything, it was almost like jogging at home. Lia breathed herself forward through the darkness.

Achatina Beach was deserted.

Lia easily picked out their van on the other side of the beach. It was near the treeline, its silhouette visible against the white sand.

The vehicle was creeping slowly through the sand. Without lights, since Dillon didn't want to attract attention.

Lia had never done anything like this. She had confronted armed men, she had tailed a criminal with Paddy, but she had never been in a situation like this.

Especially not alone. Paddy and Ron were coming, somewhere behind her, but she couldn't wait for them.

She moved further up away from the waterline. Her feet sank more easily into the sand, but once she arrived on level ground it carried her weight again.

She slowed to a light jog.

How many minutes had passed? Had Dillon killed someone in that time?

She couldn't think of such things. She couldn't think of anything.

A couple of hundred metres in front of her, the van stopped. Lia slowed as well, glancing back and to the sides, searching for any movement or signs of people.

No one.

She walked slowly through the trees, closer to the van.

Tree roots, fallen branches and foliage protruded from the sand. She had to walk carefully to avoid tripping or making a noise. And she also had to keep her eyes glued to the van and stay aware of her surroundings.

Having a weapon in her hand gave her a strange feeling of omnipotence. As if she could march straight over to the van and use the gun to set everything right.

That wasn't possible though. She stopped.

What was Dillon doing right now? What would Dillon want at this moment?

He wanted two things, Lia thought: to get away and probably to kill Rico because Rico was part of the group that had humiliated him.

Dillon was here because Achatina Beach had once been a favourite place for the boys of Stone Town. Little Farrokh Bulsara swam here. This was not a place Dillon would think of for getting away from his trackers, not so close to Stone Town. He had stopped here to kill Rico.

The vehicle remained where it was. The driver's door opened. Out stepped Philip Dillon.

He was too far away. Lia knew she wouldn't be able to hit him from this distance in the dark. He was favouring one of his feet, the one Ron had shot.

Dillon circled around behind the vehicle, grabbing the rear doors and swinging them open. Lia saw a slender figure sprawled behind Dillon in the van. Rico. Rico was alive. Rico moved, instinctively trying to get away from the killer.

Lia was fast as she ran to the van. She ran faster than she ever had.

Dillon had to hear her coming. Releasing his grip on the struggling Rico, he turned to look.

Lia loped the final metres towards him in a fog. She moved precisely, placing her feet as deliberately as she could. That was the only way to move forward and face this killer.

She saw Dillon's eyes in the dark. There was something in those eyes Lia didn't recognise. He extended his left hand towards her and for a second Lia stared at the outstretched, empty hand. Suddenly she realised he wanted her to look at it, that it was a feint.

The small knife only hit Lia obliquely. Her reflexive dodge saved her, and the dagger only grazed her upper arm.

When Dillon saw that the knife he had thrown hadn't stopped Lia, he grabbed Rico.

Lia was only a few metres from them. She saw the fear on Rico's face as Dillon dragged him out of the van.

Lia fired. She fired again.

She hit him on the outside of his thigh. She hit him in exactly the place you were supposed to hit to stop a man.

Dillon faltered. He didn't even make a sound, but he jerked backwards. Rico pulled himself away. Lia knew her shot had been accurate, and still she saw one of his hands reaching for his trouser pocket.

He still didn't fall.

Lia had to stop that hand. She shot again. And again.

It didn't feel bad. It didn't feel wrong. Firing the weapon was the only way to stop that hand and bring an end to a situation that was impossible to endure.

56.

Once they had Philip Dillon bound unconscious in the back of the van, Rico rang Mari. Now Mari answered instantly.

Rico was still half in shock from Dillon's beating, but he could talk, and Lia wanted to guard the killer. Lia heard Rico briefly telling Mari what had happened. Still she was having a hard time getting used to the idea that the incident was over.

They didn't want to take any risks with Dillon. Rico had gone through his pockets and found two more knives. Dillon had retrieved three in all from his cache behind the concrete building.

As Rico started the van and slowly drove back to the road, Lia kept her gun trained on Dillon.

He was alive. Lia had hit him in the thigh, arm and shoulder. They weren't instantly fatal wounds, but they stopped Philip Dillon. They had to get him to hospital even though Lia struggled against the idea within herself.

A desperate scene awaited them along the road near the Temple.

Mari sat on the sand with a man in her arms Lia could only just recognise as Aldo Zambrano. Mari had found a piece of fabric to cover his upper body with, but his legs showed what had been done to him. They were covered in burns, horribly painful looking ulcers. Here and there intact skin was visible, but it was also swollen. Zambrano was in such weak condition that he couldn't even keep his eyes open.

Paddy sat with Theo Durand right next to them, holding his arm protectively around the man. Durand was conscious but looked at everything with wide, frightened eyes. He stared at the van as it drove up. He couldn't grasp that his ordeal was over.

They couldn't put these men in the same space where Philip Dillon lay bleeding.

Soon Ron showed up, breathing hard. He had run after Lia and then turned back when he saw the van returning.

They didn't talk much. There wasn't much to say.

Lia saw that Mari had taken control again. Holding Zambrano in her arms, she gave Ron his instructions. They would take Dillon to the concrete building and tie him up there to wait.

'Show him to us,' Mari said.

Ron lifted the unconscious man out of the rear of the van and carried him for all to see. Lia understood why. Mari wanted Aldo Zambrano and Theo Durand to see their torturer subdued. Mari wanted to give them an assurance that Dillon and their nightmare would never return.

Durand stared at the bullet-riddled killer. Zambrano could barely open his eyes but looked for a moment at the man sprawled in Ron's arms. Then he quickly turned his head away.

Ron took Dillon to the concrete building, and while he was securing him, the others helped the former prisoners into the van.

Before leaving, Mari took one more trip to the building. She wanted to see how Dillon looked now.

When she returned, she also brought one of his shoes, the one with the micro transmitter. Ron stayed to guard Dillon.

'Will he live?' Paddy asked.

Mari nodded. Starting the car, Paddy set off driving towards Stone Town.

They took Durand and Zambrano to the city's small hospital. Two night nurses were on duty, both older men who during their careers had seen everything from scuba diving accidents to house fire victims. But both were shaken when they saw the condition Durand and Zambrano were in. One of them instantly ran off to ring a doctor.

'The police will come in the morning,' Mari told Durand.

She held a hushed conversation with him before the nurses wheeled him off on a stretcher for examination.

Durand had agreed not to reveal them to the police, Mari told the others. Mari had told him that Dillon killed one of their friends. That was enough of an explanation. Zambrano had been so detached from the world through the events of the night that he wouldn't be able to say anything to the police that could harm them.

The night nurse asked them into the reception area to collect their contact information.

'Don't worry about that,' Mari told the nurse. 'You go and ease their pain. The one with the burns could die of them.'

Blanching, the nurse rushed off to arrange first aid for his new patients. Mari, Lia and the others slipped out without anyone else noticing.

They returned to pick up Ron.

On the way, Mari and Paddy made their decision about Philip Dillon. They would leave him in the concrete building under lock and key. It was possible he would die of blood loss before the police arrived, but that was a risk they decided to take.

They didn't go into the building. Paddy went to call Ron out, and they closed the door carefully.

'He isn't going to escape again,' Ron said when he climbed in the van.

Ron had bound Dillon's wounds. He had lost a lot of blood and seemed in critical condition.

'If he ever walks again, it's going to be slowly and with a limp,' Ron said.

The receptionist at the Cinnamon Hotel was piqued when they appeared in the middle of the night, but Mari silenced him with a glance.

Mari announced they would be leaving first thing in the morning on the first flight out. The manager could start arranging them some food and writing up the bill.

Ron collected his things from his own hotel, which was close by, and joined them back at the Cinnamon. They were all worried about Rico.

'I might have concussion,' Rico admitted.

His head ached badly and his brain wasn't quite working right. When Philip Dillon had suddenly appeared at the van, he hit Rico hard, several times. They could also see the shock from the events of the night in him, but that was true of all of them, Lia thought.

Only Mari was strangely calm. At the Zoroastrian temple, she had staggered out of the concrete building, barely able to stand, utterly beaten down. Now Mari's strength had returned, and Lia thought she seemed to have regained the mental balance she had lost over the previous weeks.

Even a night with no sleep didn't seem to drain Mari's ability to concentrate any more. She simply handled things one at a time.

The first morning flight to the mainland departed a little before eight o'clock. It was already light.

As they were waiting for their flight at Kisauni Airport, Paddy made an anonymous call to the local police and told them where to find Philip Dillon near the temple and Audax Mkapinga waiting tied up in the House of Wonders.

'We wouldn't leave like this if this were just going to remain a matter for the Zanzibari police,' Mari told Lia.

And it didn't. A few minutes later, an airport official came and announced to all the passengers that their departure would be slightly delayed. No explanation was given, but it soon became apparent.

Without any prior announcement, a private jet arrived. They watched from the departure terminal windows as the passengers of the mysterious flight disembarked onto the tarmac.

'Interpol,' Paddy said quietly.

There were four police officers, easy to identify from their bearing despite their civilian clothes. The plane contained no other passengers. The police were quickly ushered through the border formalities, and Mari, Lia and the others watched from a distance as the detectives exited the terminal to cars waiting outside.

When the announcement came for their departure, Mari sighed with relief. Despite the arrival of Interpol, Durand and Zambrano's fate still weighed on them. But staying on the island was too big a risk for the Studio team.

On the return flight, they mostly slept. Afterwards, Lia remembered three things from the trip.

First was the relief when Rico visited the clinic at Nairobi airport while they were waiting for their flight to London and was given a clean bill of health. He had concussion, but it wasn't dangerous, and the other marks were just bruises.

The second was the feeling that came over Lia when she saw Mari and Paddy sitting side by side in the plane. Quietly they took adjacent seats, Lia, Rico and Ron noting it silently and letting them have their space. When Lia stood up to pace the aisles and stretch her limbs during the flight, she saw Mari and Paddy holding hands. Lia wasn't sure exactly what feeling it gave her, but it was a good one.

The third was a startling moment just before arriving home. They were waiting at Heathrow Airport in the long, winding immigration queue, numb from exhaustion and from everything they had experienced. In the queue, Rico handed Lia the Topo, which was displaying new information that had just come from Maggie. Maggie had found one more detail about Dillon's previous life.

His full name was Alexander Philip Dillon. Once she had found his original first name, which he had dropped, that opened up new avenues. Dillon had lived as a ward of court in his childhood, moving from one orphanage to another. He had good marks in school, but his records also reported constant discipline problems. Before taking odd jobs in the film industry and trying to become a paramedic, he had applied to the police force and the army. Both turned him away.

Years ago some of Dillon's amateur videos had won two small prizes. In one of them, he had cut together pieces of Queen videos to create a completely new work.

Maggie had found out that Dillon was an avid participant on several Queen fan forums. Time after time the forum administrators had tried to ban him because before long he always ended up belligerently slandering other forum members.

Dillon had a rented flat in Kensington, only a kilometre from Rich Lane where he had dumped Brian Fowler's body and shot Berg. Dillon's flat was near Logan Place, where Freddie Mercury had lived for years and also where he died. The general belief was that Mercury's ashes had been spread in the garden of his home – after his death, the star had been blessed in London in a Zoroastrian ceremony and cremated.

'That could explain the fire, Dillon's fire,' Mari said after seeing the information. 'Or part of it.'

But no one from the Studio would be going to Dillon's flat in Kensington. That task belonged to the police.

Reading simple, concrete information instantly cleared Lia's woozy head. The killer who had caused all of this, and whom they had left barely alive in Zanzibar waiting for the police to arrive, was really just a person.

'But only just,' Mari said. 'There is probably still a great deal about his background that has never been recorded.'

Someone like Dillon could spend years causing trouble and intimidating people without it ever leaving any specific evidence.

'That's all still ahead of us,' Mari said. 'He is still going to become a celebrity, in a way.'

That was why Mari had gone back to see how Dillon looked as he lay bound, shot and unconscious on the floor of that concrete bunker in Zanzibar.

'I was proving to myself that we got him.'

57.

At the Studio, Maggie had cleaned the Den.

It was a sort of sign, they knew. Maggie hadn't thrown much away, she explained, just gone through things.

Lia liked the way Maggie had arranged everything. Berg's tea tins, the Bettys and Taylors, made up a row of everyday memories.

Maggie saw immediately from their faces that asking about the trip was not a good idea yet. Mari said she would tell her in detail a little later.

But Maggie had yet more information to share about Philip Dillon. The whole time she was finding more, one bit of information leading to the next. Dillon had been convicted of a violent offence. Maggie hadn't unearthed the details yet, but one of Dillon's work colleagues at Reel remembered him getting sacked after his conviction for some sort of attack.

The employee, a woman now in her sixties, had been reluctant at first to open up about the incident on the phone. When Maggie said she was from the police and investigating a possible crime, the woman became more talkative.

'I shouldn't wonder if Philip has done something unfortunate,' she had said. 'Sometimes the things he said could make your hair stand on end. He spoke of people with such brutality.'

Videography had been an obsession for him, something he went on about constantly. Other people in the industry talked about work all the time too, but the things Dillon said gave people the feeling he didn't have much of a life.

Dillon desperately wanted to do something more than technical background work, to participate in shoots himself, but after working with him even once, no one ever wanted him on their team. He had been too uncompromising, unable to accept anyone else's decisions.

'Actually, his technical skills in the editing room were good,' the woman had said. 'And his lighting. People would say that others knew how to use light, but he knew how to use the dark.'

'Use the dark?' Maggie had asked.

Dillon had been an expert at using shadows and darkness.

'Sometimes he said that there was always more going on in the dark than people knew,' the woman had said. 'That when there was darkness in an image, viewers started to think more, to use their imaginations. The others thought his dark shots were strange and creepy, but for him I imagine they were beautiful.'

Maggie also had something to show them.

A backlash to Philip Dillon's videos had started online. His work was still spreading, still reaching new viewers. But a few days ago another kind of video had started appearing. Maggie showed one after another on the big display in Mari's office.

All of them also featured music from Queen. But all of the images were of people hugging.

The first one had come from Denmark. A young man who liked Queen had been so disgusted by the kicking videos that he wanted to do something. Going to the main square in the city where he lived, he asked a complete stranger, an old woman, if he could hug her. Confused, the woman nevertheless agreed. They stood in the centre of the small city, a young man and an old woman, hugging each other for several minutes. The images showed how after her initial embarrassment, the woman relaxed in the young man's arms. By the end, both had tears in their eyes.

The man's friend taped the hug, and then they dubbed the Queen song 'Spread Your Wings' in the background and uploaded it. Within two days it had gathered tens of thousands of views and nearly as many followers. Now similar video clips were coming in from all over the world, always with someone going and hugging a stranger to a Queen soundtrack.

The BBC had done a story about the meme during their main evening broadcast the day before. Dozens, perhaps hundreds of videos had cropped up during the following day in Britain alone. The viral campaign even had a name: *Someone Cares*.

'A self-correcting system,' Mari said.

Lia understood.

Once people had enough of evil, once their normal fascination with it was satisfied and some emotional threshold was crossed, they wanted to do something to counterbalance it. They made gestures of good will, fixing what had been broken.

How was Craig Cole doing? Mari asked.

Quite well, Maggie said. Cole and his wife were moving to Bradford so he could start his new job at The Pulse. There had even been a story about him in the local paper.

'I think he still has a long career ahead of him,' Maggie said.

But Cole still always wondered why Bryony Wade had chosen him in particular as her victim and whether she might try to blackmail him with information about his affairs, Maggie said.

Mari looked thoughtful but didn't say anything.

Lia wandered the Studio. She called *Level* and left Martyn Taylor a message saying she would be back at work the next day.

Despite her exhaustion, she had to keep finding things to do. The idea of just going home felt strange. When Mari asked Lia to go with her to see Bryony Wade, she didn't hesitate for a second.

Mari had found Bryony's phone number somehow. The girl had agreed to a meeting near her home in Newham when Mari told her she was a reporter with a new entertainment magazine that was planning a big story about her.

Bryony was waiting at a table at a café called the Grub Stop, focused on her phone. She didn't shake their hands when they sat down, just glanced at them quickly.

Bryony was a little too big for her clothes, Lia thought. Maybe she was trying to attract male attention. The straps of her bra pressed into her skin, and her tank top didn't cover quite enough.

Mari had looked into the girl's background. She had no police record. Everything indicated a peaceful, middle-class life. Her mother worked in an estate agent's, and her father was a manager in a transport company. The Elizabeth Simms School in Newham was a bit better than average, and Bryony had reasonably good marks.

The stunt she had pulled on Craig Cole didn't fit the picture at all, but meeting her face to face they saw more signs of a surprising natural callousness.

'I'm not talking to any more reporters until we agree on a fee,' Bryony announced.

Her gaze didn't waver at all as she demanded the money. She had practised this in dozens of conversations with other journalists.

'And you have to pay more to go to the house,' Bryony said. 'But no pictures unless you pay for that too.'

Nothing in the girl's background pointed to this sort of vulgarity, but somewhere she had learned to be demanding.

'I understand,' Mari said kindly. 'But we don't intend to pay you anything.'

The girl's expression changed. She wasn't prepared for this.

'Then I'm not talking to you,' she said.

'Yes, you are,' Mari said. 'I don't think you'll want your parents present for this discussion. Although of course we can get them if necessary.'

Bryony maintained her defiant silence as Mari said what she had come to say.

'You're lying,' Mari said. 'And that's fine. That happens. When I was a kid, I had to make up all kinds of self-defence mechanisms so my parents wouldn't walk all over me.'

Mari said that nothing in her allegations against Craig Cole was true. The problem was that it was difficult to prove. It was difficult, almost impossible to determine what had happened in the dressing room at the Elizabeth Simms School.

'What I know is that Cole didn't touch you. He didn't even see you,' Mari said.

'That's a lie,' Bryony snapped.

Her powers of speech had returned.

'You don't know anything about anything,' she said. 'That man groped me through my shirt. And then under it.'

She pointed to her neckline.

'Here,' Bryony said. 'He shoved his hand down and fondled my breasts. He didn't even take his ring off. I felt it.'

Mari leaned in closer and looked at the girl carefully, especially her chest.

'Do you like what you see?' Bryony asked.

Mari shook her head.

'It isn't about that,' she said. 'How did Cole put his hands on your breasts?'

'What?'

'Show me how his hands were. What position they were in.'

Bryony's chin rose.

'That isn't anyone's business. You're a perv.'

'I don't think he was even near you. You went into the same room, into the dressing room, but Cole never got anywhere near you.'

'He did,' Bryony said. 'I felt his ring when he touched me.'

'You keep talking about that ring,' Mari said. 'You've repeated it in almost every interview you've given. It sounds convincing. And sensational – to have an under-age girl feeling the wedding band of a man who's been married for decades against her skin. But you haven't mentioned any other details. You haven't known how to invent them.'

Bryony's face closed up. She was shutting them out, shutting out the world, Lia thought.

'Before we came to meet you, I thought that you really might have experienced some sort of sexual abuse in your life,' Mari said seriously.

Lia hadn't expected such directness, but Mari remained perfectly calm.

'Now when I see you, that doesn't seem as likely,' Mari said. 'You talk about it so coldly. You're too distant. I've listened to your voice, now and when you rang the radio show. What you said on the radio sounded rehearsed. That was when I realised you'd worked it all out beforehand. Your real stroke of genius was that you attacked Cole so publicly. Real victims of harassment avoid confrontations, but you went looking for one. You'd seen all the old famous blokes in the tabloids who got caught meddling with young girls, and you realised how hard it is to prove anything like that. You succeeded because you took the whole thing to a new level. You turned it into a public fight.'

The girl didn't move. They could see how much she wanted to escape. Her eyes were looking for something to latch onto but avoiding Mari. Her gaze rested on Lia but then turned away.

For a moment there was perfect silence. Then Mari snapped back to the moment.

'You poor girl,' she said. 'You didn't have any real reason for what you did. Unless you count boredom with the world and what you think life has in store for you.'

Bryony took a breath. It didn't make any sound – they could just see it on her worried face.

'You wish something would happen,' Mari continued. 'You thought you could get some attention and some sympathy, and maybe a little money. You could stand out from the crowd.'

'You don't know anything, you fucking cow.'

Bryony drew strength from swearing. She retook control of the situation by berating them. Lia and Mari watched as a stream of vicious slurs began flowing out of the girl's mouth, and they saw how alive it made her feel. Surprised glances came from a nearby table and behind the café counter.

In some ways there was something admirable in her strength, Lia thought. She brimmed with belligerent self-confidence.

Where do they come from? Lia thought. *Where do these young people come from who can be so indifferent? How does a teenager come to see other people as nothing more than either stepping stones or obstacles?*

Mari stared at Bryony, completely transfixed by her hard expression. Nothing could get at Bryony Wade. She might never feel weakness.

'You don't regret anything,' Mari said. 'You could even do it again, or something like it. It worked so well. That's why you don't regret it.'

'No, I don't,' Bryony said.

'Why Craig Cole?' Mari asked. 'Do you know him? Do you know anything about him?'

'Only that he groped me,' the girl snapped. 'Isn't that enough?'

'But he didn't grope you,' Mari said. 'Craig Cole never touched anyone.'

Lia glanced at Mari. The tactic was straightforward: if the girl knew anything about Cole's affairs, it would come out now.

'I didn't say he groped anyone else,' Bryony said. 'But we were in the same dressing room, and he touched me.'

'No,' Mari said. 'You hoped he would touch you. You hoped that something like that would happen, that a famous man would want you and give you attention. But Cole didn't even notice you. He doesn't remember ever seeing you.'

A grimace flashed across Bryony's face. She was so agitated she couldn't control her expression.

'Is that what it was?' Mari asked. 'Cole didn't even notice you. Is that why you did it? You had a brush with fame and it just ignored you?'

Bryony stood, tipping over her chair. The sudden movement startled Lia and Mari. Bryony seemed as if she wanted to attack them. But instead she walked out of the café, without looking at anyone, her coat hanging open.

'She isn't going to tell her parents about this,' Mari said.

Her parents were the last people Bryony wanted to know, Mari guessed.

Mari spent the long walk to the Tube station venting the surge of emotions she had felt in the café.

'Poor girl,' she said.

Did Mari believe that Bryony had really made her accusations just for fun? Lia asked, astonished.

'Of course,' Mari said. 'She's fourteen and she's realised what's in store for her. She doesn't want to be just anybody, so she decided to be a molested teenager. Tricky girl.'

The most important thing for Bryony was feeling powerful. She wanted it so badly she was ready to make false accusations against anyone, even a universally beloved radio announcer.

'Her parents may know on some level,' Mari said. 'But if they know, they don't want to know. It's too hard.'

And what if Bryony really had been mistreated? Lia asked.

'I doubt it,' Mari said. 'I could see how attracted she was to the feeling of having the upper hand. She doesn't act like a teenager who's been forced into anything. She was the one who wanted power. Sexual power over an adult man.'

Kummajainen, Mari said.

An oddity. Bryony was unique, but not incomprehensible by any means. Her behaviour had a logical basis. Lots of teenage girls enjoyed sexual dominance, just like anyone else, Mari suggested.

'She doesn't know anything about Craig Cole,' Mari said. 'She just used Cole because he happened to be there and she could use him. Bryony got lucky when Cole didn't mount more of a defence.'

They left the Tube at Warren Street. Lia knew where Mari wanted to go: the Fitzroy Art Museum, her favourite place in London. There was one piece of art in particular that Mari liked. She could sit for hours sometimes watching it just to calm down and let the world spin on its way.

As they walked to the museum, Mari rang Craig Cole. He answered in Bradford.

Bryony Wade didn't know anything about him, Mari reported. She had targeted him because he had visited her school and she had decided to take advantage of the opportunity.

'I don't think you'll ever hear from her again,' Mari said.

'Thank you,' Cole said.

His first broadcast on The Pulse was scheduled for the next day.

'Everything is just fine here,' he assured Mari. 'More so than in a long time, now that you've told me that about the girl.'

How could he ever repay Mari and her colleagues for their trouble? Cole asked.

'That isn't necessary,' Mari said. 'But if I ever think of something, I'll ask.'

The rustling of the thin black tape was familiar to Lia. She had sat in front of this piece of art in the Fitzroy Museum many times with Mari, watching as the two loops of plastic tape thrown between two large fans gyrated in the air current they made.

Double O, the work of a Lithuanian artist, always calmed Mari's mind. Usually she wanted to think about anything apart from the Studio's work when she was here, but now she couldn't shut it out of her mind.

'I think Craig Cole will do all right now,' Mari said.

Lia nodded.

'Maggie can keep in contact with him,' Mari said. 'And the rest of us can listen to his broadcasts online sometimes. That will tell us how he's doing. You can always tell from a person's voice.'

Lia guessed in what direction Mari's thoughts were turning. Philip Dillon and the men he had tortured in Zanzibar. It was clear that

Mari and the rest of them at the Studio were thinking about the trio's future.

'We aren't touching Dillon,' Mari said.

She said it quietly so no one walking the corridors of the museum would hear, but Lia could hear the resolution in her voice.

'Dillon belongs to the police and the justice system now,' Lia said.

'And the media,' Mari said. 'And everyone who is going to make him famous. His audience.'

Lia closed her eyes and tried not to think about it, but heavy doubt loomed in the back of her mind.

Did we make a mistake leaving Dillon alive? Should we have just let him bleed to death?

'I've been thinking about forgiveness,' Mari said as if in answer to Lia's mental questions. 'I haven't forgiven him. And I won't.'

Only the norms of civilisation and rationality had prevented them from taking Dillon's life in Zanzibar. They thought that was what they were supposed to do, so they did it.

'People have a hard time believing extremes of greed and cruelty are real, as if they were some sort of illusion,' Mari said. 'Or just a form of mental illness. They aren't. Dillon's crimes were perfectly logical acts, just completely inhuman. His brutality makes him seem sick, but he is responsible for his deeds.'

And it wasn't up to them what kind of celebrity Dillon would achieve.

Lia listened to the hum of the fans and the quick crackling of the rotating tapes and focused her thoughts elsewhere.

Theo Durand and Aldo Zambrano. They are more important now.

'I have to go back to Zanzibar,' Mari said. 'It was important to get you and Rico home, and we all just wanted out of there. But I should have stayed. I'm going back with Paddy.'

She gave a brief sketch of her goals. Only two of them needed to return to the island. Each of them would focus on one of the victims – Mari on Theo Durand because she knew a little French. Both men were in intensive care, probably detached from the world by the strong drugs they would be on. But they had to return some day, and Mari and the others had to make sure that Durand and Zambrano received the best possible care. Once the men returned home, Mari and the others would have to consider how to support their families.

'It's going to be dreadful,' Mari said.

They had to prepare the families to deal with the post-traumatic stress reactions and their own shock, and do it all with as much secrecy as possible.

'Isn't there any other way?' Lia asked. 'Can't we leave all that to the authorities?'

No, Mari said. These men would need small miracles now. They would need treatment programmes that weren't available anywhere. But they could be created, with enough money and work.

'I am a psychologist,' Mari said, and Lia understood that she was saying it out loud as much to assure herself as anything. 'This is my duty. Paddy and I are leaving tomorrow morning.'

Then Mari immersed herself in her thoughts again, watching the captivating randomness of the black loops of tape of *Double O* as they darted about in the air.

Lia looked at her friend. Just now she was filled with admiration and sympathy for Mari, but all the while doubt gnawed at the back of her mind. Would she ever know Mari completely?

58.

At home in Hampstead, Lia showered. Then she rang her parents in Finland.

She saw Mr Vong in the garden with Gro and went out to meet them. Gro was overjoyed at their reunion, even though Lia had only been gone a few days. The time had felt much longer for both of them.

Lia stroked the dog, bewildered at how happy such a mundane meeting could make them both.

Mr Vong had read the book Lia gave him. He thought it was very moving.

'I had no idea what a wonderful namesake Gro has,' Mr Vong said. 'I should follow the news more carefully.'

'I don't know about that,' Lia said. 'Maybe it's better to keep your distance.'

She didn't ask whether he wanted to keep Gro. She could see it in both of them.

'Do you know, whenever we're in the stairway, Gro's tail wags at one door every time? Your flat, if you're home,' Mr Vong said. 'If you aren't home, it doesn't wag.'

Bless you, Mr Vong. You always know the right words to say.

After her fitful night's sleep on the plane and the restless day afterwards, Lia didn't have the energy for an evening jog. After what had happened to them, in London and in Zanzibar, readjusting to normal life was difficult. It was as if she still had to be on constant alert because a new emergency could arise at any second.

On her home computer, she watched a few *Someone Cares* videos. She glanced at the news. An article about Zanzibar had appeared on the *New York Times* homepage: a major police operation was ramping up, but no details were available other than that the island was on lockdown. Due to ongoing police interviews, no one was being allowed off, not even tourists.

She wondered whether she should text Mari, but then she decided Mari had probably already seen and would want to go to the island anyway.

She considered ringing the gun range. It wasn't late, and maybe Bob Pell would have a free lane.

But maybe not.

Zanzibar was still too close, the memory of running through the dark with a pistol in her hand and shooting Philip Dillon. She would want to experience the feeling of a weapon in her hands again though. Not now, not soon, but someday. As far as the proprietor went – Bob Pell could be an extreme last resort, someone to call if being alone became utterly unbearable at some point. Now being by herself was a relief.

One person was on her mind the whole evening. She logged on to Skype and tried to ring, but there was no answer. She left the machine on and logged in. Maybe her call would be noticed.

Half an hour later, Lia heard the Internet phone app trill. Mamia was on the line just returning Lia's call.

Getting the video connection working took a few seconds. Mamia's face betrayed her irritation.

'Where on earth were you two this time?' she asked.

Mamia had been worried and vexed that Mari hadn't responded to her messages.

'You kept an old lady worried for a week,' she said reproachfully.

'Oh, we were fine,' Lia said. 'Didn't Mari send you a text message a few days ago?'

'Yes, she did. It just said, "On a trip, talk when we can."'

They had been in Africa, Lia said.

'Africa? Any more precise coordinates?' Mamia asked.

Lia laughed.

'Ask Mari.'

'I will. Is she all right?'

Lia thought for the space of a long intake of breath.

'Yes. Yes, she is. We all are.'

Mamia's face came closer to the camera.

'I can even see through this pale computer screen that you're not telling me everything again. But that's fine. Just don't think I don't notice.'

'Mamia?'

'Yes?'

'I have a question.'

'OK.'

347

'Tell me what happened that time at your family reunion, back all those years ago at Vanajanlinna Estate. Tell me all of it.'

'You certainly are persistent,' Mamia chided gently. 'You seem to remember everything.'

Lia waited. She saw Mamia weighing the limits of their confidence.

'You said once that night feels different in London from here,' Mamia said. 'Because there are more people to share it with.'

The same thing went for information, she said. Sometimes information changes according to how many people share it.

Lia nodded. Mamia's eyes glistened a little. Maybe it was from the light reflecting from the screen, or maybe she was moved.

'It wasn't anything terribly dramatic that happened,' Mamia said. 'So much time has passed since then. It was mostly just sad. Such old, sad things aren't really worth remembering.'

She hesitated, and then made her decision.

'Yes, I can tell you. You want to understand. That's important. Nowadays when so much information gets shared about people, we think knowing everything is important. Knowing every little detail. But the most important thing is *understanding* people, not knowing everything about them.'

First Lia had to promise one thing though, Mamia said.

'That I'll tell Mari what I know about her some day?' Lia guessed. Mamia nodded.

Lia looked straight into the tiny camera on the computer and at the old woman thousands of kilometres away.

'I promise,' Lia said.

Special thanks to

Samuli Knuuti, Ms Adkins, Nina Gimishanov, Jarkko Moilanen, Elisa Nurmi, Martha Pooley, Salla Pulli, Antti Sajantila, Deborah Gold and Peter Kelley at Galop UK, Joël Le Déroff at Ilga Europe, Maija-Liisa Ojala and Ulla Vanttaja at the Finnish Ministry of Education and Culture, and the WSOY Literature Foundation which supported the writing of this novel.

Biographical note

Pekka Hiltunen is a Finnish author, whose debut novel in 2011 immediately became of the most acclaimed first novels in Finnish literature. The psychological thriller *Cold Courage* was nominated for the *Helsingin Sanomat* Prize for Best Debut of the year, a rare feat for a thriller. It won three literary prizes in Finland, including the Clue Award for Best Detective Novel of the Year, and it has been nominated for the Scandinavian Glass Key Award 2013.

Critics have pointed out that Hiltunen's thrillers, called the Studio-series, started a whole new phase in Finnish crime lit. They combine global political topics with a smart urban setting and a nod to classical trickster novels.

Hiltunen also writes in other genres, and his books have been translated into six languages, including French and German. In 2013 he published a novel called *BIG*, about the tricky problem of the worldwide obesity phenomenon. Following a twenty-year career as a journalist in 2010 he received the Best Writing Editor Prize for his magazine articles. He specialises in extensive articles tackling social and political topics.

Hiltunen is a keen traveller. He loves the monthly supplements of quality British newspapers and devotes any free time to his two hobbies: holidaying away with his partner at a summer cottage by a small Finnish lake and inventing themes for imaginary surprise parties he wishes he could throw.

Under our three imprints, Hesperus Press publishes over 300 books by many of the greatest figures in worldwide literary history, as well as contemporary and debut authors well worth discovering.

Hesperus Classics handpicks the best of worldwide and translated literature, introducing forgotten and neglected books to new generations.

Hesperus Nova showcases quality contemporary fiction and non-fiction designed to entertain and inspire.

Hesperus Minor rediscovers well-loved children's books from the past – these are books which will bring back fond memories for adults, which they will want to share with their children and loved ones.

To find out more visit www.hesperuspress.com
@HesperusPress